Since winning the Ca... ...Fiction for her first ... **Wood** has published twenty novels and ... me one of the most popular authors in ... K.

... in the mining town of Castleford, Val c... ...e to East Yorkshire as a child and has lived in ...ull and rural Holderness where many of he... ...ovels are set. She now lives in the market to... ...of Beverley.

W... ...n she is not writing, Val is busy promoting lib... ...ies and supporting many charities.

Fi... ...out more about Val Wood's novels by vi... ...ng her website at www.valeriewood.co.uk

Have you read all of Val Wood's novels?

The Hungry Tide
Sarah Foster's parents fight a constant battle with poverty – until wealthy John Rayner provides them with work and a home on the coast. But when he falls for their daughter, Sarah, can their love overcome the gulf of wealth and social standing dividing them?

Annie
Annie Swinburn has killed a man. The man was evil in every possible way, but she knows that her only fate if she stays in Hull is a hanging. So she runs as far away as she can – to a new life that could offer her the chance of love, in spite of the tragedy that has gone before . . .

Children of the Tide
A tired woman holding a baby knocks at the door of one of the big houses in Anlaby. She shoves the baby at young James Rayner, then she vanishes. The Rayner family is shattered – born into poverty, will a baby unite or divide the family?

The Gypsy Girl
Polly Anna's mother died when she was just three years old. Alone in the world, the workhouse was the only place for her. But with the help of a young misfit she manages to escape, running away with the fairground folk. But will Polly Anna ever find somewhere she truly belongs?

Emily
A loving and hard-working child, Emily goes into service at just twelve years old. But when an employer's son dishonours and betrays her, her fortunes seem to be at their lowest ebb. Can she journey from shame and imprisonment to a new life and fulfilment?

Going Home
For Amelia and her siblings, the grim past their mother Emily endured seems far away. But when a gentleman travels from Australia to meet Amelia's family, she discovers the past casts a long shadow and that her tangled family history is inextricably bound up with his . . .

Rosa's Island
Taken in as a child, orphaned Rosa grew up on an island off the coast of Yorkshire. Her mother, before she died, promised that one day Rosa's father would return. But when two mysterious Irishmen come back to the island after many years, they threaten everything Rosa holds dear . . .

The Doorstep Girls
Ruby and Grace have grown up in the poorest slums
of Hull. Friends since childhood, they have supported each
other in bad times and good. As times grow harder, and money
scarcer, the girls search for something that could take them far
away . . . But what price will they pay to find it?

Far From Home
When Georgiana Gregory makes the long journey from Hull for
New York, she hopes to escape the confines of English life. But
once there, Georgiana finds she isn't far from home when she
encounters a man she knows – a man who presents
dangers almost too much to cope with . . .

The Kitchen Maid
Jenny secures a job as kitchen maid in a grand house in Beverley – but her fortunes fail when scandal forces her to leave. Years
later, she is mistress of a hall, but she never forgets the words a
gypsy told her: that one day she will return to where
she was happy and find her true love . . .

The Songbird
Poppy Mazzini has an ambition – to go on the stage. Her lovely
voice and Italian looks lead her to great acclaim. But when her
first love from her home town of Hull becomes engaged to someone else, she is devastated. Will Poppy have
to choose between fame and true love?

Nobody's Child
Now a prosperous Hull businesswoman, Susannah grew
up with the terrible stigma of being nobody's child. When
daughter Laura returns to the Holderness village of her
mother's childhood, she will discover a story of poverty, heartbreak and a love that never dies . . .

Fallen Angels
After her dastardly husband tries to sell her, Lily Fowler is alone
on the streets of Hull. Forced to work in a brothel, she forges
friendships with the women there, and together they try to turn
their lives around. Can they dare to dream of happy endings?

The Long Walk Home
When Mikey Quinn's mother dies, he is determined to find a
better life for his family – so he walks to London from Hull to
seek his fortune. There he meets Eleanor, and they gradually
make a new life for themselves. Eventually, though, they
must make the long walk home to Hull . . .

Rich Girl, Poor Girl
Polly, living in poverty, finds herself alone when her mother dies. Rosalie, brought up in comfort on the other side of Hull, loses her own mother on the same day. When Polly takes a job in Rosalie's house, the two girls form an unlikely friendship. United in tragedy, can they find happiness?

Homecoming Girls
The mysterious Jewel Newmarch turns heads wherever she goes, but she feels a longing to know her own roots. So she decides to return to her birthplace in America, where she learns about family, friendship, love and home. But most importantly, love . . .

The Harbour Girls
Jeannie spends her days at the water's edge waiting for Ethan to come in from fishing. But then she falls for a handsome stranger. When he breaks his word, Jeannie finds herself pregnant and alone in a strange new town. Will she ever find someone to truly love her – and will Ethan ever forgive her?

The Innkeeper's Daughter
Bella's dreams of teaching are dashed when she has to take on the role of mother to her baby brother. Her days are brightened by visits from Jamie Lucan – but when the family is forced to move to Hull, Bella is forced to leave everything behind. Can she ever find her dream again?

His Brother's Wife
The last thing Harriet expects after her mother dies is to marry a man she barely knows, but her only alternative is the workhouse. And so begins an unhappy marriage to Noah Tuke. The only person who offers her friendship is Noah's brother, Fletcher – the one person she can't possibly be with . . .

Every Mother's Son
Daniel Tuke hopes to share his future with childhood friend Beatrice Hart. But his efforts to find out more about his heritage throw up some shocking truths: is there a connection between the families? Meanwhile, Daniel's mother Harriet could never imagine that discoveries about her own family are also on the horizon . . .

LITTLE
GIRL LOST

Val Wood

Typeset in 11/13.5pt New Baskerville by Kestrel Data, Exeter, Devon.
Printed and bound in Clays Ltd, Bungay, Suffolk.

CORGI BOOKS

TRANSWORLD PUBLISHERS
61–63 Uxbridge Road, London W5 5SA
www.transworldbooks.co.uk

Transworld is part of the Penguin Random House group of companies
whose addresses can be found at global.penguinrandomhouse.com

First published in Great Britain in 2015 by Bantam Press
an imprint of Transworld Publishers
Corgi edition published 2016

A CIP catalogue record for this book
is available from the British Library.

ISBN
9780552171182

Typeset i͏ Devon.

futu͏ ͏ok
is ͏.

For my family with love and for Peter as always

ACKNOWLEDGEMENTS

My grateful thanks are due to Mr Christopher Evans of Haller Evans, Parliament Street, Hull, who kindly gave me a tour of his building from cellar to top floor, where I could then 'see the view' through my characters' eyes.

CHAPTER ONE

Parliament Street, Hull, May 1842

Margriet pressed her nose against the first-floor casement window and turned her head both ways, the better to see along Parliament Street towards Whitefriargate where her mother liked to shop, and then towards Quay Street and the dock from where she hoped her father would come if his ship had berthed.

'Margriet! Come away from the window.' Her mother's voice was impatient. 'You're smearing the glass.' She pressed her finger to the bell on the wall to summon the housekeeper.

'Sorry.' Margriet rubbed the pane with the cuff of her sleeve. 'I'm watching for Papa.'

'He'll be here when he's here,' her mother told her. 'No sooner and no later.' She rethreaded her needle with embroidery silk. 'It might not even be today, or tomorrow either for that matter. It depends on business.'

Margriet knew that, but Papa was already two days later than he had said he would be. Papa was fun, whereas Mama was no fun at all and only became

11

animated when trying on a new gown or running a fine piece of muslin or velvet through her fingers at the draper's. Margriet thought rebelliously that her mother didn't really mind how long Papa stayed away.

The housekeeper answered the bell and was asked to bring a cloth to clean the window. Margriet hung her head. 'Sorry,' she said again, and dropped her voice to a whisper to explain to Mrs Simmonds that she had been looking out for her father. The housekeeper gave her a complicit smile and told her mistress that she would send Florrie up to deal with the dirty window.

Margriet's father Frederik Vandergroene was Dutch, which made her half Dutch, he had told her, and he ran an import-export business. She hadn't known what that meant when she was little, but now that she was six she thought she understood. It meant that his company bought and sold merchandise between England and Netherlands and other northern countries of Europe. They took lace from Nottingham, linen and wool from Yorkshire and cotton from Manchester across the German Sea, and brought back, amongst many other things, cheese, wine, and gin which he called *Genever* and was the finest spirit you could buy. He brought her mother gifts of trinket boxes in blue and white Delft ware and for Margriet pretty little dolls with porcelain faces and rag bodies that sat on a shelf in her bedroom. Her favourite dolly had a painted celluloid face with wide-open eyes and was dressed in an outdoor gown and bonnet; if she was tipped upside down there she was with another head and her eyes closed and dressed in her nightgown, with slippers on her soft little feet.

He didn't always bring presents, but Margriet didn't mind; she just liked him to come home. The house seemed happier when he was there, the air charged with a joy that disappeared when he went away. Even the servants – Mrs Simmonds, Florrie, Cook and Lily the young maid who was so nervous she rarely spoke to Margriet – seemed much merrier once he was home, and Cook especially made lovely biscuits and cake for him that Mama never ate.

Florrie brought up a cloth that smelled of vinegar and wiped the glass, then polished it with a clean duster. 'I don't think your papa's ship will be here until tomorrow morning, Miss Margriet,' she whispered. 'Tide's not right for it to come in now.'

'Ah,' Margriet said softly. She'd forgotten about the tides. 'Thank you.'

She was given a conspiratorial smile and Rosamund Vandergroene, who must have overheard, said, 'That is all, Florence,' dismissing her, and to her daughter, 'Go to the schoolroom, Margriet, and prepare for your lessons. Miss Ripley will be here shortly.'

Miss Ripley was tall and thin and sniffed constantly even when she didn't have a cold. She also twitched her nose, and when she first came to teach Margriet the child was so fascinated by this habit that she began to do it too. It wasn't until she was spoken to harshly by her mother and then more kindly by her father that she was able to stop, but only by avoiding looking at Miss Ripley. Someone, probably her mother, must have spoken to the governess, for she now kept a handkerchief permanently pressed to her nose.

Margriet's father had taught her to read, write and add up long before Miss Ripley came to teach her, which was just as well, Margriet thought, because the lessons were probably as boring to the governess as they were to her. However, she did bring Margriet some of her own books to read, which were much more interesting than the children's books that her mother had ordered for her.

When the governess joined her in the schoolroom Margriet asked, 'Do you know about tides, Miss Ripley?'

'Tides? What kinds of tides?'

Margriet gazed at her and wondered how many kinds there were. 'Sea tides,' she said, 'that bring ships into the harbour. It's just that Papa's ship should be coming in soon, but it will have to be on the tide.'

'I see.' Miss Ripley sniffed. 'I know there's a morning tide and an evening tide, so if your father's ship has missed the morning tide . . .' She pondered, and then shrugged. 'I don't know. Perhaps it won't come in until tomorrow.'

Margriet's spirits slumped. Sighing, she wiped her slate clean with a cotton cloth and prepared to write answers to the questions that Miss Ripley was sure to ask about yesterday's lessons. Then she heard the bang of the front door and her face became wreathed in smiles. It was a joyous sound, triumphant. No one else slammed the door as her father did. No one else was allowed to. She slid off her chair and looked rebelliously at the governess.

'It's Papa,' she said jubilantly. 'He didn't miss the tide after all.'

Miss Ripley closed her book. There would be no lessons for a while; she had neither the energy nor the spirit to counter the child's devotion to her father, and why indeed should she? If she had had such a father, or indeed could have caught such a husband as Frederik Vandergroene, she too would have given him all her love and adoration. But she hadn't, and with her plain looks, long nose and melancholia she was unlikely to get the chance. She thought of Mrs Vandergroene, who would later question her on how much her daughter had learned that day. I'll just lie, she thought, following Margriet out of the nursery schoolroom and heading down the stairs to the kitchen, where Cook would be sure to offer her a cup of tea.

'I thought you'd missed the tide, Papa!' Margriet flung herself into her father's arms as he bent to catch her.

He kissed her cheek. 'No, little Daisy, I did not. We docked very early this morning and I didn't want to waken you or Mama, so I went to the office and caught up with some work.'

'So have you finished now? Can I stay downstairs with you and not go back to lessons?'

Her mother was still seated in her chair with her embroidery on her knee. 'No, you cannot, Margriet,' she said. 'Otherwise why are we paying Miss Ripley?'

Margriet looked up at her father as he let her down to the floor. He gazed whimsically back at her. 'Ten minutes only,' he said, giving a little wink. 'Just whilst I have a little chat with your mama. Then I must go back to the office. You see? We all have to work.'

'Mama doesn't,' Margriet pointed out.

'Of course not,' her father said, a slight reprimand in his voice. 'But she has other things to do.' Then he added, 'I'll try to come home early; perhaps we'll have supper together?' He looked at his wife for confirmation.

'I don't think so,' she said. 'Seven o'clock is Margriet's bedtime.'

'A story, Papa. Will you tell me a bedtime story?'

'I will,' he agreed, 'but hush now. I want to speak to your mama.'

Margriet's concentration drifted as she stood by her father's side. She knew by looking at her mother's face that she had not the slightest interest in anything he was saying, but she kept very quiet, otherwise she knew she would be sent upstairs again.

'I had dinner with the Jansens when I was in Gouda. Do you recall meeting Nicolaas, Rosamund?' her father was saying. 'I brought him here for drinks a few years ago. We've known each other since we were boys.' He looked pensive. 'He doesn't look well. Not at all his usual self.' Then he smiled. 'His son, Hans, is a fine boy. Very polite and very grown up for a ten-year-old.' He glanced at Margriet. 'They have a daughter, Klara, a little older than you. About eight, I think.'

'Is she taller than me? Is she fair or dark?'

'She's taller than you, and fair,' he said, 'like you, and Hans's hair is reddish brown, though he was blond when he was a child.'

'Did you know them when they were little?'

'I met them once or twice, but not often. I usually see their father in his office, but this time he invited me to supper at his house and they were allowed to stay up late to eat with us.'

'I wish I could stay up late,' Margriet pleaded. 'When can I, Mama?'

'Not yet. Perhaps when you're older. The Dutch do things differently from us.' She gave a resigned huff of breath. 'Off you go now, Margriet. Miss Ripley will be waiting for you.'

'Yes,' Frederik continued after Margriet had left the room, 'Nicolaas didn't look at all well. I'm quite concerned about him. He's very sallow, and doesn't have much appetite even though the meal was delicious.'

Rosamund wore a resigned expression. 'Herring?'

Frederik laughed. 'Of course herring. And pea and ham soup, sauerkraut and waffles – not together, of course! Cornelia had arranged a buffet with many different dishes. And then there was apple cake and rye bread, and you know how I love my bread.' He stood up. 'I must go back to the office. There's huge potential for business. Why don't you come with me next time I go over? I shall be visiting Amsterdam: you could go shopping. We could take Margriet.'

'I have things to do,' she said coolly. 'I'm on several committees, and besides, you know I don't like to sail. I get very claustrophobic as well as seasick.'

'But the weather is calm now. I wouldn't ask you to come in winter as it can get very cold and the sea is rough, but it's lovely at the moment

and the tulips are in flower; they are such a wonderful sight.'

'Well, I'll see,' she said, and he turned away,
knowing that she wouldn't come.

CHAPTER TWO

Margriet ate her supper at a small table in the nursery schoolroom on the top floor of the house. She hated it to be called the nursery, for that implied that she was still a baby. The room was the schoolroom during the day and she sat at the table with Miss Ripley opposite her. After she had finished her lessons and Miss Ripley had gone home, Florrie came up to move the table and chair nearer the fire to make it into a nursery again. A fire-guard was placed in the hearth so that there was no fear of Margriet's burning herself. An interconnecting door led into her bedroom, and apart from the twice-daily visits downstairs to see her parents, once after breakfast and once before bedtime, and being taken for a walk on a fine day, this was where she spent most of her life.

Margriet was convinced that her father would have allowed her downstairs more often had he not spent his days at his office near the estuary, but in practice her mother was in total control of her daughter's well-being, which encompassed the type of book she should read, the food she should eat, her religious instruction, her piano lessons and her

19

health, which meant not going out if the weather was wet or cold in case of catching a chill, or if it was too hot in case of becoming overheated. All of these things Mrs Vandergroene had been taught by her own mother, and so must be right and proper.

Her father was much more lenient. Margriet knew that the daughters of her mother's friends rarely saw their fathers, and when they did it was only when they came downstairs in their dressing gowns before bedtime, and put up their clean and shiny little faces to receive a peck on the cheek. They were certainly not read to by their papas as Margriet was; whenever he was at home her father would sit in an easy chair by her bed and read her a story he had loved when he was a child. He had once quite memorably sat beside her on the bed and she had snuggled beneath his arm to follow the words in one of her favourite books, and both had fallen asleep halfway through it. When Florrie had come up to tuck Margriet in she had had to shake his arm gently and tell him that the supper bell had been rung.

This evening he arrived home early, but not early enough for Margriet to join them for supper; that would have been a rare treat indeed and not an indulgence she expected. Her mother considered that her father spoiled her, and her behaviour today, running down the stairs to greet him, had been quite reprehensible, despite Frederik's pleasure at receiving, as he called it, such a joyous welcome home.

Frederik didn't understand, Rosamund thought. When Miss Ripley had taught her pupil to the best of her ability she would leave, and it would become Rosamund's task to teach their daughter to be an obedient, well-mannered young woman who knew her place in society. Rosamund alone must teach her the important things in life, such as running a household, in preparation for when she married and had her own establishment. She must teach her to respond intelligently to conversation but not to give an opinion lest she be thought forward, a failing which would reflect back upon her mother and not on her indulgent father.

Rosamund's friends constantly reminded her of how lucky she was to have such a tolerant husband, to be married to a man who didn't spend every night at home. She could be invited out to dine or to make up a card party whilst he was away, knowing that Frederik wouldn't object as some husbands might. But what they didn't understand was that Frederik expected her to be interested in what he was doing, and even worse to discuss business or current affairs with him, when she had no interest in either.

When Margriet came downstairs to say goodnight, her father beamed at her. 'Tomorrow I am taking a day's holiday,' he announced, turning to his wife. 'I thought we could take a walk about town and see what's happening – buildings being pulled down and others going up. Margriet can see the ships in the dock and then perhaps we could walk down to the Corporation Pier and look at the Humber.'

Margriet's face lit up, but Rosamund's lips turned down. 'It's very breezy down there,' she said. 'We might catch a chill.'

'Nonsense,' Frederik said briskly. 'You can take a warm shawl, and the weather is fine. It will do us good to walk. It will blow the cobwebs away.'

'I wish we could go for a ride on the ferry,' Margriet said. 'Could we, Papa?'

Frederik glanced at Rosamund. 'Well, perhaps another day. Mama doesn't like going on the water. You know that she has never been to my country, or even to Lincolnshire.'

'Poor Mama,' Margriet said.

'I'm so sorry that I can't, Frederik,' Rosamund murmured. 'And I regret only meeting your parents on our wedding day.'

'Yes.' He lowered his eyes. It was remiss of him too not to have taken Margriet to his homeland before his father died a year ago. His parents had never met their granddaughter, but he hoped that when his mother was out of mourning perhaps she would come back with him after one of his visits.

'Come, give Mama a kiss goodnight.' Rosamund held out her hand to Margriet. 'Sleep well.'

'Goodnight, Mama,' Margriet said dutifully and offered her cheek, glancing at her father. He nodded.

'I'll be up in five minutes,' he told her, 'and we'll have a story.'

'A short one,' Rosamund reminded him. 'Supper will be almost ready.'

'Yes,' he said irritably, bending to give Margriet a kiss. 'I know.'

After Margriet had gone up, he said, rather testily, which was unlike him, 'Please do not begrudge the child an extra ten minutes of my time, Rosamund.

She must get lonely with only the company of servants, for she has little of yours!'

'I don't understand what you mean, Frederik,' she said primly, which didn't delude him in the least. She knew very well what he meant and how irritated he was that she spent so little time with their daughter. 'I cannot indulge or cosset her in the way that you do or she will grow up to be outspoken and unconventional, which will ruin her chances of making a suitable marriage.'

He said nothing more. Rosamund was inflexible, entrenched in traditional rules of what women should and shouldn't do. For eight years he had offered her the opportunity to speak her mind and enjoy the equality and companionship of a good marriage, and she had chosen not to accept. Well, he would not in future pander to her; she could go to the devil, he thought resentfully. In a few more years, when Margriet was old enough to travel with a maid, he would take her to visit his mother and siblings and show her what family life could be like.

After giving Margriet time to get into bed, he went upstairs and pulled an easy chair closer to her bedside. 'Your mama thinks it too cold to walk out tomorrow.' He saw her expression close up. 'But you and I will still go.' He smiled at her obvious delight. 'You can ask Florrie to give you a warm scarf to wear with your coat in case you need it, though I don't think you will. It's May, after all, and quite warm.'

Margriet nodded. 'I'd like to wear my grey bonnet, because Florrie has put a new blue ribbon on it. She said it needed prettying up and that blue would match my eyes. It's not as pretty as Mama's new hat with the flowers and feathers, but I'll have to wait until I'm grown up to wear one of those.'

'I'm sure your bonnet will look lovely,' he said, 'and so will you. Now, what shall we read tonight?'

'I don't know,' she said. 'I'm a little tired of the ones we always read. You can choose, Papa.'

'Well, I was thinking that maybe I'll tell you something about history, about the old days, or perhaps Miss Ripley does that?'

She nodded and sighed. 'She tells me about kings and queens, but it's a bit boring because all she wants me to learn are the dates when they were on the throne.'

'Mmm. And has Miss Ripley told you about our young queen, or of the time when King Henry had a palace in Hull?'

Margriet considered. 'I know when Victoria came to the throne. It was in June 1837, after her uncle William died. I don't remember it because I was only a baby, but I think I remember seeing all the flags in the streets when she married Prince Albert and we went to parties to celebrate, didn't we, Papa?' Her eyes widened. 'But Miss Ripley never said that King Henry came to live in Hull. Where is his palace? Can we go and see it?'

Frederik smiled. 'I'm not sure if he ever lived in Hull, but monarchs had houses and palaces all over the country, so that they could stay in them if they were visiting the area.'

'Could they not have stayed with friends?' she asked. 'I'm sure people would have loved to have them visit. Mama would be very pleased to have the queen here to stay if ever she came to Hull, and her friends would be very jealous, but . . .' She frowned and contemplated. 'I'm not sure which bedroom she would have. I wouldn't mind if she had mine, but of course she would bring lots of servants, so perhaps we wouldn't have room – maybe that's why they have their own palaces to stay in.'

'I think you have worked that out very well, Margriet. So where do you think she would stay if she did come to Hull?'

Margriet shook her head. 'I don't know. I don't think there is anywhere that would be suitable. Perhaps someone should build a palace for her, just in case.'

He saw that she was getting sleepy, so he tucked her blankets around her. 'I think that tomorrow we'll look at all the buildings and think about where she might like to stay, and about what went before.' He smiled. 'Do you know the name of the street that was here before Parliament Street?'

'No,' she murmured, her eyelids drooping. 'It's always been called Parliament Street.'

'It was called Mug-House Entry!'

'Oh, Papa,' she chided sleepily. 'You are joking of me!'

He kissed the top of her head. 'No,' he said softly. 'I am not joking of you. Sleep well, *mijn lieveling*. And tomorrow we will go and look for King Henry's palace.'

CHAPTER THREE

The following morning was bright and sunny. Margriet had an early breakfast and was dressed and ready for their walk when her mother came into her bedroom.

'Why do you have your coat on, Margriet? Where are you going?'

Margriet licked her lips. 'For a walk, Mama. Don't you remember?'

'Don't be impertinent,' her mother admonished her. 'Of course I remember, but I don't recall that we agreed that you should miss your lessons with Miss Ripley. You must do at least an hour's work before you go out.'

Margriet's mouth trembled. 'I'm so sorry, Mama,' she mumbled. 'I – I didn't realize – I thought Papa meant after breakfast.' She began to unbutton her coat and take off her bonnet. She looked up at her mother. 'Will you be coming too?'

'Of course I will. Why not?'

Margriet managed a smile, though she would rather have had just her father's company. 'Oh, good,' she murmured. 'That will be very nice. We're going to look for King Henry's palace.'

'What?' Her mother frowned. 'A palace?'

'Papa said. He said that King Henry had a palace in Hull.'

'Your father fills your head with stuff and nonsense. I have never heard of such a thing and I have lived here all my life. Miss Ripley!' Rosamund called as she heard the governess come into the adjoining schoolroom. 'Have you ever heard of a king's palace in Hull?'

Miss Ripley patted her mouth. 'Erm, I vaguely recall something,' she offered hesitantly, not knowing whether yes or no would please her pupil's mother.

'Well, have you or haven't you?'

'It's possible,' she said. 'I believe King Henry commandeered a manor house in medieval times. It – erm – isn't here now.'

'So there you are, Margriet. What did I say? Miss Ripley,' Rosamund continued, 'Mr Vandergroene wishes to take Margriet out this morning, but first she must have an hour's lesson. You may then take the rest of the morning off, but I will expect you to make up the lost time on another day.'

Miss Ripley dipped her knee. 'Of course, ma'am,' she said. 'Thank you. Well,' she said to Margriet, 'we'd better get started and then you can go off and enjoy the sunshine.'

'I expect there's a chill wind, isn't there?' Rosamund asked.

'Oh, no, ma'am,' Miss Ripley smiled, unable to believe her luck at being given the morning off on such a lovely day. 'It's warm and sunny. Just perfect for a walk.'

Rosamund left the room and met Frederik coming

up the stairs. 'Miss Ripley has arrived,' she told him. 'She's going to give Margriet an hour's lesson before we go out.'

'Oh, is she?' He seemed astonished. 'I would have thought she would have jumped at the chance of having a day off. Well, I suppose I could have another cup of coffee whilst we wait.'

'I'll ring for Florence,' Rosamund said. 'If you'll excuse me, Frederik, I must take a powder before I get ready. I have a beastly headache starting and I want to nip it in the bud if I can.' She gave a stoical sigh. 'I don't want to spoil our walk by making us all come home again.'

'No indeed,' Frederik agreed. 'But the fresh air will do you good.'

'Oh, I don't think so,' his wife murmured. 'There are so many infections lurking about, with that dreadful workhouse at the bottom of the street. Something should be done about it. It isn't right to have it situated so close to where decent people live.'

Frederik nodded. He had heard this opinion often; it seemed to be the only topic that Rosamund discussed.

By the time Margriet met him in the hall wearing her coat and her newly trimmed bonnet, he was waiting with increasing impatience for Rosamund to come down and say she was ready. Half the morning had been wasted, and he wished he had gone into the office. Then Florrie came hurrying downstairs, followed by Miss Ripley.

'Beg pardon, sir.' Florrie dipped her knee. 'The mistress isn't well and asks to be excused from coming out – her headache . . . She says that Miss Ripley could go with you instead.'

'I see,' Frederik murmured. 'And what does Miss Ripley say about that?'

Florrie glanced at the governess and the three of them waited for her to speak. Her nose twitched and she uttered something that could have been a hesitant stammering excuse or an apologetic erm.

'You don't have to come, Miss Ripley,' Margriet said kindly, giving her an option to refuse. 'You might prefer to go home.'

'Of course you'd like to go home,' Frederik said firmly, 'or indeed anywhere you please. You can have the rest of the morning off, and goodness me,' he glanced at his pocket watch, 'how the day is flying by. Off you go.'

As Miss Ripley rushed out of the door as if worried he might have a change of heart, Florrie asked, 'Shall I tell Mrs Vandergroene of the new arrangements, sir?'

Frederik stood for a moment as if considering, then said, 'No, I don't think so. She's better resting, don't you agree? Best not to disturb her in the slightest.'

'Very good, sir.' Florrie seemed relieved. She smiled at Margriet. 'Don't you go losing that pretty bonnet, Miss Margriet,' she said, 'for you'd never get it back again.'

Margriet put her hand into her father's. 'I won't, Florrie,' she said. 'Thank you. I'll take great care of it.'

When father and daughter had left the house, Florrie heaved a sigh and went into the kitchen.

Cook was rolling pastry and Mrs Simmonds was drinking a cup of coffee.

'Mistress is in bed,' she said, 'and 'master has tekken Miss Margriet out. We might get a bit o' peace for an hour or so.' Cutting a slice of bread and smearing it with marmalade, she said, 'I think that this is not a very happy household.'

'Well, that doesn't concern us,' Mrs Simmonds said sharply. 'Though I feel sorry for 'little lass in 'middle of it.'

'She's happy today.' Florrie took a bite from her bread and munched appreciatively. 'And who wouldn't be with such a papa? She told me when I was dressing her this morning that they were going to look at 'king's palace and when I said I'd never heard of such a place she told me that King Henry used to live here.'

'He's teaching her history, then,' Mrs Simmonds said. 'But I can't think it'll be of much use to her. She'll be married off to somebody when she's old enough and be in 'same role as her mother.' She curled her lip. 'And live a most useful life.'

Margriet and her father walked along Parliament Street and crossed into Quay Street, where they stood looking at the busy dock in front of them. It was packed tightly with sailing ships, steamers and schooners, barges and tug boats with barely any space between them.

'Hull is a great shipping town,' he told her, 'and when this dock was built it was the largest in the country. That was when they made Parliament Street, to give access to it from Whitefriargate. The ships come in to the River Hull from the sea and the Humber and unload here. You know where the Humber Dock and the Junction Dock are, don't you?'

Margriet shook her head.

'The Junction Dock is at the top of Whitefriargate, a mere two-minute walk from our house. How is it that you don't know? It links together the other two. It's a ring of docks.' He shook his head; it was remiss of him not to have shown her before. Had she been a son and not a daughter he would have done so.

'I'm sorry, Papa,' she said, looking crestfallen. 'I didn't know. But please, when are we going to see the king's palace?'

He laughed. She was still a child and believed in fairy stories, so he would take her. 'First of all we will go back into Parliament Street,' he said, 'and I will show you a secret place.'

'Oh?'

'You have probably passed it with your mama or Florrie and not even noticed it, although I'm sure Florrie must know it.'

They walked back a few yards and Frederik paused by a narrow opening between the buildings. 'This is a short cut, a passageway through to another part of the town.' He gazed down at her. 'Shall we take a look?'

Margriet peered down the entrance and clutched her father's hand. 'I don't know. It's very dark.'

'It's dark because the buildings are high and no sunlight can get in, that's all. Shall we try?'

'All right,' she agreed, 'but I don't think that Mama would have liked it.'

'I'm quite sure she wouldn't, but there's nothing to fear, Margriet, or I wouldn't bring you.'

She knew that was true; Papa would never let her come to any harm. She followed him trustfully, holding on to the hand he held out behind him. It was too narrow for them to walk side by side so she kept as close as possible without treading on his heels.

There were doorways along the passage, leading into houses, she supposed, and as Papa had said the buildings were very high, but some had windows at the very top to catch what little light there was. They turned a corner that brought them into a slightly wider area, where the buildings had yards and washing hanging out and children playing in the dirt; her father said it was called Duncan's Entry. A few moments later she could see an opening ahead of them leading out into a sunny, busy street.

'Once upon an ancient time,' her father began, 'by the confluence of the River Hull and the Humber estuary, the monks of Meaux owned a piece of land and on it a hamlet they named Wyke. The people of Wyke lived in wooden houses and there were no paved or cobbled streets such as we have today, but only the rough earth. Then one day King Edward I realized that Wyke was well protected from any enemies coming from across the sea and bought it from the monks. He called it King's Town upon Hull, but everyone came to know it as Hull.'

'Oh,' Margriet said, disappointed. 'So it wasn't King Henry after all? And what about the palace?'

Frederik took firm hold of her hand as they walked on; the road was busy with carriages and traps and carters' vans. 'The reason that the king wanted it was because of its position,' he went on. 'He enclosed the town with boundary walls, gates and a moat, and where there was no wall there was the barrier of the estuary and the River Hull to keep the people safe from any invaders.' He looked down to see if she was listening, and she appeared to be. 'And over the centuries,' he continued, 'inside these walls, various royal personages came and made improvements. Rich merchants and ship owners lived in High Street, and there were craftsmen, wood carvers and silversmiths, and warehouses full of goods to trade with other countries. Most important of all was Holy Trinity Church in Market Place, where shopkeepers and stallholders clustered around it selling their wares, much as they do today.'

'I sometimes go there with Florrie,' she said eagerly, as if wanting to be included in this rich tapestry of life.

Her father nodded. 'It became a bustling medieval town, and,' he paused dramatically, 'many important people lived here.'

'Like the king!' Margriet piped up as they came to the top of Silver Street.

He stopped and pointed out the old church of St Mary's and now she knew they had walked in a circle and were not far from home. Here were shops selling silver and gold jewellery and regalia where her mother liked to linger.

'Noble families like the De la Poles served under

many kings, and one of them, the earl of Suffolk, built a mansion which he called Suffolk Palace.'

'For the kings to stay in when they visited!' Margriet exclaimed. 'So where is it, Papa?'

'It was right here where we are standing,' he said, 'and it was a splendid building with a great gateway and a fine tower.'

Margriet looked about her, but there was no splendid palace, only some commercial buildings that she had seen before and hardly noticed. She turned a disappointed face to her father.

'I think that's enough history for the time being,' he said, smiling. 'Let's take a walk down High Street by the Old Harbour and look at the ships, and then we'll go to the pier to see the Humber. Perhaps we might stop for a dish of ice cream, *ja*?'

'*Ja*,' she agreed, and thought how she loved being out with him.

From High Street he led her down one of the staiths to look at the congested River Hull, clogged with barges and cobles and fishing vessels. The wharf was stacked with wooden crates and coils of ropes and all the paraphernalia of shipping, too dangerous, Frederik considered, for Margriet to walk along, so they cut back into High Street again, heading for the Vittoria Hotel and the promised ice cream.

They were sitting at a window table overlooking the estuary, Frederik sipping coffee and Margriet scraping her dish for the last of the ice cream, when a figure loomed beside them.

'Vandergroene!' The man was stocky and rather portly, as if he lived well, and was holding out his hand. Frederik stood up to greet him and shake it.

'Webster! How are you? Won't you join us? This is my daughter Margriet. Margriet, this is my lawyer, Mr Hugh Webster.'

Hugh Webster gave a polite bow. 'Charmed to meet you, Miss Vandergroene. How are you?'

'Very well, sir, thank you.' Margriet gave a slight nod of her head, as she had seen her mother do on meeting an acquaintance, and then offered her hand, which Mr Webster bent over.

'Delighted,' he smiled, before seating himself. 'This is a great pleasure.' He turned to her father. 'So, not working today, Frederik?'

'No. I decided I would take the day off and enjoy the company of my wife and daughter. Unfortunately, Rosamund felt unwell and was unable to join us.'

Webster glanced at Margriet. 'So you have your papa all to yourself?'

Margriet couldn't help but give a happy smile. 'Papa is telling me about the kings who used to live here. Or at least . . .' She hesitated. They hadn't quite got to that part. 'They had a palace here, so I expect they stayed sometimes.'

'Really?' Mr Webster seemed astonished. 'I didn't know that.'

'Opposite St Mary's Church,' she informed him. 'But it isn't there now.'

'Teaching history, are you?' Webster asked Frederik. 'How is it that you know so much about a town you weren't born in?'

'I've known Hull for many years.' Frederik ordered another pot of coffee for them both and a lemonade for Margriet, who sat happily in her chair looking out at the choppy estuary waters and feeling very grown up sitting here with her father and his friend. 'I first came here when I was eighteen and about to join the family company. We had recently opened a Hull office. I liked the town and got to know it very well on my visits, and five years later I married Rosamund and came to live here.'

'I see. I hadn't realized you had known it so long, longer even than I,' Webster observed, 'for I have been here only five or six years.' He leaned confidentially towards Frederik. 'Speaking of marriage, do you recall the broker Smithson? He died about two years ago?'

'I do remember, *ja*; he left substantial assets to his widow, or so I heard.'

'You heard correctly. He was not my client, so I am free to speak of it.' Webster lowered his voice. 'His widow married a much younger man shortly after her mourning period was over; I have recently learned that within six months he has spent practically all her money, has taken a mistress, and is now threatening to sell the house to raise capital, which will leave the former Mrs Smithson and her two daughters virtually penniless.'

He gazed keenly at Frederik. 'Smithson was not well advised. I suppose he thought that as his wife was of middle age she would not be tempted by another suitor after his death, but he was quite wrong. I tell you this, Frederik, as I am telling all my clients, to be sure your will is watertight, however fit and hearty you may be at present.' He smiled at Margriet, who was listening to the conversation with her head on one side. 'You must take steps to ensure that if, heaven forbid, anything should happen to you, your wife and daughter will be secure.'

CHAPTER FOUR

At last the lawyer rose from his seat. 'I'll see you some time soon, Frederik, and we'll sort out the details.' He turned to Margriet. 'I won't detain you from your activities any longer, Miss Vandergroene. It has been a great pleasure meeting you and I am always at your service.' He gave her a courtly bow of his head, his hand to his chest.

'Thank you,' she said. 'I'm much obliged.'

Frederik gave an indulgent smile and shook hands with Webster, who murmured 'Charming' as he left them.

Frederik turned to his daughter. 'Shall we continue our walk, Margriet, or are you tired?'

'Oh, no,' she assured him. 'I want to know what comes next.'

They walked away from the pier with their backs to the estuary, and Margriet felt the cool wind at her neck. Soon they came to Market Place, where the gleaming statue of William of Orange, or King Billy as he was affectionately known in the town, sat astride his horse.

'What you have to imagine, Margriet,' her father said, 'is that in the olden times, before these buildings were here, this was open land. When King Henry came on a visit he liked what he saw and took Suffolk Palace for himself, renaming it the King's Manor House and laying out elaborate gardens with fish ponds, flowering bushes and trees that stretched all the way down here.'

'And did the king walk in the gardens?' she asked, her voice rising in wonder. 'Did he come down here where we are now?'

'I expect he did, along with his advisers and noblemen, and perhaps noblewomen too.'

'I expect the ladies liked the gardens more than the gentlemen did,' she said. 'Mama would have liked them.'

'Mmm,' her father said. 'Perhaps so.' He was thinking that Rosamund had never shown any interest in visiting the tulip fields of his home country. Entertaining or being entertained was what she liked most of all.

'Can you see them in your mind's eye?' he asked her. 'The gentlemen dressed in doublets made of the finest material, and linen shirts with wide sleeves, with gold chains round their necks and rings on their fingers to indicate their wealth, and the noblewomen wearing so many layers of petticoats under their velvet gowns that it would have taken them hours to get ready before being seen in public.'

'Oh,' she murmured, 'I wouldn't have liked that. It takes Florrie a long time to dress me before I go out with Mama. I have to wear three petticoats. I much prefer it when I stay in for lessons and only need to wear one. And I expect those ladies wouldn't have

39

wanted to get their lovely gowns dirty if the weather was wet, but how uncomfortable they would have been if the days were hot!'

They continued along Market Place, past the stalls near Holy Trinity Church where the traders were calling out their wares, their voices mingling with the squawks of caged hens and the bleating of goats and the rattle and rumbling of wheels on the cobbles, until Margriet said abruptly, 'But what about the poor people?'

'The poor people?' Frederik's thoughts had turned away from the past to the present day and his conversation with Webster. He had made a will in Rosamund's favour, with provision for Margriet and any other children they might have – although he considered that highly unlikely – but he hadn't given any thought to Rosamund's position if by chance he should die suddenly and she should marry again.

He recalled the sinking of a passenger ship only the previous year, when a sudden storm had blown up in the German Sea and many people had drowned. He spent a considerable time travelling overseas, he thought, and the worst could happen. Rosamund was not yet thirty, and she was not wise enough to look after her own interests. Just like poor Mrs Smithson and her daughters, she and Margriet could be in a very precarious position if she should marry a bounder.

Margriet was pulling at his sleeve. 'Papa! What about them? Were there any, or was everyone rich?'

He gazed vaguely at her. 'Ah, the poor who are always with us. They would rub along as usual, I suppose,' he said thoughtfully. 'They would try to keep alive by whatever means possible. Work, if they could find it.' He wondered whether there were workhouses in those far-off days, and considered it unlikely. 'In order to buy their bread and lodgings,' he added.

'Well, that would be very unfair,' Margriet said indignantly, 'especially if there were rich people who could have helped them.'

Frederik sighed. 'Yes,' he said. 'But it was always so. It is an unfair world.' He looked down at her sweet little face, which was wearing an unaccustomed scowl. 'So how do you know about poor people, my dear Daisy? Who has told you?'

'I've seen them from my window. They come to the workhouse at the end of the street and wait outside the gate to be let in; and when Mama goes shopping they hold out their hands to her.'

But, she thought, Mama says, 'Don't look at them. Come away, come away, don't look at them,' and never gives them a single copper, unlike Florrie when she comes with us to carry the parcels. She slips a coin into their hands, especially the old beggar women who are dressed in rags and can barely walk in their torn boots. Mama says I mustn't touch them as they are probably diseased, and Florrie nips her mouth up very tight when she hears that. She doesn't say anything in front of Mama – she's afraid to, I expect – but she tells me afterwards that they are to be pitied for having fallen on hard times.

'I have one more place to show you,' her father was saying, 'but if you're tired we can cut across in front of the church and go home.'

'I'm not tired,' she said quickly, even though she was, but she didn't want the outing to end. 'I'd like to see it.'

He led her on until they reached the top of Silver Street once again and were looking down the length of Whitefriargate, within minutes of home.

'Down here is a street that you might have passed without noticing,' he said, 'and there are many stories of how it came to be named.'

Margriet looked up at him quizzically. 'Mama says we must hurry past all the little streets – entries, she calls them – for fear of robbers and ne'er-do-wells hiding in them. I can see one of them from a window at the back of our house. Florrie says it's called Winter's Alley. I hadn't been down the passage to Duncan's Entry before, but sometimes if I go on an errand with Florrie we cut through some of the others.'

She hesitated, fearing she had been indiscreet and might have got Florrie into trouble, but her father simply smiled and said that he was quite sure Florrie would not let her run into danger. A moment later he pulled her to a halt. 'Now, do you know where we are?'

Margriet looked round. 'I do know this street,' she said, 'but not its name.'

'Then look up and find it, and then tell me what you think of it.'

Margriet gazed up at the high walls on either side. It was an unremarkable street with an inn on the corner, and it was not as elegant as their own Parliament Street; most of the buildings had tall doorways leading straight off the street, and she saw that what she had thought was a small lane led into a courtyard and the narrow passage they had come down earlier. She spun round and saw Bowlalley Lane behind her, then lifted her gaze again and saw the name he was referring to.

She drew in a breath and mouthed, 'Oh.' On a grimy metal plaque, too high for her to have noticed before, she read, *Land of Green Ginger*.

CHAPTER FIVE

The stories might not be true, her father told her as he led her up the short street, but no one could dispute them, for there wasn't anyone left alive who could remember how it had come by its name.

Margriet nodded her head and listened as he told her that there had been a street here for hundreds of years, and it was marked on old maps as Old Beverley Street. He said that he had become interested in the name when he was a young man just arrived from Amsterdam, and had been told that a Dutch family named Lindegroen had once lived here. 'Some people think the street name is a corruption of theirs, but there are others who say that ginger was once grown here, so—'

'In the king's gardens?' Margriet asked eagerly.

'Possibly so,' he agreed, 'for the street was very close to the palace. Other people say that the ginger was preserved here and stored in jars and the name came from that.'

Margriet tugged on his hand and looked about her. 'Could there have been a shop here and it sold ginger? Because I think this is the place where the little girl lives.'

'Which little girl?'

'The little Dutch girl, from the family that you said. Lindegroen. Green lime trees.'

'How do you know it means green lime trees?' he asked, astonished. '*Spreek je Nederlands?*'

She shook her head and gave a little hop. '*Nee!* But the little girl does.'

'Does she?' Frederik raised his eyebrows. 'How do you know?'

'She's Dutch.' Margriet looked up at the roofline of one of the buildings and pointed. 'She said this is Lindegroen Walk.'

Frederik followed her gaze. The building she was indicating seemed unused; the door had a bar across it and the upstairs windows were dirty. He was startled when Margriet gave a sudden smile and a wave of her hand before turning back to him. 'She's gone now. Perhaps I'll see her again another day.'

He felt he should mention this encounter to Rosamund once they were home. Margriet had gone upstairs to her room, where Florrie brought her a meal of soup made from yesterday's chicken and a small bowl of rice pudding, and then suggested she had a lie down on her bed for an hour after her long walk. 'Perhaps read a book?' she said, but Margriet shook her head and said, 'No thank you, Florrie, I have some thinking to do.'

Frederik preferred to eat their main meal at seven o'clock, so he and Rosamund were just served cold chicken and bread and butter, followed by coffee and cake.

'How is your headache?' he asked solicitously. 'Has it gone?'

'Just about,' she said wearily, drawing her hand over her forehead. 'I rested in my room and did a little sewing.'

'Margriet and I had a good walk,' he told her. 'Right down to the pier.'

'Oh!' She gave a slight exclamation. 'Then I'm so pleased I didn't come. That would have been much too far.'

'Margriet enjoyed it. I gave her a history lesson.' He told Rosamund about showing Margriet Land of Green Ginger. 'She took to heart what I said about the Lindegroen family, and said she knew their little girl.'

'Who are they? I don't know them. Are they new to the area?'

He laughed. 'Don't tell me you haven't heard of the myth that surrounds the street name?'

She clearly hadn't, and he explained again. But she frowned and he saw that she was displeased and not in the least amused. 'You are filling her head with foolishness,' she said.

'Not at all,' he said brusquely. 'I want her to be interested in what is around her, otherwise she will be unaware of the history of her birthplace.' Much as you are, he thought, but didn't say, and wondered how anyone could live in a town all their life and only be interested in who said what, who gave the best supper parties and where they bought their fashionable clothes.

'And I still believe she's lonely,' he went on in the same tone. 'Why else would she make up a story

46

about a little Dutch girl? Some of your friends have children; could you not take her with you when you visit?'

'Sometimes I do,' she countered. 'But it is not always convenient.'

'Then they could come here,' he said impatiently. 'Perhaps share lessons together?'

'That would hardly be fair to Miss Ripley.'

He leaned across and touched her hand. 'Rosamund,' he said softly, 'perhaps we should have another child? There would be a big gap, of course, but Margriet would love to have the companionship of a younger sibling.'

She stiffened, and her expression froze. 'You have forgotten, Frederik,' her voice was tight and cold, 'just how much I suffered in giving birth to Margriet. I have tried to be a good wife and I hope I have not been neglectful of my wifely duties, and of course if you insist it is not my place to refuse, but—'

He pulled his hand away, spreading his fingers in dissent, almost as a shield against her suggestion that she would agree in spite of her dread. It was true that she never refused him, but any loving advance he made towards her was, he knew, quite abhorrent to her. It was enough, he thought, to drive a man into another woman's arms.

Margriet was indeed thinking as she lay on top of her coverlet; she was considering how she could persuade her mother to allow the little Dutch girl to visit her. She had called down her name but Margriet couldn't recall what it was. Was it Klara,

47

like the daughter of Papa's friend? Anika or Liesel? It was something like that, she was sure. Margriet closed her eyes, the better to think; her own name in English was Marguerite, which was why her father sometimes called her Daisy. She liked that, but she preferred Margriet to Marguerite because it was easier to spell.

Anneliese. The name came suddenly as she had known it would if she didn't think too hard about it. If only I could go out alone I could knock on their door and ask if I might speak to her, or perhaps we could take a walk in the gardens? Surely the king wouldn't mind if two little girls walked in his shrubbery. She turned her head on the pillow and sighed. But how to find the gardens again? Then she smiled to herself; of course, Anneliese would know the way. She lived in the Land of Green Ginger, after all. She'd be sure to know.

She thought about it for a while and then made a decision. Papa and Mama were downstairs in the sitting room. Florrie and Mrs Simmonds would be busy with chores and Cook hardly ever stirred out of the kitchen. She slipped off the bed and put on her shoes. The weather was nice so she wouldn't need a coat, and she could be out of the house and down the street before she was missed. She wouldn't be long, could be there and back quite quickly, only needed time enough to introduce herself and arrange a meeting for another afternoon.

She was quite sure that Mrs Lindegroen wouldn't mind her calling without an appointment. The Dutch were very liberal, she had heard her mother say so. Margriet wasn't quite sure what liberal

48

meant, but it sounded comforting, she thought. She had a picture in her head of Mrs Lindegroen, plump and kind, wearing a skirt of dark material and a pretty white blouse, her fair hair tucked under a white cap with small white wings, like the pictures she had seen of Dutch ladies. Anneliese had long golden hair dressed in plaits just like the miller's daughter in *Rumpelstiltskin*, the story Papa had read to her.

She ran down the stairs, crossed the hall and the lobby and quietly opened the front door. Closing it behind her, she sped down the seven steps and along Parliament Street into Whitefriargate; none of the shoppers took any notice of her as she ran towards Land of Green Ginger. She paused at the top and looked up. The window where she had seen Anneliese was open and there she was, waving her hand, beckoning Margriet to come inside.

Margriet and Anneliese met often after that, during the afternoons when she had finished her lessons with Miss Ripley and was supposed to be resting. Sometimes they played at Margriet's house and climbed up to the top floor and into the maids' room, where they stood on a chair and looked out of the window over the rooftops of other houses to where the estuary showed as a thin silver line, and sometimes they played at Anneliese's house, where her mother, Mrs Lindegroen, was just as friendly and welcoming as Margriet had thought she would be. And occasionally the two little girls walked hand in hand in the king's garden, down long paths that were bordered by small trees and spicy-smelling bushes, or sat in the sunshine on carved wooden seats with little dogs playing by their slippered feet until ladies and gentlemen of the court walked by, when they would rise and curtsey as children were meant to do.

Anneliese's mother, who said Margriet should call her Mevrouw Lindegroen, would then come to fetch them home herself instead of sending a servant, and take Margriet to the top of Parliament Street where the girls would say goodbye and promise to meet the following day. But the strangest thing, Margriet thought, was that her mother didn't seem to notice her absence, or even Anneliese's presence, in the slightest.

CHAPTER SIX

'Must you go, Papa?' It was June and Frederik was about to sail again to Amsterdam. Margriet clung to his hand as he picked up his portmanteau. 'When can I go with you?'

'Not yet. I have a lot of work to do on this trip. When you are ten I'll bring my mother over to stay and then you can travel back with her.'

'That's a long way off. Could my grandmother not come here to visit before then?'

'I'll ask her,' he said, bending towards her. 'I might not have time to see her on this visit, though. Now, kiss me goodbye and be a good girl for your mama.'

Later, when he had stowed his belongings in the small cabin, Frederik went back on deck and leaned on the rail as the ship prepared to sail out of the dock, through the lock, down the Humber and into the choppy German Sea. He was a good sailor and had been making this voyage for many years. Since his father's death he had been running the family business alone, although his mother retained a keen interest in it. He had good managers both in Hull and in Amsterdam and he trusted them absolutely, but he still liked to keep his hand on the tiller, meeting clients and making sure that everything was running smoothly. His younger brother Bartel had settled for a quieter life and moved with his wife and daughters to Alkmaar, where he became a trader in the local cheese and other dairy products, shipping them to England through the business. Their sister Anna lived with her husband and children, in Amsterdam, near to their mother.

Frederik's thoughts drifted to his daughter, who, he was still convinced, was a lonely child. She was meditative, yet not shy or reserved; he laughed softly as he recalled the meeting with Hugh Webster and how she had behaved like a small adult, giving the lawyer her hand in greeting, just as Rosamund would have done.

Rosamund. He remembered fondly how charmed he had been at his first introduction to her, not only by her fragile beauty, but also by her discreet and delicate manners, her refinement, her shyness. He had supposed then that it was the complete contrast with his own boisterous and noisy family that drew him to her, for his mother, a farmer's daughter, believed that children should have not only freedom of expression, but freedom to get dirty if they wished, and as children he and his brother and sister had roamed the meadows near their childhood home, swum in the dykes in the summer and skated on them to school in the winter.

His father, always involved with his business activities, had viewed his children with a mild and humorous eye, as if they belonged not to him but to someone else. Not until the boys reached fourteen and sixteen did he take a hand and introduce them to the business, where they were expected to start in humble positions so that they would realize just how lucky they were to have had such a privileged childhood. They hadn't known until they were much older that they were more than fortunate; their father had had a shrewd head for investments during Amsterdam's lean years; he had become a bondholder in railway companies, had invested in tobacco, coffee and diamonds, and then had sat tight until the economy improved. On his death they were astonished to learn just how wealthy they were, for their father had divided his fortune equally between his wife, his daughter and his sons, after making provision for his grandchildren when they came of age.

Rosamund's father was a gentleman of private means, and Frederik gathered that he had expected Rosamund to marry someone in a similar position. Her mother, a merchant's daughter, however, having successfully married off three of her daughters, decided that although Frederik was not a gentleman as her husband understood the term he had a very successful father with a business that would one day belong to him. She thought him both charming and socially acceptable, and decided that if her youngest daughter would entertain his proposal her duty towards her girls would be fulfilled.

After their second meeting, Rosamund thought that of all her suitors he was the most promising. He did not try to impress her with the superiority of his admirable self as some young men did, nor treat her as a suitable candidate to be the mother of his children; he did try to engage her in conversation, which she found a little disturbing, particularly when he asked her opinion on subjects of which she knew nothing. But he was an attractive man with a slight accent that she found appealing; and she was becoming rather fearful that as the only daughter left she might have to stay at home and look after her ageing parents. Knowing her mother as well as she did, she was aware that that would mean being at their constant beck and call: not a choice she would have accepted gladly.

Frederik sighed, and moved away from the rail. Why had Rosamund accepted his proposal, he wondered. Had she just wanted to leave home, to remove herself from an overbearing mother? He had loved her then, or thought he did, but they had nothing in common, nothing to bind them together – except, of course, our beautiful daughter, he told himself now.

He returned to his cabin as they left the Humber and the ship rose to the challenge of the open sea, and lay on his bunk thinking of Margriet. He would ask his mother if the child could stay with her for a while. She was an outgoing woman with many interests and often had her other grandchildren to stay.

It would be good for Margriet to meet them, perhaps even learn their language; she'd like that, he thought. He didn't want her to grow up knowing only people from Rosamund's narrow social circle. He wanted her to be a well-rounded person, aware of other cultures and nations, able to know her own mind, express her own opinion. Lying on his bunk, feeling the swell of the ocean beneath him, he decided that he would definitely ask his mother to come back with him after his next visit. She and Margriet could get to know each other, and after that, perhaps next spring, Margriet could go and stay with her. Yes, he thought, that is definitely something we can do.

The ship came in to Amsterdam by way of the New Holland Canal, built only twenty or so years before to shorten the long sea route, and Frederik booked in at his usual small hotel. He changed his clothes, ate breakfast and ordered a carriage to take him to the railway station. His first visit was to the head of a company in Gouda, who asked him if he knew that Nicolaas Jansen was ill. 'I believe he's a colleague of yours?'

'More than a colleague,' Frederik said. 'A friend.'

'Perhaps you should visit him,' Beulen suggested. 'I have heard it isn't good news.'

Frederik was shocked. Nicolaas hadn't been well on his last visit but Frederik had hoped that he would have regained his health since then. He made one more call and then decided he would visit Nicolaas and continue with his business activities the following day.

He took a carriage to the house on the outskirts of Gouda. A maid answered the door to him, but Cornelia was already hurrying down the stairs and through the hall to greet him, having seen him arrive from an upstairs window.

'What a tonic,' she exclaimed. 'Nicolaas will be so delighted. We were only saying a few days ago that we hoped you would call soon. He wants to talk to you.'

Her voice broke as she spoke and Frederik saw her eyes, suddenly full of grief, well up with tears. He caught her by the hand. 'How is he?' he asked anxiously.

She shook her head, strands of thick auburn hair escaping from her cap. 'Much better,' she murmured. 'Much better today,' and he thought that she was saying it for the benefit of the maid rather than him. 'Will you have coffee before you go up?'

'He's in bed?'

'In his chair in the bedroom. He likes to stay up there for the view, he says.' She lowered her voice as the maid slipped away down the hall. 'But really it is because he finds the stairs so difficult. Come, I will make the coffee and you can have it up there with him. Can you stay? We would be so pleased if you could.'

'Thank you, if it's convenient. I wouldn't want to trouble you.'

'It is and you won't,' she said. 'It will be a pleasure. Nicolaas must tire of my company sometimes, and – well, friends – people, they don't always come when there is sickness.'

The Jansens' home had once been a farmhouse and although little had been changed structurally, the dimly lit rooms with their tall shuttered windows and mullioned glass were enlivened by brightly coloured cushions and patchwork covers on dark and heavy furniture and tapestry hangings on the walls. The kitchen where Cornelia now led him was tiled in blue and white, a deep-set inglenook with cooking accoutrements held a cheerful fire and a great oak lintel supported the chimney above it. In the centre of the room was a large table scattered with cups, plates and books.

Cornelia invited him to sit whilst she put water on to heat, ground coffee beans, took a pewter jug from a tall cupboard and set a wooden tray with cups, saucers and plates. Lastly, she lifted a sweet cake from a tin and put it on the largest plate.

He watched her admiringly. Nicolaas was able to afford servants, there was no doubt about that; the maid who had answered the door and then taken herself off to the other end of the hall would not have been the only help they employed, yet his wife clearly preferred to carry out some of the housewifely duties herself. He tried to imagine Rosamund doing anything of the kind but no image came to mind.

'There,' she said. 'All done.' She smiled as she poured hot water on the coffee grains. 'I know what you're thinking. You're thinking why does she do this herself instead of asking one of the maids!'

'I was indeed thinking that,' he laughed. 'You are a mind reader, *ja*, as well as a coffee maker?'

'I make good coffee,' she said simply and without conceit. 'Much better than Miriam does.' She turned to him. 'Will you carry it upstairs?'

He rose from the chair, took the tray from the table and followed her up the wide staircase. On the landing Cornelia went to an open doorway and in a cheerful voice proclaimed, 'Look who we have here, *liefje*. A new manservant for you.'

Frederik felt a sudden pang of envy. Never in

their life together had Rosamund used a term of endearment and certainly never such a word of love – 'sweetheart' – as Cornelia did now to Nicolaas. What a lucky man his friend was, he thought, until he stepped into the room and saw him.

Nicolaas sat by the window in a high-backed chair with a blanket over his knees and a shawl over his shoulders, even though the day wasn't cold. He turned to greet his visitor, and Frederik saw the gauntness of his face, the skin stretched across the cheekbones, and the deep salt cellars in his neck. His hands on the chair arms were skeletal, like an old man's.

Frederik was shocked, unable to believe how quickly Nicolaas had deteriorated since his last visit. He placed the tray on a low table and covered his disquiet by saying with forced merriment, 'Well, how are you, old fellow?'

'Fine, fine. What about you?' Nicolaas put out his hand to shake Frederik's and Frederik held it gently, as if fearful of breaking the fragile bones. 'Come and sit by me,' he went on in a rasping voice. 'Sorry I can't get up. My knees are a little weak today.'

Cornelia poured coffee for them both, giving Nicolaas only half a cup and then adding milk. 'Look what I've come to,' he joked. '*Kinder* coffee. I cannot stomach anything stronger.'

She offered Frederik a slice of cake. 'Coffee cake,' she said. 'I made it myself.'

'What an amazing wife you have, Nicolaas,' Frederik said. 'Makes her own cakes, grinds her own coffee beans.'

'I am a lucky man, *ja*? I know it,' he smiled, looking up at Cornelia. 'Of course I was a very good catch all those years ago, let's not forget that.'

'Indeed you were,' Cornelia returned. 'The prime of Holland, but it was my baking that settled it; he only decided on me because of my pancakes and *appeltart*.'

Frederik smiled as he listened to them and thought how well they were coping with the shadow of sadness hanging over them. There was no apparent misery or woe, no sense of misfortune, and yet it was there, hidden beneath the thin skin of their laughter. He realized the teasing was for his benefit, to put him at his ease, to accustom him to the perception of what they had already accepted.

They chatted of this and that, of people they knew, and when he had finished only half of his milky coffee Nicolaas said to his wife, 'Cornelia, *lieveling*, I want to talk to Freddy about boring business things. Why don't you take the opportunity to go out for an hour? It's a nice afternoon – you could sit in the garden, or take a walk. You need some fresh air; always you are cooped up with me. Why not?'

He smiled so sweetly and lovingly at her that it broke Frederik's heart to see it.

'Ah,' she said scornfully. 'You will talk of men's secrets, I know it.' She got to her feet. 'Well, yes, I will escape for an hour. Frederik, will you stay with us tonight?' She had already asked him, but this was for Nicolaas's cognizance. 'We would like that, wouldn't we, Nicolaas?'

'Oh, yes. Please do. Perhaps I'll come down for supper.'

'I'd be delighted to,' Frederik agreed. 'Thank you. Where are the children?'

'With my mother,' Cornelia said. 'She asked if they could stay and keep her company for a few days and of course they love to go, and it is easier for them to go to school from her house, so we can have a quiet supper, just the three of us. How lovely. I'll think of what we shall eat whilst I am out.'

Nicolaas gazed out of the window until he saw Cornelia go out of their gate and then look up, when he gave her a wave.

He sighed. 'I'm so pleased you have come, Frederik. It is as if you have answered my call. I wish to ask you something, my friend; a very great favour.'

CHAPTER SEVEN

'Forgive me, I haven't asked,' Nicolaas said. 'How is your wife? And your daughter?'

'Very well,' Frederik replied. 'I hope one day to bring Margriet over to meet my mother. She's too young to come yet – but yes, I'm making plans. I will bring her to meet you.'

'I'd like that,' Nicolaas said, and both were aware that that plan wouldn't come to fruition. 'And Cornelia would too, of course. She loves to have a houseful of children.' He settled himself back in his chair and straightened his blanket. 'You will perhaps realize, Freddy, that Cornelia and I have gone well past any pretence about my condition. The way we acted just now was entirely for your sake. But, good friend that you have been for so long . . . how long is it, do you think? We were students together in Amsterdam, and even when we went our separate ways we always kept in touch, did we not? I have always known that in any difficulty I could approach you, and I hope that you felt the same about me.'

Frederik swallowed. 'Indeed I did,' he said with difficulty. 'What times we had. Do you remember when you fell in the Herengracht canal?'

Nicolaas laughed, and then broke into a fit of coughing. 'Yes. And the night you were locked out of the Athenaeum and spent the night sleeping under an archway.'

'And then my father found out and decided the time had come for me to join him in the business where he could keep an eye on me!'

Nicolaas nodded. 'It was good to have such friendship,' he said quietly, 'and I hope I do not break that bond with the question and favour I am about to ask you.'

'I'm quite sure that you won't,' Frederik answered. 'You may ask anything at all and I'll do my best to comply with your wishes.'

Nicolaas nodded his thanks. 'I thought you would say that, but it is a great thing to ask, particularly as you live in England.'

'But I come home often,' Frederik demurred and was surprised to realize that he still regarded Netherlands as home, even though his life with his wife and child was firmly entrenched in England.

'I have little time left,' Nicolaas murmured. 'A month or two if I'm lucky, a few weeks if I am not.' He sighed. 'But the waiting – for Cornelia particularly it is very hard.'

Frederik felt a quickening of his pulse. What was Nicolaas going to ask of him? Life, however long or short, was precious.

'It is of Cornelia I speak,' Nicolaas went on. 'She is still a relatively young woman.' He smiled fondly. 'We were married when she was eighteen. She is a woman with a huge heart, a zest for life; she deserves happiness. She has been happy with me – we have been happy together – but it is wrong that she should be deprived of any contentment with someone else.'

Frederik thought of Hugh Webster's words and remembered that he still hadn't been to see his lawyer about renewing his will. He made a mental note to do so when he returned to England. 'But you are anxious that she might choose someone who will not take care of her as you have done?' he said.

'Yes, and no,' Nicolaas answered. 'I cannot rule her life from the grave and she may well choose someone that I wouldn't care for, but I want her to find happiness with someone, not live the rest of her life alone. Nevertheless, she will be vulnerable for quite some time, and I would hate to think that anyone might take advantage of her. So what I am asking you, my friend, is will you watch over her, when you can, of course, and be her friend as you have been mine? Care for her, if you will, so that she can trust you and ask your advice if she should need to?'

Frederik pondered. Cornelia seemed to him to be a strong woman and not vulnerable at all, unlike his own wife, who he thought might possibly make some wrong choices. However, Cornelia would undoubtedly be well provided for by Nicolaas, and there was no question that a comely widow with a large fortune might well be targeted by a scheming seducer.

'I want someone to love her as I have loved her,' Nicolaas said simply. 'To make her happy again.'

*

It would be easy enough for anyone to love her, Frederik mused as he sat downstairs by the window in their sitting room, waiting whilst Cornelia prepared food and Nicolaas took a rest. Presently he got up and went into the kitchen to find her, but she wasn't alone. The maid and an older woman who was scrubbing potatoes in the sink were also there.

He thought of an excuse for his intrusion and asked, 'Do you mind if I walk in your garden?'

'Of course not.' Cornelia looked up and smiled, but her smile was wistful, he thought, and the sadness was back in her eyes. 'And whilst you're there, will you pick me some herbs? Chives, mint, oregano, rosemary.'

'I will, if I recognize them,' he said wryly.

'Chives look like thick-stemmed grass. You'll know the mint and rosemary by the scent, and possibly the oregano too, for it has a distinctive smell, and like rosemary it has excellent healing properties.' She lowered her eyes. 'So they say.'

'And what else is rosemary for? It sounds familiar.'

'For remembrance,' she said softly. 'In *Hamlet*. Ophelia says, "There's rosemary, that's for remembrance".' She sighed. 'It is believed to have medicinal qualities too.'

He couldn't find any words, none that would comfort her anyway, and stepped out into the paved and gravelled garden, which had a dyke at the bottom of it.

The area was small but full of flowers and shrubs. Growing out of cracks in the paving were plants which smelled sweet and aromatic as he crushed them beneath his feet. He bent to draw in the fragrance of a white rose, its petals pure and unblemished perfection. He strode the few yards to the edge of the swiftly running water and gave a small smile as he remembered the dyke at the foot of their own garden when he was a boy. He wondered if the Jansen children played in the water as he once did. Nicolaas had told him that they both attended local schools and didn't have tutors or a governess, like Margriet.

That was the answer, he thought suddenly. Margriet must go to school! To a local school, not a boarding school, so that she could come home every afternoon. There must be many private dame schools in Hull, and she would be with other children and not alone as she was now. Why hadn't he thought of it before? He would discuss it with Cornelia to gauge her opinion, and then he would put it to Rosamund, although he feared she would raise objections.

He found the herbs that Cornelia had asked for growing together in a sunny corner, and behind them a tall clump of white marguerites which made him smile and think of his daughter again. It was a pity they didn't have a garden in Hull, he pondered, but only a yard where the servants emptied the slops and hung their dusters. He vaguely considered the possibility of moving somewhere with a garden, but he loved the house they were in and it was in a convenient position both for his business and for Rosamund's shopping and social activities. Perhaps at some time in the future, when he was finished with business and had more leisure time on his hands, he might think of it again.

He wondered if Cornelia would stay in this house alone, but then berated himself for being morbid, even though Nicolaas's life was hanging by a thread.

Frederik helped his friend downstairs for an early supper. Nicolaas's bony frame was light and angular and he winced at every step, which he took one at a time. 'Well done,' Frederik murmured as they reached the bottom.

'*Ja*,' Nicolaas muttered breathlessly. 'A small but significant success. I haven't been downstairs for several weeks. I can't ask Cornelia to help me, she isn't strong enough.'

'Indeed not,' Frederik agreed, thinking that he would try to rework his appointments to give his friend the pleasure of coming downstairs to sit with his wife. 'Could I make a suggestion?' he asked as they entered the kitchen.

Cornelia smiled. 'Please do.' She placed a tureen of pale green soup on the table and hurried to settle Nicolaas in his chair.

'How would it be, if it is agreeable to you, if I stayed here with you for this visit rather than at my hotel? Then, Nicolaas, when you feel up to it, I can assist you downstairs before I leave for work in the mornings so that you might spend all day with your lovely wife, and even perhaps see your friends when they call to enquire how you are?'

Nicolaas smiled. 'Rather than greet them upstairs as an invalid! *Ja*, I would like that. Cornelia? What do you think? Would that be a nuisance to you?'

'Of course it wouldn't be a nuisance,' she said warmly. 'I would love you to be downstairs where I

66

can talk to you. We can put your chair by the window where you can see the garden, and when it is sunny we can open it wide or even – perhaps – you could sit outside in the herb corner? Thank you, Frederik. That would be splendid.'

She began to serve the soup into bowls. 'This is a spring broth,' she said, 'with chicken meatballs. It also has celery, carrot, onion and the chives that Frederik kindly picked.' She gave a sudden laugh that lit up her face. 'And grass!'

Frederik apologized profusely, thinking how very beautiful she looked when she laughed. She wore an open expression of merriment and he caught a glimpse of how she had been before sadness over-took her. He glanced at Nicolaas and saw that he was watching her as well, a small poignant smile hovering on his lips as if he too was remembering how she once had been.

As they ate the rest of their supper of tender duck breast with asparagus and salad, he understood why Nicolaas wanted her to be happy when he had gone. It was what any man would feel who truly loved his wife: he wished her to know the joy of loving, and being loved, again.

CHAPTER EIGHT

Frederik stayed with the Jansens until the end of the week but then reluctantly had to leave. Before he went to his last appointment he made sure that Nicolaas was safely back upstairs in his room, though he was a little disturbed that his friend asked to be helped into bed rather than into his chair.

'I hope being downstairs so much hasn't overtired you, Nicolaas?' he said compassionately.

'Not a bit.' Nicolaas shifted about to make himself comfortable and then settled with a sigh. 'But no matter, anyway. I shall be getting plenty of rest before long and would rather not welcome that respite too soon. I must make the most of the time I have left and I thank you most sincerely for helping me to do that. I have enjoyed our time together immensely, and I know that Cornelia has too.'

Frederik nodded. He and Cornelia had sat talking until midnight after Nicolaas had gone to bed, and he had heard so much about the family that he felt he knew them better than he ever had before.

'I've cancelled my afternoon appointments so that I can see my mother before catching the ship home this evening,' he said in as normal a tone as he could manage, reluctant to utter the words of farewell.

'I'm sorry if we've curtailed some of your business.'

'It's of no consequence, none at all. I've done enough, and I've enjoyed the opportunity of being here with you and Cornelia.' He laughed, although he felt not in the least merry. 'Friendship is far more important than selling cheese and gin, after all.'

Nicolaas put his head back on his pillow. 'Try telling that to the purveyors of cheese and gin,' he said croakily. 'I think you'll find they have a different opinion.'

Frederik told him that he hoped to be back in Netherlands within three weeks and Nicolaas said he would look forward to it and he must stay with them again. He put out his hand. 'Take great care, my good friend, and thank you for your friendship. I shall rest more easily now that I know you will watch over Cornelia, although I won't hold you to any commitment that you can't easily accomplish.'

Frederik took the offered hand and tears fell unbidden down his cheeks. 'Farewell,' he said huskily. 'Not goodbye, for I look forward to seeing you next time,' and bent and kissed his boyhood friend tenderly on the forehead. '*God zegene u.*' God bless you.

At the bottom of the stairs he held his fingers to his eyes to quell the tears before he went to say goodbye to Cornelia. 'Forgive me,' he whispered as he took her hand. 'I do not have your strength to withstand such anguish.'

'It is a matter of taking one day at a time, one hour at a time, one minute at a time,' she said softly. 'And that way the whole day passes and you are through it and ready for the next one.' She gently brushed his wet cheek with her fingertips. 'We shall hope to see you again soon, and if anything should occur before then, perhaps I might write to you?'

'Of course,' he murmured. 'Do not hesitate. I can be here within a day.'

'You have been a good friend,' she said. 'To both of us. It is appreciated; you have gone beyond the bond of friendship.'

He shook his head. 'I have done nothing. I wish that I could have done more.' He kissed her on both cheeks and then, without thinking, he put his arms around her. For a moment only, he held her close. He felt her take a sudden breath before he released her.

'I beg your pardon,' he began, but she gave a tremulous smile.

'It is best not to be too kind to me, Frederik, or my questionable resolve to be strong will weaken,' she whispered.

As the carriage bowled along the road to Amsterdam, he mused on the week just past. He'd felt like one of the family as they had sat and chatted after supper. Cornelia had found him a pair of slippers and a woollen jacket belonging to Nicolaas so that he could be more comfortable than dressed in his formal coat, and after Nicolaas had gone to bed she had taken off her white cap as she talked and unplaited her braids, running her fingers through her thick hair without a thought for the impropriety of such conduct in front of a man who wasn't her husband. He had never seen Rosamund with her hair undressed except in bed, and more often than not she wore a bed cap. There was something, he reflected, quite pleasurable about such long, soft and luxurious tresses. With the undulating waves falling around her shoulders, Cornelia was not the usual image of a Dutch woman one might see in a painting, calm and peaceful, her passions and emotions controlled in much the same way as her hair was confined beneath a cap.

Lost in his musings, he barely noticed the familiar landscape of rich green fields interspersed with dykes and ditches and only vaguely glanced at the polder mills in the distance as their sails turned and the pumps drained the land. It was all so familiar and well loved, and although it seemed not to have changed since he was a boy he was aware that there was constant renewal as engineers worked to keep the low-lying land safe from the invading sea.

Making a quick decision, he asked the driver to take him to his mother's house. After the time he had spent with Nicolaas and Cornelia, his conscience told him that he didn't see enough of his family, and that business could wait.

She was delighted to see him even though she was entertaining guests. He greeted them all, then drew his mother aside to tell her that this was a fleeting visit only and he would come again next time he was over. 'I didn't want to leave Amsterdam without seeing you,' he said. 'But you know how it is when business calls.'

71

'Of course I do. Your father was just the same, but you must make time for friends and family as well. They are important too.'

He told her about Nicolaas, whom she remembered well. She clasped her hands together and murmured '*God zegene hem*', then patted her son's arm. 'Go, then. Next time I'll ask your sister to come too.'

He travelled back to England on the evening tide and the following morning strode home the short distance from the dock. He ran up the steps, rang the doorbell and let himself in with his key just as Florrie came hurrying to the door, pushing her hair beneath her cap. He smiled, remembering Cornelia's long tresses.

'Oh, sir,' she said. 'You startled me. Mrs Vandergroene is still abed. I've taken her breakfast.'

'And Margriet?'

'She's up and dressed, sir, and having her gruel. Shall I tell her you're here?'

'No. I'll go up and surprise her, but perhaps you will tell my wife I'm home. She won't like a surprise,' he added jokingly.

'No, sir, mebbe not.' Florrie dipped her knee and ran up the stairs in front of him.

Frederik continued up the staircase to the top floor and was about to knock on Margriet's door when he heard voices. He paused. Who was in there with her? Miss Ripley? But she didn't usually come so early, and Florrie would surely have mentioned her. He put his ear to the door and listened. Margriet was saying, 'What I think we should do,

Anneliese, the next time we visit the garden, is to say quite emphatically' – she pronounced the word firmly – 'that we would like a little dog of our own to play with.'

Another voice replied, a child's voice but shriller than Margriet's. 'Oh, but Margriet, we must ask *emphatically* for two little dogs so that we can have one each.'

Frederik frowned. Who was that? He tapped softly on the door and slowly opened it. Margriet was sitting at her table with her back to him, a dish of gruel in front of her, but there was no one else in the room. She hadn't heard him come in, so he slowly backed out again, knocked briskly and entered once more.

Margriet jumped, startled, but on seeing her father pushed back her chair and ran into his arms.

'Hello, *lieveling*.' He kissed her cheek. 'Are you pleased to see your papa?'

'Oh, yes!' she said. 'You've been gone such a long time.'

'Not really,' he said. 'Only a week.'

'It seems much longer,' she pouted. 'Miss Ripley has been sick and hasn't been for our lessons, so I haven't had much to do and the days were very long, even though Mama set me some work to do.'

'Did she? Was it interesting?'

Margriet sighed. 'Not really.'

'When I came upstairs,' Frederik said casually, 'I thought I heard you talking to someone.'

Margriet's mouth opened and then closed. 'Oh?'

'Yes. I thought that perhaps you had a friend here.'

She looked at him, her eyes wide, and then she

licked her lips. 'N-no.'

He made a pretence of looking round the room and under the table and then raised his eyebrows. 'She's disappeared! I must have frightened her away.'

She gave a nervous laugh, as if unsure how he was going to react, which bothered him. He wanted her to know that she could always confide in him.

'I was thinking whilst I was away,' he remarked, and sat down in the other chair at the table. He noticed that she watched him carefully, as if trying to anticipate what he was going to say. 'I was thinking about you being taught on your own, without any other children to exchange ideas with.' He thought she seemed to relax, although her eyes remained alert. 'And I wondered if you'd like to go to school,' he continued. 'The children in Gouda I told you about go to a local school, and I understand they enjoy it. What do you think? I haven't discussed it with your mama yet, but I'm sure we could find a good school in Hull.'

Her face brightened. 'Oh, yes please, Papa. I would. I really would like that. When? When could I start?'

'Perhaps next term. We must find somewhere suitable first and make sure there's a place for you.' He got to his feet. 'I'll speak to Mama later and ask her opinion.'

'Will she mind, do you think?' she asked anxiously. 'She likes me to be at home.'

He patted her head. 'I'll persuade her.' He smiled conspiratorially. 'I know how.'

Closing the door behind him, he stood for a moment, pondering, and then heard Margriet saying eagerly, 'What do you think about that, Anneliese? Won't that be such splendid fun?'

And then the other piping voice, but undoubtedly Margriet's own, saying, 'But will I be able to come with you, Margriet? It won't be fair if you leave me behind.'

'I won't do that,' Margriet replied. 'Not ever. You are my very best friend.'

CHAPTER NINE

Rosamund was dubious. 'She might pick up bad habits at a dame school,' she complained. 'She will not be taught to be a lady.'

'Perhaps not,' he said. 'But you are able to teach her those attributes. I'm more concerned that she's always alone and doesn't know any other children. She needs to be integrated with others.' He didn't tell Rosamund what he had overheard. He knew she would be concerned and would probably question Margriet about it.

But he told her about the Jansen children, and about Nicolaas. She was horrified. 'But he is still young, is he not? Much too young to die. Your age, if you were at school together. That is so sad, so difficult to comprehend.' He was heartened by her sympathy for his friend, although musing that it was unusual. 'And his wife,' she continued in the same dismayed and apprehensive tone. 'How ever will she manage without her husband's support? Is she young enough to marry again? Can she go back home to live with her parents?'

'Her parents?' He frowned. 'Why would she do that? She's not a young girl; she has a home and children to take care of. Nicolaas will have made provision for her and the children, but she will have to make a new life without him.'

'But how can she?' Rosamund said. 'Who will make decisions for her?'

He shook his head in bemusement. 'Women can make their own decisions,' he said. 'You make decisions. You will decide whether or not Margriet should attend dame school.'

'But I might choose the wrong school,' she floundered. 'And besides, I meant on important matters. I can make rules for Margriet and attend to the servants, but affairs of significance are left to you.'

She didn't say what affairs of significance she was referring to and he thought she meant money matters. She was clearly agitated, and he wondered if she had awoken to the possibility that she too might be left a young widow. It was plain, he considered ruefully, that she wouldn't stay widowed for long but would look for a husband to take his place. Although he was mildly amused, he reminded himself that he still hadn't been to see Hugh Webster and must do so immediately, for if such an unlikely event did occur Rosamund would be a very rich widow indeed.

He made enquiries about dame schools, for he knew that Rosamund wouldn't, and came up with several quite close to home. He asked some of his associates if they knew anything about them, but it seemed their wives attended to the schooling of their daughters; sons, of course, went away to their father's choice of school. But one day as he was crossing Market Place he saw Hendrik Sanderson, a businessman whose mother was Dutch, taking his leave of a man in cap and gown outside the grammar school.

'Good day to you, Sanderson,' he called out as he caught up with him. 'How nice to see you.'

Sanderson greeted him warmly; he had gained much by helpful conversation with Vandergroene in the past. They chatted about this and that until Sanderson said, 'I must tell you – I'm so delighted. The headmaster of the grammar school – my old school – has just told me that my son has gained a place there.'

'Excellent,' Frederik exclaimed. 'A very prestigious school, I understand.'

'Indeed yes; so many illustrious past pupils. It was an honour for me to receive my schooling there and I'm thrilled that my son will do so too.'

'Do you have daughters?' Frederik asked. Here was a man who had given thought to his son's education and hadn't just sent him away to boarding school because that was the thing to do.

'Yes.' Sanderson's face lit up with pride. 'I have two intelligent, beautiful daughters. Imogen is ten and Julia is eight.' He pointed down North Church Side. 'They attend the dame school with George, just along here. Excellent headmistress; I can't recommend her enough.'

'Oh, tell me more!' Frederik exclaimed. 'I'm looking for such a school for my own daughter.' He hesitated. 'Does your wife approve?'

'Oh, indeed. She's a very forward-thinking woman, believes in girls having the same opportunities as boys.' He grimaced. 'She's in the minority, I fear, and will have to wait a long time to see her ideas come to fruition, if they ever do.'

'Well, perhaps for our daughters?' Frederik suggested.

'I'm a realist, Vandergroene.' Sanderson shrugged and shook his head. 'Not even for them, but it's a start, isn't it? We must do what we can.'

Frederik was so uplifted by the conversation that he went immediately to the school to see the headmistress, Miss Dorothy Barker, who requested that he bring his wife and daughter to talk to her.

'I have only a small school, Mr Vandergroene,' she explained, 'and I must be sure that my pupils will not only integrate well, but also be willing to learn.'

'Excellent.' He rubbed his hands together. 'Margriet is six and can already read and write well.' He thought how wonderful it would be that she would have at least six more years of education to improve her mind and vocabulary as well as her knowledge.

He couldn't wait to get home and tell Rosamund and Margriet. Rosamund was still unsure about the prospect. 'Can you be certain that Miss Barker has the proper credentials to be in charge of children? Will she insist on good manners and correct behaviour? We don't want Margriet to become lax in matters of decorum.'

Frederik sighed. 'She won't. But you can judge for yourself when we take her to see Miss Barker.'

'But surely I don't have to come with you? Not when you have already met Miss Barker?'

'You do,' he insisted. 'If you want to be sure that

Miss Barker comes up to your exacting standards, of course you do.'

Rosamund was shirking her responsibility, he thought as he climbed the stairs to Margriet's room; it was clear that she didn't want to be pressed into giving her opinion. Regretfully, Frederik concluded that she probably didn't have an opinion to give.

Margriet, on the other hand, was overjoyed. 'Will there be other little girls there, Papa? Will I be able to play with them?' Her expression became cautious for a moment, as if she was thinking of something else.

'You will be there to learn, Margriet, but I dare say there will be a chance to play too.'

'And who will take me?' she said. 'Will Mama? Oh, but then she would have to walk home alone and she can't do that.' Her face clouded for a moment, and then cleared. 'Florrie will take me, I expect. She doesn't mind walking by herself; she's quite used to it.'

How strange it was, he thought, that women like Florrie had more freedom than someone like Rosamund, who considered it unseemly to walk along the street alone, without the company of a maidservant, even during daylight hours. He gave a deep sigh. Would it ever be any different?

'And what shall we tell Miss Ripley, Papa? I think she will be sad if she can't come to teach me any more.'

'Mama will explain that you will be going to school next term . . . but we are jumping our hedges too soon. First we have to go and see Miss Barker and find out if she is willing to take you as a pupil.'

'Oh.' Margriet considered. 'You mean she might not? Then I must practise my curtsey and how to say how-de-do to please her.'

Frederik laughed and patted her cheek. 'I think, Daisy, that you will impress Miss Barker more if you ask her what she will be teaching you than if you can do a wobble-free curtsey!'

Frederik decided that he would act in the manner of a masterful husband even though it went against his better nature, and he insisted that Rosamund went with them to meet Miss Barker. Rosamund said little after the initial greeting, but Frederik noticed her surveying the parlour that served as a schoolroom and the five children – three girls and two boys – sitting at the table with books and slates in front of them. A young woman of about eighteen sat with them.

'This is my assistant, Miss Chambers,' Miss Barker said, and the young woman got up to shake hands. 'As you will see, I take only five pupils, but we shall be losing George this summer, and so will have room for another.' She smiled at one of the boys. 'He will be attending Hull Grammar School in the autumn. We are all very proud of him.'

The boy tried to hide a grin, but it was easy to see that he was pleased by the praise.

'Sanderson's son?' Frederik asked. 'It was Sanderson who recommended you to me.'

'Ah! Did he? That is very gratifying.' She took them back into her office, which doubled as another schoolroom; there were exercise books on the table, a small desk with an oil lamp, and in one corner a pianoforte and stool. When they were seated, she turned to Margriet. 'It's Margriet, isn't it? How old are you?'

Margriet got to her feet and gave a small dip of the knee. 'I'm six, Miss Barker.'

'Ah, so you know my name.'

'Yes, Papa told me.'

Miss Barker nodded. 'And is there anything you'd like to ask me? Anything you'd like to know or are anxious about?'

Margriet worked her mouth as she thought. 'I'm not anxious about anything, but I wondered if you will be telling us about King Henry?'

Miss Barker raised her dark eyebrows. 'Which King Henry?'

Margriet's lips shaped into an orb, and she glanced at her father. She only knew of one. 'The one who had a palace in Hull.'

'Henry VIII? I see. You are interested in history, are you?'

'Papa took me to see where the palace and the gardens used to be, but it was a long time ago so the palace isn't here any more, although the gardens . . . the gardens might be.' She paused. 'At least – I think I know where they are, and that the ladies of the court like to walk in them.'

'You know where they *were*, I think, Margriet,' Miss Barker suggested. 'They would have been built upon long ago.'

Margriet pressed her lips together. 'Yes,' she murmured. 'That's what I meant.'

Before they left, Miss Barker asked Margriet to go back to the other room and say hello to the other students whilst she spoke to her parents. 'She seems a very bright intelligent child,' she said, when the door had closed behind her. 'I think she will make a welcome addition to our school. I was intrigued by her question about the royal palace; there are few adults who know of its existence, let alone a child.'

'But I must expect the cane for not telling her which King Henry came here,' Frederik said contritely.

Miss Barker gave a faint smile. 'There is no such thing as the cane in my school, Mr Vandergroene, not even for the boys.' She looked at Rosamund. 'Is there anything you would like to ask, Mrs Vandergroene?'

Frederik held his breath, hoping Rosamund wouldn't mention decorum or ladylike manners. 'I think my husband has covered everything that is necessary, Miss Barker,' she said after a moment. 'Thank you for your courtesy.'

CHAPTER TEN

Miss Ripley was informed that her services would not be required after the end of July, which gave her ample time to look for another position before the following term began. 'We will of course give you an excellent reference,' Rosamund told her. 'Had it been left to me I would have asked you to stay much longer; we have found nothing lacking in your teaching of Margriet.' She gave the merest lift of her shoulders as if to say that the matter was out of her hands. Miss Ripley was disappointed, but understood very well that Mr Vandergroene would want a higher education for his daughter than she could give. She would send an advertisement to 'Positions Required' in the local newspaper; Mrs Vandergroene promised that she would enquire amongst her friends and acquaintances for suitable situations but Miss Ripley privately thought it highly unlikely that her employer would take such trouble.

Barely a month after Frederik's return from Netherlands, Mrs Simmonds brought him a letter bearing a Dutch postage stamp. He didn't recognize the writing; it was a bold though shaky hand,

and with some dread he guessed just whom it was from and what its contents must be.

It was from Cornelia telling him of the death of Nicolaas.

I write to advise you as I promised I would. The funeral will be held in two days, but I do not expect you to come at such short notice. If you feel you can visit us at some time in the future, then my children and I will be more than pleased to welcome such a good friend.

He saw by the date of the postmark that he would be too late for the funeral, but nevertheless he decided he would sail that same evening and stay with his mother. Rosamund expressed surprise. 'Surely Mrs Jansen will not be receiving visitors so soon after her husband's death? Is that the Dutch custom?' She gave a little shudder. 'I wouldn't be able to face anyone.'

'Would you not be comforted by sincere well-wishers?' he asked. 'Would you not be glad of the fact that friends wanted to offer their help and condolences?'

'Oh, no!' she said. 'I would want to hide away in a darkened room.'

Frederik gave a wry smile. 'I am heartened, *nee*, gratified, Rosamund, that you would miss me so much!'

She gazed at him blankly, and he realized that she wasn't thinking of her feelings if such a tragedy should take place, but of the unfortunate situation she would be left in.

'Well,' he sighed. 'I am going on this evening's tide, and even if I should be turned away at the door I will at least have tried to offer some comfort and support.'

He told Margriet why he was going away again so soon and she said how sad the lady must be. 'I would cry, Papa. I expect her children will cry too, now that they have no papa.' Her own eyes filled with tears. 'Please will you tell them that I am very sad for them?'

'I will, Margriet, and I'm sure they will take strength from your kind thoughts.' He kissed the top of her head. 'I will return soon.'

When the ship docked the next morning he called first of all on his mother, and then took a train to Utrecht and a cabriolet to Cornelia's house. The window shutters were closed and he wondered if Rosamund had been right after all and he was calling too soon.

He gave a cautious knock on the front door and inhaled the sweet perfume of the roses and honeysuckle that were climbing up around it. A moment later the door was opened by Klara, who was dressed in white threaded with black ribbon, and gazed silently up at him as if not recognizing him.

'Hello, Klara,' he said quietly. 'I'm Frederik Vandergroene. Do you remember me? I was a good friend of your father's. Would you give your mother my kind respects, and ask if I might call at a convenient time?'

She nodded and said, 'Please wait one moment,'

and leaving the door ajar she turned away and pattered down the hall. He heard her voice and then her mother's and then Cornelia came hurrying to greet him.

'Oh, Frederik, how kind of you to come so quickly. Please come in. Klara said she was sorry she didn't recognize you.'

'Not at all; I didn't expect her to,' he said. He thought how regal and dignified Cornelia looked. Although her face was pale, accentuated by the deep black of her gown, she smiled at him as she led him to the kitchen. He looked up the stairs as he passed and remembered helping Nicolaas down them so that he could eat with them at the table, and was suddenly devastated by his loss.

He put his hands to his eyes, and as Cornelia turned to ask him to be seated he murmured, 'Forgive me. I came to offer comfort and find that I am in need of it too.'

She patted his shoulder in a maternal manner, but didn't say anything, allowing him to sit quietly until he had suppressed his emotion. Klara sat on the arm of her mother's chair until Cornelia whispered something to her. The child dipped her knee to Frederik and left the room.

'I'm sorry.' He cleared his throat. 'When I received your letter I was saddened, although the news was not unexpected, but now, here in your home, his loss has hit me hard.'

'I understand,' she said softly. 'I, of course, had time to adjust to the inevitable, and yet when it came—' She broke off, fingering a black pendant at her neck, and paused a moment before continuing. 'It was harder than I thought. But I am so glad that you are here. So very glad.'

'My wife thought it too soon to come,' Frederik told her. 'That you wouldn't wish to be disturbed until your mourning period was over.'

'I would not wish my friends to stay away,' she said simply. 'I want us to share our happier memories. Nicolaas requested a simple funeral ceremony and asked me not to observe a long period of mourning. He knew that it is not in my nature to be sombre. I will wear black for a year, so as not to shock my neighbours, but I know Nicolaas would not mind if I began quietly to go out again after six months.' She gazed into the middle distance. 'But I am worried about Hans. He misses his father very much. I am not able to comfort him.'

'He's young, but too old to want to show his feelings in front of others. He's hovering between boy and man, I think?'

'He is,' she agreed. 'I believe he considers that he is now the man of the house and should be taking on responsibilities, but he's not ready for them.'

'Would he allow me to speak to him? Perhaps I could tell him about his father when he was a boy?' Frederik glanced out of the window overlooking the garden. The shutters were open here and the sun shone brightly through the glass; Hans was pacing about with his hands thrust into his trouser pockets.

'You could try,' Cornelia said. 'Yes, please. Perhaps now, whilst I prepare coffee and cake.'

Frederik got up immediately and Cornelia pointed to the door leading out to the garden. Outside, he closed his eyes and stood with his head back for a moment or two before opening his eyes and looking about him. Hans was watching him.

As if startled, Frederik said, 'Hans. I'm sorry. Did I disturb you?' He took a step towards the boy and held out his hand. 'I am so very sorry about your father. We were friends from when we were young, you know – younger than I imagine you are now.'

Awkwardly, Hans returned a limp handshake and nodded briefly.

'I admit it was very difficult for me in the house,' Frederik confided. 'I don't want to upset your mother, but I couldn't help but dwell on the last time I was here, not thinking that—' He pressed his lips together and swallowed, filled with a genuine emotion. 'That's why I came outside. I'm sorry to disturb you,' he said again. 'It must be much more difficult for you.'

Hans nodded again. 'You have children, don't you? How would they feel?'

'A daughter,' Frederik said. 'Margriet asked me to tell you that she is very sad for you and your sister.'

'Please thank her, sir,' Hans muttered. 'Most of our friends haven't spoken to us, although some have sent cards.'

'That's because they don't know what to say. They're afraid of upsetting or embarrassing you. When you get older you are able to control your feelings better.' He chanced a weak smile. 'Well, that's the theory, but it doesn't always work.' He looked away as a single tear rolled down the boy's cheek. 'My own father died only a short time ago, and although it doesn't compare to losing a father when you're as young as you are, I found that having a good weep alone in my room helped me to cope later when I was in the company of others. And talking about him helped,' he added hurriedly, fearful that Hans was about to take his advice and bolt away, 'because it made sure that I didn't forget all the witty things he used to say. And that applies to my friendship with your father too. I'd very much like to talk to you about him one day, if you would permit me.'

'Yes,' Hans croaked. 'Of course. Will you excuse me, sir?' and he dashed for the house door.

Frederik wandered around the garden, bending to examine the roses and running his fingers through lavender and marjoram to release the pungent aroma. Cornelia came outside carrying a tray, and they sat at a small wrought-iron table where she poured them both coffee from a jug.

He smiled. 'Don't you have servants, Cornelia?'

'You know I do. But why would I interrupt their cleaning and polishing and scrubbing floors, work that I don't like to do, just to do something simple like making coffee or baking cake? Besides,' she laughed, 'it keeps them on their toes. They see that I can manage some things and so do their utmost to show me how much better they are at the others than I am.'

'I think they are also fond of you, Cornelia,' he murmured, and thought, why wouldn't they be? There would be no raised voices, no sharp or demanding words from the mistress of this household.

She nodded. 'They are. They idolized Nicolaas

and they look after me and the children for his sake, especially now.'

He sipped his coffee. 'I've spoken to Hans. I don't know if it's done any good. It's early yet – he's sunk in misery and will take some time to heal. Adjustment to his father's loss will be part of his growing up.'

She turned to look at him. Her eyes were large, soft and grey. 'I at least am grateful for your kindness,' she murmured.

His impulse was to reach out and touch her hand and he stopped himself just in time. What was he thinking of? Here was a woman recently widowed; how abhorrent it would be for her to feel another man's hand on hers. He felt his pulses racing and a quickening sensation he hadn't known in a long time. It wasn't mere sympathy that had caused the impulsive instinct to reach out towards her. It was something much more, and he realized he must tread carefully or he would lose her trust and ruin the memory of the lifelong friendship he had shared with Nicolaas. There was only one word for what he was feeling. It was desire.

CHAPTER ELEVEN

Frederik travelled back to Amsterdam that evening. He had kissed the back of Cornelia's hand, shaken hands with Hans and given Klara a courteous bow. The little girl had dipped her knee in return.

'Thank you so much for coming,' Cornelia had said. 'Please come to see us again.'

He had said that he would, but as he was driven away from the house he determined that he would wait a few months before returning. He was still shocked by his earlier revelation, and told himself that it could only have been because his emotions were still in turmoil. Nicolaas, after all, had been his very good friend and was the first of his contemporaries to die. He was not invincible after all.

He stayed overnight at his mother's house; she had cooked supper for the two of them and as they ate they talked about Nicolaas. 'You will miss him,' she said, 'but when you return home you will have much else to occupy your mind. His wife will take longer to recover.'

'She's strong,' he said. 'Just like you, Moe. You women are much stronger than men.'

'So we are,' she sighed. 'Or appear to be.'

He told her about his wish that she might accompany him to England after one of his trips and then bring Margriet back to Amsterdam. 'I would like her to sample Dutch life,' he said. 'Perhaps learn the language, spend time with Bartel and Anna and their children.'

His mother agreed. 'It isn't good that they don't know each other, but you must wait a little while longer before I can travel. I am not yet strong enough to meet your wife again.'

He gave a sharp gasp. 'You've only seen her once, on our wedding day!'

'I know. It is the thought that she might have grown to be like her *moeder* that worries me. *She* was a formidable woman. I believe she was expecting to see me wearing wooden clogs and an embroidered apron and carrying a bunch of tulips.'

'Well, sometimes you do,' he prevaricated.

'Not at an English wedding! If you'd married here I might have done.'

'Rosamund is not a good sailor,' he began, but his mother tutted impatiently and he desisted. He had heard her opinion often enough to know that he couldn't win that argument. 'She is not like her mother,' he said instead, 'who by the way moved away from Hull quite some time ago. You wouldn't have to meet her if that's what's worrying you.'

His mother gazed cynically at him. 'It is not. You should know me better than that, Frederik. Now,' she said, changing the contentious subject of her daughter-in-law and her family, 'tell me about my English *kleindochter*. Ask Margriet to write and tell

93

me about herself. She is old enough now to do that, isn't she?'

'She is. She can read and write very well. Let me tell you about the school that she will be attending in the autumn. She's really looking forward to that.'

He travelled home two days later. He had spent the time reading reports and going over sales figures in his Amsterdam office, and was satisfied that the manager and his staff ran the Dutch side of the business as well as he could have done himself. He decided that he would look into the possibility of giving them shares in the company to keep them from moving elsewhere.

He did not sleep well in his narrow bunk even though the sea was relatively calm; it was not the weather but his restless thoughts that kept him awake on this voyage. His mother had chastised him for not insisting that Rosamund should overcome her distaste for travel and bring Margriet to visit her. He thought too of young Hans, adrift without his father, trying so hard to be a man before his time. Did he have uncles to whom he might turn for guidance? Nicolaas had two sisters, he recalled, but no brother, but what of Cornelia? Had she mentioned siblings? Cornelia! The image of her arose sharp and strong: her perfect face and skin, the luxuriant hair, her soft lips.

He sat up with a groan and reached for a warm jumper. When he was fully dressed he sat for a moment on his bunk with his head in his hands, confused and melancholy. He knew there was no need to return to the Dutch office for some time; even in Hull they could manage without him at present. Slowly, an idea took root in his mind. He, Rosamund and Margriet would take a holiday. They would hire a house in Scarborough or Bridlington for a month. Margriet would like that. Yes, that was what they would do.

He stood up, and opening his cabin door made his way up the companionway and out on deck. The wind was fresh and strong, thundering in the sails and whistling through the rigging as the ship made good headway. He took several deep breaths to clear his head and gazed up at the dark sky with its millions of scintillating stars.

We are nothing in the scheme of things, he thought as he sought to follow the path of a shooting star. We worry ourselves over the trivialities of a life which is so short, and there are few of us who make a mark to be remembered by. So why do we torment ourselves? He tipped his head back and gazed up at the firmament, feeling dizzy as the gremlin of desire came back to torment him and ruin his previous decisive conclusion. *I want to see her. I must. I have never wanted anything more in my whole life.*

To avoid thinking about Cornelia he set about trying to find a suitable house for hire in one of the nearby seaside towns. Surprisingly, Rosamund had agreed to the suggestion, but had said she would prefer somewhere in the south, like Bournemouth, where the weather would be warmer. Frederik had demurred, saying he didn't want to make such a long journey when there were other resorts within easy reach. 'Scarborough is a spa town,' he said. 'You'll know lots of people there.'

'It's very small,' Rosamund said. 'And I believe that taking the waters is not as popular as it once was, so of course it won't attract the London crowd.'

Her manner was so cutting that Frederik became more determined to find somewhere closer to home. He was sure that Rosamund had only mentioned Bournemouth because her sisters had always gone south for their vacations.

He trawled the advertisements in his daily paper without success, and then resorted to his wife's fashion magazines, but there was nothing in there either, nor in the *Illustrated London News*, a recent quality publication to which he subscribed. In addition to topical news features it carried book reviews, crime reports and select advertising, but nothing on houses for hire in Scarborough or Bridlington.

He was on the point of giving up when quite by chance he once again bumped into Hendrik Sanderson, and stopped to thank him for recommending Miss Barker's school. Sanderson was delighted to hear about Margriet's success.

'She'll love it there,' he said. 'My daughters do, and even George says he'll be sorry to leave. But he'll soon forget about it when we start to plan our holiday. We go to Scarborough, and take a maid to look after the children so that my wife and I can listen to the music at the Spa. We spent our honeymoon there, you know, and it's a favourite place. Quiet and peaceful, and the children play on the sands all day.'

'You're just the man I need,' Frederik said enthusiastically. 'I'm looking for a house to rent in Scarborough.'

Sanderson gave him the name and address of the agent he used and within the day, fired up by the idea of a month by the sea, Frederik had asked his clerk to write and enquire about a suitable house for a family, with a view of the sea and near the new promenade.

Within the week came news of two cottages close to St Nicholas Cliff, one with three bedrooms and the other with four. Both were vacant for the month of August.

'If we take the four-bedroomed house we could take one of the servants, Florrie perhaps,' Frederik suggested, thinking of what Sanderson had said, 'and use the spare as a dressing room.'

'We'll take Florence, if you are still determined on Scarborough,' Rosamund said coldly. 'I don't suppose she'll mind walking on the sands with Margriet.'

'I don't suppose she will,' Frederik muttered, feeling deflated. 'I must search out my cricket bat and balls. I'll teach Margriet how to play.'

Rosamund turned a horrified face towards him. 'She's a girl!'

'And – what? My sister used to play games with Bartel and me when we were young.'

'Well, you need more than two players.'

'I'm sure that Florrie will know how to play,' he snapped, irritated. He simulated an overarm throw just to torment her. 'It's only bat and ball, Rosamund, for heaven's sake. It's just a game.'

Florrie was delighted to be asked to go with

them, and as she said to Mrs Simmonds it wouldn't be hard work as she surely wouldn't be expected to do more than a little dusting if she were to be in charge of Miss Margriet. Cook too was looking forward to taking it easy for the month as there would be little cooking to do, but Mrs Simmonds said she was going to ask for another girl to come in and help whilst Florrie was away. They'd take the curtains down to wash and give the rugs and carpets a good beating.

Margriet, of course, was thrilled. 'We'll be able to paddle in the sea, Florrie,' she said animatedly. 'Will you come in with me?'

'I certainly will,' Florrie enthused. 'I've never been to 'seaside. I'm so excited. Your mama will probably go into the water from a bathing machine, but I don't think we'll have to.'

When Margriet asked her mother if that were so, Rosamund seemed confused. 'I'm not sure,' she said. 'I believe there are rules. But there will be separate bathing machines for ladies and gentlemen, and we must be very careful not to stray into areas where gentlemen are bathing.' She considered for a moment. 'Oh, dear,' she said. 'I know so little about it. My sisters and I only once went to the seaside and we were not allowed on the sands. My mother would never have considered it proper for us to bathe in public. I'm not even sure I will, though it is considered to be very beneficial to immerse oneself for five minutes twice a day.'

When Margriet asked her father the same question and told him what her mother had said, he – rather strangely, she thought – simply raised his eyebrows and rolled his eyes but didn't give her an answer.

Rosamund bought bathing costumes: a long tunic made from dark navy flannel trimmed with white with matching turban and pantaloons for herself, and a similar tunic for Margriet in pale blue; for Frederik she found a striped all-in-one costume which came down to his knees, the sight of which made him put his hand over his mouth to hide a grin; and as an afterthought a costume for Florrie, for, as she murmured to her husband, it wouldn't do at all for their maidservant to be dressed inappropriately at the seaside whilst known to be in their employ.

At last the day came for them to depart. Early in the morning a dog cart collected the trunks and carpetbags containing their clothes and the bed linen which Rosamund insisted they should take with them rather than use anyone else's, and at ten o'clock the clarence rolled up to the door. The driver rang the bell and took the last few bags while Frederik handed his wife and Margriet into the carriage. It was a fine sunny day, so Florrie said she wouldn't at all mind sitting up front next to the driver.

Margriet was thrilled. She had a little fold-away seat opposite her parents, who settled themselves on to the cushioned leather upholstery. She waved to Mrs Simmonds and Cook, who had come to see them off, and even her mother smiled and gave them a nod. The driver cracked his whip, the two bay horses whinnied and they were off and away for a whole month in Scarborough.

CHAPTER TWELVE

The cottage was tucked down a narrow lane behind the houses on St Nicholas Cliff. Rosamund said she would have preferred to be on the main street; she also proclaimed that the bedrooms were rather small.

'Next year we'll apply earlier,' Frederik said. 'Everyone wants to come to Scarborough for the music at the Spa. And of course the cottage is smaller than our house, but it's delightful, isn't it? Besides, we're not going to be in very much, and when we are we can see the sea from the upstairs windows. In fact,' he added, 'I'll take some chairs and that small table upstairs to the spare bedroom' – he pointed to a small round table with barley sugar legs – 'and we'll sit there of an evening if we're not out walking.'

Margriet came rushing in. 'Mama, Papa! That little garden at the front – Florrie has found some cane chairs and a little table that she can put out there and she said we could have tea or supper outside because it's quite warm enough. Can we? Please?'

'What a splendid idea,' Frederik enthused. 'A

picnic. Excellent! But first of all we must unpack.'

He glanced at Rosamund, who was inspecting cupboards and drawers. Without stopping what she was doing, she said at once, 'Yes, Florence must certainly unpack and make up the beds before we think of picnics. Perhaps tomorrow.'

Margriet's face fell, and Frederik said quickly, 'Whilst Florrie is unpacking, why don't we go out for a short walk and get our bearings? We've been sitting in the carriage for a long time; we ought to stretch our legs.'

'Why don't you take Margriet?' Rosamund said. 'I'll supervise Florence, and perhaps have a cup of tea if we can find the grocery basket.'

Frederik and Margriet didn't take any further persuading. Margriet put her bonnet on again and Frederik picked up his grey top hat and together they cut down the lane towards St Nicholas Cliff. Margriet clasped her father's hand. 'I'm so excited,' she said. 'Look, there it is!' She waved her free arm as the sea came into view. 'Oh, I can't wait! Papa?' She jumped up and down as they walked on. 'Will you take me if Mama doesn't want to bathe?'

'Oh, we'll persuade Mama to take a dip in the briny,' he declared. 'We'll tell her that it's very good for her health.'

'And is it?' Margriet asked astutely.

'Mmm, not sure.' He wiggled his eyebrows. 'But it can't do any harm, can it?'

Margriet giggled. 'Of course not.' Directly in front of them a cast-iron footbridge spanned a narrow valley, and they could see a terrace built out over the sea. 'What's that, Papa? Is that a private place?

I think Mama would prefer to sit there than on the sands.'

'I think you're right, she would. It's the Spa; you can take a glass of water from the wells, and in that rather splendid building there's music to listen to, or you can just sit outside and enjoy the view.'

Coming from the flatlands of Netherlands and living in low-lying Hull, Frederik had been totally entranced by the steep cliffs and woodlands as they dropped down steep ravines towards Scarborough on the journey. They had driven through Ramsdale valley, which was overhung by ancient trees and filled with birdsong, where streams of crystal-clear water ran down the hillside, burrowing into the earth and resurfacing in the cliffs to tumble down into the sea. He gazed now at the green cliff, where paths had been cut to make walking safer as the steep incline rolled almost to the sands. A small whitewashed cottage with a wooden bench and table outside the door stood halfway down and he guessed that someone had spotted the opportunity to sell refreshments. Here and there greenhouses and old cottages were being dismantled and surveyors stood with measuring sticks and plans making notes.

Building is bound to happen, he thought. This is a beautiful area, and many people will want to come and share it. If it was true that the taking of the waters was not as popular as it had once been, he guessed that the town fathers would want to encourage visitors in other ways. The Spa itself had recently been rebuilt after a great storm had washed the original away, and there were plans for further developments.

'We've lots of walking to do, Margriet. Are you fit for it?'

'Oh, yes,' she said breathlessly. 'I am.' She squeezed her father's hand. 'This is the best time of my whole life!'

'Is it, *lieveling*?' He smiled down at her bright eyes and animated expression. 'I do believe it's mine too.' And he thought that it probably was, until unbidden another image stole into his consciousness: Cornelia sitting in her garden amidst the sweet-smelling herbs and roses. He tried to brush it away.

Margriet couldn't wait to paddle in the sea, but best of all was having her father to herself, just as she'd had when they'd walked in the streets of Hull. I wish that Anneliese could be here, she thought. I do so want a friend of my own to play with. Perhaps if I wish hard enough she will come.

'What would you like to do?' Frederik asked. 'Cross the bridge to the Spa or follow the path down the cliff to the sands?'

'Oh, can we cross the bridge, please? I've never been across such a long one!' In fact the only bridge she had ever crossed was Hull's North Bridge that spanned the River Hull as they began their journey this morning, heading out of town towards Holderness and the coastal road.

As they stepped on to the bridge she looked down into the valley below and thought that she had never been so high, either. She felt quite dizzy as she watched the carriages pass below them, and she clutched her father's hand as they crossed.

They passed the Spa terrace and promenade, where Frederik lifted his hat to the ladies who were taking tea, and then went down the steps to the sands. Men and women were strolling together or standing in groups chatting; children were racing about with kites, balls and bats, and dogs were chasing and barking at the waves. Above them, heavy-winged seabirds were swooping and screeching and making much more noise than those that flew along the Humber or above the docks in Hull.

'Come along then, Margriet; let's take off our shoes and stockings.' Frederik sounded very boyish. 'We'll have a paddle in the sea.'

Margriet gazed at him in astonishment. 'Really?' she asked. 'Is it allowed?'

He laughed. 'Of course it's allowed.' He hopped about on one foot and then the other to take off his leather shoes. 'Come on, there are lots of people in the sea. Don't be coy.'

Margriet blinked, and then sat down on the sands to unlace her boots. 'If you're sure it's all right, Papa. I'm not sure Mama—'

'It's perfectly all right,' he said, slipping his feet out of the stirrups that kept his fine wool trousers neat and tight, and rolled the legs up to his knees, showing his pale calves. Throwing caution to the wind, he shrugged off his grey frock coat and put it over his arm. 'We're on holiday, so we're allowed to do all kinds of things we wouldn't do at home.'

Margriet looked up at him as she took off her shoes and stockings. Never had she seen her papa in such a state of undress. She giggled; he looked so comical standing there on one foot, taking off his stockings, in his rolled-up trousers, white waistcoat and pale grey cravat. It was a good thing, she thought, that Mama wasn't there to see him – especially when he removed his top hat, stuffed his stockings into it, and crammed it back on his head.

Cautiously they entered the water. Margriet's giggles ended abruptly and she shrieked, clutching her father's arm. 'It's so cold! Ah!' She stumbled back as a foam-crested wave headed towards them, and then stopped and jumped over it instead. Frederik smiled. It was good to see her so full of high spirits. This was what had been missing from her life, the chance to be a child and not a miniature adult. He thought back to his own childhood and realized how lucky he had been.

He jumped over the next wave with her. The tide was coming in and the sea was becoming boisterous. Further north were the bathing huts; women were sheltered from public view by tent-like canvas canopies, but men were swimming in the open sea, some in costumes like his and others naked to the waist. He smiled again. That was how he and his brother used to swim in the dykes, but not his sister: that was one pleasure that she was not allowed as they grew up, even though their mother was so broad-minded; Anna had to bathe in long drawers and a tunic top.

Margriet shrieked again as the waves became bigger, and grabbed her father's arm once more. He struggled to keep hold of his clothing and shoes, and as he stumbled a breeze caught his hat and took it tumbling along the sands. He set off in hot pursuit and saw it hurtling towards a man and a group of children who were playing beach cricket.

The man caught it and held it up in the air. It was Hendrik Sanderson.

'I have a thing, a very fine thing,' he called. 'Who is the owner of this fine thing? Frederik! How very nice to see you.' He held out his rather sandy hand as Frederik approached. 'So you were able to find a house?'

Frederik shook his hand and took the hat, looking back at Margriet still trying to catch his wind-blown stockings by the water's edge. 'We were, thanks to you. It's quite delightful. We've only just arrived, so Margriet and I escaped whilst my wife is organizing the maid and unpacking. This is Margriet's first visit to the seaside.'

'Oh, she must be introduced to my daughters. Imogen! Julia!' He called to two young girls. 'There's another friend for you. Go over and say hello to Margriet.'

The two girls looked across to where Margriet had just trapped the second stocking. 'We know her,' Julia shouted. 'She's coming to our school.'

'Do you know how to play cricket?' Imogen asked as Margriet approached.

Margriet paused for only a second. 'Yes,' she said. 'I think so.'

'I'm afraid we must get back,' Frederik said, and then felt guilty when Imogen as well as Margriet looked very disappointed. Hendrik looked from one to the other.

'Why don't you leave Margriet with us and we'll bring her back in half an hour or so?' he said. 'We'll be packing up by then.'

Frederik saw Margriet's pleading eyes and agreed.

He gave Hendrik the address, rolled down his trousers and walked back across the sands to put on his shoes and stockings. He brushed down his coat before putting it on and placed his hat at a jaunty angle on his head. When he looked back towards the cricketers, Margriet had abandoned her coat and bonnet and was barefoot with the bat in her hand, looking as if she had been playing the game all her life. She did not look his way, and he was smiling as he made his way back to the cottage, sand crunching between his toes.

'You left her?' Rosamund was horrified when he explained that Margriet was still playing on the sands. 'But are they suitable children for her to be associating with?'

'I know their father and he was there,' he said irritably. 'He won't leave her alone, and she will be associating with the girls at Miss Barker's dame school in another month.'

She was somewhat mollified by his explanation, and when Sanderson arrived at the house with four dishevelled cricketers she relaxed enough to ask Frederik to invite him in to be introduced.

Sanderson declined her offer to be seated and said they must be getting back, as the children would need to bathe before their supper.

'Of course. Your wife will be waiting for you.'

'Oh, I shouldn't think she'll be back yet. She's gone walking up to the castle and across the cliffs to the North Bay. Alice likes to walk, but the children were eager to play cricket.'

Rosamund seemed bewildered. 'Are you holidaying with friends?'

'Sometimes we do, but not this time.'

Rosamund wanted to ask if Mrs Sanderson had gone walking with a companion or a maid, but sensed that it might be considered an intrusion. Sanderson, however, seemed to read her thoughts.

'My wife is very sociable,' he said tolerantly, 'but also quite comfortable with her own company. She's happy to walk alone whilst I take care of the children.'

'I see.' Rosamund quite clearly did not see, and after a moment's hesitation she asked, 'Are you not afraid for her well-being or her reputation, sir?'

He shook his head. 'No, Mrs Vandergroene, I am not. Alice is a very capable and competent woman and would not thank me if I thought her any less.' Incredulous, she raised her eyebrows, and he added, 'She believes that she has every right to walk unaccompanied if she wishes to do so, and she wouldn't take any unnecessary risks.'

Both men realized that their wives would be quite incompatible.

'I don't understand him,' Rosamund said after the Sandersons had left. 'What kind of man is he to let his wife go jaunting off on her own? Did you say he was half Dutch?' She raised her chin as if to say that perhaps that accounted for the lack of discernment. 'Does he not realize how bad it looks, let alone the fact that something disastrous could happen to her? Do they not have a maid who could accompany her?'

'I understand that they do,' Frederik sighed, bored with the conversation almost before it had begun, 'but you heard him: his wife is capable of going out alone.' He put such heavy emphasis on the word 'capable' that Rosamund, raising her chin, remarked sharply that she too was quite capable, but would not dream of doing such a thing.

'You care too much about what others might think, Rosamund,' he said wearily, 'when it really doesn't matter.'

'Well, it matters to me,' she protested. 'I am beginning to wonder if their children are suitable companions for Margriet after all. And what's more, Frederik, I will not be inviting Mrs Sanderson to join me for tea on the Spa terrace. Do not expect it of me.'

Frederik had not yet met Mrs Sanderson, but he responded to his wife's determined expression with an ironic bow. 'Such a pity, my dear,' he said in mock sorrow. 'I'm sure she will be quite devastated if perchance she should hear of it.'

CHAPTER THIRTEEN

The month at Scarborough was wonderful for Margriet once her mother had reluctantly agreed that the Sanderson children were well mannered and well behaved, and allowed Margriet to be in their company. Rosamund's own daily routine began when Florrie walked her to the Spa terrace and settled her at a table. She then dismissed the maid to do whatever she wanted for an hour, but said that she must return to walk with her down to the sands where Frederik and Margriet were engaged in games with the Sanderson family. It was on one such occasion that Mrs Sanderson came across to introduce herself.

She might have been warned by her husband of Rosamund's sensibilities, for she was perfectly charming, and not at all controversial. 'Mrs Vandergroene,' she said, 'I am thinking of bathing tomorrow. Would you care to join me?'

Rosamund had been intrigued by the bathing huts, and sufficiently interested to have walked quite close to where they were lined up in the sea to assure herself that the canopies were perfectly private and the occupants invisible to anyone on the sands.

Alice Sanderson saw her hesitation. 'The bathers are quite secluded,' she advised her. 'No one can see them, except of course those who are already in the sea, but the swimmers tend not to come near the huts; the water isn't deep enough.'

'I – I can't swim,' Rosamund told her, 'although I feel sure I would like to bathe if I felt I wouldn't fall.'

'There's a rope to hold on to, and a female attendant to help you in. It's great fun, and very exhilarating.' She nodded towards Florrie, waiting at a respectful distance. 'Your maid could come too. There are bathing costumes for hire if she doesn't have one.'

'Oh, I bought one for her,' Rosamund said. 'I thought she could accompany me into the water.'

'Well there we are then. Shall we say at about eleven? I believe the weather is staying warm for the whole week.'

The next morning Florrie packed a bag with the bathing costumes and escorted Rosamund down to the sands. Frederik and Margriet had gone ahead; the Sanderson children had promised to teach Margriet to swim and Frederik had also taken his costume. Rosamund didn't want her husband or daughter to see her embarrassment.

There was room for four in the hut but Mrs Sanderson commandeered one for the three of them. It had a door at each end, one for entering fully clothed and the other to be exited once the machine was pulled into the sea. It was painted white on the inside and had mirrored cupboards for personal belongings such as hairbrushes and combs. A drawer held clean towels and there was a rubber bag for wet towels and costumes after bathing; the floor was peppered with holes to allow any water to drain away.

Once they were on board the doors were closed, and the horse-drawn hut rumbled forward across the sands and into the sea. Rosamund sat on a bench whilst Florrie helped her out of her stockings and petticoats. Then Florrie unfastened her mistress's corset and withdrew it, slipped the pantaloons beneath her unbuttoned gown, popped the tunic over her head and withdrew the gown so that Rosamund was never seen uncovered. Mrs Sanderson had no such modesty; she was not wearing corset or stockings but only a simple gown with one petticoat, and these she removed before pulling on her knee-length pantaloons and tunic, unafraid of showing her nakedness.

Mrs Sanderson must have been aware of Rosamund's shock; Florrie gave her a sidelong glance before she began her own undressing. Mrs Sanderson smiled. 'Don't mind me, my dear,' she said. 'We're all the same under our clothing. If Mrs Vandergroene were not here today I would swim naked, like the men. Some women do, you know.'

'Surely not, Mrs Sanderson!' Rosamund was horrified.

'If we were pulled well out into the sea, yes indeed.' She tucked her hair under a swimming hat. 'No one can see your body when you're under water, and it's such a liberating feeling to be unrestricted by clothing.' She sighed. 'But there we are, prudery reigns, I'm afraid. Come along then, ladies, we've arrived. Shall we bathe?'

112

She opened the door and dived straight into the water, coming up gasping. 'Wonderful,' she cried, and dipping in again she swam away.

Rosamund clung to the attendant who helped her down the steps and into the water. It was freezing cold and came above her waist. She screamed. 'Oh, no, I can't bear it, it's so cold! Let me out. Let me out!'

'Get back out again then, ma'am,' the woman said, 'and then come back in. It's not so bad a second time. Come on, miss,' she said to Florrie, who was dithering above them. 'Just jump in; you'll not drown.'

Florrie took a deep breath and, used to obeying orders, did as she was told. The splash as she jumped in made Rosamund shriek.

'Mama, Mama! Florrie, look at me!'

Rosamund, her teeth chattering, looked around for her daughter, and as she did so the attendant pulled her into the water again. It wasn't true that it wasn't as bad the second time. It was.

'Mama, I'm swimming!'

Rosamund steeled herself to look up and saw Margriet on her father's back as he swam only yards away from her. 'Oh, be careful, be careful,' she cried out. 'The water is deep.'

'No it's not.' Frederik laughed and stood up, showing that the water only came to his waist. Margriet clung on to his back.

'It's such fun, Mama. I can nearly swim.'

After five more minutes Rosamund got out, shivering uncontrollably. Health-giving or not, nothing would ever induce her to sea bathe again. She sat

113

on the bench and waited. Where was Florence, the wretched girl? The attendant seemed to have disappeared too, and Rosamund wondered how long she would have to wait. She rubbed her feet and legs with a towel and then, not liking the feel of wet clothing on her, she wrapped the towel round her waist and pulled off the pantaloons and tunic.

'So undignified,' she muttered, but as she rubbed her arms and shoulders her body began to glow. Knowing she couldn't fasten her corset by herself, she slipped on her petticoat and then her gown and jacket, and soon she was warm.

Florrie had loved the water, she said, as they walked back up the hill towards the Spa for a cup of hot chocolate. She and Mrs Sanderson would have stayed in longer if it hadn't been for Rosamund's insistence that she had had quite enough, thank you, and must be pulled back up the beach. To make up for it, Rosamund had rescinded her vow and invited Mrs Sanderson to join her for a hot drink, but Mrs Sanderson had politely declined.

For Margriet the month went far too quickly. She had made great friends of the Sanderson children, and Mrs Sanderson had taken them up to the castle several times and didn't seem to mind if they climbed on the ancient walls. Frederik saw a huge difference in his daughter. Rosamund did too; the girl was showing another side of her personality, a merry, unrestrained side, not one Rosamund felt she could understand. Sometimes she was disobedient too, removing her bonnet when she thought her mother wasn't watching and ignoring

114

Rosamund's warnings that her face would freckle in the sun. For some reason Margriet didn't seem to care about freckles.

On the last day before they were due to go home, Frederik and Hendrik Sanderson sat side by side on the sands watching the boats coming in to the harbour and keeping an eye on their children, who were playing a game of Catch.

'I'm so grateful to you for telling me about the letting agent,' Frederik said. 'This holiday has been wonderful for Margriet; she was such a solitary little girl before she met your children.'

'She's your only child?' Hendrik asked. 'That's a pity.'

Frederik nodded. 'Yes. We haven't been fortunate enough to have more.' He paused. Rosamund's frigidity wasn't a subject for discussion. Even here on holiday she had rejected his loving advances, alarmed that Florrie or Margriet might hear in the small cottage. He wasn't the kind of man to insist, but he was frustrated and often felt depressed by the situation. It was grounds for separation, but he couldn't do that either. Rosamund would die of shame and humiliation.

'We're expecting another.' Hendrik drew on a cigar and blew smoke rings in the air. 'Alice is delighted, and I am too. She's had a couple of miscarriages since Julia was born and so we waited until she was fully recovered.' He grinned. 'It was difficult, but she threatened me with all kinds of ghastly accidents if I should stray. Not that I ever would. She's my whole life.'

Frederik thought of Alice Sanderson swimming

in the sea and trooping off with the children for adventures at the castle, which meant a steep walk up the headland and some strenuous games at the top. On the way back she led them through the boat yards to explore the old streets and the harbour before she treated them to tea and cake. The children were exhausted by the time they reached their lodgings again, but she didn't appear to be.

'She's an amazing woman,' he murmured. 'I trust everything will go well this time.'

Hendrik nodded. 'So do I. It must be rotten being a woman and having to go through all that. It frightens me to death even thinking of it.'

'It frightens women too, I should think,' Frederik said, knowing that it frightened Rosamund.

The next morning they all met to say goodbye before the Vandergroenes departed for home. The seabirds screeched overhead and Margriet was sure they were saying 'Don't go. Don't go'. She was so pleased to have met Imogen and Julia and built up a friendship before starting school that she shouted and waved when she saw them, and was admonished by her mother for being unruly.

Most of their luggage had already gone off in the cart. Florrie was helped up to sit beside the driver of the clarence and Margriet hopped from one foot to another as she waited for her father to assist her mother into the carriage. The driver cracked his whip and the carriage jerked as they drew away, and Margriet craned out of the window for the last glimpse of the sea, eagerly remarking on what she could see. Her mother interrupted. 'Settle down now, Margriet. The holiday has come to an end. There will be no more lax behaviour, only decorum, if you please. Remember your manners.'

Margriet pressed her lips together. 'Yes, Mama.' She sat back on her little seat and glanced across at her father. He had his head back against the seat and his eyes were closed, but he slowly opened one of them and pulled his mouth down into a comical pout, and she felt a bubble of mirth creeping up which she hastily changed into a cough.

'I've had such a lovely time,' she said. 'I do hope we can come to Scarborough next year. Although,' she added thoughtfully, 'Mrs Sanderson is going to have a new baby, so perhaps they won't be able to come. It won't be able to play on the sands with us for quite a long time.'

Rosamund drew in a breath. 'What! Whoever told you that?' She put her hand to her forehead. 'Oh, my word! I can't believe I'm hearing such a thing from my own child's lips.'

Margriet opened and closed her mouth. What had she said? She looked from her mother to her father. Rosamund seemed on the point of collapse, whilst her father's face was set. He reached over and put his hand on hers. 'It's all right,' he murmured.

Margriet thought he was cross, and miserably wondered if she was the unwitting cause of his anger and her mother's obvious distress. But he turned to her mother. 'Rosamund,' he said patiently, 'the Sanderson children are aware of the happy news, which they learned from their parents. I too was told by Hendrik that his wife is with child after several difficult years. For them it is a time for rejoicing.'

Rosamund cast him a cold glance. 'It is not a subject for general discussion and certainly not for children to know. I am once again forced to consider the suitability of Margriet's attending the same school as the Sanderson children. They are not a good influence.'

'Is that so?' he muttered so quietly that Margriet barely heard him. 'We will discuss this at home, but I am telling you now that I will have the final say on the matter.'

CHAPTER FOURTEEN

Frederik longed to return to Netherlands and visit Cornelia, yet he had no real reason to do so. He was busy in his Hull office; there had been many orders whilst he'd been away and although his staff was capable of dealing with enquiries and ongoing business he liked to follow up new contacts with either a personal letter or a visit. He decided that he wouldn't sail to Netherlands again until at least the end of September, by which time Margriet would be settled in her new school.

He told Rosamund that he would walk Margriet to school with Florrie every day for a week, until she was sure that their daughter was in no danger of running into any unsavoury character who might ruin her reputation before she even possessed one. September began with Margriet enthusiastically ready for school early each morning and at the end of the day eager to tell of the things she had been taught. Florrie collected her every afternoon, and on the way home they would stop to chat to people she knew and tell them about Scarborough.

Frederik wrote to Cornelia, asking how she was and insisting that she should not hesitate to ask him for help or advice if she should need it, or just write in friendship, he hoped. *Do not think that you must have a reason to correspond*, he urged her. *I am your friend too, as I was Nicolaas's.*

He asked about her children and added that he expected to be in Netherlands at the end of September and would like to call on her if it was convenient.

I want to see her now. The thought tormented him, and if she had written to say he might visit whenever he liked he would have booked a passage immediately.

During his discussion with Rosamund he had told her that as he was not sleeping well due to his overload of work, he would move into the guest room so as not to disturb her. He thought he detected a note of relief as she replied, 'Of course, Frederik. I quite understand, and you must be careful not to become overtired. I have noticed that you've been rather on edge since our return from Scarborough.'

And there was every reason for him to be so, he thought irritably, since he had seen at close quarters how a happily married couple might behave. Perhaps the Sandersons were unusual in their open fondness for each other, but it was what he wanted for himself; friendship and affection was surely not too much to expect in a marriage, especially within the bedroom.

The month for him passed slowly, unlike for Margriet, who found the weekends irksome and couldn't wait for Mondays. She gobbled up her lessons and made great advances in reading, writing and arithmetic, but especially in storytelling. Miss

Barker asked her one day to read out something she had written on the history of Hull.

'It's quite short,' Margriet explained as she stood up in front of the small class. 'If there was time I could make it longer?'

She looked hopefully at Miss Barker, and was disappointed when the teacher said, 'Perhaps you will write another episode for another time. For the moment just read what you have written, as the others too have stories to tell.'

Margriet cleared her throat. 'This is the tale of a little girl who lives – lived,' she corrected herself, 'with her parents quite close to here in a street named Land of Green Ginger. Her playground was the garden which used to belong to King Henry VIII, who had a beautiful palace in Hull hundreds of years ago.'

As she told the story of the little girl and her friend playing with her pets in the royal gardens, she was reminded that she hadn't thought of Anneliese for some time, and not at all since she had returned from Scarborough and started school. She decided that she would call on her, and wondered if she could persuade Florrie to let her walk home alone one day as the Sanderson girls did.

'Thank you, Margriet,' Miss Barker said, when she had finished. 'That was very interesting. Can you tell us if your story is true? This is a history lesson, after all.'

Margriet hesitated for a second and cleared her throat again. 'It's true about King Henry,' she said, 'and . . .' She remembered playing in the garden with Anneliese and curtseying as the ladies of the

121

court walked by, but the picture wasn't quite as sharp in her memory as it had once been. 'I – yes,' she said, not wanting to deny her friend. 'I think it's true about Anneliese.'

'Anneliese?' Miss Barker asked. 'Was that the name of the little girl?'

'Yes,' Margriet whispered. 'It is.'

'And what was the name of her friend?'

Margriet let out a whispered breath. 'I don't know, Miss Barker.' She didn't want to tell an untruth, but she knew that if she confessed that she was the other child in the story Miss Barker would not believe it. Yet it is most sincerely true, she reassured herself, and she would visit again just to prove it.

Towards the end of September Frederik received a letter from Cornelia saying that they were looking forward to his visit. *I am feeling much better and more settled in my new life,* she wrote, *and although it is not long since Nicolaas's death I am slowly adjusting. Please come when you can.*

So that he didn't appear too eager he waited until the final days of the month before booking his passage. Margriet didn't make as much fuss as usual and he was pleased that she was enjoying school so much as not to miss him. Rosamund said she had many things to do whilst he was away, luncheons to attend, card parties and so on, and added gaily that she needn't feel guilty seeing as he was away and Margriet was at school. Frederik was puzzled by this, as he hadn't realized that she ever did feel any guilt, or had any reason to.

He stayed with his mother whilst attending to business in Amsterdam, and then left for Gouda early one morning, telling his mother that he might be late back that evening.

'What takes you to Gouda?' she asked. 'Is there much business there?'

'Not a great deal,' he said honestly. 'But whilst I am there I will call on Nicolaas's widow.'

'Ah!' she said perceptively. 'Be careful for her reputation, Frederik. A woman in her position is vulnerable to gossip.'

'Her children are there,' he said huffily, very conscious of her shrewd insight. 'And I am – was – Nicolaas's friend.'

'Even so,' she murmured. 'Even so.'

And of course she was right, he thought as he journeyed again by train and cabriolet. How was it that his mother could always read him like a book? Cornelia would not want any gossip-mongering to reflect on her or her children. What a fool he was, he thought. What an absolute fool.

Because of his mother's warning and his own deliberations, and then discovering that Hans and Klara were not at home to be a safeguard against tittle-tattle, he was awkward and reticent during the visit. They had coffee and made light conversation, he not wanting to speak of Nicolaas because he felt guilty about his feelings towards Cornelia, and she, somehow, absorbing his reserve and only asking him about business and talking about her garden, saying she was not looking forward to the winter ahead.

When he finally rose to leave, she gazed at him for a moment and then said softly, 'I realize it is difficult for you to come here, Frederik, now that your memory of Nicolaas is fading and you must continue with your life, as I must with mine.' She lowered her eyes, and when she lifted them again he saw that they were moist. 'Please don't feel obliged to call every time you come to Gouda. I know that Nicolaas probably asked you to support me, but I don't expect it, even though I appreciate your friendship and hope that it will always continue.'

He gazed back at her. What? His lips formed the word but he didn't speak it. Did she mean that she didn't want him to come any more? Had he said something he shouldn't? Offended her in some way? But how could he bear not to see her?

Although he was conscious of the maid clattering pans and crockery somewhere in the distance, he felt that he was trapped in a bubble, unable to connect, unable to say or do what he wanted most of all. He reached for her hand and held it. It was soft and warm and he tried to tell himself that she wasn't excluding but excusing him.

'Frederik?' she said.

'I . . .' He sought to find some kind of expression. 'Do you not want me to visit?'

'Of course I want you to come,' she said huskily. 'I look forward to your visits. But you seem distant today, not your usual self. I don't want you to think that you have to call on me; I understand that you are a busy man with your own commitments.'

His relief was so enormous that he gently kissed her hand before lowering it. 'I *am* a little ill at ease,' he explained. 'I'm staying with my mother in Amsterdam and told her that I was coming to see you. She warned me that I must be careful of your reputation; she said that you might be the subject of gossip if I called too often.'

She laughed. 'And so I might be,' she said. 'But I care nothing for gossips. My friends understand me and are loyal, and that is what counts. So you will still visit, and not just because you feel obliged to? The children would like to see you too; Hans will be disappointed that he has missed you today.'

'Will he be here tomorrow? I can come back.'

'Yes,' she said eagerly. 'Come after school, as we would like to discuss his future education. I'm sorry,' she gave a wry smile, 'but, as your mother will understand and to dispel her anxiety, I cannot ask you to stay. Not just yet, anyway.'

His mood had lifted completely; he felt light-hearted and happy. Not only was he coming back tomorrow, but he was welcome at any time. He was heartened to think that at some time in the future . . . not just yet, but soon, perhaps, he could spend a much longer time with her, for wasn't that exactly what he had promised Nicolaas?

He tapped on the roof of the cab to attract the driver's attention. 'Take me to the cheese market first, if you please,' he said, thinking that he would placate his mother by buying her a wheel of cheese, even though his brother was in the cheese business. Gouda was famous for its cheese, as well as for the manufacture of clay pipes and he remembered that his father had enjoyed a pipe of tobacco.

The rounds of cheese were laid out on sheets in the centre of the marketplace and he paused for a few minutes listening to the cries of the porters in their straw hats as they extolled the perfection of their product. The big buyers would have made their choice in the morning, negotiated a price, and on agreement clapped hands with the sellers before the cheese was taken off to the weigh house. During the afternoon it was the turn of small shopkeepers and *huisvrouwen* to purchase what they needed. He chose a small mature wheel for his mother, knowing her preference, and then a larger vintage one to take home to Hull, justifying, at least to himself, his visit to the town. He decided that he would not tell his mother that he was returning the following day.

CHAPTER FIFTEEN

Margriet had sent her first letter to her Dutch grandmother, beginning it with *Dear Grootmoeder,* but Gerda Vandergroene had written back to say that Margriet should call her Oma, as her other grandchildren did. In her second letter, Margriet wrote about school and how much she loved it and about her friends Imogen and Julia who had Dutch blood the same as she had. Then she told Gerda about her friend Anneliese Lindegroen who lived in the next street.

She's a proper little Dutch girl, she wrote, *because she was born in Amsterdam. I don't know why they live here in Hull, but it is something to do with ginger. I think her father grows it in his garden and then sells it.*

When Frederik returned to his mother's house after his second visit to Cornelia Margriet's letter had arrived, and Gerda said she was pleased that her granddaughter had made a Dutch friend. 'Do they speak Dutch together?' she asked.

'Imogen and Julia?' Frederik said. 'I think they only know a few words, the same as Margriet. Their father's mother is Dutch but as she lives in The Hague they don't see her very often.'

'*Nee, nee,*' Gerda protested. 'This little girl lives with her parents near to you. She's called Anneliese. Her father grows ginger, apparently, which I was surprised to hear. I didn't know there were gardens to your houses.'

Frederik laughed. 'There aren't,' he said. 'Margriet is telling stories.' He explained about their walk in Hull. 'She has taken it to heart. I thought she had created this friend because she was lonely, but she's at school with other children now and still talks about her.'

'It's rather sweet,' his mother said indulgently. 'There's no need to worry about such a thing. She will grow out of it eventually.'

He didn't worry about it very much as Margriet seemed to be content, and neither did he mention it to Rosamund on his return home; he and his wife seemed to have little to talk about and his departure from their bedroom had brought them to a point where they rarely spoke to each other except for a few desultory words at supper. He had on a few occasions knocked on her door at bedtime and hearing no refusal from within had gone inside. He had whispered her name but she was always either asleep or feigning it.

Sometimes he had gone in without waiting for a reply and found her either sitting at her dressing table or reading in bed. When he asked if he might stay, she made the excuse of a headache, or implied that it was untimely. He didn't argue or plead with her but simply turned round and walked out. As he sat on the edge of the spare bed with his chin in his hand he pondered on his options in this impossible situation. He could leave her and set up another house, but what then of Margriet? He would never abandon his daughter, and neither would he take her away from her mother as was his right, but how could he go away on business knowing that Rosamund virtually ignored the child in his absence? It was a dilemma. He was angry and frustrated and he determined that he must speak seriously again to Rosamund, perhaps even tell her this was not normal behaviour and frighten her with the possibility of divorce. He thought of when they had first been introduced and how charmed he had been by her serenity and calm manner. He had had a vision of returning home in the evenings or from his travels abroad to be greeted by a loving and welcoming wife; instead he had found that she was indifferent to his views, had no opinions of her own and rejected his loving advances. He was patient with her in the beginning, but after giving birth to Margriet she seemed to think her duty was done, and even though he patiently explained that he would be careful not to get her pregnant again she wouldn't even discuss it, finding the whole matter quite distasteful.

He did not feel that he was an immoral man, but he knew without a shadow of doubt that if temptation should ever come his way, he would undoubtedly fall. His greatest fear was that he would make his feelings for Cornelia apparent without intending to, thus losing her friendship and trust. He liked her children, too. Hans in particular was becoming easier with him, and had asked him questions about when he and his father were in school together.

'I shall miss him when he goes away to school,' Cornelia had said, 'for I think he will have to board rather than spend so much time travelling there and back every day. What do you think, Frederik? Will boarding suit him?' He had been flattered that she should ask his opinion, even knowing that she and Hans would make the final decision.

Christmas came swiftly. The Vandergroene family went to the Christmas service at St Mary's and came straight back home as the weather was so cold. After Boxing Day the holiday dragged for Margriet, who was bored and wished she could go back to school. Frederik set her some work to do each morning involving either arithmetic or history, and then one day he went to her room and told her that he would be going back to Netherlands in January. She sighed and said plaintively that she would be glad when she was old enough to visit her grandmother. Frederik considered this, and then went downstairs.

He found Florrie in the dining room polishing the table and chairs and asked her if she knew where her mistress was.

'In 'upstairs sitting room, sir,' she said. 'I'll be taking her coffee up in ten minutes.'

It struck him that Rosamund hadn't asked if he would like to join her. 'Perhaps I'll have some too,' he said, 'and then Margriet and I will go for a walk before luncheon.'

'Very good, sir.' Florrie smiled, and straightened her apron.

She was a presentable young woman, Frederik thought as he nodded and smiled back. She was fairly tall and robust and carried herself well. 'Tell me, Florrie – do you prefer Florrie? I've noticed that Mrs Vandergroene always calls you Florence and Margriet says Florrie.'

'I don't mind, sir,' she said. 'Florrie's more friendly, isn't it, but 'mistress prefers Florence.'

'I was wondering, Florrie.' He put his hand to his beard and scratched thoughtfully and she studied him warily. 'Have you ever travelled – abroad, I mean?'

'Me, sir? No, sir, except when we went to Scarborough. That's 'furthest abroad I've ever been.'

'So you don't know if you'd be seasick if you went on a ship?'

Florrie's mouth went slack and then she closed it and grinned. 'No I don't, sir, but I'd give it a try if 'opportunity came up.'

'Mmm,' he said vaguely, smiling in return. 'Would you? Very good, Florrie, thank you.'

Frederik went upstairs to seek out his wife and Florrie finished her dusting in double quick time and scurried down into the kitchen. 'Guess what!' she said in an awed whisper. 'Master's just asked me if I'm a good sailor. What do you think that means?'

Mrs Simmonds was sitting with Cook at the scrubbed table, both of them waiting for Lily to make their coffee. She folded her arms across her chest. 'Best be careful, Florrie. What sort o' question is that? I know that Mr Vandergroene is a gentleman, but even so you shouldn't risk your reputation by travelling on a ship wi' a married man.'

'She hasn't got a reputation,' Cook said bluntly,

'so how can she risk it? And besides, 'master hasn't said why he wants to know.'

'I think he's thinking of Margriet,' Florrie said. 'She's told me that he's going to take her to see her Dutch granny one day. I reckon that's what he's planning. Mistress won't go cos she gets seasick and he can't tek 'little lass on her own.' She heaved a breath. 'I hope I'm right. I'd love to go with 'em.'

Mrs Simmonds grunted disparagingly. 'What clothes would you wear for that sort of trip?'

'Same as I wore for Scarborough. Nowt wrong wi' them, is there?' She turned to the kitchen maid. 'Come on, Lily, look sharp. I'm supposed to be tekkin' coffee upstairs.' She went to the sink to wash her hands, then changed her apron and tidied her hair. 'This might be a good opportunity for me and I'll tek it if it's offered.'

Upstairs, Rosamund seemed startled when Frederik came into the sitting room. 'Oh,' she said. 'I thought you'd gone out.'

'No, not yet. I've been upstairs with Margriet. She's very bored with being banished to her room.'

Rosamund put down her sewing. 'She isn't banished,' she said curtly. 'She is in her own room as I am in mine.'

'And so do you mind if I join you?' he said, taking a seat anyway.

'Of course not. It's not often that you're here.'

'It's still the Christmas holiday, in case you've forgotten.'

'Why would I have forgotten?' She seemed astonished at his remark. 'We still have the Boxing Day ham to finish.'

He sighed. 'Rosamund, I've been thinking—' He was interrupted by a knock on the door, and Florrie came in with a tray of coffee and biscuits.

'Beg pardon, ma'am,' she said. 'I've tekken 'liberty of bringing in these Dutch biscuits that you brought home after your last trip, sir. I recall you said they were your favourites. I thought they'd mek a change from Christmas cake.'

'Oh, yes indeed.' Frederik sat up. 'Spice biscuits,' he said. 'My mother always makes them for the start of the St Nicholas feast, Florrie, which begins earlier than Christmas in England.' He took one of the star-shaped biscuits and bit into it. 'I hope you've tried them down in the kitchen. Cook will like them, I think – they're full of nutmeg and cloves. Perhaps she'd like to try her hand at baking some?'

'I'll tell her, sir,' Florrie said, dipping her knee.

'Perhaps you'd ask Margriet to come down? She can have some hot milk with us.'

Florrie glanced at Rosamund's stony expression, and said that she would.

'You are very familiar with Florence,' Rosamund said coldly when the girl had left the room. 'You really had no need to tell her what your mother does.'

Frederik took another biscuit, determined not to argue with her. 'I thought she might be interested. Shall I pour or will you? Anyway, as I was about to say—'

'I'll pour.' Rosamund picked up the coffee pot, which was heavier than usual as Florrie had brought a larger pot than when she had coffee alone; she gave an impatient tsk with her tongue as she

133

gripped the handle.

'I thought,' Frederik went on, 'that I'd take Margriet to meet my mother at Easter.'

'Alone!' Rosamund drew in a breath. 'How can you possibly do that? You know that I—'

'Not alone,' he interrupted. 'Of course not. I thought I would ask Florrie to accompany her.' He paused for a moment for his suggestion to sink in. 'She seems to be fond of Margriet judging by the way she took care of her in Scarborough, and I think she'd be the perfect travelling companion for her.'

'But – she's a housemaid.' Rosamund was astounded. 'She's not a suitable companion at all. She doesn't speak well—' She would have brought up several other reasons that would preclude a housemaid from travelling with their daughter, but Frederik interrupted her.

'Margriet likes her,' he said. 'Florrie would look after her on board ship and she'd fit in perfectly at my mother's house. My mother wouldn't notice her local accent at all, as her own English is limited.'

Rosamund's lip curled. 'I dare say,' she replied in a low voice, but said no more as the door opened and Margriet came in.

'Florrie said I'd to come down for some hot milk,' she said, as if astonished.

'And biscuits,' her father said, and put out his arm for her to come closer. 'It's still Christmas after all – or at least it's only just over.'

'I'll know it's over when you go back to Amsterdam, Papa.' Margriet hovered over which shape of biscuit to choose: a star, a heart or the wheel. 'I wish I could

134

go with you.'

'Your mama and I were just this minute talking about that,' Frederik said, 'and . . .' He paused. 'We have decided that at Easter, if the weather is good, perhaps you might make the journey with me.' He smiled at her obvious delight. 'You will of course be much older by then, as I seem to remember you have another birthday coming along very soon. You'll be very grown up. What do you think about that?'

'Oh, Papa,' she squealed. 'I think you are joking of me again!'

CHAPTER SIXTEEN

On his next visit to Amsterdam, Frederik told his mother of his plan to bring Margriet at Easter, and as he had expected she was as delighted as Margriet had been. Gerda's apartment was roomy, with spacious living and dining rooms and three bedrooms, so there was space for both Margriet and the maid.

'Oh, how lovely,' she said. 'I will tell your sister and we will arrange outings for the children.'

Before he had left home Frederik had asked Florrie if she would be willing to travel with Margriet and stay for the duration of her holiday. 'We'll arrange temporary help here whilst you are away,' he told her, and wondered why he was discussing this when his wife should be dealing with it. But Florrie was thrilled, even though he saw that she was trying not to show it.

'It'll be a pleasure, sir,' she had said, quite flushed with excitement. 'And – erm, I'll speak to 'mistress, shall I, sir, as to what Miss Margriet will need to tek with her? Like we did for Scarborough?'

'Indeed yes.' He'd made a mental note to ask Rosamund to buy a suitable gown for Florrie and a warm coat or cloak for travelling if she hadn't already got one.

Rosamund hadn't been pleased, but since it wouldn't do for Margriet to be travelling with anyone unsuitably dressed she had taken Florrie to buy a ready-made dark blue gown and a warm coat that would be eminently suitable for a governess or companion or someone in a similar situation. So that's all arranged, he thought as he travelled once more towards Gouda. It's something for Margriet to look forward to.

He hadn't told Cornelia that he would be calling; the weather was cold and icy, the dykes were frozen and the roads treacherous, but the trains to Utrecht were running and he'd decided impetuously that morning that he would make the journey, hoping that he would find a driver willing to take him on the final stage to Gouda. He told his mother not to expect him back that evening; he would find hotel accommodation.

'Yes, yes, you must do that,' she urged. 'Do not travel tonight – there will be a hard frost. Have you forgotten our winters?' He kissed her cheek and said that he hadn't forgotten, wondering how Cornelia and her children had coped over their first winter holiday period without Nicolaas.

The train was on time in Utrecht and he made a few calls, not selling or buying but simply acknowledging his thanks for his customers' support throughout the year and assuring them of his; keeping in touch he felt was an important part of business.

The sky began to darken by mid-afternoon and

he felt an icy chill, a threat of snow or a blizzard. He pulled his fur hat over his ears and looked about for a cabmen's stand to enquire if there was a hackney driver willing to take him to Gouda. There were some who flatly refused on the grounds of the worsening weather, but eventually one offered to take him and asked for twice the usual price.

He agreed, deciding that he would find an inn or a lodging house in Gouda and travel back to Amsterdam the next day. As they began the journey the snow started to fall and soon became a blizzard, so that he could barely see his surroundings through the carriage window. The driver knew the district, and slowed his horse at the end of Cornelia's lane to ask his passenger if he would walk the rest of the way.

'For I won't be able to turn round, sir, and if I got stuck you'd have to give me a bed for the night.'

'No, this is fine, thank you.' Frederik gave him an extra coin for his trouble. 'Take care on the way back.' The driver tipped his hat and cracked his whip and Frederik heard the slush and grind of wheels turning through the deepening snow.

The shutters at Cornelia's windows were firmly closed and bolted, and he couldn't see a light. He cursed beneath his breath for not having written to say he was coming, but he hadn't wanted her to stay at home on his account. He knocked sharply on the door and hunched his shoulders against the bitter wind, listening for footsteps within. Then he heard her voice through the door.

'*Ja, wie is daar?*' Who is there?

'It's Frederik!' he called back.

He heard the sound of the lock being drawn back and a key being turned, and the door opened. 'I'm so sorry, Cornelia,' he said. 'I didn't mean to disturb you.'

'Come in, come in.' She was holding up a lamp, and drew the door wider when she saw him. 'Whatever are you doing out on such a night?' She sounded agitated, not like her usual self, and he wondered if he had alarmed her.

He tapped the snow off his boots and shook his hat before entering the hallway. 'I was in Utrecht, and thought that—'

'No need to explain.' She brushed off his apologies. 'You are welcome, as always.' She took his coat and hat and hung them on a coat stand. 'Come up. I have made a sitting room upstairs for the winter. It's very warm and cosy.'

Indeed it was, he agreed. In a small room at the top of the stairs a wood stove stood on a tiled hearth and was sending out radiant heat. A small sofa with a rumpled wool blanket was where Cornelia must have been sitting, for there was an open book on it, and there were two easy chairs made welcoming with soft cushions and shawls. A brightly coloured rug lay on the wood floor, adorned by a black cat stretched out in perfect luxury who didn't even turn her head to look at him.

'You're alone!' He was perturbed.

There was a pot of coffee on a side table; after asking him to be seated she took a cup and saucer from a cupboard before answering. 'I am,' she said. 'The children are staying with my mother for a few days and I've sent Miriam home. Her mother is sick and the weather is set to worsen. You were lucky to get here.'

She poured him a cup of thick black aromatic coffee and he drank it gratefully, warming himself by the stove. Cornelia sat on the sofa, and kicking off her slippers drew her feet up beneath her skirts.

'I've disturbed you. I should have written,' he murmured. 'But I wasn't sure if I would be able to come.' Which was a lie, he thought. I knew I would come. I can't keep away. 'Had I known that you were alone—'

'You wouldn't have come?' she said abruptly.

He turned his head to look at her directly and saw then that she wasn't wearing black, but a plum-coloured gown. Her hair was tied back loosely with a ribbon. 'It wouldn't have been fitting, would it?'

She gave him a wry, derisive half-smile. 'Fitting?' It was almost an admonishment. 'I suppose not, but you see that I am not wearing mourning attire, at least not at home. Going out I wear a dark cloak and bonnet, but you cannot imagine how black drags my children down.' Her voice rose slightly. 'They are afraid to laugh or act normally. They whisper, and tiptoe about, and so I have put aside my black clothes for their sake and I don't care a jot what people say, for my children are more important to me than the views of any tittle-tattling gossip who doesn't know anything about me.'

It was the first time that he had ever heard her speak with such bitterness, and he guessed it was because she was feeling the effect of being without Nicolaas; she could no longer maintain the brave face she had put on during his illness and following his death. He saw that her eyes were red, as if she had been crying.

She spoke about Hans and Klara, how she had explained to them that their father would have wanted them to continue with their lives, to have fun with their friends, and suddenly there was a great outpouring of grief, anger and hard words, as if a dam with a hairline crack had burst and a torrent of foaming water had rushed through.

She kept wiping her eyes and between sobs repeated, 'Sorry. Sorry. Forgive me.'

Frederik put down his cup and moving towards the sofa sat down next to her, drawing her towards him so that his arm was around her.

'Shh, shh,' he murmured as she put her head against his chest and sobbed. 'No need to say sorry. Let it all out.'

Her tears wet his jacket and shirt as she wept and said how sad she was, and he closed his eyes and felt the warmth and softness of her as she leaned against him and he felt no guilt whatsoever, for hadn't Nicolaas asked him to take care of her?

'She deserves happiness,' he had said, and that he wanted her to find love again. But Frederik also recalled that Nicolaas had said that Cornelia would be vulnerable for some time, and that he hated the thought that someone might take advantage of her. But wasn't that what Frederik was doing? Was holding her in his arms and offering her comfort a prelude to something less innocent? He determined that Cornelia should never be given reason to suspect his integrity.

Cornelia drew away and put her feet to the floor.

Frederik gave her his large clean handkerchief and she took it and blew her nose. 'Whatever will you think of me, Frederik?' she said shakily. 'I am sorry if I've embarrassed you. So very sorry. This has been building up and up, and I have been so cross and sharp with everyone; that's why I sent the children to my mother. Why should they spend time with such a miserable wretch as me? And poor Miriam couldn't do anything right for me, so I sent her home so that I could drown alone in my misery.'

He patted her shoulder in sympathy. 'And then I came barging in and disturbed you.'

She turned a tear-stained face towards him. 'I'm glad that you were here,' she said, her voice hoarse with crying. 'I'm only sorry that you had to witness my distress.'

'It was quite natural,' he said softly. 'You wouldn't be human if you weren't able to show it.'

'I'm so lonely, Frederik,' she said simply. 'I'm used to being loved, and that has been taken away from me.'

He swallowed. 'You and Nicolaas had a very special marriage,' he said softly, and as she nodded he saw her eyes fill up again. 'How lucky you were.'

'We did,' she said. 'And we were lucky. I know that eventually I will believe that, but at present it makes it more difficult. Do you understand what I mean?'

'Yes, I think so.' He did, of course. To be so close to someone and then lose them must be heartbreaking.

'Do you have a good marriage, Frederik?'

'No,' he said. 'If I'm honest, we don't. Not like you

142

and Nicolaas, which was why I said how lucky you were.'

'Oh, I'm sorry. I didn't mean to be inquisitive.' She wiped her eyes. 'I assumed . . .' Her mouth formed a moue as if the idea that anyone might not have a good marriage hadn't occurred to her, but he dismissed her apology with a shrug as if the discussion was of no account.

She offered to make them a light supper, so he followed her down to the kitchen and sat on a stool whilst she sliced up cold meat, boiled eggs and took rye bread out of the crock and pickled herrings from the larder. She put the food on to a tray and gave him a bottle of red wine to open. As he did so she put her hand over her mouth and Frederik saw her eyes fill up with tears again.

'What?' he said softly.

'I'm so very pleased you came,' she said, her voice choked. 'I was at rock bottom and feeling so sorry for myself, when really I have no need to be. I have so much – my beautiful children, a lovely home and such good friends. Thank you, Frederik. Thank you.'

He longed to take her in his arms, to kiss her cheeks and stroke her hair, but he had to be content with reaching for her hand and gently squeezing it.

They ate at the small table by the stove upstairs in the soft glow of lamplight. He couldn't recall a time when he had felt so content. When they had finished eating and talking the evening had lengthened, and the clock ticking on the wall told him that it was almost half past ten.

'I should be going,' he said.

'You won't get a cab tonight.'

'I was going to walk,' he said. 'I'll find a local guesthouse, won't I?'

Cornelia gazed at him for a moment, and then turned her gaze to the flickering fire. Then she sighed and turned back to him.

'Won't you stay, Frederik? I'd like you to.'

CHAPTER SEVENTEEN

Within the second's pause before he answered, he wondered whether or not she had already been compromised by his visit. She had been alone when he arrived and he had been here for several hours, so what difference would it make if he stayed until morning? What was more, the idea of venturing out into the cavernous blackness to look for accommodation was hardly appealing on such a wintry night.

'There is a guest bed ready,' she added, as if assuring him that it wouldn't be inconvenient. 'It is a habit I have always had in case of unexpected guests.'

'That's very kind of you,' he said. 'I admit that I'm not keen on walking out into a blizzard, so, if you're sure, yes, thank you, I'd be pleased to stay.'

She seemed happy, giving him a sunny smile, and half rose from her chair. 'I'll find you a robe and run the warming pan over the sheets.'

'The robe, yes, but I'll be quite warm enough, thank you. But there's no hurry, unless of course you are tired, which I'm sure you must be.'

Suddenly they were polite to each other, embarrassed perhaps because he was staying the night.

'I'm not in the least tired,' she said, sitting down again. 'I have really enjoyed talking to you, Frederik, but I am talked out and you must be bored with my moaning, so now it's your turn. Tell me about you and your family, and your business too. It's good that you still have so many ties with Netherlands. How is your mother in Amsterdam?'

He assured her that he wasn't in the least bored, and discussed his business interests in both England and Netherlands. He told her about his plans to give shares to the people who worked for him in Amsterdam. 'It's important that they feel included in a business for which they work very hard and enthusiastically, and it seems the right thing to do. My lawyer agrees, and we are in the process of setting up the detail.' He realized as he spoke that although he had mentioned the idea to Rosamund, she hadn't made any comment. It was refreshing, he thought, to discuss it with someone who seemed interested.

Eventually they agreed that it was time to prepare for bed. Frederik carried the tray downstairs, Cornelia took the wine glasses and the empty wine bottle and they stacked everything by the deep sink in the kitchen. He smiled when he thought of how he and his siblings had done things like this when they were children.

'Why are you smiling?' Cornelia asked.

'Just thinking of the past,' he said. 'We were all expected to help when we were children – not a lot, but to know how to. Rosamund was brought up in a household where they had servants to do everything for them, and so it continues at home now. Margriet

146

has never moved a dish or a piece of cutlery in her life.'

'Oh, but that's dreadful,' Cornelia exclaimed. 'She should be taught how a home is run, or how will she know what to expect from the servants?'

He agreed, but knew that Rosamund would never countenance such a concept.

Cornelia showed him into the guest room and lit a bedside lamp, and then pointed out the robe hanging behind the door and the towels on the wash stand. She offered to bring up a jug of hot water but he reassured her there was no need as he could wash as easily in cold, and awkwardly they stood in the small room and said goodnight. She thanked him for his company and he gently kissed her hand and closed the door behind her.

He sat on the bed and put his head in his hands. The more he saw of her, the more he wanted to be with her, yet he could ruin her life just by being here, and ruin his marriage into the bargain if Rosamund discovered that he had spent the night with her, however innocently. On the other hand, would she even care? Did she expect him to remain celibate all his life? Sighing, he climbed into bed and turned down the lamp so that there was just a small glow that threw flickering shadows on the walls. Then he put his hands behind his head and wondered how to make sense of his difficulties.

Sleep must have overtaken him at some point, for he awoke to the sound of Cornelia softly calling his name. 'Frederik? Are you awake?'

He sat up. 'Yes,' he said throatily. 'Yes. Are you all right?' The lamp was still burning and he saw her standing just inside the open door. She seemed almost ghostlike in a light-coloured robe, that glorious hair hanging loosely over her shoulders.

'I woke you,' she whispered. 'I'm sorry.'

He reached for the dressing robe that he'd thrown on the bed and slipped his arms into it, covering his nakedness as he stood up. 'What is it? Are you unwell?'

'No,' she murmured. 'But I'm – I can't sleep, and I keep thinking of all the things we spoke of . . .' She turned away. 'I'm being foolish – I'm sorry for disturbing you.'

'No, wait.' He went towards her and took hold of her hand. 'Shall I sit with you? Are you nervous?'

'Nervous? No. But I'm very lonely. Will you – would you sit with me until I go to sleep?'

Frederik's heart hammered; how difficult that would be. 'Do you trust me, Cornelia?'

'I do,' she said, and began to weep.

He put his arm round her and led her back to her room. A low lamp burned there, and he saw how tumbled the bed sheets were, as if she had tossed and turned for hours. Somewhere in the house he heard a clock strike two. 'Shall I make you a hot drink?' he suggested, almost as if she were a child.

She shook her head. 'No. No, thank you. I'm so tired, but I can't sleep.'

He straightened the sheets and the blanket and the eiderdown and plumped up the pillows. 'Come on; back to bed.'

She took off her robe, revealing her long white cotton nightdress, and Frederik suppressed an inward breath as she climbed into bed. He tucked her in, smiling. 'I should tell you a bedtime story.'

Cornelia gave a weepy laugh. 'I can't believe I'm asking you this, but will you sit with me?'

There wasn't a chair in the room, but it was a double bed and after a brief hesitation he went to the vacant side and swung his legs on to it. It was a very comfortable feather mattress, and he thought that this must have been where Nicolaas slept before his illness forced him to move into the other room.

'Thank you,' she said simply; she was half propped up on the pillow and gazing at him. 'I didn't want to be by myself. I should never have sent the children away.'

'You did it for them, which was the right thing to do. Come here,' he murmured. Easing her up, he put his arm round her so that her head rested within the crook of his shoulder. 'How's that?'

She sighed. 'So comforting. What a good man you are, Frederik.'

If she knew what it was costing him, he thought, she would think him a very good man indeed. Her hair was tickling his face and he could smell her skin, an aroma of soap and something else, of flowers and lavender, and he inhaled deeply. 'You smell nice,' he said softly, wanting desperately to kiss her cheek, but not daring to in case he frightened her. She'd said that she trusted him; he had to be satisfied with putting his head lightly against hers and saying, 'Try to sleep now, Cornelia. Think of all the good things you have in life.' And he should do the same, he thought, and this was one of them.

He lay still, not daring to move, as Cornelia's breathing became steadier and he felt her relax against him. When he turned his head towards her he saw her eyelids were closed, and he kissed her lightly on the forehead. She made a small sound and snuggled closer, and then to his dismay she put one arm across him, her skin touching his where his robe didn't fasten. He was trapped, and to extricate himself he gently moved her.

Sound asleep, she turned over so that her back was facing him. He eased himself out of the bed, then lifted the blanket and crept back under it, keeping the top sheet between them. For heaven's sake, he thought, what am I doing? He could feel the warmth of her, and in the half-light of the lamp saw her long hair draped across the round curve of her shoulder, more than was proper to see of a woman who was neither wife nor lover. He wanted to turn towards her, but dared not – if she should wake! It was almost more than any man could bear.

Eventually he dropped into a light slumber, and dreamt that Cornelia held him in her arms and was giving him soft kisses while he kissed her cheek and her lips and ran his hands through her hair. He woke to find that they had turned to each other and she had her arm round him in a close embrace. Gently, he rolled away from her and buried his face in the pillow, breathing hard. The lamp had spluttered out and faint streaks of dawn were coming through the window before he silently left Cornelia's bed and tiptoed back to his own.

He awoke several hours later. He hadn't closed the curtains the night before, and a harsh bright light reflected from the snow streamed through the window. He wondered what time it was. He could hear the murmur of voices downstairs and guessed that the maid had come in to work. Presently he heard footsteps on the stairs and a knock on his door. It was Miriam, who had brought up a jug of hot water for shaving.

'Thank you,' he said. 'Please tell Mevrouw Jansen I will be down in ten minutes.'

She seemed not at all put out that a gentleman visitor had stayed the night. 'Pardon, *meneer*, but there is coffee ready when you are, and *poffertjes*.'

He groaned. Was there nothing Cornelia couldn't do? Baby pancakes, such as his mother used to make: an absolute favourite.

Miriam beamed. '*Zeer goed!*'

Quickly he washed, shaved and dressed, repacked his overnight bag and went downstairs, where a delicious smell of coffee and pancakes greeted him. Cornelia looked up from setting places at the table and gave him a hesitant smile.

'Good morning. Did you sleep well?'

'I did, thank you. And you?'

She murmured that she had, keeping her eyes lowered, and poured him coffee, thick, black and aromatic, and as they sat down Miriam turned from the stove with a dish piled high with pancakes, a jug of syrup and a dish of apple butter to spread on them.

'Cornelia, are you going to tell me that you made these?' he said teasingly.

'Well, actually, no, Miriam made them. But I can.' She laughed. 'They are a favourite with Hans and Klara.' She passed him the plate to help himself

151

and dropped her voice when Miriam left the room. 'Frederik! Whatever do you think of me? I behaved so stupidly last night. Please forgive me. I am mortified.'

He reached for her hand. 'There's no need. You were unhappy, and needed comfort.' Gently he squeezed her fingers. 'There's no harm done.'

'You could have taken advantage of me.' Her voice broke. 'And yet you didn't.'

He smiled and, lifting her hand to his lips, whispered, 'Believe me, Cornelia, I was very tempted. I wanted to.'

'Don't joke,' she said, drawing her hand away, but it broke the tension. 'Eat your pancakes.'

Miriam put her head round the door when they had almost finished eating and told Cornelia she was leaving and would see her the next day. Frederik stood up, wiping his mouth with a napkin, and thanked her for the lovely breakfast.

'I told her she needn't stay, as there's nothing much to do,' Cornelia said as she heard the front door close. 'The children will be home tomorrow and we'll be back to normal.' She took a deep breath. 'As I was saying, I'm so embarrassed. So ashamed of what I asked of you. I cannot believe that I was so weak.'

'Don't be,' he said firmly. 'I am honoured that you trusted me. I'm glad I was here.' He couldn't tell her that he wasn't joking when he said that he was tempted, and really did want her. It was too soon, far too soon to say that he had fallen in love with her. She wasn't ready to hear it – might not ever be ready.

She helped him on with his greatcoat and handed him his hat, then said, 'Thank you again for coming, Frederik.' She smiled up at him. 'You arrived in my hour of need, and . . .' she hesitated, 'you exceeded the bonds of friendship.'

Silently he gazed at her, remembering the warmth of her body next to his, seeing now the pale flush of her cheeks, her soulful grey eyes, her soft lips curved in a half-smile, and without thinking of the consequences he bent his head and kissed her tenderly on the mouth.

CHAPTER EIGHTEEN

Back at school at last, Margriet proudly told Miss Barker and the other pupils that she was being allowed to visit her Dutch grandmother at Easter because she was now old enough to travel without her mother. 'I'm quite grown up now,' she proclaimed.

Julia said that she was very jealous as she could barely remember her own Dutch grandmother, but added that she didn't mind too much now they had a new baby brother. She and Imogen had been allowed to help bathe him, and could talk of little else.

'I wish I could have one. Where did he come from?' Margriet asked during morning break as they drank their milk. 'I mean, how did your mama get him?'

Imogen looked at her and said solemnly, 'He was sleeping inside Mama until it was time for him to come out.'

'Inside her!' Margriet was astonished. 'But how did he get in there? Wasn't he too big?' She had seen the new baby, Hugh, in his perambulator when Mrs Sanderson and a nursemaid had come to collect her daughters from school.

Julia wiped her mouth free of milk with the back of her hand. 'He wasn't as big then as he is now. He was only a little seed when he first went in.'

Margriet opened her mouth to ask further questions but Miss Barker called them to attention and they went back to their desks. Margriet's mind was working hard. Who could she ask about this mystery? Not her mother; she had made her feelings plain when Margriet had told her that Mrs Sanderson was going to have another baby and Margriet had gathered that it wasn't something to be talked about. It was a big secret, she decided, but perhaps her grandmother would tell her when she went to visit.

Miss Barker, after much thought, had decided that the time had come for her well-off charges to be told about children who were less fortunate than they were; those whose parents could barely afford to buy bread for their tables or shoes for their feet, let alone pay for their children to sit in a comfortable schoolroom, learn their tables and go home afterwards to a good meal and a warm bed. It was time her privileged pupils were taught about real life.

After learning about the many difficulties that the poor faced every day, the children were subdued. Margriet put up her hand for permission to speak. 'Miss Barker, I'm going to ask my papa if he has any spare money they could have, and ask Mama if I could give away a pair of boots that are too small for me now.'

'Very commendable, Margriet.' Miss Barker smiled. Catch children whilst they were open to suggestion and teach them about humility and humanity before they became caught up in the complacent world of adulthood, and perhaps they wouldn't turn into copies of their parents. On the other hand, she did not want them to think that handing out money or a pair of old boots would solve the problems of a society where some people were starving and others feasting on roast pheasant and syllabub.

She knew there were exceptions: the Sandersons, for instance. Mrs Sanderson was an educated and articulate woman, who with her husband's support funded food kitchens in the winter and took young girls from the workhouse into her employ, and no one but a few knew of it. She did not advertise her philanthropy as some did.

When Florrie came to collect Margriet at four o'clock the child was buzzing with ideas about helping the poor and needed a ready ear. Florrie listened and nodded or pursed her lips as her charge suggested asking Cook to make extra bread every day, and collecting clothes that they didn't often wear to give away. And as soon as Papa returned from Amsterdam she would ask if he had some money to spare.

Florrie hid a grin. She didn't have any money to give away, and her only decent clothes were the ones her employer provided, which she certainly wasn't going to hand out to all and sundry. Besides, she was beginning to form ideas of her own about bettering herself, once she had been to Amsterdam.

'Well,' she said, as Margriet took a breath. 'If you want to ask your papa for something, Miss Margriet, look ahead of you, and here's your chance.'

Margriet lifted her eyes and there striding towards them was her father. He was smiling, she was pleased to see, for he had seemed rather sad lately, and he was waving to her. With a squeak of joy, she dropped Florrie's hand and ran to meet him.

Frederik picked her up and swung her in a circle until her skirts flew out and she had to cling on to her bonnet. 'Oh, Papa, I'm so pleased to see you. I've lots of things to tell you. Did you see my grandmother? I sent her a letter.'

'I saw her, she loved your letter and she's looking forward to your visit.' He turned to the maid. 'Do you want to get off, Florrie? I'll bring Miss Margriet home.'

'Oh, thank you, sir,' Florrie said. 'I have an errand to see to.' She hadn't, of course, but it would be foolish to pass up the opportunity to do a little window shopping and maybe stop for a gossip if she ran into a friend.

As they walked, Frederik told Margriet about the snow he had encountered in Netherlands and how much colder it was there than here. 'But when we go in the spring it will be warmer, though it might be rather windy. It's a very flat country and there are no mountains to stop the wind.'

'And there are lots of ditches to keep the water out, aren't there? I remember you telling me, Papa.'

'Good girl,' he said, pleased that she had been listening. 'Dykes, we call them, but yes, they are ditches.'

He led Margriet towards a coffee house. He didn't want to go back to the house yet. He'd arrived early this morning and gone straight to his office before heading home at midday. Rosamund had been about to leave to have luncheon with Lydia Percival followed by a game of bezique; she offered to send word that she couldn't come and stay at home with him for a light lunch of bread and beef, but it was said in such a way that he knew that cancelling her luncheon would displease her. This is a pretty kettle of fish, he had thought. How have we come to this, tiptoeing around each other and not wanting to be in each other's company?

'Are we going to have coffee?' Margriet asked.

'I am going to have coffee,' he said, 'and you can have hot chocolate and a piece of cake.'

He wanted to think and he could do that whilst Margriet looked around the coffee house and told him what she had been doing at school. He was filled with a warm glow whenever he remembered Cornelia and her reaction to his kiss as he'd said goodbye to her.

She had touched his face tenderly. 'I took advantage of you,' she had said softly. 'It was unfair.'

He'd smiled and nodded. 'You most certainly did. It was a wicked thing to do.' He had been trying to keep the moment light, not wanting her to think that he might expect more than she was prepared to give if she invited him to visit again.

She had blushed and lowered her eyes, then smiled and looked up. 'You're teasing me.'

'When I tease Margriet she says to me, "Papa, you are joking of me,"' he told her. 'But I don't want you to be embarrassed. I want to come again. To be your loving friend. Would that be permissible?'

She murmured, 'Yes, I would like that, Frederik.

I would like that very much.' She raised her head towards his and he bent to receive her kiss. 'Thank you.'

He had been euphoric. The warmth of the kiss, even though on his cheek, had been enough to carry him through the snow until he managed to hail a cab to take him to Utrecht. The train to Amsterdam was late and it was early evening by the time he reached his mother's apartment, cold and hungry and wanting only to eat and retire to bed. The next day he had boarded the ferry and spent another restless night as the ship tossed and rolled on a big sea and several times he almost fell out of his bunk.

'And so, Papa,' Margriet was saying, 'I am going to ask Mama if I can give away some of my clothes to the poor children.'

He stared at her. What on earth was she talking about?

'Because it's winter now and they must be very cold if they haven't any warm clothes to wear.' She noticed his uncomprehending look. 'The children!' she emphasized. 'The ones I've been talking about.'

'Oh, yes,' he said. 'Of course. Indeed you must ask your mama.'

As they were leaving, Margriet asked, 'Can we go the long way round, Papa? Past where the king's palace used to be and then home along Silver Street? Florrie always cuts across the square because she says it's quicker.'

'It is quicker,' he said. 'But Florrie has duties to get back to and hasn't time to go the long way round.' He looked down at her and took hold of her hand as they crossed the road. 'Why do you want to go this way?'

She chewed on her lip. 'Erm – because I haven't been that way for ages. I only ever go along there with you and it's so interesting.'

Amused, he was sure she had another reason. How was it he always agreed with her suggestions? Was he spoiling his only daughter? He thought he probably was, but then why not? It was unlikely that he would have another child and he wanted Margriet to know that she was loved, that she could ask him and discuss with him anything she wished.

They continued along Lowgate and away from the shelter of the church, feeling the chill of the wind blowing at their backs from the estuary; then they turned into Silver Street to walk towards White-friargate. They had almost reached the top of Land of Green Ginger when someone hailed Frederik.

'Vandergroene! Just the man I need.' It was Farrell, a business associate, a wholesale supplier of goods. 'I was talking about you only the other day. I'd like to have a discussion with you.'

'All right. I'll come along to your office. Would next week be early enough? I only arrived back from Amsterdam today.'

'It's Netherlands I want to discuss,' Farrell told him.

Casting a glance at her father, Margriet cautiously moved away a little, taking a few steps at a time until she was at the top of Land of Green Ginger.

'Margriet. Wait there,' her father called to her. 'Don't wander off.'

'I won't,' she called back, but she edged just a

little down the street until she could see Anneliese's house. She glanced back at her father and his associate and saw that they were walking slowly in her direction, talking earnestly as they did so.

She's not there, she thought as she looked up at the house; perhaps they're away, maybe in Netherlands. Where do they buy their ginger from, I wonder? Or do they grow it here? Then she glimpsed a movement at an upstairs window, a small hand on the curtain and a child's face; she lifted her own hand to wave. There she is! I think she's been waiting to see me and it's such a long time since I was here.

Her father and Mr Farrell were standing beside her, still chatting. 'I've been thinking exactly the same thing,' she heard her father say. 'There's quite a brisk trade already but room for more. We'll probably be too late for this spring, but I will enquire.'

Margriet glanced up when he went on, 'I see that house is still empty. Why is that, do you suppose? It's a good solid building.'

'A bit of a mystery about it, so I understand,' Farrell answered. 'I heard tell it's believed to be haunted.'

'Really!' Her father laughed.

Margriet turned. They were looking at Anneliese's house, and Anneliese had dropped the curtain.

CHAPTER NINETEEN

Rosamund wasn't back from her outing. Margriet ran upstairs to take off her outdoor clothing and change into her slippers, then ran down again to talk to her father before her mother returned.

'Papa, what does haunted mean?'

He waggled the lobes of his ears to show he knew she'd been eavesdropping. 'What do you think it means?' he said.

'I don't know. I don't think I've ever heard the word before.'

'Have you heard of ghosts?'

'Y-yes, I've read ghost stories. They're very eerie and might frighten little children.'

He stretched out his legs in front of the fire. 'Well, that's what haunted means. If someone believes that there's a ghost in an empty building, they say that it's haunted.' He put his hands in the air and made a whoo-ing sound, like an owl.

She was about to say that it was Anneliese's house he and Mr Farrell had been talking about, and if Anneliese lived there how could there be a ghost? But then she remembered that her father didn't know about Anneliese or Mevrouw Lindegroen and

162

decided that she would approach the subject in a different way.

'Papa, you know when we were talking about Land of Green Ginger?'

'Were we?'

'Yes,' she answered. 'You remember – about growing ginger.'

'No, I don't remember,' he said. 'But go on.' He heard the front door open and close and the murmur of voices and knew that Rosamund was home. Margriet had heard them too and said hastily, 'Oh, I just wondered if we could grow some?' Her eyes travelled the room and Frederik knew that she hadn't been going to ask that at all but something else entirely, something she didn't want to discuss in front of her mother.

When Rosamund came into the sitting room, Margriet was sitting demurely and swinging her crossed ankles. She smiled sweetly at her mother and got up to offer her her chair.

'Thank you, Margriet,' Rosamund said, taking it. 'Have you had an interesting day at school?'

'Oh, yes,' Margriet said enthusiastically. 'I have. We've been learning about the deserving poor.'

Rosamund glanced at Frederik, who raised a quizzical eyebrow. 'Really? Well, how very – erm, commendable. What subject does that come under?'

Margriet pressed her lips together, not properly understanding, but her father broke in. 'The Poor Law, wasn't it, Margriet?'

Margriet's expression cleared. 'Yes, I think that's what it was, and,' she hurried on before her mother lost interest, 'we have to think about the poor

163

people among us. So can we give them some of our things that we don't need any more, Mama? Like old clothes and boots?'

'Well, I – we don't know any poor people, Margriet. And in any case I already give clothing and suchlike to Florence and Mrs Simmonds to pass on to anyone they might know.'

Margriet considered. She had hoped to present a parcel of clothing or a small bag of money to the first poor person that she happened to chance upon, but now it seemed that might not be possible.

Florrie knocked on the door. 'Beg pardon, madam, sir, but Miss Margriet's afternoon tea is ready. Shall I serve it here or upstairs?'

'I'd like it upstairs, please, Florrie, if that's all right, Mama?' Margriet said. 'I have some reading homework to do.' She knew that would please her mother.

Frederik hid a smile. Little minx, he thought. She hadn't at all; she was just bored. She needed the company of other children; he could see the difference in her since she started school.

Upstairs in her bedroom, Margriet opened her wardrobe door and looked at the clothes hanging there, then went to fetch a stool to stand on. She began to move the dresses and coats she didn't like to one side, pushing them close together and carefully rearranging those that she liked, spreading them apart so that no one would notice that she had moved any. At some point, she decided, she would ask Florrie to take those she didn't like and give them away to the deserving poor.

When Florrie came upstairs with her tray, she was

sitting reading. She put down her book. 'Florrie,' she said, 'don't you wish that Easter would hurry up and come so that we could go away to Netherlands?'

Florrie arranged the contents of the tray on a small table. 'I'm looking forward to it, Miss Margriet. It'll be very exciting for me.'

'And for me too,' Margriet said. 'I have never met my grandmother before. I'm to call her Oma, which is a pet name for grandmother.'

'Oh!' Florrie grinned. 'I used to call mine Gran.' She changed the subject. 'We'll have to sort out 'clothes you're to tek, won't we? You'll need a large trunk.'

'I expect so,' Margriet agreed vaguely. 'I can't wait.'

Florrie too was eager to be going. This was her chance. She had been listening in to her employers' conversation, not to eavesdrop but to improve her own use of language, knowing that if she wanted to better herself she needed to improve her deportment. Her imagination began to soar as she thought of the applications she might write, telling of looking after her charge both at home and abroad. She thought too of a time when she didn't have to dust and polish and run errands and help in the kitchen. She'd had enough of being a maid of all work.

At the beginning of April Florrie began to prepare Margriet's trunk and her own canvas bag. The clothes that Margriet had put to one side, telling her mother that she had outgrown them, Florrie was charged with finding a suitable home for, which she did, giving them to her own nieces, and

Margriet was satisfied that she had done something to help the poor.

The day before they were due to sail, Margriet suddenly felt sorry for her mother, about to be left alone. 'Wouldn't you like to come, Mama?' she asked. 'I wish you would.'

Frederik felt a sudden charge of unease. Conscience-stricken, he realized that he was praying she would say no.

'Much as I would love to,' Rosamund sounded grieved, 'I fear I would be too ill. I wouldn't dare to make the return journey home.'

'Mama won't be on her own for long,' Frederik told Margriet. 'I won't be staying a whole month as you will, Daisy. I shall come home and keep her company.'

A whole month! Florrie hid a smile. Mrs Simmonds had been most put out when given this information and had nerved herself to speak to Mrs Vandergroene, saying she must have more help than had been originally arranged.

'I didn't know it was going to be so long, ma'am,' she said peevishly.

'No, Mrs Simmonds,' Rosamund had sighed. 'Neither did I.' She had wondered whether she would miss her daughter's presence. Being without Frederik for a week or more didn't disturb her, because it meant that the threat of any night-time visit to her bedroom was removed. Indeed, he rarely made such visits now, and it was a huge relief to be done with such disagreeable occasions, although she did sometimes wonder if he had found consolation elsewhere. Her friend Lydia had reliably informed her that a man had to find comfort with another woman if his wife wasn't willing, and although Rosamund had pretended incredulity that a wife should so behave, she decided that perhaps she wouldn't mind too much if Frederik did take a mistress, although she thought that he was probably far too honourable to do such a thing.

She walked with them to the dockside, accompanied by the new temporary maid. Jane, she thought, was very presentable; someone she would be happy to be seen with when she went shopping.

Margriet was so excited she could barely keep still as they waited for the luggage to be taken aboard, hopping about on first one foot and then the other. Then it was their turn to cross the gangplank. She felt quite tearful as she kissed her mother goodbye, but once on board she waved her hand cheerfully and went below with Florrie and a steward to find their cabin.

Florrie heaved a deep breath. 'I'm a bit fearful, Miss Margriet,' she said, 'I don't mind admitting. I've never sailed afore.'

'I've never sailed before either, Florrie,' Margriet said. 'But I'm sure we'll be all right. We'll just have to be brave.'

'We will,' Florrie agreed. She thought for a moment, and then said, 'Do you think you could call me Florence, Miss Margriet? I think perhaps it would be more proper now I'm your travelling companion.'

Margriet agreed, but when she told her father he laughed and said that Florrie was going up in the world.

Florrie was slightly sick as they emerged into the German Ocean, but she soon became used to the rise and fall of the ship and joined Margriet and her father for a short stroll along the deck before going below for supper. Margriet wasn't queasy at all and slept soundly in her bunk that night.

Frederik did not sleep well; deep in the pit of his stomach he had a churning sensation at the thought of seeing Cornelia again. He wondered whether he should take Margriet to meet her and, if he did, would Margriet mention the visit to Rosamund on their return? And if she did, he thought, lying in his bunk with his arms stretched above his head, would it matter? Surely he was allowed friends, just as Rosamund was. So, perhaps he would do it. He sighed. On the other hand, perhaps not.

CHAPTER TWENTY

On disembarking in Amsterdam, Frederik ordered a carriage to take them to his mother's apartment. Margriet was filled with excitement and Florrie was apprehensive.

'You'll like my mother, Florrie,' Frederik said. 'You needn't be nervous.'

'What should I call her, sir?' Florrie asked. 'Do I say ma'am, like in England?'

'You say *mevrouw* – muh-frow. You'll soon become used to it,' he added, seeing consternation written on her face. 'And you can also say *alstublieft* – alst oo bleeft – for "if you please, ma'am".'

'I'll never get used to it, sir.' Florrie was beginning to panic.

'I'll help you, Florrie,' Margriet said. 'Florence, I mean.' She giggled. 'We'll practise together, because I can't speak Dutch either.'

Gerda swept her granddaughter up in her arms when they arrived, giving her a great squeeze and several kisses and then patting Florrie on the shoulder in welcome so that the girl immediately felt more comfortable but still unsure of what role was expected of her. Gerda too had taken the trouble to improve her English. 'I will call you Floris,' she said to Florrie. 'It means the same.'

Frederik stayed until midday to have lunch with them and was surprised when his mother set a place for Florrie. He saw that Florrie was slightly embarrassed, but she helped to dish up and when they were finished at table she cleared away and washed the dishes, taking it upon herself to become a servant once more. It will be all right, he thought, standing up to leave.

'I must go,' he said. 'I'll see you tomorrow or the day after. Will you be all right without your papa, little Daisy?'

'Of course she will,' his mother answered. 'This afternoon, Margriet, we are going to meet your *tante* Anna, and your cousins are going to show you the flower gardens.'

Margriet beamed with delight and Frederik smiled. He was pleased that he had brought her.

'I am going into the tulip business, Moeder,' he said. 'I've been asked about supplying them to growers in England.'

'How interesting!' she said. 'Bulbs or flowers?'

'Bulbs, probably. It isn't yet decided.'

He took his leave then, giving Margriet a kiss, and booked in at his usual hotel as there wasn't enough room for him to stay at his mother's. Then he called at the Amsterdam office and said he would come in again the following day as he wished to discuss several things; within minutes he was walking away from the building and once round the corner he set off at a run to catch a train to Utrecht. I'm like a lovesick schoolboy, he thought as the train rumbled and chuffed towards its destination. What was the matter with him?

It was not yet a year, he mused as the hired carriage bumped and swayed towards Gouda. Not a year since Nicolaas died – yet what had he said? That he wanted his wife to be loved, so why did he, Frederik, feel as though he was betraying him by having such feelings for her? He put his hands to his forehead. It was too soon to say anything, however desperate he might be to declare his love and affection. He took a sudden breath. But I am a married man and this feeling within me is totally immoral.

Miriam answered the door to his knock. She invited him in, explaining that her mistress had taken Klara to visit friends but wouldn't be long. She offered to make coffee for Frederik in the meantime.

'Should I come back?' he asked, but she shook her head and said that it would be quite all right for him to wait.

'Mevrouw was very much cheered by your last visit, *meneer*; please come in.' She led him into the sitting room and he sat facing the garden, which was full of pots of daffodils, hyacinth and early tulips. It was a very pleasant room, lit today by bright sunshine, and he noticed an upright piano by the back wall that he couldn't recall from his previous visits.

Miriam brought him coffee and cake, and he was just wiping the last crumbs from his mouth when he heard the front door open and Cornelia and Klara calling to Miriam. The maid answered them with the news that they had a visitor.

Cornelia put her head round the door, a slight

apprehension in her expression until she saw who the visitor was, when he was delighted to see her face break into a warm smile. 'Frederik! How lovely.' She came towards him, holding out both her hands to clasp his as he rose to greet her. 'I'm so pleased to see you.'

'You look well, Cornelia,' he said, his voice husky with nervous emotion; he was overcome at seeing her again. 'So very well.'

'I am well,' she said. 'My spirits have lifted with the arrival of spring. The trees are in leaf, and my garden is flourishing. It was such a long, long winter – I thought we were never coming to the end of it. Those never-ending dark nights . . . well, you saw how I was. I was so grateful for your last visit.'

She invited him to sit again, and after opening the doors into the garden she took a chair next to him. 'Miriam has given you coffee, I see. Can I get you anything else?'

'Nothing, thank you.'

'But you will stay the night?' She lowered her voice. 'I promise that my behaviour won't be as foolish as last time.'

He shook his head. 'You were not foolish,' he insisted, speaking softly. 'You were unhappy and distressed and needed a friend and I happened to come along at the right time.' He was about to say that he would always be there if she needed him when the door opened and Klara came in.

'*Lieveling*,' Cornelia said, 'come and say hello to Meneer Vandergroene. Tell him what you have been doing, why don't you?'

Frederik stood up as Klara dipped her knee. 'Call

me Frederik, please,' he said, putting out his hand. 'Or Uncle Freddy? Would you prefer that?'

'Yes, please,' she said. 'I would.' She smiled, and turned round to point at the piano. 'That was my *oma*'s piano and she's given it to me. I'm learning to play.'

'I used to play when I was young,' Cornelia remarked. 'So did my mother, but she no longer does and said that Klara could have the piano. She loves it, don't you, Klara?'

The little girl nodded. 'I could play you something if you like, Uncle Freddy. I'm not very good yet but Mama says I will improve, don't you, Moe?'

'Of course you will.' Her mother smiled at Klara as she went to the piano and then at Frederik. Lowering her voice again, she murmured, 'She has lost her sadness since learning to play. It has made a great difference to her, and Hans too is mixing with his friends again.'

'They just needed time,' he said. 'It is a great healer.'

He broke off as Klara began to play and his eyebrows lifted in delight. He could recall his sister Anna playing the same simple piece when they were young, and remembered too that he and Bartel used to tease her whenever she hit a wrong note. He clapped his hands when she had finished. 'Well done, Klara,' he said kindly. 'That was lovely.' She got down from the stool and dipped her knee and asked her mother if she might go upstairs.

He told Cornelia that he had brought Margriet with him on this trip, with a maid to accompany her on the voyage.

'I wish you could have brought her here,' she said wistfully. 'I would love to meet her.'

'Perhaps another time,' he said. 'She's meeting my mother for the first time, and my sister and her children, and maybe my brother and his family too. But I would like to bring her; she and Klara would get on well together I think.' What would Rosamund make of that, he thought.

'So do you have to get back to her tonight? Or can you stay for supper?'

'I don't have to rush back. I have business to attend to in Gouda tomorrow, and in any case I am staying at a hotel in Amsterdam. My mother doesn't have enough room for all of us.'

'Then you must stay with us. There's no need for you to stay in hotels when we have space. It will be lovely if you can, and you can see Hans too. He needs a man to talk to.' A shadow fell across her face, and she bent her head. 'As I do too. I also need grown-up company.'

When Hans came in he seemed very pleased to see Frederik and shook his hand, giving a little bow. He sat down to talk and said that he would soon be going to school in Amsterdam. 'My father's old school, and yours too, *meneer*,' he said. 'I shall have to board, as it's too far to come home every day.' He looked towards the kitchen, where his mother had gone to supervise supper, and lowered his voice. 'I shall worry about my mother, though, alone here with Klara, so I will come home every weekend until I am satisfied that she's all right.'

'That is most praiseworthy,' Frederik said approvingly. 'But your mother is a strong woman and

I think she will cope very well.' He hesitated, and then said, 'And you know that I will call and see her whenever I come over from England.'

Hans nodded. 'Thank you, *meneer*. I hoped you would say that. She looks forward to your visits.'

Frederik suggested that Hans too might like to call him Frederik or Freddy. He didn't mention uncle as the boy would soon be twelve and probably thought of himself too grown up for that, but Hans grinned and asked if he could call him Uncle Freddy anyway. He added that he would like to speak only in English, and Frederik said he could do that.

The four of them ate supper together. Frederik hadn't brought a change of clothing but only the razor blade and shaving brush that he kept in a small cardboard box in his travelling case; he hadn't wanted Cornelia to think that he assumed he would be staying. Cornelia had come down in a dark blue full-skirted silk gown patterned with small flowers, with a pointed waistline and a low neckline that emphasized her creamy skin, which was bare of jewellery.

Afterwards, Hans and Frederik began a game of chess and Klara played the piano whilst Cornelia sat and watched them. Presently Klara went up to bed, and Cornelia got up and poured two glasses of wine.

'I'm going up now, Moe,' Hans said as they reached stalemate and declared the game a draw. 'I've to be up early in the morning. I have an exam tomorrow.' He turned to Frederik. 'I might see you in the morning, sir, or perhaps tomorrow evening?'

'I have to be in Amsterdam tomorrow, but perhaps before I return to England I might call again. But in any case I will be back before the end of the month to collect Margriet, and I will see you then.'

Hans nodded. 'Good. I'll look forward to it. Goodnight, Uncle Freddy.'

'What a splendid young man he is,' Frederik said after he had gone. 'I would have loved to have had such a son.'

'He is quite special.' Cornelia smiled. 'But then I am very biased.'

'And quite rightly so. We should be proud of our children, and yours are a credit to you.'

'Yes,' she said softly. 'And to Nicolaas too.'

'Of course.' He sighed. 'What a good fellow he was.'

She nodded but didn't say anything, and they sat quietly drinking their wine. Then he asked, 'Won't you play me something?'

She shrugged and laughed. 'I'm rather rusty.'

'It doesn't matter. Please do – I never hear music. We have a piano, but Rosamund is too shy to play in front of anyone.'

'All right,' she said reluctantly, rising from her chair. 'Will you turn the pages?'

He laughed. 'You'll have to tell me when.'

He took his glass with him and stood slightly behind her as she began, taking sips of the full-bodied red wine. Cornelia faltered a little at first but as her confidence grew she began to play more fluently. Frederik didn't really care if she made mistakes; he was happy just to stand near her, watching her fingers on the keys and the movement of her head and shoulders as she gently swayed to the melody.

He reached across to the nearby dresser and put his glass down as she indicated that he should turn the page, and leaned over her to do so. He was mesmerized by the wisps of hair that had escaped from the braids around her head and were touching the back of her neck, quivering as an aspen leaf might. I'm drunk, he thought, on one glass of wine. He gently touched the nape of her neck and his fingers trembled as he teased the wisps of hair between them. Cornelia stirred slightly but wavered only briefly in her playing as he ran his hands down the smooth slope of her bare shoulders to the narrow silk piping of her neckline.

Her hands paused in their movement and she slowly turned round to face him. Her lips were parted as his were too.

'Forgive me, Lia,' he whispered. 'It's more than I can bear.'

She stood up, and with the piano stool between them she gazed at him. Then, with barely a second's pause, she leaned towards him and kissed him tenderly on his lips.

Upstairs in his room, Hans lay sleepless, waiting as he always had since his father's death for the click of the latch on his mother's door. Once he heard her he could relax, knowing she was safely in bed, although he often heard her weeping. He had heard the faint notes of the piano and was pleased that she was playing again, and now he heard footsteps on the stair. Two pairs of feet, the quiet tread along the corridor to her room and the click of the latch to open the door and close it. Only one door.

He gave a huge sigh and slid down beneath the sheets. He was glad. At last, his mother would be happy again. He was sure of it.

CHAPTER TWENTY-ONE

'What about the children?' Frederik had whispered as Cornelia placed a guard against the fire and turned down the lamp.

He'd returned her kiss, drawing her to him and leading her to a chair where she'd sat on his knee and wept. He kissed her wet cheeks and smoothed back her hair and told her he loved her and that there was no need for tears.

'I won't ever hurt you, Lia,' he murmured. 'I will cherish you and take care of you always.'

She placed her finger on his lips to silence him. 'Don't make promises,' she whispered. 'We don't know what is in front of us. Let us make the most of what we have now. You have already given me joy by your caring friendship, and—'

Now it was his turn to put his finger to her mouth, gently tracing the outline, feeling the moistness as she parted her lips. 'I have told you I love you,' he said softly. 'I don't want only friendship.'

It was then that she stood up, drawing him to her and asking him to come again to her bed. 'But this time not as a friend, but as my lover.'

And then he had asked, 'What about the children?'

She kissed his hand as she led him to the door, carefully closing it behind them. 'They'll be asleep,' she whispered as they mounted the stairs. 'They sleep well.'

Once inside her room he took off his jacket and threw it on a chair, and when Cornelia turned her back to him he fumbled to unfasten the lacing that reached below her waist. The sleeves of the bodice slipped off her shoulders, her gown falling to the floor in an abundant cascade, leaving her in only her linen chemise.

He took in a deep breath as she turned towards him and raised her arms, and he lifted the chemise over her head so that she stood naked before him. He gazed at her and then fell to his knees, and as he knelt she lifted first one foot and then another so that he could take off her dainty slippers. He kissed each foot in turn, murmuring her name. Not Cornelia, but Lia. That was his name for her, and never in his life had he felt such emotion, such strength of passion as he was feeling now. Not once had he seen a woman unashamed to show him her body in all its beauty, and as he knelt before her she bent to unfasten his shirt, her breasts touching his face, and he felt that he was in heaven.

It was not as if he had never felt any affection for Rosamund, he told Lia many weeks later on one of his many return visits. She was the mother of his daughter, after all, but he felt that she didn't return his affection and his feelings for her had dwindled after so many years of her reluctance to share her bed or have another child.

He turned to Lia as she stroked his cheek. Her thick luxuriant hair was strewn across her pillow and he told her again how much he loved her.

'I would gladly give you a child, Frederik,' she whispered. 'But I fear that because you are a part-time husband and I am a widow it would not be to our advantage.'

'I could leave her,' he said. The prospect of that had filled his mind constantly. 'I have every reason to do so.'

'*Nee, lieveling*,' she said. 'I would not wish that on any woman. Your wife would be ostracized, and from what I gather about her she would not cope with that. She would be condemned to living a life without friends or family.'

They were alone in the house. Klara had gone to stay with Lia's mother and Hans was now at school in Amsterdam, but before he had departed the boy had asked to have a private word with Frederik. He had blushed, and said, 'I wanted to tell you, Uncle Freddy, that I'm pleased that you have brought my *moeder* some happiness, but I wonder what will happen to her if you return to your wife.'

Frederik was startled. He and Lia had tried to be discreet, but Hans was old enough – and mature enough, it seemed – to see through their veil of discretion. Honesty appeared to be his only option.

'I haven't actually left my wife, Hans. We are still married, and although I am willing to leave her your mother is against it. She says that my wife would be shunned by society if I follow that line, and she doesn't want that.'

Hans gave a little smile. '*Mijn moeder* always

181

thinks of others. It is a generous trait.'

'I love your mother,' Frederik said. 'And I would give anything to be with her, but she is right. I must think not only about my wife but about my daughter too, for our separation would reflect on her as well.'

Hans nodded. 'Margriet. Yes. I wish we could meet her.'

'I promise that I'll bring her one day. She is coming to stay with her *oma* again in the summer; perhaps I will bring her then.'

And so he did. When summer came along he once again asked Florrie to accompany Margriet to his mother's and she agreed immediately. She liked Gerda Vandergroene, and her daughter too, and her plans for improving her position were still in her mind. Mrs Simmonds asked Jane to step into the breach once more.

Margriet stayed for a week this time, visiting her cousins and learning to speak Dutch. Often Floris, as the Dutch called her, took the children out alone without Gerda or Anna. Then Frederik arrived from his office one day and told Margriet he would like her to come with him to meet a friend and her children.

'Do you recall, Margriet, that a very dear friend of mine died and you asked if I would tell his children, Hans and Klara, that you were very sad for them?'

'Yes, I do remember,' she said. 'I said that I would cry if you died.'

'Well, I would expect at least a bucketful of tears, Margriet,' he joked, patting her head. 'I've seen Hans and Klara a few times since then and they would like to meet you, so could Oma spare you for a day, do you think?'

Although he wasn't meeting his mother's eye he was conscious of her gaze, but she said mildly, 'We haven't planned anything for tomorrow, Margriet, so perhaps then? Were you thinking of taking Floris, Frederik? If not, she could come shopping with me.'

'No, no. Margriet and I will be fine together, and tomorrow will be perfect as Gouda has the cheese market on Thursdays. We must go early, though, as it closes at half past twelve prompt.'

He didn't want Florrie to go with them. She was an astute young woman, and she must have realized that the bedroom situation at home was not normal. He was not yet ready to have it known that he was being unfaithful, although he was sure his mother suspected the truth.

Margriet skipped alongside her father to the railway station the following day. 'You like it here in Netherlands, don't you, Papa?' she said as they boarded the train. 'I think you're happier here than at home in Hull.'

'No, no,' he said quickly. 'I like Hull very much, and it is my home and where you are, but I'm happy in my own country too, and especially now that you're here with me. I've wanted you to come and meet your relatives for such a long time.'

She smiled and nodded. 'And now I'm going to meet some new friends and I'm really looking forward to that, although I expect that Hans is too old to play games.'

They were in time for the cheese market and

183

Margriet was delighted by the colourful costumes of the porters and the way that the traders clapped hands to seal a bargain. Her father told her that this part of Netherlands was called Holland, and that she would probably see many people in traditional dress and wearing clogs like the ones she had at home.

'I ought to have another pair, Papa,' she said. 'I've grown out of the old ones.'

He laughed and said he'd buy her another pair and a winged cap too, and then she'd feel like a proper Dutch girl. He bought them both waffles and they ate them sitting on the canal wall before he took her to see the weigh house and the ancient town hall. She licked syrup from her fingers and he gave her a handkerchief to wipe her mouth and hands. 'I don't think we should tell Mama that we've been eating outside, Papa,' she murmured. 'I don't think she would like it.'

He nodded solemnly. 'I quite agree, Daisy. I think this must have to be our special secret.'

Klara had been watching for Margriet's arrival, and opened the door to them. 'Hello, Margriet. Are you going to stay with us? Can she, Uncle Freddy?'

'I'm sorry, but not this time, Klara,' Frederik answered, seeing Margriet's eyes open wide at 'Uncle'. He knew there would be questions later. 'Margriet's *oma* is expecting us back tonight.'

'Well, come up to my room now.' Klara reached for Margriet's hand. 'But first you have to meet Hans. He's up in his room studying, even though it's the holidays, but he wants to meet you too.'

'Wait, wait.' Cornelia came out of the kitchen. 'I must say hello to Margriet first.'

Margriet dipped her knee. '*Hoe doe je, Mevrouw Jansen?*' she asked in perfect Dutch.

Cornelia smiled delightedly. 'I'm very well, thank you, Margriet. You've been practising your Dutch!'

'Papa taught me,' she said. 'He said it would be polite if I knew a few words.'

'You have a very good accent,' Cornelia said. 'But we can all speak English, so that will be easier for you, and you may call me Tante Lia if you wish. Klara and Hans call your papa Uncle, but they have known him a long time, of course.'

'Ah, I see!' Margriet exclaimed. 'I thought they might be more cousins. I've met my Amsterdam cousins already.'

'No, not cousins,' her father said. 'But very good friends, which is why they call me Uncle.'

The two girls ran up the stairs to see Hans, and Lia led Frederik into the sitting room. He closed the door and kissed her tenderly. 'I can't bear being away from you,' he whispered. 'It's agony to be within a few miles and not able to hold you in my arms.'

'We must be careful,' she said. 'Margriet is young, but she just might say something untoward to her mother.'

He shook his head. 'I don't think Rosamund would care, quite frankly. But you're right: I wouldn't for the world want Margriet to be confused or worried.'

'She won't be, *lieveling*.' She kissed him. 'We'll be discreet.'

*

185

Back home in Hull Rosamund already had her suspicions. Frederik was much more light-hearted than he had been for some time; in fact more like the man he had been before and during the early days of their marriage. It was her fault, she confessed only to herself; the change began in their marriage bed. She wouldn't mind his having an affair if he were discreet, especially if his lover lived abroad. She had noticed how eager he was to be back in Amsterdam. Separation, on the other hand, was unthinkable. What if he were to leave her on the grounds that she had refused him his conjugal rights? Her friends had long noses for scandal and would soon put two and two together; even a hint that her marriage was not as perfect as she made it out to be would be all over town in no time, and she couldn't bear that. She nipped the skin on her fingers with her teeth in her anxiety. She really couldn't.

CHAPTER TWENTY-TWO

November 1846

The last four years had passed quickly and Margriet was happier at ten years old than she had ever been before. She had met her Dutch cousins and had Dutch friends; she and Klara corresponded regularly, with Margriet using the few Dutch phrases she had learned and Klara practising her English.

Margriet had travelled three times to stay with her grandmother during the school holidays and at Easter, but she had also holidayed with her parents in Scarborough, taking a larger house in St Nicholas Cliff as Rosamund had wanted and again meeting up with the Sanderson family.

Rosamund had relaxed her severe hold on Margriet, allowing her more freedom than she had enjoyed previously. Although she was still accompanied to school by Florrie in the morning, she was sometimes allowed to come home with Julia Sanderson; they walked together to the top of Parliament Street, where Julia was met by Imogen, who had now left the dame school, or by the nursery maid.

On one such occasion, having waved goodbye to the Sanderson girls and knowing that her mother would not yet be home from one of her tea parties, instead of continuing down Parliament Street Margriet about-turned and retraced her steps along Whitefriargate to Land of Green Ginger. She hadn't seen Anneliese at her window for a while and was curious to know where she was. The street was busy, with people cutting through into Bowlalley Lane or heading towards Broadley Street or Quay Street, and Margriet stood in a doorway as if waiting for someone and kept an eye on the Lindegroens' house. After waiting ten minutes without seeing even a twitch of the curtains, she knew she had to go home, but she worried that Anneliese might think that she had neglected her. It's because of school, she told herself in excuse, that's why I haven't been to see her so often.

Nowadays she ate at seven in the evening with her parents, but had a glass of milk and a biscuit in her room when she got home from school. Florrie brought it up on a tray. 'You were late home today, Miss Margriet,' she said. 'You didn't go wandering off, did you?'

'Oh, no,' Margriet said innocently. 'Julia and I were talking and I suppose we dawdled and didn't realize the time.'

'Well, you mustn't dawdle but come straight home,' Florrie said. 'I was on 'point of coming to look for you. If your mama hears about it I'll have to start fetching you home again, especially now that winter's here and 'nights are drawing in. It gets dark very quickly.'

Margriet heaved a sigh. 'All right,' she agreed. 'But I'm old enough to come home on my own.'

'Well, mebbe,' Florrie said. 'I went everywhere on my own when I was your age, but your mama would have a fit if I told her about you being late, so you'd better not do it again.'

'I won't, I promise. Please don't tell, Florrie.'

'Tell who what?' Neither of them had heard her father come upstairs. 'What has Margriet been up to, Florrie?'

Florrie decided to tell the truth. Mr Vandergroene was much more understanding than her mistress. 'Nothing much, sir,' she said. 'Just that she was a bit late home from school and I said I'd have to start fetching her back again if Mrs Vandergroene heard about it.'

'Oh ho!' Frederik said with mock severity. 'So what do you suggest? Bread and water in her room tonight instead of supper downstairs?'

She nodded in collusion. 'That's about right, sir.'

'Which would be a pity,' he went on, rubbing his beard, 'especially as I'm leaving for Netherlands in the morning and I won't see her for a week.'

'Oh, Papa!' Margriet jumped up and put her arms round his waist. 'Please, no! Are you joking of me again?'

He laughed and ruffled her hair. It amused him that she still asked the question in the same way and he never corrected her. 'I'm joking about the bread and water,' he said. 'But you must always come straight home. Florrie is responsible for you when your mama isn't here, and it's not fair to worry her.'

Margriet hung her head. 'I'm sorry, Papa. Sorry,

189

Florrie.' She sighed. 'When will I be old enough to do things on my own? Or will I always have to have someone with me, as Mama does?'

He patted her cheek. 'When you're grown up you can make your own decisions, Daisy,' he said softly. 'I promise you that.'

At supper that night he told his wife and daughter that he was about to take delivery of a massive consignment of tulip bulbs from Amsterdam, for which he had taken orders from growers all over England.

Rosamund nodded politely. 'Is this instead of your other supplies or as well as?'

He looked at her in surprise; she didn't normally ask any questions. 'As well as. There'll still be cheese and Genever and other commodities coming in, as well as timber.' Although his father had set up the Hull office to export English wool and English oak and import wood from the Baltic, when Frederik took over the business he had decided to add selected perishables with a quicker turnaround. That trade was now flourishing, but he was excited by the success of the bulb venture.

'I love tulips,' Margriet said. 'Tante Anna took us to see the bulb fields last spring, and' – she spread her arms wide – 'there were millions!'

Frederik smiled at her enthusiasm. 'Well, there will be cut flowers coming too, for the local market. Tulips, hyacinths and narcissi. We'll fill the town of Hull with them.'

He was leaving early the next morning on a steamer packet carrying produce and a dozen or so passengers. The owner, Captain Simpson, had said he could travel out on any of his ships whenever he wanted, as they made daily sailings to both Amsterdam and Rotterdam. Frederik was keen to have the option of frequent carrier travel for the import of bulbs, flowers and foodstuffs, and Captain Simpson seemed keen for the business, so he had decided to try him out. For his other contingents of timber and heavy goods he would still use the bigger trading vessels.

As always, he was eager to see Lia. His life now had a kind of pattern to it, and although it was not ideal, he thought as he stowed his travel bag in the tiny cabin – the bunk was too short to stretch out his legs and the overhead locker was on a dangerous level with his forehead – he was prepared to endure it in order to be with the woman he loved and the daughter he adored, for he wasn't prepared to give up either of them.

One day, he thought, when Margriet was older and able to understand, he would tell her. She knew Lia now and seemed to like her, and Rosamund didn't appear to think anything of it when she mentioned Tante Lia and Klara in conversation.

It was a very rough crossing and he barely slept. This was such a spiteful sea, he thought irritably as he struggled to dress in his outdoor clothes early the following morning. One day it was like a millpond and the next it was trying to take back the land that had been stolen from it.

All Dutch children grew up with the knowledge that the sea must be treated with caution. Dutch engineers were known the world over for the great feats of engineering that kept the sea from their low-lying marshy land, but sometimes the hungry tides tricked them and colluded with the hurricane force winds and swept in, driving a great force of house-high water that engulfed all that lay before it.

He had to use all his strength to open the door on to the deck. When he looked out the deck was awash and he knew he would be putting his life in danger if he left the cabin. He saw a wall of water rise, about to break above the deck, and swiftly shut the door again. These seamen, he thought, as he sat back again on his bunk. They do this every day of their lives, delivering our goods and fishing for our food, and most of us just take them for granted.

As they neared the Dutch coast the wind eased a little and it became less rough, so he ventured out on deck in search of the galley – the caboose, as the Dutch seamen called it – and a hot drink. Captain Simpson was in there, swaying easily on his feet in front of the stove and making cocoa from a steaming kettle. He handed a cup to Frederik and told him to help himself to rye bread.

'Did you sleep, sir?' he asked. 'It was a rough old night.'

'Not much,' Frederik admitted. 'Are we going to be late in?'

'An hour, maybe, and we might have to make a detour if the port is flooded.' He shrugged. 'But it is how it is; we can't control the sea, no matter how we try.'

Frederik repeated the captain's words to his mother and Lia when he eventually saw them, and both expressed concern that he should travel in such dire weather. 'You don't need to come in the winter,' his mother said crossly. 'You are just like your father – you must always do things yourself even though you have plenty of staff to do them for you.'

Lia said she would rather wait longer for a visit than worry about his safety. 'It is a vicious sea,' she said vehemently. 'Wanting always to reclaim the land! People should live up on a mountain, not on the ocean bed as we do in Netherlands.'

He kissed her cheek and laughed. 'But here we are, as we have been for a thousand years, and the engineers are coming up with new ideas all the time to keep us safe. The Dutch are the best in the world at building sea defences.'

But she wouldn't be convinced and only implored him not to travel again before spring, until at last he agreed. 'But I can't wait until Easter to see you,' he insisted. 'I'll come early in the New Year, after Margriet's birthday.'

She gave a shiver. 'It will still be winter, *lieveling*,' she said. 'January is as cold and windy as November.'

'You're tired of me,' he teased.

'Never,' she said. 'Never, never, never!'

And so he didn't come, but he wrote to her and she sent letters to his Hull office. Christmas came and went and Margriet was thrilled by a visit to the newly opened theatre in Paragon Street as a special eleventh birthday treat. A week later they took a train ride on the railway line from Hull to Bridlington, also newly opened only a few months previously. In Bridlington, wrapped warmly because of the icy wind, they walked through the village and along the seashore before returning to the station.

'So what do you think about rail travel, Margriet?' her father asked her as the train huffed and chuffed its way back to Hull, emitting great clouds of smoke and sounding its whistle as they passed through the intervening villages. 'We are a little late in getting this line, but it will open up many opportunities for the people of Hull.'

'I love it, Papa,' she shrieked above the screech of the wheels. 'It's just like Amsterdam, isn't it, when we go to Utrecht to see Tante Lia and Klara and Hans?'

Frederik swallowed, but smiled guilelessly as Rosamund, wrapped in blankets and shawls, turned her eyes from Margriet to him. However, she said nothing except to remark on how well travelled Margriet appeared to be.

By February he was desperate to see Lia, but the weather was atrocious and a ship was lost on a voyage to Hull from Hamburg; he knew it was foolish to attempt travelling and he wrote to her again, assuring her of his love and wishing that they could be together more often.

I am tempted, he wrote, *to ask if you would consider living on this side of the cruel sea that divides us as I have considered moving back to Netherlands, but I am only too aware that we both have responsibilities to our families and this, alas, keeps us apart. But I will come, my dearest love, just as soon as I am able.*

And in turn she wrote to say that just knowing that he wanted to be with her was enough for the time being. *I will keep you warm in my heart for ever, even whilst we are apart.*

At the end of February the weather was still cold, but it was less windy and he decided to make the journey, but on a bigger passenger ship. The packet was still crossing most days and bringing in his goods to the docks.

The journey was uneventful, but his mother scolded him for travelling. Amsterdam was still freezing, but he conducted his business as usual and then caught the train to Utrecht. By now he had a regular coach driver willing to drive him to Gouda whatever the weather, and the man accepted his extra tip with gratitude.

'You have been away a long time, *meneer*,' he said. 'I trust business has been good. Your wife will be pleased to have you back at home.'

Frederik took in a breath. 'I hope so,' he said amicably, 'but she won't be when I tell her that I shall be leaving again in two days' time.'

'Ah, tut! Work is not everything. But there again, I know how it is. We must work to eat.'

Cornelia had opened a shutter when she heard the rattle of the carriage wheels and now she hurried to let him in. She kissed him tenderly before calling upstairs to Hans and Klara that Uncle Freddy was here.

'Hans?' Frederik queried. 'Not at school?'

Hans came down the stairs to greet him. 'Studying,' he said. 'I have another exam next week.' He shook hands with Frederik, who remarked that the boy was now as tall as he was.

'I'll be sixteen in June,' Hans said, 'and I'm still growing. Will you excuse me, sir? Perhaps we can talk over supper? I'd like to ask you a few things, if I may.'

Klara came down and gave him a kiss, and then she too disappeared back up to her room. Lia smiled.

'You see how it is,' she said. 'My babies are growing up and don't need their *moeder* any more.'

'I think they always will.' He kissed her mouth. 'Just as I do. What fine children they are. Hans is so sensible, and handsome too; he takes after his mother.'

She laughed. 'So he does. He wants to talk to you about his future. He's very good at maths and has a head for business, so his tutors say, rather than the classics. He's not sure that he wants to go to university, and that's why he would like to talk to you.'

Frederik nodded. 'He is a very personable young man. I will help him all I can, and if he decides to go into commerce perhaps he might like to start in my office, when the time is right?'

'That, I think, is what he was hoping you would say.'

CHAPTER TWENTY-THREE

As he travelled back to Amsterdam Frederik mused that this had been the happiest visit yet. The only flaw was that Margriet wasn't with him. One day, he thought, she could choose for herself where she would like to live, but he hoped that it would always be close to him.

He had had a long talk with Hans about his future and had told him that there would be an opening for him in his Amsterdam office if he decided to go into business. 'I'll put your name down,' he had joked, but the boy had said very seriously that he would be pleased if he did. Accordingly, on arriving back at his office he discussed with his manager the prospect of employing Nicolaas Jansen's son when he finished his schooling.

'If he is anything like his father,' said Aarden, who remembered Nicolaas, 'he will be a welcome asset. Are you staying a few days? I wanted to talk to you about how well the bulbs are selling. We have had a huge number of growers contacting us and wanting to use us for cut flowers in the spring as well as bulbs in the autumn. A fantastic success, I would say.'

'Then let's hope it will continue,' Frederik said. 'And it's down to you and the team who have worked so hard to make it so. I'm returning to England tomorrow night, so we'll discuss everything in the morning; now I must go to see my *moeder* and give her some of my time before she feels neglected.'

Aarden grinned. 'My *moeder* is the same. Please give Mevrouw Vandergroene my kind regards, sir, and tell her she is very welcome here at the office at any time.' He was well aware that Frederik's mother was a major shareholder.

Gerda welcomed him back with a smile. 'How's the tulip business?'

'Thriving,' he answered. 'You will be pleased to hear that we are having great success with them, so you have no need to worry about a poverty-stricken old age.'

'Pah!' she said. 'You can't fool me, not when I've fooled so many.' She put the kettle on the stove, and with her back to him remarked, 'It is the widow I think who brings you back, is it not? Not the tulips at all.'

He was silent for a moment and then sat down in one of the easy chairs and folded his arms. He sighed. Sometimes he grew tired of the secrets. He didn't want to hide Lia away; he wanted to talk about her and explain that his wish was to be with her, that his empty life with Rosamund gave him no happiness at all.

His mother turned to face him, curious about his silence when normally he was quick to respond. She sat down opposite him.

'You can tell me, *kindje*,' she said softly. 'Anything.'

198

'But I'm no longer an infant, Moe,' he said in a despairing voice. 'I am a grown man, and I'm split in two.'

She leaned forward and patted his hand. 'You will always be my *kindje*, just as Anna and Bartel are,' she said. 'So tell me, is it the widow Jansen who gives you such heartbreak?'

'No!' He shook his head. 'She doesn't give me heartbreak. My heart breaks because I can't be with her and I'm trapped in a loveless marriage.'

'Ah! Does she love you, this widow?'

'Her name is Lia, and yes, she does.'

She considered. 'I cannot condone separation, but—'

'Neither can I hurt Margriet,' he interrupted, adding adamantly, 'and it would. She is a kind little girl and wouldn't want to see her mother unhappy, as she would be if we separated. I'd be condemning Rosamund to a life alone, looked down on by society.'

His mother sat back and sighed. 'You were always such a principled child. I thought that one day those principles would floor you.' She pursed her mouth. 'Then you must wait. Wait until Margriet is grown up and has her own life, then buy your wife another property where she can entertain her friends.' She wrinkled her lips as if to say that she doubted she had any. 'And you can then make your own arrangements.' She shrugged. 'How long will that be? Ten years? Less. Time travels so fast.'

He smiled wryly. She had always been positive, always sure that she knew best, when often she didn't. 'What a great help you are, Moe,' he murmured. 'Of course you are right. I must be patient.'

199

He said goodbye to her the next morning after breakfast and tenderly kissed her cheek. He was planning to spend the rest of the day at the office discussing with Aarden the possibility of selling even more horticultural products. In addition, he intended to put something on file to ensure that Hans Jansen would be taken on as a member of the company if that was what he wanted.

At four o'clock he packed up his briefcase, had a few final words with Aarden and left the office to go to the docks. He hadn't booked a passage but there was always plenty of room at this time of year.

It was already dark. There was a strong blustery wind, and he realized that it would be a very rough crossing. He was heading for the passenger ferry when he heard his name being hailed. There were few lights except for the oil lamps positioned by the gangplank, but someone was walking towards him and waving his arm in greeting.

'Goodness, you've got good eyesight, Hendrik,' he said as Hendrik Sanderson approached him. 'Are you coming or going?'

'I *was* going home. I've been visiting my *moeder*, but the ferry is cancelled. There's a storm expected.'

Frederik blew an exasperated breath. 'Oh, no!' Now he saw the chain across the gangplank and a seaman positioned by it. 'What about the packets? Are any of those running?'

'I haven't enquired. Alice would have my hide if I sailed in one of those old tubs.'

Frederik laughed. 'They cross constantly! They're perfectly safe, just a rougher passage, that's all. How is she? Alice?'

'She's expecting another child; she reckons she's going to lock me in the basement after this one is delivered. That's why I will only travel on a passenger ship; she made me promise.'

Frederik shrugged. 'Ah well, in that case . . .' He pondered for a moment. 'Well, I've travelled several times on Simpson's packet, the *Mary Brown*, and if she hasn't already left I'll go on her. I trust my cargo to her so I should trust myself.'

Sanderson was obviously weighing up the question of whether to overrule his wife's command or wait until the following day. 'No,' he decided. 'If Alice should find out, I'll be in the doghouse for weeks. Women, eh? We're ruled by them, aren't we?'

Although Frederik said he agreed wholeheartedly, he reflected ruefully that Rosamund probably didn't give much thought to how he travelled or when. Margriet, however, always asked him which ship was he crossing on, and had said that she too would like to go on the 'little ship' sometime.

He shook hands with Hendrik and they went their separate ways, Frederik towards where he thought the packet might be berthed and Hendrik back towards the line of carriages waiting outside the dock. Hendrik paused, turning to look back but Frederik had disappeared into the darkness. The wind was getting stronger and more blustery, whistling and rattling through the riggings and furled canvas of the many ships, and as he climbed into a cab Hendrik felt a sudden unease. He wished he'd persuaded Frederik to come back to his hotel, where they could have enjoyed a companionable supper, sharing a bottle of wine and a chat. Still, he thought philosophically, he's made this journey often enough; he knows what he's doing.

The gangplank on the *Mary Brown* was open and Frederik boarded. He called to the captain, who was about to go below with a bucket of water in each hand.

'Are you sailing tonight, Captain?'

Captain Simpson put up his thumb. 'Aye. Are you coming with us?'

'Please. If you have space.'

He put down the buckets. 'Enough,' he said. 'Only three passengers, but plenty of cargo, so I'd like to sail tonight.'

'What about the weather?'

'It'll be rough, no doubt about that, but she's a sturdy little lady. The firemen are re-laying the fire bed; the trimmers are standing by so we'll be ready to sail in half an hour. Find a bunk and help yourself to coffee. You know the drill.'

'I do,' Frederik said. 'Thanks.'

He went below at the fore of the ship, finding a cabin at the same level as the boiler room where he could hear and feel its thrum. He took off his coat and put on a warm jumper and the fur hat that covered his ears, and put his coat back on again. It would be cold on deck once they were under way. He went up to the caboose, where the kettle was steaming gently on the stove, found some cocoa and made himself a hot drink with a lot of sugar in it.

He was only halfway through it when he felt movement beneath his feet. We're away; good. Let's hope for a steady voyage.

Captain Simpson came up as he was finishing the

cocoa; his face was rimed with coal dust and sweat. 'It was touch and go,' he said, reaching for a cup and the kettle. 'Damned boiler, although 'fireman says it's not the boiler, but the coal. Reckons it's not right, that it doesn't lay well, but I told him it's 'best Yorkshire coal, can't better it. I should know – I worked as a coal trimmer before I got my own vessel.'

He quickly drank from his cup and put it down. 'Once we're out of port you'd be better off going below. It's going to be a stormy night. One passenger's already changed his mind and gone ashore.' He grinned. 'It's the tough ones who stick it out.'

'Do you think it will be bad?'

Simpson lifted his head to look at him. 'Aye. Reckon we'll have to batten down. But we'll be all right, God willing.'

Amen to that, Frederik thought. Maybe I should have waited after all. We all make mistakes; maybe this is one of mine.

He began to suspect that it was the worst mistake he had ever made when they were struck by the towering waves of the open sea and he was thrown out of his bunk, crashing to the floor. He climbed back in again and felt the churning of the cocoa he had drunk and wanted to be sick. It was pitch dark in the cabin and he wondered if there was a bucket should he need one.

He lay still, trying to sleep, but once more the ship tilted and he slid off the bunk again. Sighing, he took the blanket and pillow off the bunk and arranged them on the floor. He didn't sleep, what with the pitch and roll of the ship and the shouts of the crew, but at some point he must have dropped into an uneasy doze that was full of voices calling things like 'bear down' or 'luff to starboard'; at other times he thought he could hear Margriet calling 'Papa, where are you?' and Lia crying 'Frederik!'

Someone banged on his door. 'You all right, sir?'

'I think so.' Frederik raised himself up on his elbow as Captain Simpson entered. 'Where are we? How much longer?'

The skipper's face was grey with fatigue. 'We can see land, but it'll be a while yet. We're still having problems with the boiler. It's making too much steam.'

Fredrik frowned. 'Isn't that good?'

'No, it's overheating. Might even blow. Put on your warmest gear and come up on deck. We might need every man to the pumps.'

'Dear God!' Frederik scrambled to his feet and put on his boots. He was still dressed in his jumper and trousers, and pulling on hat, coat and scarf he staggered after the captain to the nearest companionway. Up on deck the wind thundered through the sails and the sky couldn't be seen from the deep troughs of heavy seas.

The captain gave him a length of rope and told him to fasten it round his waist and tie the other end to a spar or a bulwark so he wouldn't be washed overboard. And if he did that, he thought, and the ship went down, then he'd go with it. He said as much to the skipper, who said, 'Aye, or we might all be blown to kingdom come,' and ran to the stern and disappeared below.

Frederik clasped his hands tightly together and only then noticed the other passenger further along the deck. He appeared to be muttering prayers.

Is it too late for prayers? he thought. Have I lived a good enough life? What do I believe? That if I should go down with this ship I will one day be with my loved ones again?

Margriet. He gave a small sob. What would become of her if he should die? Who would take care of her? Lia was a strong woman, but how would she cope with the loss of a second love? But Margriet – *mijn lieveling dochter.* Rosamund won't be able to manage. Would his mother take her if he should be lost? He tried not to think of it, to be positive, but dear God in heaven, what a stupid mistake. To rush home as if time was so important that life should be put at risk.

There came a sudden explosion as the boiler blew and black smoke issued from the aft companionway; a figure staggered out with his clothing on fire and then the captain behind him. Frederik started towards them to help.

'No! Get back!' It was the skipper's voice, husky as if scorched. 'Abandon ship! Save yourselves!'

Then came another bigger, mightier explosion and the sea and the sky were filled with searing light and roaring flames that turned the crashing towering waves to scarlet and the ship to matchwood, and Frederik knew no more.

CHAPTER TWENTY-FOUR

It was Hendrik Sanderson who first heard the rumour that a ship had gone down between Amsterdam and Hull. He caught snatches of the seamen's conversation on his voyage home the next day, and noticed that some of them were searching the surrounding sea with telescopes. Eventually, feeling uneasy, he found his way to the bridge to make enquiries of the captain.

'It's true,' the captain told him. 'It's feared that a ship is lost. There were reports early this morning that an explosion was heard last night close to the English shore.'

'What kind of ship? Have you heard?'

'No, I'm sorry, I don't know anything more. But there was debris suggesting it was a small vessel, perhaps a cargo packet.'

Hendrik turned away feeling sick to his stomach. It couldn't be. Surely not. He couldn't curb his anxiety for the rest of the voyage and as soon as they were berthed in Hull he made his way to the Dock Office to enquire. But they couldn't or were unwilling to say whether a ship was missing.

'Come back later, sir, if you would. We'll have a better idea once we've logged everyone in. Many ships might have delayed their sailings because of the weather and not arrived back yet.'

It gave him some small hope, but he was still uneasy. At home he confessed his fears to his wife, who put her arms round him and held him tight. 'Thank God you didn't take that ship,' she wept. 'We must hold fast to the hope that it wasn't Frederik's.'

But although Hendrik nodded, he didn't feel much hope, for when he had asked the shipping clerk if the *Mary Brown* had returned, the man had evaded his question.

He had coffee with Alice and then made his way to Frederik's office by the dockside, where he asked to speak to the manager.

'I might be worrying unnecessarily, Reynoldson, but have you heard anything from Mr Vandergroene? I met him in Amsterdam the night before last.' He cleared his throat. 'I, erm, that is . . .' He took a deep breath. 'The passenger ferry was cancelled, and he said he was going to come home on the *Mary Brown*. I don't suppose . . .' He didn't need to say any more, for the expression on the manager's face told him all he needed to know.

'Is there a chance that he changed his mind, sir?' Reynoldson asked in a low voice. 'Perhaps took a ship the next morning?'

'Would he not be home by now? And if he had taken the passenger ship I would have seen him; it wasn't full. But you're right, he might have changed his mind; we must hope that he did.'

'Yes,' Reynoldson murmured. 'And if our worst fears are realized . . . as you are a friend of Frederik's would you be so kind as to accompany me and whoever in authority might need to be there when we visit Mrs Vandergroene? I – that is . . .' It was as if he had run out of words to say.

Poor man, Sanderson thought. He's overwhelmed. He knows more about the missing ship than he's admitting. 'As soon as you have news, one way or another, will you send for me?' he said quietly, and Reynoldson nodded and opened the door to see him out.

A message came the following morning, confirming his fears. Alice asked her husband if he would like her to go with him to visit Rosamund, along with Reynoldson and the official from the port authority. 'Or will there be too many of us?'

'I'm fearful of upsetting you in your condition,' he said. 'I don't want anything to happen to you.'

She rested his hand on her belly. 'This child is quite safe and you know that I am strong, but I'm thinking of Margriet. That poor child adored her father.'

Rosamund's reaction was much worse than they expected. After her initial refusal to believe the news, she began to scream at them, demanding that Florence go at once and bring Margriet home from school.

'What are we to do?' she shrieked. 'How can we survive alone? This can't be right. There's been a mistake!'

Alice whispered to her husband that she would go to fetch Margriet herself and that Florrie should go at once to the Vandergroenes' doctor and ask him to come to Rosamund immediately. He didn't want her to go alone, but after speaking to the maid

Alice came back into the room and whispered that the two of them would go together as the doctor's residence was close by the school.

'What's happened, ma'am?' Florrie asked as they went down the steps and headed towards Market Place. 'What's wrong with 'mistress?'

'It's unhappy news, I'm afraid, my dear.' Alice linked her arm. 'You must be strong, not only to assist Mrs Vandergroene but most of all to help Margriet, for it will be more than she can bear.' She told Florrie what had happened, patting her hand and uttering soothing murmurings as the girl began to weep.

They called in at the doctor's first and delivered their message, and when they reached the dame school Alice explained to Miss Barker the reason why they were there. The teacher took them into her own small sitting room and brought Margriet to them.

'Margriet, my dear,' Alice said gently, 'I'm so sorry to have to tell you that the ship your father was travelling on is missing. I have come to take you home to be with your mama.'

Margriet seemed confused by the term 'missing' and wrinkled her brow, pressing her lips together. 'But Papa will be all right, won't he? He'll find his way home again?'

'I don't know, my dear,' Alice said softly, and added a small lie. 'We are waiting for news. But you must be prepared to be strong and help your mama.' Although, she thought, it should be the other way round.

When they arrived back in Parliament Street,

the doctor's carriage was outside the door and the doctor had already administered a strong sedative to Rosamund. She was calmer, but on seeing Margriet she gave a moan and uttered, 'Margriet! We are lost. What will become of us without your papa?'

Margriet stared silently at the solemn group of adults gathered there. Her lips moved, but nothing came out until she eventually whispered, 'Papa!'

CHAPTER TWENTY-FIVE

Rosamund refused to let Margriet out of her sight until one day in April, when the regular doctor wasn't able to come and his younger colleague came in his place. Dr Johnston took due note of Rosamund's full mourning gown of black bombazine, the widow's white cap and the black pearls around her neck, and having already wondered at the amount of medication she had been taking for several weeks, reduced it. He also noticed Margriet's pallor, dull eyes and monosyllabic answers to his questions.

'I understand that you have had a tragedy in your lives, Mrs Vandergroene,' he said quietly, 'and this has brought great sorrow to you and your daughter.'

'I don't want to talk about it,' Rosamund said bitterly. 'It makes it worse.'

'I understand,' he answered softly. 'But I was thinking of your daughter. Margriet, is it?' He turned to the little girl. 'A very pretty name. You were called after a flower?'

Margriet nodded. She too was wearing a black dress to her ankles and a black ribbon in her hair. 'It's Marguerite in English.' Her voice was so husky that he could barely hear her.

211

'Ah! And Margriet is . . . ?'

'Dutch,' she whispered, and then, with her eyes filling with tears, she said, 'Papa sometimes calls – called me Daisy.' As she spoke a trickle of tears ran down her cheeks.

'How lovely,' he said. 'And what a wonderful memory for you; one you will always keep.'

She nodded again and took a white handkerchief edged with black stitching from her skirt pocket to dry her eyes.

Dr Johnston sighed, and then, as if considering the matter, asked, 'But what do flowers need to make them grow, Margriet?'

She blinked and gazed at him. 'Rain,' she murmured.

He gave her an encouraging smile. 'And what else?'

Margriet's lips parted. 'Warmth – and sunshine.'

'That's right.' He looked to the windows. The blinds were half drawn so that very little light was coming into the sitting room. 'On a day like today when it's very sunny and bright, the seeds and plants will be stretching themselves and growing, which is what you should be doing.' He turned to Rosamund. 'Might I suggest that your daughter takes a short walk as it's such a lovely day? I would guess that she hasn't been out much lately.'

'She can't!' Rosamund was scandalized. 'We're in mourning.'

'Yes, I realize that, Mrs Vandergroene,' he said patiently, 'and I wasn't suggesting that you went with her, of course not. But perhaps Miss Margriet might go out with one of the servants to stretch her limbs and gain a little colour in her cheeks.'

Margriet gazed towards her mother. She'd like that. She had spent so much time inside the house that her mind was dull; she couldn't think of anything except that her darling papa hadn't come back as she had so vainly hoped. She had written to her *oma* to say as much, and Gerda had written back to say she must always keep him in her heart.

'She is extremely pale,' the doctor was saying, 'and we don't want her to become ill, do we?'

'Well, no, I suppose not,' Rosamund said. 'But, well, I'm not sure if it would be acceptable. It has not been very long since – since . . . well, only a few weeks.'

'Acceptable? To whom, Mrs Vandergroene?'

'Why, society, of course! We must conform.'

'But your daughter is surely too young to be out in society? And is it not more important to consider her health rather than what other people might think of a little girl who is simply taking a walk with a servant?'

Rosamund was silent as she weighed up the consequences should anyone she knew recognize Margriet. Then she realized that none of her friends had met her daughter on more than one or two occasions, and rarely in the last twelve months or so. Only the Sandersons would be sure to recognize her, she thought, and they didn't count, for Mrs Sanderson didn't give tuppence for society.

'I will consider it,' she said. 'I will give it some thought. Is there a chill wind blowing today? I would hate Margriet to catch a cold, for then I should catch it too. I am very susceptible to colds.'

He smiled and closed up his bag. 'It's a most beautiful day, but perhaps she might take a warm wrap as this is her first time out for a while.'

Margriet rose to her feet. 'I'll see Dr Johnston to the door, Mama.'

Rosamund nodded and picked up her sewing. 'Good day, doctor,' she said stiffly. 'Thank you for your advice.'

He gave a small bow and followed Margriet into the hall and towards the front door.

'Thank you, Dr Johnston,' she said politely. 'I would like to go out. When do you think I can go back to school?'

'If I could choose I'd say today,' he said softly, inwardly cursing society's intolerable rules, 'but that is your mother's decision. A few steps at a time, Margriet. Going out into the fresh air will make you feel better, and although it won't take away your sadness, being healthier will help you to accept the loss of your father.'

Margriet's lips trembled. 'I miss him such a lot,' she whispered. 'He taught me so much. I just miss him not being here. I want to ask him so many things.'

He could see the grief in her face and hear it in her voice, and patted her shoulder. 'It's very hard to lose someone you love, especially when you are so young. I'm sure, though, that your papa wanted you to grow up into a strong and resilient young woman, and although he isn't here to guide you any more you will always remember what he has taught you.'

'When the parson came to see us he said Papa would be watching over me,' Margriet told him. 'Do you think he will be? Only, if he went down with the

214

ship, I don't understand how he can be.'

The doctor had some theories of his own about an afterlife, but he believed that people should find comfort in their own way following the death of someone they loved.

'I expect the parson meant your papa would be watching from heaven,' he told her.

'Yes, that's what he said, but only if he'd been a good man. And he was,' she added fiercely. 'I know he was.'

'Well, there you are then.' He smiled at her. 'In that case you have nothing to worry about.'

When Margriet and her mother had finished their lunch and Florrie had come to clear away, Rosamund said, 'I'm going to have my afternoon rest, Florence, but the doctor has recommended that Margriet should take the air to improve her constitution.'

Margriet looked at her mother in astonishment. Had he really said that? Constitution? What did that mean?

'He suggested a short walk, so as it seems to be a nice day I'd like you to accompany her, as of course I can't venture out myself at present.' She sighed as if she were being deprived of a treat, and went on, 'Margriet must wear a warm coat or cape and carry a scarf or shawl so as not to take a chill, and you should walk in the direction of Albion Street, because there is often a breeze blowing down by the river. You may come back down Prospect Street.' Then she added firmly, 'But you must walk on the opposite side from the Infirmary in case there are any noxious diseases drifting from the building.'

Florrie stared open-mouthed at her mistress and then, recovering herself, bobbed her knee and mumbled, 'Yes, ma'am. Of course. It's a lovely day and it'll do Miss Margriet 'world of good to go out.' She beamed at Margriet and thought that at last the poor bairn could get back to something like normality. 'It'll put 'roses back in her cheeks, ma'am.'

They had all felt the master's loss, even Lily, who had cried so much that Cook had threatened to sack her as she was upsetting everybody, but their hearts had gone out to his daughter, who had adored her father so much.

That first night, after they had heard the dreadful news, Margriet had been unable to sleep, and after thinking only of how would she manage without her papa she had got out of bed and gone down the stairs and along the landing to her mother's room.

'Mama,' she had whispered. 'May I come in with you?'

There was no sound from her mother, who was lying so still that for a terrifying moment Margriet thought that she had died too, until she recalled that the doctor had given her mother some medicine that he said would help her sleep. He'd given Margriet a bottle of cordial that he said would settle her too, but she hadn't taken any.

She climbed into her mother's bed anyway, but her mother made no movement, and after lying there for some minutes she got out and padded back to her own room. The cordial bottle was on her bedside table and Florrie had told her that it wouldn't do her any harm if she took a dose. Margriet picked it up and looked at the label. There was a picture of a sleeping baby on it so she unscrewed the top and took a long drink from the bottle before getting back into bed.

Memories of her papa came pouring back, mingled with images of Anneliese. The young girl appeared at the bottom of her bed, looking at her kindly, and then climbed in with her and put her arms round her, murmuring that she would make things better. Then she brought her mother, Mevrouw Lindegroen, who picked Margriet up and put her on her knee and comforted her. Margriet thought she looked very much like her own grandmother. Then she slept until morning, when Florrie came up with her breakfast.

A memorial service for Frederik was held at St Mary's Church at Reynoldson's suggestion. He invited the manager of the Amsterdam office, and Aarden brought Mr Vandergroene's mother, brother and sister with him. Other members of the Amsterdam business community also came over to Hull as a mark of respect, for Frederik was as well known in Netherlands as his father had been before him.

As became a widow, Rosamund had chosen not to go to the memorial service and had said that Margriet shouldn't either, but Gerda was determined to see Margriet and had insisted on calling on Rosamund at home. It was upon seeing her grandmother and hearing her loving voice that Margriet had begun to cry as if her heart were truly broken.

She had agreed with her grandmother that one day she would come to visit her, explaining that she couldn't leave her mother alone just now. 'It's because of our mourning, Oma,' she'd said quietly. 'Mama can't leave the house at present.'

'I know that, *lieveling*,' she'd answered. 'But next year she can, and then you will be able to come. Perhaps Floris can bring you?' and she'd glanced at her daughter-in-law for confirmation. Rosamund had given a tight little smile and put her hand wearily to her forehead and said they would see what the year would bring.

'I am too grieved now to think about what the future holds for us,' she'd said plaintively.

To which Gerda had replied robustly that life must go on. 'You have Frederik's daughter to think of. She is the one who matters now. And,' she added decisively, 'if Floris cannot bring her, Bartel or Anna will come to fetch her.'

Florrie, listening to their conversation as she cleared away the teacups on that sad day, thought that when the time was right she would try to find a way to persuade her mistress to let her take Margriet to Amsterdam alone. She was perfectly capable, she thought. There was no reason at all why she shouldn't, if only Mrs Vandergroene would allow it.

But several weeks had passed and still there had not been an appropriate moment. 'I'll fetch Miss Margriet's warm cape down,' Florrie said now. 'And mebbe a warm bonnet?'

'Yes please, Florence,' Rosamund said, rising from her chair, 'and I'll go up now for my rest.

Don't keep Margriet out too long.'

'No, ma'am.' Florrie dipped her knee. 'I won't. We'll just have a brisk walk.'

Margriet discarded her bonnet as soon as they'd turned the corner of Parliament Street. It was a glorious day. She could smell the tang of the sea, and looking up she saw seabirds wheeling, screeching and soaring above them. It reminded her of their last holiday playing ball on the sands at Scarborough with her father and the Sanderson children, and although she had a great heaviness in her chest and a lump in her throat when she swallowed, she felt glad that she had been so happy then.

Florrie decided that walking down Whitefriargate was a better option than skirting the side of the dock, in case the sight of the ships' masts might remind Margriet of her father. Although they couldn't avoid Junction Dock, she led her charge briskly towards Savile Street and through short cuts, of which she knew many, down Bond Street and into Albion Street as Mrs Vandergroene had suggested. When they reached the street, Margriet gave a deep sobbing breath.

Florrie gently squeezed her hand. 'You all right, ducky?' she said before remembering that she was speaking to her employer's daughter and not one of her many nieces.

Margriet gave a watery smile. 'You are funny, Florrie.' The girl's request to be called Florence was long forgotten.

'I am, aren't I?' Florrie grinned. 'But I thought you seemed sad.'

'I am sad,' Margriet agreed. 'I was thinking about when I once came this way with Papa and we called on the Sandersons. I don't suppose we could do that now, could we?'

'Your mama said nothing about calling on anybody.' Florrie considered; it didn't seem much to her, just calling on friends, but she thought Mrs Vandergroene might be displeased. She rather suspected that her mistress might not consider Mrs Sanderson a friend. She had been quite frosty towards her when they were in Scarborough. 'I think I'd better ask your mama first,' she said. 'We don't want to do the wrong thing and not be able to come again, now do we?'

'I suppose not,' Margriet agreed reluctantly. 'It must be very hard being a grown-up and having to obey so many rules.'

Florrie looked down at her charge. Poor little mite, she thought. 'When you're grown up, Miss Margriet, I think you should make your own rules.'

Margriet nodded. 'I think I'd like to,' she said. 'It seems to me that it will be very difficult otherwise.' She thought for a moment. 'But it's not so difficult for you, Florrie, is it? You can walk down the street on your own, and go shopping without anyone with you, but Mama can't.'

She looked up at the houses, searching for the one where the Sandersons lived, and then frowned. 'But Mrs Sanderson doesn't always have a maid with her,' she said. 'I've seen her sometimes; she goes to the library in Parliament Street. So how is it that she can do that and Mama can't?'

Florrie sighed. 'It's a matter of choice, Miss

Margriet. Mrs Sanderson doesn't care what society thinks about her. She's her own woman and is proud of it.'

Margriet listened. That's what she would like to be, she thought. But she wasn't sure how to go about it.

CHAPTER TWENTY-SIX

Lia sat in her small garden with her eyes closed. She could feel the sun on her face and hear the trickle and gurgle of the water in the dyke as it flowed down to the wider ditch. The dyke was very full this spring, as they had had a great deal of snow in the winter. They had been confined to the house during the worst blizzard she could ever recall, when Klara couldn't get to school and Hans had been unable to travel home from Amsterdam.

She opened her eyes and looked about her. The tulips and hyacinths in their pots were in full bloom in this sheltered sunny garden, but even their bright colours did nothing to cheer her as once they might have done. She could hear Miriam clattering in the kitchen; what a blessing she was, putting order into Lia's life when there would have been only chaos, making her meals and standing over her whilst she ate them.

She remembered that cold bleak day when she had answered a knock on her door and opened it to an older woman, older than her own mother, and beside her a younger one of about her own age. Although she didn't know them, she greeted them cordially, feeling an uneasy curiosity.

'Mevrouw Jansen?' the older woman asked. 'Lia?' the younger said, and as no one but Frederik had ever called her that she had felt a sinking feeling travelling down her body.

'I am Frederik's *moeder*,' Mevrouw Vandergroene had said. 'This is his sister Anna. May we come in?'

How had she known that something was wrong, she wondered now. They could have been here only to warn her not to break up Frederik's marriage, and yet she did know. Perhaps she'd always known that the happiness they'd shared wouldn't last for ever, that their dream of a mountaintop hideaway was only a figment of their imagination; that such dreams would never, could never come to fruition.

Anna had said that they hadn't come earlier because it was over a week before they had found out that Frederik's ship had gone down. The communication between Hull and Amsterdam had been poor because of the atrocious weather, and the manager of the Hull office had come over himself to tell the Dutch employees before taking the news to her mother. 'We came as soon as we could,' she finished.

'I am grateful that you came at all,' Lia said huskily. 'I hadn't heard. I am . . . so . . .'

'You don't need to say anything,' Gerda Vandergroene said softly. 'We understand how you must feel, how we all feel when someone we love has been taken from us.'

Lia had looked at her. 'You know that I loved your son?' she whispered. 'Did Frederik tell you about me?'

Gerda nodded and her voice had broken. 'Just

before he took that last voyage he told me that he loved you – that you loved each other – and he wanted to be with you.'

Miriam came in then with a tray of coffee and cakes, and when she had put them down on the table Lia caught her by the hand and told her who her visitors were and whispered that Freddy was no more, that his ship had gone down in the sea. Miriam pressed a hand to her mouth and closed her eyes. 'He brought such happiness with him, *mevrouw*,' she said to Gerda. 'How will we ever recover?'

'You see?' Lia said, when Miriam had gone, weeping, back to the kitchen. 'How everyone loved him. I don't know how I will break the news to my children – they will be devastated for the second time in their young lives. And dear little Margriet, how she adored her father.'

Anna had told Lia about the memorial service, and that they intended to call on Margriet and her mother. 'We would be pleased if you would come to the service with us,' she said. 'You could be part of our family; no one would know who you were.'

Lia had shaken her head; she had no place there.

'We don't think that Rosamund will attend,' Gerda had explained. 'It won't be expected of her, so if you should wish . . . ?'

'No. Thank you, but no,' Lia had said. 'If I came it would be too final a parting. I will say my goodbye to him here. Here in the place where I know he was happy.'

Gerda had given a wistful smile. 'I am so glad that we came, for I see now that he would have been content here with you. Alas, it was not meant to be. But one day, perhaps, we could bring Margriet again to visit you?'

Lia had told Klara when she came home from school and the child had cried, but she was young and resilient and had told her mother she would write to Margriet when she could find some comforting words to say. She was yet to write them. Lia had written to Hans at school and he had asked for leave of absence to be with her, and she was touched by his generosity of spirit that he would think to do so.

Now, as she sat alone in her garden on the day that the memorial service was to be held in Hull, she wondered how she would fill her life. The love that she and Frederik had shared had been brief, unlike the longer love she had known with Nicolaas. The two could not be compared for each was different, but both were so special that she felt she had been singled out for happiness. This morning she had lit two candles on her table, one for each of them. How blessed she had been, she thought, but there would be no other. Only the love of her children would comfort and support her now.

CHAPTER TWENTY-SEVEN

Rosamund had allowed Florrie to take Margriet to call at the Sanderson house. Margriet had enjoyed the visit, especially on being allowed to see the new baby, another boy, but when they called a second time they were told that the family had gone to Scarborough for the whole of August and this had made her miserable again. That was one of the reasons Rosamund had decided that Margriet should go back to school in September; it had been her own judgement and she felt rather smug about it. Dr Johnston had stressed that Margriet shouldn't be confined to the house and she had discussed the matter with her friend Lydia Percival, who had called to see her. Lydia had concurred that it was within the bounds of protocol; no one would think it improper. Margriet was still only a child, after all.

'Dr Johnston!' she had exclaimed. 'The young doctor? He's charming, is he not? If only I had some medical reason to ask him to call, but unfortunately I am in good health and of course I couldn't invite him to a soirée. It wouldn't be at all the thing.'

Rosamund had sighed as she gazed down at her

black bombazine and crape, longing for the time when she could go into half mourning and wear grey or mauve. She had ordered a sweet little dress for Margriet in black and white that she could wear for school, and the child had perked up considerably.

'You know, I've been thinking, my dear.' Lydia had called again and was having coffee with her one late-November morning. 'I know that you can't go out yet – the year won't be up until February, will it? – but I see no earthly reason why you shouldn't invite one or two friends here. It wouldn't be as if you were stepping out into company. Don't you agree?' She helped herself to another biscuit. 'Your biscuits are always so delicious.'

Rosamund nodded and said vaguely, 'It's a Dutch recipe. Cook likes to make them in Frederik's memory. So, what was it you were saying? You think I could invite friends here?'

'Indeed! Only those you know well, of course, and only those who would be discreet. And it must be before Christmas comes too close, so it couldn't possibly be considered to be any kind of celebration.'

Rosamund gave a little gasp. 'Oh, I wouldn't want anyone to think that. Certainly not. I still feel Frederik's loss deeply.' And, she thought, it was true: not hearing his key in the lock or his footsteps on the stairs and Margriet's feet running down to greet him. The poor child missed him so much. Allowing her back to school had been the right thing to do.

'But perhaps two or three people,' she went on, 'no more than four would be acceptable, I suppose.' She mused over whom to invite. Lydia, of course, as it had been her suggestion, and her husband, but who else? 'You and Vincent would come, Lydia, wouldn't you?'

'Vinny will come if he's not tied up, you know how he is with his clubs and what not. Let's think who else would be suitable.' She put a finger to her mouth and idly brushed away a biscuit crumb. 'I have an idea,' she said triumphantly. 'My brother William is coming to visit us the week after next. I've lined up one or two parties for him. I don't know if you've ever met him, Rosamund; he's younger than me, about your age I should think, and he would be the perfect guest. He's not from this area, he lives near York, so you needn't worry that he'd tell anyone round here where he'd been.'

'Oh, but he wouldn't want to be visiting a widow still in mourning, surely? And will he not have his wife with him?'

'Not yet married, m'dear. He can't seem to find anyone he's really attracted to. I've tried introducing him to suitable young women but I've given up. I dare say he'll remain a bachelor all his life!'

Rosamund considered. She would be comfortable with Lydia and Vincent. Lydia was never short of conversation and never really expected any comment on her wisdom, her husband often fell asleep in company, and if she brought her brother he wouldn't be worried about being set up in any matchmaking scheme as she was still in mourning. It would be a start, she thought, to easing herself back to a normal life.

'I've just remembered something that Vinny asked me to tell you,' Lydia said, breaking into her thoughts. 'If you need his advice on money matters, or anything at all, he will always be glad to give it.' She lowered her voice sympathetically. 'We ladies are hardly competent to be thrust so unexpectedly into such issues.'

'Oh, please thank Vincent very much. It's kind of him to offer, but Frederik was meticulous about such things. His lawyer came to see me and explained that I would have no worries on that score, and of course the business is very strong.'

'Such a relief,' Lydia exclaimed. 'Whom do you use?'

'Hugh Webster,' she said. 'He has an office here in Parliament Street. He seems very efficient.'

Lydia pulled a face of disapproval. 'They all do,' she answered, standing up to leave. 'But there are some who line their pockets, so one must be careful. I'll ask Vincent's opinion of him.'

After bidding Lydia farewell, Rosamund wavered over whether she should invite her guests for the morning or the afternoon, and after some indecision decided that she would ask them to come for a light luncheon and eat in the dining room. The room needed an airing as it hadn't been used since Frederik had died.

She discussed with Cook what would be required. 'I think cold chicken and ham, don't you? And possibly veal cutlets as well, do you think, Cook, as gentlemen have larger appetites than ladies?'

Cook suggested that she could serve the cutlets hot with mashed potatoes and peas, and perhaps begin the meal with a consommé as the weather was becoming very cold.

'Excellent,' Rosamund nodded.

Later, down in the kitchen, Cook told the others that the mistress had looked quite merry as she decided that rather than serve a dessert they would have coffee and cake and then adjourn to the sitting room for a game of cards.

'Well,' Florrie said. 'What do you mek of that?'

Rosamund was quite excited about the prospect. So bored had she become with her life that on the day of the visit she sent Florrie out for flowers to grace the dining room table. 'I'm not sure what will be available now,' she said. 'If there are no flowers in the market then bring some greenery – ivy,' she stipulated, 'not holly, for red berries will appear far too frivolous.'

Florrie came back with a trail of ivy and a small bunch of white and purple winter pansies that Rosamund deemed very suitable as a centrepiece. It was as Rosamund was placing the small oval dish holding them on the table that it suddenly struck her that she had never taken as much trouble arranging the table for Frederik as she was doing now for her guests. She stood with her hands clasped lightly together beneath her chin, wondering whether she had been as considerate towards him in their marriage as she might have been. She did not move until Florrie came in with the table settings, and then she blinked as if a dusty mote had flown into her eye.

The cabriolet carrying her guests arrived at twelve fifteen. Florrie opened the door to them and dipped her knee to Mrs Percival, whom she had met several times. She dipped again to the gentlemen, guessing Mr Percival to be the portly one with the full set of whiskers who handed her his top hat and coat without looking at her. The other, a dark stocky man with a short beard and piercing blue eyes that appraised her from top to toe, also handed her his hat and murmured a greeting.

Hiding a smile as she guessed he'd been told to be on his best behaviour, she led them into the drawing room, where Rosamund was sitting quietly waiting, a magazine on her knee as if she had been reading. She rose gracefully as Florrie announced her visitors, greeting Lydia and Vincent and holding out her hand as Lydia introduced her brother, William Ramsey.

He bent over her fingers, and kept hold of them as he murmured that he was sorry to hear of her loss. She blinked rapidly to clear her tears as she accepted his condolences.

'Please, do be seated,' she said, and the men lifted their coat tails as they perched on graceful chairs while Lydia and she sat side by side on the sofa.

'Well, this is very nice, Rosamund,' Lydia said. 'You are looking much brighter already. You have been quite dragged down recently.'

'Hardly surprising, Lydia,' her brother remarked reprovingly. 'Mrs Vandergroene has been through a very difficult time, and a sad one. It isn't something one can shake off like a bad cold, you know.'

Rosamund looked gratefully at him. It was gratifying to know that someone understood. She didn't think that Lydia ever had, although she remonstrated now, saying that her remark had been misconstrued.

'I wasn't trying to belittle what Rosamund has

been through,' she said petulantly. 'I understand, of course I do. I was merely trying to say that the loss of dear Frederik was taking its toll on her. It is especially difficult for women, you know, William; gentlemen can't possibly imagine what it must be like to be housebound for so long. That is why I suggested that Rosamund should invite one or two friends in for company.'

'Quite right,' Vincent muttered, looking around longingly for a glass of something. Florrie appeared as if on cue, with a tray of decanters and glasses that she placed on a side table.

'Leave them, please, Florence. Perhaps the gentlemen will be so good as to do the honours.' Rosamund glanced at William Ramsey as she spoke, hoping he would offer rather than the ungainly Vincent, who she was sure would upset the whole table.

William Ramsey rose immediately. 'My pleasure,' he said. 'Ladies, what can I offer you?' He looked at the tray. 'Sherry? Whisky? I think this jug might contain lemonade.'

'I'll have sherry, please, William,' Lydia said. 'Rosamund, won't you have the same?' she added as if she were the hostess.

'I will, thank you, just a small one.' Rosamund smiled at William Ramsey and gave a little sigh. How nice it was to be looked after again; she had almost forgotten how much she missed being asked her preference for this or that. Again she thought how considerate Frederik had always been and how heedless, alas, she had been of it.

The gentlemen's cutlets were cooked to perfection, slightly pink and very tender, and the potatoes were creamy with a hint of herbs. Lydia chose the chicken, and Rosamund decided on a thin slice of ham with a small amount of potato. When they had finished and William Ramsey had sent his compliments to the cook they adjourned to the sitting room, where a bright fire was burning. Florrie had drawn the chairs to the fireside and lit the lamps so that the room was very cosy and inviting.

'Delightful,' William said.

'Would you care for cards?' Rosamund asked him.

'I'd like just to chat,' he answered, before his sister could comment. 'We can play cards any time, can't we? Oh, I'm sorry, of course you haven't been able to, Mrs Vandergroene. What would you like to do?'

'Well, actually I would quite like to talk,' she said. 'It's some time since I had any conversation, although Lydia does come and keep me up to date when she can.' She leaned forward. 'What brings you to Hull, Mr Ramsey? Are you here on business?'

'No, I'm not in business.' He uncrossed his legs and stretched a little. 'I'm here to visit Lydia and Vincent. I generally come before the Christmas festivities begin and before the roads become impassable should it snow.'

Vincent Percival grunted. 'If you will drive a curricle,' he said. 'You'd be better with a brougham in winter.'

Ramsey smiled, and Lydia raised a cynical eyebrow. 'Vincent has forgotten what it's like to be young and free,' she said. 'William enjoys his curricle, don't you?'

'I do,' he agreed. 'One day when I settle down with someone special, and I will, then I'll buy a fine carriage and team of horses, but a barouche, Vincent, not a brougham! But for now I'm happy with my curricle and pair.' He smiled at Rosamund.

Rosamund felt delightfully relaxed as she walked with them to the door two hours later. Florrie helped them on with their outdoor coats and Lydia and Vincent thanked Rosamund for a lovely luncheon, with Lydia cooing that it wouldn't be long before Rosamund would be out and about. William Ramsey lingered over releasing her hand as he said goodbye, and expressed a hope that they would meet again under happier circumstances. She answered that she hoped so too.

As they went down the steps to the waiting carriage Hugh Webster happened to pass by. Seeing the departing guests, he paused in his stride and raised his hat to them. She saw Vincent do the same in return and Lydia inclined her head. Then Webster looked up at her in the doorway and raised his hat again, holding it momentarily to his chest. He nodded, replaced it and walked on, and though she couldn't think why, she felt slightly disturbed, as if caught out in a misdemeanour.

CHAPTER TWENTY-EIGHT

Christmas Day was dismal for Margriet. Although her mother had given her a box of French bon-bons obtained from an advertisement she had seen in the *London Illustrated News*, and several books she had ordered by post from a bookseller, she still felt unhappy. She missed her papa so very much. Because her mother still couldn't go out into the world, they couldn't even go to the Christmas morning service.

'I don't think that life will ever be happy again, do you, Mama?' she said as the two of them sat down to a breakfast of crisp bacon and coddled egg.

'It will be different, certainly,' Rosamund answered. 'But you will be happy one day, I expect.' Privately, she wondered if she herself ever would be or indeed had ever been truly happy. If she was honest with herself, she didn't think she had that joyfulness of spirit that most people seemed to have, at least at some time in their lives.

'Will I?' Margriet said. 'Will I ever be as happy as when Papa was here?' Her mouth trembled as she spoke and her eyes filled with tears. 'I don't think . . .' she shook her head and swallowed, 'I ever will be.'

Rosamund didn't know how to respond. Having had a distant, disinterested mother herself, she didn't know how to console her, so she simply said, 'Get on with your breakfast, Margriet, before your eggs go cold.'

Florrie had been given the day off to visit her sister and wouldn't be back until the evening, so Margriet didn't even have her company after breakfast. Cook was roasting the Christmas birds, pheasant for Margriet and her mother and a fowl for herself, Mrs Simmonds and Lily, so they wouldn't want her in the kitchen, and her mother had gone up to her own small sitting room to read and sew.

Giving a huge sigh, she picked up the books that her mother had given her and carried them up to her room. Lily had lit the fire and it was blazing away merrily so she sat down and idly turned the pages. Miss Barker had said she might find consolation in books and words; she thought of the teacher's sympathetic understanding on her return to school, and her advice that she should try to take comfort from happy memories of her father. One of the books contained an anthology of poetry, ballads and sonnets from Tennyson and Thomas Carlyle and other writers of long verse, but some were sad and others she didn't understand and she wasn't in the mood for reading anyway.

She shuffled down in her chair. She could paint or draw, she thought, or start the sampler her *oma* had sent her as a Christmas present. She had said that embroidery might help to take Margriet's mind off her sorrow, but it wouldn't, Margriet thought miserably. She didn't think anything would.

Although she wasn't cold, she pulled a shawl over her shoulders and stared into the fire. The sun was shining outside her window and creating coloured motes that danced around the room. If only she could go out, she thought, but Florrie wasn't there to take her. Would anyone notice if she slipped out alone after luncheon? Her mother would have gone to her room, Mrs Simmonds and Cook would be eating their own lunch, and Lily wouldn't notice one way or the other.

A smile played around her lips. She would slip out and take a stroll about the town. Maybe she'd walk down to the pier and look at the Humber and then come back through Market Place and the king's gardens and call at Anneliese's house and ask if she was at home, even if it was Christmas Day.

At lunch Margriet was allowed a small glass of wine mixed with water with which to toast happier times, but she was not very enthusiastic either about the wine, which she found too bitter, or about the toast to the future, which she couldn't believe would ever be happy again. To please her mother, however, she raised her glass and murmured, 'Happier times.'

After they had eaten and Mrs Simmonds and Lily had cleared away, Margriet's mother, as predicted, said she was going up to rest in her room. She asked Margriet how she would pass the time.

'Oh, I'll do the same, Mama, and perhaps read one of the books you gave me.' Margriet had embroidered her mother a pretty bookmark and she saw that it was already in use inside a magazine that Rosamund was taking upstairs with her.

'Very well. I'll see you at teatime, then,' her mother said, and Margriet thought wistfully of the times when her father would come upstairs and share afternoon tea and crumpets by her fireside, and then go down and have another tea with her mother. Now she was allowed to have tea downstairs to keep her mother company. She gave another sigh. She seemed to sigh a lot, she thought. It was as if she were trying to move a heavy weight that was sitting on her chest.

She went upstairs and took her warm coat from the wardrobe and placed it on her bed, and instead of her bonnet she brought out a shawl. She thought she would wrap it round her head, so that no one would recognize her. Not that there would be many people about on Christmas Day now that the church services were over. The market and the shops would probably be closed and the town quite still.

She lay down on her bed and waited. Waited for her mother to settle into her rest; waited for Cook and Mrs Simmonds to finish their meal, and waited for Lily to finish washing the dishes. When she thought it was safe, she climbed sleepily off the bed and put on her coat, slipped on her outdoor boots and gloves and lastly draped the shawl over her head. She quietly crept downstairs to the front door, closed it softly behind her and ran down the front steps towards Whitefriargate.

It was colder than she had thought it would be and she wrapped the shawl firmly round her head, tucking the ends inside her coat. She reached the end of Whitefriargate and sped along Trinity House Lane towards the King Billy statue, where several children were playing on the plinth beneath the feet of the golden horse. She waved to them as she went past and they glanced towards her; she crossed over into Blackfriargate and on to Queen Street towards the Humber and the pier.

She leaned over the railings and saw the rough waves crashing against the wooden uprights, filling the slope where at low tide market traders and others would bring their horses to wash the mud off them.

"Ere, who are you? What 'you doin'? You're not from round 'ere. What 'you doin' by 'oss wash?'

Margriet turned and gazed at the dirty-faced, ragged boy standing behind her with his arms crossed against his thin chest. 'Sorry. What did you say?'

'Ooh, la-di-da! Who are you?'

'I'm . . .' Perhaps she shouldn't tell him her name.

'Don't ya know who you are?' the boy asked. 'Are you lost or summat?'

Margriet could barely understand what he was saying. She stared at him, thinking he might have been one of the children she had seen near the statue. 'I'm not lost,' she told him. 'I've come out for a walk.'

'Where d'ya live?'

'Erm, near Whitefriargate.'

'In an 'ouse?'

She laughed. 'Of course in a house. Where else?'

The boy shrugged. 'I dunno. Anywhere. Have ya had your dinner?'

'Yes, thank you. Have you had yours?'

'Yeh. Sandy brought it and Immi came as well.

We had pork 'n' mash an' loads o' gravy an' then a plum puddin'.'

'Oh,' Margriet said. 'That sounds nice. Is Sandy your mother?'

It was his turn to laugh, wrinkling up his dirty face. 'Nah! She's Immi's ma. They brought dinner for all of 'bairns, cos of it being Christmas. Did you know it was Christmas Day?'

'Yes, I did.' Margriet didn't know what to make of this boy. She thought her mother would have called him an urchin and wouldn't have allowed her to speak to him, but he had a cheeky grin and although he didn't look very clean she liked him. 'But we couldn't go to church this morning because my mother is in mourning and isn't allowed out.'

'Why's that then? Who's she in mourning for?'

Margriet's lips trembled and her eyes filled with sudden tears. 'For my father,' she whispered and wiped her eyes on a corner of the shawl.

'Aw! Don't cry,' he protested. 'Do ya want to come ower and talk to us? Most of us don't have a fayther an' some of us don't have a ma either. But we all manage one way or another, 'specially when Sandy or some of 'other women bring us summat to eat.'

She began to walk alongside him, sniffling into the shawl. She hadn't understood what he meant at first, but now she realized that if these children hadn't any parents, then perhaps they might be the deserving poor she had learned about at school. The ones for whom she had collected her unwanted clothes and given them to Florrie to distribute. She couldn't ask him if they'd got them, she thought, in case he might be offended by the act of charity.

By the time they reached the King Billy statue, some of the children had gone and there were only four of them left, sitting below the plinth.

'Who's that wi' you, Billy?' one of the boys asked. 'Is she new round 'ere?'

'Says she lives in Whitefriargate.' He grinned at Margriet. 'Didn't tell ya I had 'same name as King Billy, did I?' He turned to the others. 'She's just lost her da, so I says for her to come ower to us.'

'She can't live with us,' one of the girls said. 'There's not enough room.'

'I don't want to live with you – thank you,' she added, not wanting to appear ungrateful. 'I live with my mother. I only came over to talk to you.'

'What 'you want to talk about?' the other girl asked.

'I – I only wanted to say hello, that's all,' Margriet answered hesitantly, thinking that these children, a couple of whom were slightly older than her, seemed very grown up and sure of themselves. 'I'm on my way to call on a friend.'

'Where does she live?' Billy was asking questions again.

'She lives on Land of Green Ginger.' Margriet smiled. 'Do you know the story about the name?' She thought that if they'd like her to she would tell it to them just as her father had told her. But they all nodded and said that they knew it and that some of them had lived down there. 'So do you know Anneliese Lindegroen?' she asked eagerly, and was disappointed when one after another they shook their heads and said they'd never heard of her. 'I'll have to be going now,' she said. 'It's getting late but

241

it's been very nice to meet you all,' and she wondered why they all grinned at each other and the boys larked about and gave each other little bows and one of the girls got up and dipped a curtsey.

But Billy didn't. He just gazed at her curiously and then said, 'Sorry about your da. You can come back sometime if you like and talk about him. Was he a fisherman and lost at sea, like mine?'

'He wasn't a fisherman,' she said, 'but he was lost at sea. I didn't really know what it meant at first, and then we were told that the ship's boiler had blown up and everyone was killed. Instantly.'

Immediately they were sympathetic, and one of the girls came and put her arm round her. 'Poor little lass,' she said sorrowfully. 'That's really hard.' She patted her shoulder. 'You come an' talk to us any time you want. We're generally round here about teatime. We wait to see if there's owt left ower from 'market stalls.' She seemed to cotton on to Margriet's bafflement, and added, 'You know – food 'n' that.'

'Of course,' Margriet said. 'Thank you. I'd like that. Goodbye, then. Goodbye, Billy.'

Billy silently nodded and lifted his hand and she set off down Market Place towards Silver Street, still determined to call on Anneliese in Land of Green Ginger.

She stood in her usual position and looked up at the window. Daylight was diminishing and clouds rolling in, whilst above her seabirds were heading inland. She shivered. There was no light in Anneliese's window and she felt a shred of disappointment. Perhaps it was true what her father had said all that time ago, that the house was empty. What was it that his colleague had answered? That the house was haunted! She had asked Papa what it meant – she took a small breath and felt that she could almost see his face as he'd waggled his ears to tease her for listening – but what answer had he given her?

She gazed up at the window and thought for a second that the curtain had moved slightly; did it or not? Yes, there it was again. She saw a small hand lift the muslin. Papa had said that if a place was haunted it meant that there was a ghost living there, or something like that anyway. She laughed and waved but knew it was too late to call; Florrie would be home soon and would demand to know where she had been. But there was Anneliese, not a ghost at all, waving back to her.

CHAPTER TWENTY-NINE

January 1848

Margriet had told her mother at Christmas that she didn't want to mark her forthcoming birthday. 'It's almost a year since Papa – since Papa . . .' She swallowed. She didn't want to say the words. If she said the words it would make it true that her father wouldn't be coming back, and she still clung to the hope that he had been washed ashore on some tiny island and was living off fish from the sea and rabbits he could snare and cook over a fire.

She had said as much to Miss Barker one day when the teacher had taken her to her own room after she had been overcome by a fit of weeping for no reason that she could explain, except that it was just a few days before her twelfth birthday and her father wouldn't be here to share it.

'It's very hard to lose someone you love, Margriet,' Miss Barker had said gently, holding her pupil's hand. 'But if you try to accept it, then you will find that the pain will lessen eventually.'

It was then that Margriet had told her about her father being washed up on an island. 'He might be waiting for a boat to rescue him,' she sniffled.

Miss Barker sat thinking for a moment, and then got up and went to her bookshelf. She brought down an atlas and put it on the table.

'Come here, Margriet, and let us look at the area of the German Ocean – which is sometimes called the North Sea – between Hull and Amsterdam and see if we can find an island. We know, don't we, that many fishing boats go out to sea from this town and head off towards the Arctic regions. So if seamen saw an island they would mark it on a chart. Rather as Sunk Island in the Humber is marked.'

Margriet nodded eagerly and wiped her tears. Then her eyes filled up again as she remembered that the boy Billy had said that his father had been lost at sea, so he must have meant drowned. She gave a small shudder, and Miss Barker, seeing it, took a shawl from the back of a chair and draped it round her shoulders before opening the atlas at the appropriate page.

'So, now, Margriet.' She sat the child down and bent over her. 'Here is a map of the British Isles. Tell me what you see.'

Margriet scanned the map. 'We're very small, aren't we, Miss Barker?' Her finger traced up the coastline. 'But here's an island, and another! Orkney,' she said, peering at the tiny print, 'and Shetland.'

'But look where we are, Margriet,' said Miss Barker, taking hold of Margriet's hand and bringing her finger back down to the small spit of land pointing into the sea. 'Here is Hull, and across this stretch of water is Amsterdam.'

Margriet stared at the width of water separating England and Netherlands. It seemed as if a mere stride would cross it, but she had sailed over the sea to visit her grandmother and she had seen it at Scarborough, and knew that in reality it was very wide; too wide to stride across and deep enough to hide a ship beneath its waves.

'Yes,' she whispered. 'I understand now. There are no islands where he might have been washed ashore.'

'No,' Miss Barker said softly. 'But you must try to think that whatever happened was an accident and couldn't have been foreseen. Your father, being the man he was, brought you up to be a good, kind and clever girl, and he would have wanted you to continue doing all the things he taught you.'

'And do you think he's watching over me, as the parson said?'

'I don't know,' the teacher said honestly. 'Perhaps when you're grown up you will discover for yourself whether or not you believe that to be true.'

Margriet took a deep breath. 'Thank you, Miss Barker,' she said. 'I feel better now that I understand more, although I'm still sad. I think I always will be.'

Miss Barker shook her head. 'Your papa wouldn't want that,' she said. 'I think that above all else he would want you to be happy, and to think of him with joy.'

'Oh, yes, and I do. There won't ever be anyone else like him.'

Miss Barker, remembering the handsome, charming man who was so keen to have his only daughter educated, said, 'You are quite right, Margriet. There won't ever be anyone quite like him.'

Strangely enough, Margriet did feel better and more grown up now that she had reached twelve, and she was determined to learn as much as she could so that her father would have been proud of her. Although she had told her mother she didn't want a birthday present or a special tea for her birthday, her mother, who wasn't in the habit of giving surprises, had one for Margriet.

'I know you said you didn't want to mark your birthday, but I decided that you deserved something,' she said and gave a smile, hunching up her shoulders. 'I've booked a house at Scarborough,' she went on. 'For a month, in August. I know how much you enjoy being there and by then I won't have to wear black all the time, although I might still wear a black hat and veil. I think I quite suit black, and it will go very well with grey.'

Margriet had mixed feelings about staying in Scarborough without her father. She asked Julia whether the Sandersons would be going this year and Julia said she hoped they would be, now that baby Richard was old enough to play on the sands without putting sand in his mouth and eating it.

By mid March, Margriet and Julia walked home together every day, parting at the top of Parliament Street, where Julia continued on to Albion Street. Occasionally Margriet would surreptitiously turn back and head for Land of Green Ginger. She rarely saw Anneliese, though, which she put down to the fact that the days were much lighter now and the family was probably out in their garden tending the ginger plants. Sometimes she caught a glimpse of Billy or one of the girls whose name she didn't know, but they didn't seem to notice her and always looked to be in a hurry as they scurried off into one of the many narrow passageways.

And so the winter and spring passed. Rosamund had received a letter from Gerda saying that she would like Margriet to visit her, but had replied that it was too soon and not convenient at present, and in any case they were going away in the summer. She didn't tell Margriet of the request and neither did she pass on the letter that came for Margriet shortly afterwards.

She began to hold one or two more lunches at home whilst Margriet was at school and gradually eased herself back into society, even on two occasions accepting invitations to Lydia's card parties, which Lydia assured her would be very discreet. The only other guests were people Rosamund knew, and one of these was Lydia's brother, William Ramsey, who was his usual courteous and solicitous self, asking about her health and telling her how delighted he was to see her looking so well.

When school broke up for the summer holidays, Margriet felt quite excited at the thought of going to Scarborough, although she wondered how they would manage their luggage without her father. Florrie was going with them again, and she told Margriet that the coach driver had said he would bring along his lad to help them. They were taking a smaller house this time, as the one they had rented previously wasn't available, and although her mother was cross about it Margriet was pleased. She didn't want to be in a house where she and her father had enjoyed previous holidays so much.

'Hmm,' Florrie said down in the kitchen. 'Can't think why 'mistress would have wanted 'bigger house just for 'two of them. It isn't as if she'll be entertaining.' Then she pursed her lips and muttered, 'Or mebbe she will be.'

'Why, who would she entertain?' Mrs Simmonds asked. 'Unless it's them folks as she's had here for luncheon.'

'In that case I should be going 'stead of Florrie,' Cook said. 'She can't cook like I can.'

'And neither can you mek 'beds and keep 'place tidy like I can,' Florrie pointed out. 'Nor I don't think you'd fancy tekkin' Miss Margriet swimming in 'sea like I do.'

'No,' Cook huffed. 'That I would not, not at any price.'

But their curiosity deepened when a few days before they were due to depart Rosamund asked Cook if she would cook a ham for them to take so that they could use it for cold meat instead of having to buy it. She also asked her to make biscuits and a cake just in case she invited any ladies for morning coffee.

'You see!' Florrie said. 'What did I say?' But who would she ask, she wondered. As far as she knew her mistress wasn't acquainted with anybody in Scarborough except the Sandersons, and somehow Florrie didn't think it would be them.

When they arrived in St Nicholas Cliff Margriet helped Florrie to unpack. They put foodstuffs and crockery in the cupboards and cutlery in drawers, for as usual her mother had insisted that they bring their own and not use any that were left in the house, and then she helped to make up the beds. She had her own room and Florrie had a small room next door, whilst her mother had the larger bedroom, but there was no upstairs sitting room this time, only the parlour downstairs and a very small dining room and kitchen. Margriet thought it cosy but her mother puckered up her lips and tutted.

When all was done, the three of them walked across the Spa bridge. Rosamund went straight to the Spa terrace and sat at one of the tables to order tea, but Margriet was anxious to go down to the sands.

'You'd better go with her, Florence,' Rosamund said. 'Come back in about half an hour and we'll take a stroll. There will be plenty of time for playing, Margriet. We've got a whole month.'

Margriet pouted. 'It's not going to be the same,' she huffed as she and Florrie walked down the steep path. 'Mama's going to want me to be with her all the time.'

'No, she won't, miss,' Florrie reassured her. 'Your mama is probably feeling just as lonely being here without your papa as you and me are.' She caught hold of Margriet's hand. 'We all miss him, you know, even us down in 'kitchen.'

'Oh, I'm sorry.' Margriet was immediately repentant. 'Of course you do. And poor Mama. How sad she must be feeling. We'll just take a short walk on the sands, shall we, Florrie, and then go back and keep her company?'

Florrie nodded, and looked up the cliff, but

could no longer make out Mrs Vandergroene on the terrace. She sighed, silently agreeing with her charge. The holiday wouldn't be the same at all; the only saving of it, as far as she could see, would be when the Sandersons arrived.

It was going to be very boring, Rosamund decided, unless more people arrived. Previously she had chatted with other ladies taking lunch or tea on the terrace, but today there was no one. She felt very lonely, and hoped that Scarborough hadn't lost any of its charm. Perhaps it had been a mistake coming back so soon, but she had genuinely thought it would be good for Margriet to come and meet other children; soon, Rosamund thought, she would be too big to be playing on the sands. Maybe in another year she would not want to be building sandcastles or digging dams. Yes, perhaps next year Margriet would accompany her on strolls around the town or in the flower gardens, or doing some window shopping, and wouldn't even think of wanting to play cricket or swim in the sea.

She was beginning to get restless, and also a little chilly. Margriet and Florence had been gone almost half an hour; it was time they were back. She stood by the rail and looked out across the sands. There were very few people about, only some who were walking their dogs, and she couldn't see Margriet or Florence at all. She looked down the various paths that led to the sands; perhaps they were walking up and temporarily hidden from sight. She took a deep breath and turned back to her table, and then stood stock still.

'Mrs Vandergroene! How are you?'

She put her hand to her throat. 'Mr Ramsey! Goodness. I didn't expect to see you here. You're a long way from home.'

William Ramsey took off his smart black silk hat and bowed. 'I am indeed, as you are too.'

'We come to Scarborough every August. Except last year, of course.' She cast him a pensive glance. 'But I felt I should make an effort this year for the sake of my daughter.'

'Of course.' He put out his hand, indicating that she should retake her seat at the table. 'And how is your little girl?'

'We are all having to, Mr Ramsey. There is nothing else for it.'

'Indeed,' he said. 'Well, this holiday will do wonders for you both. You do know that my sister is coming to Scarborough?'

'She said she wasn't sure.' Had Lydia said for certain? She had intimated once or twice that they might be coming, and that was why she had brought the ham, but she was sure Lydia hadn't confirmed it.

'Oh, she can be such a scatterbrain sometimes,' he said indulgently. 'Yes, they've booked in at a small hotel in the Crescent and I'm staying there too, except that she gave me the wrong date. She and Vincent are arriving tomorrow, not today as she told me.'

'Oh, how lovely. I shall look forward to seeing them, and I'm delighted of course to see you too. How long are you staying?'

'Sadly only a few days, so it's a shame that I'll be

252

kicking my heels until they arrive tomorrow evening.' He hesitated. 'I wonder – would it be permissible to meet you for coffee tomorrow? Or lunch?' His eyebrows rose. 'You are out of mourning? Being a mere man I'm not sure of the indications of dress.'

Rosamund was wearing a grey gown with black vertical stripes down the skirt and a grey hat with a black spotted veil. 'I am advised that as it is eighteen months since my husband's demise I may now consider myself to be out of full mourning and free to be seen in select society.'

'Really?' His eyebrows twitched. 'And would taking coffee with a gentleman be considered select society or will you be shunned for ever more?'

Rosamund considered. Apart from the Sandersons, there would be no one here who knew her from home. The ladies she had chatted to previously were strangers, and as Lydia and Vincent were coming what harm would it do to have coffee out here in the open air with Lydia's brother? It would be almost as if they had met by chance. She wasn't too sure about lunch, but certainly coffee would be perfectly safe.

She smiled at him and then looked away. 'I think that coffee tomorrow would be perfectly acceptable, Mr Ramsey.' She gave a trilling laugh. 'Even if it might be considered by some to be living dangerously!'

CHAPTER THIRTY

Rosamund dressed carefully the next morning in a lilac two-piece: a buttoned fitted jacket and a full skirt, both trimmed with black piping. On her head she wore the same grey hat and veil as yesterday.

'You look very nice, ma'am,' Florrie said, as she helped her fasten the tiny buttons. 'It must be such a relief to wear some colour after black.'

'I think it's quite appropriate though, wouldn't you say?' Rosamund said. 'Lilac is perfectly suitable after eighteen months of mourning.'

She had never before asked Florrie's opinion about anything, but there was no one else she could ask except Lydia, whose opinions were so entirely her own that she couldn't be relied upon.

'I think it's time you came back into 'world, ma'am.' Florrie picked up the dainty hat and adjusted the veil. 'Whatever colour you're wearing doesn't mean you're not thinking about 'person you've lost.'

'How right you are, Florence. I have to get back to some kind of normality.' Rosamund perched the hat on her head and pulled the veil over her eyes. Tomorrow, she decided, she would exchange the veil for a grey one. The black spots made her

254

feel dizzy and she wasn't sure that they were very flattering after all. Not that she was looking to attract anyone, but it would be nice to have some male company for a day or two and Mr Ramsey was very charming and considerate. Very like Frederik in some ways, she thought.

Rosamund hadn't known many young men in her girlhood. She never really knew what to talk about with young men. Her mother had put her off with odd remarks and whispered conversations with her older sisters when they were contemplating marriage, and Rosamund had never really known what to expect from a male companion.

'Trot along then, Margriet,' she said gaily after choosing a table on the terrace close by the railing and overlooking the sands. 'I've brought a book to read, and if I get tired of it then I'll take a stroll down to meet you.'

'Do you want me to come back for you, ma'am?' Florrie asked.

'No, no,' Rosamund assured her. 'I will come down alone. I'll be perfectly safe; we're in full view, after all.'

Florrie was astounded by the change in her mistress. Amazing, she thought, what a change of clothing could bring about, or maybe it was the Scarborough air. It was supposed to be very bracing. Margriet was racing ahead with her skirts flying, for she had spotted Julia on the sands, and Florrie hoped that her mother wasn't watching, as she was sure to say that it was most unseemly.

Julia was chasing after Hugh, then came George carrying a picnic hamper, Imogen carrying a rug and behind her Mr Sanderson carrying various pieces of paraphernalia, whilst Mrs Sanderson brought up the rear of the cavalcade holding on to the toddler Richard.

Florrie smiled. Margriet would have fun after all. She hailed them as she reached the sands, catching up with Mrs Sanderson, who had stopped to take off her shoes. 'Mrs Sanderson; how are you, ma'am?'

'I'm well, thank you, Florrie. I'm so glad that Mrs Vandergroene decided to come this year. Margriet was looking very peaky the last time I saw her.'

'Yes. They're both in need of some fresh air and a change of surroundings.'

'I'm quite sure they are,' Mrs Sanderson agreed. 'I've told Mr Sanderson that should he depart this earth before me I won't spend long in widow's weeds, and he agrees with me. After all, men can go back to work or business straight away if their wives die first, so I really don't think it fair that women should sit at home all day wearing black and never seeing anybody. It's not natural. Phew!' She exhaled.

'Are you all right, ma'am?'

'Oh – yes, after a fashion. I'm tired, that's all. I'll be all right.'

'Let me take your bag, ma'am. Is Polly not with you?'

Mrs Sanderson stopped to take a breath and handed over her bag. 'No, she gave in her notice. She couldn't handle Hughie. My husband says he should go away to school but I don't want that. Not yet, anyway. He's all right when George is here to entertain him but not when George is away at school, and Miss Barker can't take him for another year.' She glanced thoughtfully at Florrie. 'Polly wasn't firm enough with the young ones. They need someone a bit older yet young enough to keep them occupied. Goodness,' she said, setting off again, 'I really need this holiday.'

The Sandersons spread themselves about on the sands with their blankets and picnic baskets and Mrs Sanderson invited Florrie to sit with them. Margriet and Julia were already paddling in the sea and then both girls came racing back to ask if they could swim.

'We haven't brought a change of clothes for you, Miss Margriet,' Florrie said. 'You'll have to dry off in the sun.'

'That's all right, I don't mind,' Margriet said, and off they dashed again.

'I'd better go in too and keep an eye on them,' Mr Sanderson told his wife. 'Will you be all right with Hughie or shall I take him in?'

'Take him, darling, will you? He's old enough to learn now.'

'Oh, yes, do take him, Papa,' Imogen pleaded. 'Then we can have some peace for half an hour.'

'I'll come too,' George said. 'Come on, trouble.' He grabbed his young brother. 'Let's go and swim.'

The three of them headed towards the bathing machines and Mrs Sanderson sighed.

'Are you going to swim, ma'am?' Florrie asked her. 'I don't mind looking after 'baby and all the things here.'

'Oh, that would be nice,' she said. 'Are you sure you wouldn't mind? What about you, Immi? Would you like a swim?'

'Later.' Imogen, who was growing into an attractive young woman, looked about her. 'I'd quite like to take a stroll towards the lighthouse and the harbour and see what's happening, if that's all right, Mama?'

'Of course, dear. Just be careful who you speak to.' Mrs Sanderson, so daring herself, was cautious over her daughters' welfare. She watched Imogen walk away across the sands and then turned to Florrie. 'It is a worry,' she said. 'Trying to find the balance between giving a daughter freedom and making sure she's safe.'

'I think you do it better than anyone else I know, ma'am,' Florrie said quietly.

Mrs Sanderson nodded. 'Immi's very sensible and I want her to have as many opportunities as her brother. It's not fair that women should not be allowed to do things that are well within their capabilities. I don't suppose . . .' She hesitated. 'Perhaps I shouldn't say this when you're working for someone else, but if ever you thought of a change of employment, Florrie; I would be very pleased to discuss it with you.'

'Oh.' Florrie was almost lost for words at the proposal. Her hopes of bettering herself had been dashed when Mr Vandergroene had died, for she knew she couldn't leave Margriet to cope with her grief alone. Her mistress, Florrie considered, would be no help to the child at all. 'Well,' she said, 'perhaps when Mrs Vandergroene is out of mourning . . .'

Mrs Sanderson smiled. 'You are a very caring young woman,' she said. 'I knew that already, and now you're thinking of Margriet. I quite understand. I'm managing, but would dearly like someone reliable to help with the two boys until they go to school. Well, let's talk again. Maybe early next year, if you think you might be interested. What is your role now?'

Florrie pondered. 'General maid of all work, ma'am,' she said. 'Housemaid, companion to Mrs Vandergroene, and chaperon to Miss Margriet.'

'Dogsbody?' Mrs Sanderson laughed. 'I thought as much,' and Florrie laughed too. 'Well, you wouldn't be that in my house. I have house and kitchen staff already, and as soon as the younger children are old enough to travel we shall venture further abroad for our holidays. To France to begin with; nothing like hearing a foreign language to improve speaking skills.'

'Oh, yes, ma'am, I quite agree. When I was in Netherlands with Miss Margriet—'

'Ah, of course. I'd forgotten that you'd travelled abroad already. Excellent! Well, have a think about it, but right now,' she got to her feet, 'I'm going to take advantage of your generous offer and take a dip in the briny. Won't be long.'

At midday the Sanderson family gathered for their picnic. 'Margriet can stay for lunch if she'd like,' Mrs Sanderson told Florrie, 'and you too, of course. There's plenty of food – we brought our cook with us. There's chicken and ham and pies and lots of cake—'

'Oh, please, may I, Florrie? I'm still very damp and Mama might not be pleased.'

Florrie gave a wry grin. Little minx, she thought,

but why not? And there was no doubt that Mrs Vandergroene would dislike very much seeing her daughter dishevelled and wet.

'That's very kind of you, Mrs Sanderson.' Florrie got to her feet and dashed the sand off her skirt. 'Mrs Vandergroene said she might walk down to join us, but as she hasn't I'll go up and see if she needs anything.'

Mrs Sanderson nodded. 'Margriet will be fine with us. Immi, pass Margriet a plate and some chicken.'

Florrie saw Margriet look up and glance at Imogen as if she were about to ask her something, but she didn't. 'I'll come back later,' she said. 'Be good, Miss Margriet.' She turned to walk back along the hot sands and up the steep cliff.

The sun was beating down and she was hot and sticky by the time she got back to the Spa terrace, but Mrs Vandergroene wasn't there. She must have gone back to the house, Florrie thought. She looked over the railing and saw all the Sanderson family and Margriet sitting together eating their lunch and thought that her mistress might have seen them too and decided to go off on her own. Or perhaps she had just got tired of waiting for them to come back. Whatever the reason, Florrie thought, it was a considerable improvement on previous holidays, when she had been at her mistress's beck and call because she wouldn't go out on her own.

As she walked back up St Nicholas Cliff a man was coming towards her. He looked like a gentleman by the manner of his dress; he was wearing a top hat and jauntily swinging a cane. She moved to one side of the footpath to give him room and as he passed he didn't lift his hat but gave her a saucy wink.

Blooming cheek, she thought. Who did these swells think they were? And this one looked familiar. She walked on towards the house, and as she went up the path to the door she remembered where she had seen him. Stunned, she saw Mrs Vandergroene through the parlour window, gazing at her own reflection in the mirror on the wall.

He's been here! Mr Ramsey. Mrs Percival's brother. He's been here visiting Mrs Vandergroene!

'I'm sorry if I'm late back, ma'am,' she said as she entered the parlour. 'I lost track of 'time.'

'Oh, that's all right, Florence,' her mistress said. 'I've had quite a nice morning chatting to – people. In fact I've had an invitation to supper tonight. Mr and Mrs Percival have invited me over to the hotel where they're staying. An early supper, about six.'

'Oh, that's nice, ma'am. I'll see to Miss Margriet's supper.'

'Margriet! Where is she?'

'Having lunch on 'sands with 'Sanderson family. I'll go back later to collect her. Could she take her swimming costume tomorrow, ma'am? She really wants to swim, and all the others are going in.'

'I'm really not sure about that, Florence. I don't know if it's safe.'

'I'll go in with her, ma'am.'

'Will you? Well, perhaps . . . I'll think about it.'

'Very well, ma'am. Would you like a drink now and something to eat?'

'No, I don't think so. I've had coffee and a cake, and I'll be eating early.'

'Yes, of course. Did Mr and Mrs Percival arrive this morning?'

'Erm, no, they haven't actually arrived yet. I – I had a message to say they would be here this evening and would like me to dine with them. They'll send a carriage for me.'

'Well, that will be very nice, ma'am,' Florrie repeated. 'Very nice indeed.'

And that evening as she filled the tub for a very tired and sandy Margriet's bath, she reflected that it would indeed be very nice for her mistress to go out into company. Mrs Vandergroene had even said she would be perfectly all right to drive alone for the short distance to the Crescent. Except, Florrie thought, as she sponged Margriet down with soapy water, dried her and then popped her nightgown over her head before putting her to bed, she wasn't alone on the carriage journey – another figure had been waiting inside.

CHAPTER THIRTY-ONE

'Of course I shouldn't really be saying this . . .' Lydia Percival took a dainty sip. She and Rosamund were taking afternoon tea in one of Scarborough's hotels. The day had turned dull; Margriet was visiting the Rotunda museum with Julia and Imogen Sanderson and Florrie, and Mr Ramsey had returned home.

'Especially,' Lydia continued, toying with her fork and deliberating whether to take another slice of cake, 'as I was asked not to mention it, but when someone says something like that I always think they actually want the matter to be discussed.'

Rosamund made a mental note never to tell anything to Lydia unless she wanted it to be circulated far and wide.

'And of course I know it is far too soon. I said, my dear boy, she just isn't ready yet. It is far too soon.'

'I have no idea of whom you are speaking, Lydia,' Rosamund said, wishing her friend would get on with whatever she wanted to say. 'Who isn't ready for what?'

Really, Rosamund thought, she would be quite pleased when Lydia and her husband returned home. Mr Ramsey had left yesterday after a few delightful days during which she had not only strolled through Scarborough with him but had taken lunch and two suppers, for one of which Lydia and Vincent hadn't joined them. It had been quite proper, as they'd dined in the hotel where the Percivals and Mr Ramsey were staying, but since his departure she had found Lydia's company boring.

'I'm speaking of my brother, of course.' Lydia glanced slyly at Rosamund, and then sighed. 'Shall I have the cake or not? Oh, why not?' She popped a forkful into her mouth. 'Mmm, delicious.' She wiped her mouth with the napkin. 'And you, you didn't guess?'

Rosamund sat back and looked at her blankly. 'Guess? About what?'

'Why, that William is totally smitten with you! I could see it instantly; in fact right from the start, when I brought him to your house for luncheon. But of course, you poor dear, you wouldn't have noticed.'

Rosamund's heart thumped. Smitten? Whatever did she mean?

'But I said to him that he must tread very carefully, for you are still very fragile and won't be looking for anyone else for years.'

Years? Rosamund had thought she would spend the rest of her life alone. It had not occurred to her that anyone would be in the least interested in sharing it with her.

'Whether he would wait for years is another matter,' Lydia prattled on. 'I rather think he might, but there again he's very eligible and someone might come along and snatch him away – catch him in a weak moment, you know.'

'Lydia, what are you talking about? Has Mr Ramsey discussed me with you?' Rosamund put her hand to her throat. 'He has been most attentive, very polite and courteous, but I'm sure he does not have any intentions towards me.'

Lydia smiled. 'Well, that is your opinion, but I am William's sister and I know him better than most.' She waved her hand towards the waitress for the bill. 'But we don't have to discuss it any further, because, as I said to William, I know that you wouldn't even consider it.'

Rosamund was fuming as they walked back towards St Nicholas Cliff. How dared Lydia presume to tell her brother what she, Rosamund, would or would not consider? And as for its being too soon after Frederik's death, how could she possibly know what it was like to be alone, unable to emerge from one's own front door until society decreed that it was the right and proper time to do so?

'Are you all right, Rosamund dear?' Lydia asked. 'You're very quiet. Would you like me to walk you to the house? I can always get a cab back to the hotel.'

'I'm perfectly able to walk to the house by myself, Lydia,' Rosamund said sharply. 'I am not an invalid.'

'Indeed you're not,' Lydia agreed. 'You look so much better for these few days of sea air. You've got quite a bloom to your cheeks, if it is indeed the sea air that has put it there!' She gave a knowing smile. 'Goodbye, my dear. We're off tomorrow, so I'll see you when you return home at the end of the month. Give my love to dear little Margriet.'

She touched Rosamund's arm lightly in farewell and walked on towards the cabriolet box at the top of the street. Rosamund saw her wave her parasol at one of the drivers, who obligingly shook the reins and drove his horse and cab towards her.

Enviously, Rosamund watched Lydia climb into the carriage. Lydia didn't really care what society thought one way or another, she reflected, even though she pretended to set so much store by it. And perhaps she was right. Who, after all, was really affected by what Rosamund did or didn't do, and who really cared? She thought longingly of the amusing tales that William Ramsey had told her of the horse racing at Beverley and York.

'The Knavesmire in York is the place to be,' he'd said enthusiastically, 'and then afterwards at the Assembly Rooms, where everybody who is anybody dines and dances. Oh, you must come, Mrs Vandergroene, you'd love it – but oh, I do beg your pardon! How very crass of me.' He had been so penitent. 'For a moment I quite forgot that you have suffered a tragedy.' In his distress he had taken her hand and gently squeezed it. 'Please say that you'll forgive me?'

And of course she had. She sat now in the parlour gazing out of the window, watching the rain pouring down and bouncing off the footpath, and the holidaymakers scurrying home to their lodgings under their umbrellas. She had never been to a race meeting; it wasn't the kind of event that interested Frederik and anyway he was always so busy. As Mr Ramsey had talked she had found herself longing to go to one, forgetting for a moment that as a widow she was not in a position to do so; it wouldn't be the done thing. Tears came to her eyes. It just wasn't fair!

Her malaise continued for the rest of the holiday. The weather changed and became cold and misty – a sea fret, Margriet told her the locals called it – and the Sandersons decided to cut short their holiday and go home.

'Mrs Sanderson isn't very well,' Margriet told her. She pressed her lips together as she imparted the news, and when her mother said she hoped Mrs Sanderson didn't have anything infectious Margriet shook her head and said she didn't. She glanced at her mother and said, 'It's something only women get. It's not catching.'

The sun came out again but without its former intensity. Margriet had no one to play with and confessed that she'd like to go home too. 'It's no fun playing on the sands or swimming by yourself,' she told Florrie, who agreed that it wasn't and told Mrs Vandergroene that Margriet wouldn't at all mind if they went home early. So they packed up their belongings, found a local driver to transport them and went home a week before they had planned to.

Rosamund pondered on her situation all that autumn. One afternoon she told Florrie that she would accompany her to collect Margriet from school and they would walk home together.

'Miss Margriet likes to walk home with her school friends, ma'am,' Florrie told her. 'I don't always collect her.'

Oh!' Rosamund had forgotten she had agreed to

this arrangement. 'Well, nevertheless, I will come with you today and Margriet and I will have a stroll around town, or maybe stop for a cup of tea. I think she'll enjoy that.'

No, she wouldn't, Florrie thought, but if that was what the mistress wanted she must do as she pleased. Florrie was becoming increasingly unhappy in her situation; she felt that she was neither nursemaid nor housemaid. Margriet didn't really need her any more and she was fed up with being at Mrs Simmonds' beck and call as far as housework was concerned. Since they'd returned from Scarborough the housekeeper had taken it into her head that Florrie thought herself a cut above everyone else, and she didn't like it.

I think I'll tek that position with Mrs Sanderson if she still wants me, she thought. I hope she's all right. That was a bad session of sickness that she had at Scarborough, Mr Sanderson was right bothered about her. If I see Miss Julia today I'll ask her how she is.

Margriet and Julia came out of school together and Margriet expressed great surprise at seeing her mother waiting.

'Is everything all right, Mama?' she asked anxiously.

'Yes,' Rosamund said. 'Why would it not be?'

'I thought there might be bad news or something. You never come to meet me.'

Rosamund frowned. 'There's no bad news. I thought we could take tea somewhere. Perhaps you'd like to come too, Julia?'

'No thank you, Mrs Vandergroene,' Julia said.

'My mother will worry if I don't go straight home.'

'We walk home together, Mama,' Margriet explained. 'If I don't go with her it means she'll have to walk by herself.'

'I'll walk back with Miss Julia,' Florrie offered. 'I don't mind.'

Rosamund was quite put out. She had thought it would be a treat for her and Margriet to have tea together but Margriet sat in sullen silence and refused any cake and didn't discuss anything at all about her day at school.

Florrie asked Julia how her mother was.

'She's all right now, but she had to go to bed for a few days. She's expecting another baby. Are you going to come and live with us, Florrie? Mama says that she asked you to. I wish you would. Mama really needs some help.'

Florrie nodded. 'I think I might, Miss Julia. It's just that I worry about Miss Margriet.'

'Yes, she'd miss you, I know. But she could come and see you, couldn't she? It's just that you'd be living at our house instead of hers.'

Florrie thought about it as she walked back to Parliament Street, and she made up her mind when she saw the curricle outside the door and Mr William Ramsey mounting the steps to ring the bell. Florrie foresaw changes ahead.

He heard her behind him and turned. 'Good day to you.' He lifted his top hat. 'Is Mrs Vandergroene at home, or may I leave my card?'

Florrie dipped her knee. 'Mrs Vandergroene is out with her daughter at the moment, sir,' she began, but stopped as she saw Rosamund and

Margriet turning the corner into Parliament Street. Mr Ramsey smiled.

'What perfect timing,' he murmured, handing her his visiting card. He walked back down the steps and again lifted his hat, this time to greet Rosamund. 'Mrs Vandergroene! I have just this second given my card to your servant. I hope I might have the pleasure of calling on you tomorrow? I'm staying with my sister for a few days.'

'That would be very nice indeed, Mr Ramsey.' Rosamund's spirits lifted. 'I am at home tomorrow. Shall we say at about eleven?'

Florrie had quietly let herself into the house and was waiting in the hall when her mistress and Margriet came in.

'Why is Mr Ramsey coming tomorrow, Mama?' Margriet was saying. 'What does he want?'

'Want?' her mother said sharply. 'Where are your manners, Margriet? It's a social call. You know very well that's what grown-up people do. They call on each other.'

'Oh,' Margriet said. 'To talk, do you mean?'

'Yes. To talk.'

Margriet considered. She knew that Mr Ramsey had been at Scarborough. She had seen him talking to her mother once or twice on the Spa terrace, and she knew that he was Mrs Percival's brother. She had a funny feeling about him; she didn't like him at all. 'What does he want to talk about?'

Rosamund took a deep breath. Really! Margriet was becoming a very annoying child; she had hardly spoken to her over tea. 'I have absolutely no idea, Margriet, and whatever it is has nothing

270

whatsoever to do with you. As I said, it is a social call.' She glanced at the hovering Florrie, waiting to take her coat. 'At last your mother is coming back into the world.'

CHAPTER THIRTY-TWO

Lia paused in the unpacking of her precious crockery to look out of the first-floor window of the tall canal house that looked out over the Amstel. It had been hard to give up her delightful home on the outskirts of Gouda, which had been so full of life and love, but it had become empty with loss.

At Easter, when the bulbs in her garden were beginning to unfurl their colours, she had realized that it wasn't enough, that she needed a fresh impetus in her life. She had called together her mother, her son and her daughter and put it to them that she would like to suggest a change.

'It will break my heart to leave this place,' she said softly, after she had made her suggestion, 'but my heart is already in several pieces, and I would like it to be mended.'

She had thought of Amsterdam in the first place because of Hans who, kind and generous soul that he was, so much like his father, used his precious time travelling from there to Gouda to spend his weekends with her and Klara. It would be easier for him if they were closer, she had thought, and started looking at academies in the city that

Klara could attend in the autumn.

'Living in Amsterdam will be so very different from living here that we will not be able to compare it in the least,' Lia had told them. She had added that she was very lonely now, but would make new friends in the hustle and bustle of a place like Amsterdam, especially as the children didn't need her as much as they had done when they were small.

'We will always need you, Moe,' Klara had said, shedding a few tears, 'but I agree. I don't need anyone to collect me from school now,' she had added on a choking, laughing sob, 'and it would be quite nice to find out what it's like to live in a city.'

Lia's mother had said she would be happy wherever Lia and the children were and would relish meeting new people. Hans had looked at his mother seriously and said, 'Don't do this just for me, Moe. Do it for yourself too,' and she'd smiled and said it was what she wanted.

At the beginning of August, they had moved. Hans and Klara were thrilled with the house and the fact that their bedrooms were five floors up with a view of the city; Lia's mother had rooms on the ground floor with windows where she could sit and watch the passers-by. In no time at all she was exchanging waves with the boatmen on the barges and the tourist-filled canal boats.

The city was full of leafy green trees, and tubs of bright flowers adorned every corner. As Lia looked out, she thought that if she were ever to be happy again, it would be here. The only regret was leaving Miriam behind; she had been such a support when Lia had needed her, but she was a country girl and didn't want to move. Besides, she had shyly told Lia that she had a young man in her sights whom she was fond of.

Lia finished arranging her crockery in a cupboard, put away the empty boxes and washed her hands. She would write to Mevrouw Vandergroene and give her their new address. Frederik's mother, of course; not his wife, who had not answered her letter of condolence. It would be nice to meet Gerda and Anna again, and hear news of dear Margriet.

She mentioned it to Hans and Klara, and Klara said she had written to Margriet but hadn't yet received a reply. 'Perhaps they have moved too,' she suggested.

'Whilst we're speaking of the Vandergroenes, Moeder,' Hans said, 'I'd like to talk to you about my future. When I finish school I would very much like to go into the import-export business. Uncle Freddy always made it sound so interesting, so instead of going to university I'd like to take a business course and start work. His company is very successful and I wondered, do you think they might consider me for a junior position?'

His mother looked sad and he wished he hadn't mentioned it yet, realizing it was too soon, but his school tutors were keen to have him make up his mind about a university scholarship. Instead, he wanted to be out in the world and making his living.

Lia shook her head. 'I don't honestly know, Hans,' she said, 'but I do know that had Freddy been here he would have been delighted.' Then she smiled, her eyes lighting up her face. 'But how foolish they would be to refuse you. What a loss it would be to them not to take on my brave, handsome, clever son. You should write and tell them about yourself, your father and your connection with his friend Frederik, and see what happens.'

Gerda Vandergroene read Lia's letter telling her that she had moved to Amsterdam and was pleased. She would call, she thought. Lia had taken a positive step, and Gerda was interested in that son of hers whom Frederik had been so taken with. She sighed. She was more than disappointed in her English daughter-in-law, whom she suspected of deliberately stopping Margriet from writing to her. Margriet had never replied to her letters, though she sometimes wrote as if she had never heard from her grandmother, asking, *Will you please write to me, Oma?* as she had recently on a postcard showing sea and a sandy beach. Margriet had forgotten to put a stamp on it and Gerda had had to pay extra postage. Not that she minded that, but she thought it was strange.

Lia would have made Frederik happy; unlike Rosamund, she was warm and loving. Gerda sighed again. Life, she thought. Life was hard sometimes, so she would welcome Lia, show her that it was all right to fight back.

CHAPTER THIRTY-THREE

It wasn't fair, Margriet fumed. Nothing was going right. The odious Mr Ramsey was forever trying to worm his way into her favour and she was having none of it. For her thirteenth birthday he had bought her a fur muff and matching hat, telling her that now she was almost a young lady she could wear something fashionable that would keep her warm and cosy too. She'd thanked him but she definitely wouldn't wear them. She'd moaned to Florrie that it would be like wearing a dead cat.

And that was another thing. Florrie had chosen to tell her on her birthday of all days that she was leaving at the end of the month and going to live at the Sandersons' house to look after the younger boys and the new baby when it came. She had gone now and her mother had brought Jane back as a permanent housemaid, and Jane had barely anything to say to Margriet.

Florrie had said she could go and see her at the Sandersons' whenever she wanted, Mrs Sanderson had said so, but she didn't want to; it would only remind her of how everyone was deserting her. That meant not only Florrie, who had been with them for as long as she could remember, but Julia too, as she had left school at Christmas.

Margriet wouldn't mind leaving school in July either, she thought glumly, for the girl who had taken Julia's place was only seven, and too young for conversation. But what would she do? Her mother was taken up with Mr Ramsey; he was always in Parliament Street, and Margriet wished he would go back to his own house. And then she was struck with the terrible fear that her mother might marry him and he would live with them all the time. She would run away if he did, she decided. He's all smiles and chatter but he doesn't mean it. He's only pretending.

She said goodbye to Miss Barker at the beginning of the summer holidays. She would miss the teacher, who had taught her so much and was always willing to listen to any problem that her pupils might have.

'You are a bright and clever girl, Margriet,' Miss Barker said. 'I have written to your mother suggesting that you would profit immensely by going on to another school for young ladies. Do you think you'd like that?'

'I don't know, Miss Barker. I don't know anyone who has done that, but I might like it. And I don't know what else I could do.'

'Well, perhaps your mother has ideas of her own. You will need to discuss them with her.' She put out her hand. 'Come to me for advice, Margriet, if ever you feel the need.'

Her mother had indeed some ideas of her own. When Margriet arrived home her mother was sitting in the window watching out for her. 'Well, Margriet, you finished school today!' she said enthusiastically as her daughter came into the sitting room and slumped into a chair. 'Don't slouch, child. It is so ungainly. You must try to remember that you are almost a young woman now.'

'Are we going to Scarborough this summer, Mama?' she asked, ignoring her mother's admonishment. 'I don't really want to. The Sandersons won't be there, not now they've got a new baby. It's another boy,' she added. 'I've seen Florrie pushing the bassinet. He's called Conrad.'

'Really?' Her mother was totally uninterested, as Margriet had known she would be. 'No, we're not going to Scarborough this year. We have other plans.'

We? Margriet thought uneasily. We haven't discussed any other plans. 'So are we going somewhere else? I'd like to visit Oma. I think she might not be well, because she hardly ever writes to me.'

'I don't know why you would think she's ill,' her mother answered. 'But no, you can't. Had Florence still been here I might have considered it, but as she's not—'

'When I'm old enough I'll go alone,' Margriet said defiantly. 'Once I'm twenty-one, I can.'

Rosamund drew in a deep breath. This was not going to plan. She had realized there might be difficulties with what she was going to say but Margriet's desire to visit her grandmother was nothing to do with the subject in hand. 'When you're old enough we will find a companion to travel with you, but in the meantime I have some news for you.' She gave a nervous smile. 'I'm sure you will be delighted.'

Margriet frowned, narrowing her eyes. 'What news?'

Rosamund folded her hands across her lap. 'As you know, Mr Ramsey has been calling frequently since last summer, and we have become – we have become – shall I say – close. Yesterday when he called . . .' She hesitated. It was a big step to take and she had taken her time over her answer, debating whether or not it was the right thing to do. He had been very understanding, saying she must not hurry her decision, that he was a patient man and would wait, but then he had smiled and said he hoped she would not keep him waiting too long, for he was very fond of her and surely she must want someone to look after her as Frederik had done so ably.

She had agreed that it was a lonely life and then, impulsively, which was not like her at all, had said that she would marry him. It would be so very nice to hand over the decision-making to someone else, she had thought. Frederik had never harassed her over accounts, never questioned her expenditure – not that she'd ever been a spendthrift, she thought. But now Mr Clayton, the accountant Hugh Webster had appointed to keep an eye on her shares in Frederik's company, kept sending her sheets of figures that she didn't understand and asking her if they were satisfactory and was there anything she'd like to discuss.

'Yes?' Margriet stood up from her chair as if about to take flight. 'When he called . . . ?'

'He asked me to marry him,' Rosamund said simply.

Margriet drew in a breath. 'You didn't – you didn't say you would? You can't! What about Papa? What about me?' Her voice broke. 'Mama! What about me?'

Rosamund put out her hand but Margriet stepped back, crossing her arms in front of her chest as if to ward her off. 'No.' She shook her head. 'No!'

'Margriet! Dear! Your papa is gone.' Rosamund's voice cracked too as she spoke. 'Don't think that I don't miss him, because I do, but I need someone in my life and so do you. Mr Ramsey will look after us both. He has promised that he will and he says we won't have to move, but can stay here and perhaps travel – you'd like that. He's mentioned going to France and London – what do you think of that? We've never been.'

Margriet looked miserably at her mother and shook her head. She didn't want to go anywhere with Mr Ramsey. If her mother wanted to go, she would stay at home alone. Or . . . 'Miss Barker said I'd benefit from going to another school,' she blurted out. 'I'd like to do that.'

'Well, we'll see,' her mother said. 'We'll discuss it in due course.'

What she meant was that Mr Ramsey would decide, Margriet thought, resolving immediately that she would do the opposite of what he wanted. He's not my father and he's not going to make decisions about me. 'I'm going to my room,' she said. 'I need to think about my future.'

She ran upstairs and climbed on to the high bed. Sliding beneath the blankets, she pulled them over her head and curled into a ball. She felt betrayed by everyone, not only her mother but by Florrie and, yes, her father too for leaving her alone.

'Why?' She began to sob. 'Why did you have to go on that ship and not come back? Papa! Why did you leave me?' She sobbed and sobbed until her chest ached. Her stomach and head ached too but eventually she felt herself slipping away into sleep. When she woke up, she thought drowsily, perhaps she'd be grown up and able to do whatever she wanted with her life. She put the tip of her thumb into her mouth for comfort as she used to when she was an infant. Or perhaps she would be a child again and none of this would have happened. Papa would still be alive and she'd ask him not to go away. As she drifted towards slumber, she thought she heard the slam of the front door, the pause in the hall as he gave his coat to Florrie or hung it on the coat stand, and then his light tread on the stair as he ran up to see her. The sound stopped outside her door, and she smiled as with a deep contended sigh she fell asleep.

Downstairs, Rosamund thought wryly of Margriet's last comment. There was no need for her to think about her future as it was already planned out, just as her own had been. She would grow up, learn how to behave, meet some suitable young man whom she would marry and live the rest of her life in comparative ease, without too many difficulties. It was unfortunate that Frederik had been taken so young, leaving her to make decisions on her own, but now Mr Ramsey could fulfil that role and everything would fall into place again.

Margriet slept until the following morning. She

was vaguely aware of Jane coming in to mend the fire and draw the curtains and then, unusually, she thought that her mother came in too, bending over her to move wisps of hair from her face and turning down the lamp, but still she didn't stir until the door opened again and Jane came in with a breakfast tray. 'Your mother said you should have breakfast in bed, miss, as you're not very well.'

'Thank you.' Margriet sat up and rubbed her eyes. 'I'm perfectly well. Just tired, that's all.'

'Mebbe you're starting your flux, Miss Margriet.' Jane put the tray on the bed and then drew back the curtains. 'I'm allus tired at that time of 'month. No chance of stopping in bed for me, o' course.'

'Perhaps I am,' Margriet said, not going to admit to Jane that she had only recently discovered what the flux entailed. 'Bring me up what is necessary, will you, please.'

Jane bobbed her knee. 'Yes, miss.'

Margriet drank her tea and ate the toast and thought that nothing had changed from the evening before. She was still neither child nor adult. If her mother really did mean to marry Mr Ramsey, then she'd have to put up with him, but she wouldn't go away to school, she decided. If she left him here with her mother, she was afraid he'd take over the house. She would educate herself, she thought – ask her mother to take out a subscription at the library and borrow books from there. She'd seek Miss Barker's advice on what to read.

When she finally rose from bed, she knew that her life had changed after all. She washed, brushed her hair and from her wardrobe took a striped fine wool dress that she wore on the rare occasions when she went out visiting with her mother. It had a front-buttoned bodice so she was able to fasten it herself, and beneath it she wore two petticoats so that the skirt was full. She tied a ribbon in her hair and went downstairs to her mother, who was in her sitting room writing letters. She looked very nice, Margriet thought, in a pearl grey gown, and much brighter-eyed than she had for some time; perhaps she too had been unhappy.

'Margriet,' her mother said. 'Are you going some-where?'

'No, Mama, I am not, at least not yet, but I might later. I'd like to talk to you about several things, but first of all I must tell you that today I have reached womanhood.'

Womanhood. Rosamund mouthed the word. Then she put her hand to her mouth. 'Oh dear,' she whispered. 'You poor dear girl.'

Rosamund took out a year's subscription at the library. It seemed that she was willing to do anything to keep Margriet sweet before her impending marriage. Margriet and Mr Ramsey had little to say to one another as Margriet generally left the room whenever he visited, but the die was cast and a wedding was arranged for mid-October with a quiet ceremony at St Mary's Church.

'Do I have to be there, Mama?' Margriet asked.

'Of course you do. You're not old enough to be a witness so Mr Ramsey has asked Mr and Mrs Percival, but I'd like you to be there. Perhaps you can hold my flowers.'

It was not what she wanted, but she realized there was no other option, unless Rosamund changed her mind at the last minute. But Rosamund wasn't likely to do that, as Mr Ramsey had bought her both an engagement and a wedding ring and jokingly told her that she was now committed and there was no getting out of it. Rosamund had asked her dressmaker to style her a new gown of deep violet with a pink rosebud pattern. It had deep flounces at the hem, a silk fringe on the bodice and three-quarter sleeves, beneath which she wore silk mittens. For Margriet she ordered a white-spotted ankle-length muslin with long sleeves edged with lace, a matching silk shawl with pale green tassels, and white slippers for her feet.

There were just five of them at the ceremony. Mr Ramsey hadn't wanted a fuss, Rosamund said, and she didn't mind as it was not very long since she came out of mourning. Afterwards they went for a celebratory luncheon in a private room at a local inn; Mr Percival and Mr Ramsey had too much to drink but Mrs Percival was rather quiet, Margriet thought, and not her usual talkative self.

When they all arrived back home, Rosamund had excused herself for a moment and Mr Ramsey had sidled up to Margriet. Seizing one of her curls, he twirled it round his finger and whispered to her that he had a favour to ask. He said that he had booked a room in a hotel in York for the night as he wanted to take her mother to the races the next day.

'What do you think?' he murmured. 'Are you old enough to stay at home by yourself with just the servants to look after you?'

She backed away from him and declared that of course she was.

'Oh, good,' he said. 'Because I have another present coming for your mama, and,' he reached for a small box that he'd placed on one of the side tables, 'this is for you.'

'What is it?' She didn't want to take it. He needn't think that he could wheedle himself into her affections by giving her more presents.

'Open it. Go on. Every young lady likes receiving gifts, doesn't she?'

'I'll wait for Mama to come back,' she said, and sat down opposite Mrs Percival, who was gazing into the fire.

Presently Lydia looked up, and glancing at her brother said, 'Just watch what you're doing, William, or you'll come a cropper.'

'I don't know what you're talking about, Lydia.' He turned as Rosamund came back into the room, followed by Jane and Mrs Simmonds with trays of glasses and decanters.

When the servants had gone, he served wine for everyone and Mr Percival staggered to his feet and said, 'A toast! A toast to the happy pair.' He took a slurp of wine, spilling much of it down his waistcoat. 'A long and profitable life.'

Both men raised their glasses, and then Mr Ramsey raised his again and said, 'And to our daughter Margriet, who looks so very charming.'

Aghast, Margriet stared at him. 'But I'm not your daughter,' she gasped. 'And I never will be. I'm Margriet Vandergroene. Frederik Vandergroene's daughter.' She put down the glass of lemonade she'd asked for and would have dashed out of the room, but William Ramsey seemed to have anticipated her flight and caught her arm, forestalling her, his fingertips firm on her wrist.

'Not in flesh, I quite agree,' he said calmly. 'But I trust, Margriet, that you will be as obedient a daughter as if you were my very own.' He smiled at her, but he had narrowed his eyes. 'Now, my dear, open your present.'

CHAPTER THIRTY-FOUR

When Margriet reluctantly opened Mr Ramsey's box it was to reveal a sparkling bracelet of glittering stones. Her mother exclaimed at its prettiness when she showed it to her, and Mrs Percival murmured, 'How lovely,' but didn't show as much enthusiasm as might have been expected.

Margriet whispered her thanks and fortunately attention was diverted from her when Mr Ramsey turned to the window, glanced out and said triumphantly, 'Now it's your turn, Rosamund. Here is your wedding gift arriving. Come and look.'

Everyone rushed to the window. Margriet followed more slowly and was astonished to see her mother grow pale and put her hand to her mouth.

'But William,' she said. 'I have never driven.'

Margriet looked out and saw by the steps a smart black and green two-horse curricle and a liveried driver.

'I will teach you,' Mr Ramsey said. 'Don't you love it? I've had my eye on this for some time.'

'Very smart, dear boy,' Vincent Percival said, glancing at his wife. 'Isn't it, Lydia?'

'Very nice,' she murmured. 'Is it new?'

'Of course it's new! Would I buy second-hand for my new wife?'

Rosamund gave a nervous laugh. 'It's very generous of you, William, but if there's a coachie, why do I have to learn to drive?'

'Oh, he's only delivering it. We won't be keeping him; there's only room for two in any case, and now the best thing of all is that we are going off to the York races in it, so hurry and pack an overnight bag and we'll be off.'

Rosamund glanced about her as if not quite knowing what was happening. 'Come, Margriet,' she said. 'What will we take?'

'Margriet isn't coming,' her husband said. 'We have an understanding, haven't we, m'dear?' He gave Margriet a complicit glance and dumbly she nodded.

'I'll come and help you pack, Mama,' she murmured, and led the way out of the room, pausing at the bottom of the stairs. 'He told me that he was taking you to York tonight so that you could go to the races tomorrow, and asked me if I'd be all right on my own. He didn't say anything about buying a carriage.'

'Will you be all right?' her mother whispered. 'If it's only for one night? Mrs Simmonds is here, and Jane. They'll look after you.'

'Yes, I'll be all right,' she said defiantly. 'I don't need anyone to look after me.'

They decided what her mother would wear at the races and rang the bell for Jane to pack the valise, and then Margriet helped her mother to change into something suitable for driving to York. The seats of the curricle were set high and Rosamund didn't think she would be splashed if the road was muddy, but Margriet suggested she take a blanket in case the weather was cold on their return the next day.

'How sensible you are, Margriet.' Her mother was quite tearful. 'My little girl is grown up after all.'

But I'm not, she thought as she stood on the top step and watched Mr Ramsey hand her mother into the curricle. I'm not grown up at all. Mr Ramsey went to the other side of the curricle, handed an envelope to the driver, who pocketed it and hurried off, and then climbed in himself. He stood on the small platform, waved the whip in farewell and shook the reins. Her mother waved also, but nervously, Margriet thought, and she held on to the side of the vehicle as the horses moved off to the top of Parliament Street and then turned left and out of sight.

Margriet raced down the steps and up the street, her muslin skirt flying as she ran to watch the curricle's progress along the road. She couldn't see her mother beneath the hood but could make out Mr Ramsey's top hat and an arm as he flourished the whip, causing several people to scurry out of the way, until the carriage was finally lost to view.

She walked slowly back to the house. Mr and Mrs Percival were standing on the steps waiting for her.

'My dear,' Lydia Percival said. 'We were wondering if you might like to return home with us for to-night rather than stay alone. You are very welcome.'

Margriet shook her head. 'No thank you, Mrs Percival,' she said politely. 'I have several things to attend to,' which was a lie. 'And I also have some studying to do.' This wasn't exactly the truth either, but it might be.

'Some studying!' Lydia Percival trilled as they came inside for their coats. 'Well, my word, what a clever girl.' She lowered her voice. 'Just one thing, Margriet. When you are out, don't run; walk more slowly, as befits a young lady such as yourself. Your mama wouldn't have been pleased to see you race along the street as you did just now. It isn't becoming. And take care if you are out alone not to speak to anyone. Be circumspect at all times.'

Margriet bobbed her knee. 'I will, Mrs Percival. Thank you so much for coming today.'

Mrs Percival's eyebrows shot up at her effective dismissal. Margriet's hand remained firmly on the door as she waited for them to leave, and Mr Percival touched his hat and ushered his wife out.

'Oh, please be careful,' Rosamund begged, one hand on her hat and the other clutching the blanket. 'Please don't drive so fast.'

William Ramsey plonked himself beside her and tightened up on the reins. 'Don't be a spoilsport, Rosamund. What fun this is. I've longed for a smart curricle like this for such a long time. They're so very sporty. Built for speed.'

Rosamund glanced at him. She'd thought he bought it for her, though actually she would have preferred a dog cart for getting about; it would have been more convenient. 'Where shall we stable the horses?' she asked.

'Oh, erm, at my place to begin with, and then

we'll find stabling in Hull until we decide where we're going to live.'

'But – you said we'd stay in Parliament Street. It's a nice house, very convenient—'

'Yes, yes,' he cut in brusquely. 'Don't let's worry about that now.' He turned to her and smiled. 'Let's just enjoy the next few days. We'll dine in the hotel tonight; I've invited a few friends over, by the way. The Knavesmire races tomorrow and then we'll see what comes next.'

'I don't want to leave Margriet too long on her own,' Rosamund told him.

'She'll be fine. She's a very sensible girl, and besides, this is our honeymoon, Rosamund. Don't let's spoil it by thinking of Margriet.' He leaned towards her and planted a kiss on her cheek. 'We're going to think about us!'

And that was something she was afraid of. She had intended telling him that she didn't want any more children, that childbirth terrified her, but she hadn't. Neither could she tell him that the whole bedroom business was abhorrent to her.

Her entire body ached by the time they reached York. He had, it was true, tried to avoid the many deep ruts and wheel tracks on the road, but that meant swerving and she'd had to hold tight as he didn't slow down but let the horses keep up their breakneck speed.

'Almost there,' he said, as they rumbled beneath the archways of the walls of York. 'Have you been here before?'

She confessed that she hadn't, and he told her that it was only a small market town and the only thing to recommend it in his opinion were the races held on the Knavesmire just outside the town. 'There are lots of Irish immigrants here now,' he said. 'They came to escape the potato famine and there'll be work for them now that the railway has come. Things should look up.' He grew thoughtful. 'Maybe we should invest in the railways, Rosamund; there'll be money to be made.'

He drove more slowly through the narrow streets, and as Rosamund looked about her she saw the overhanging top storeys of buildings almost touching each other and blocking out any light from the darkening sky. She wrinkled her nose at the stench coming from some of the unmade muddy roads.

'This is it,' he said at last, reining in beside the timbered frontage of a very old building. 'Here, take the ribbons for a minute whilst I shout for the lad.'

Gingerly, Rosamund took the reins. She hoped that nothing would startle the horses and make them bolt, but they seemed docile enough; their coats were sweaty and she thought that they had been driven too hard.

William came out again with the landlord and she was helped down. 'This is my wife, Isaac. We were married today. Say how-de-do to her.'

The landlord turned to look at her. He drew in a breath and his mouth formed into an O. He glanced at William and then he grinned, showing only half a mouthful of teeth. Ushering her inside, he put her valise down on a not very clean wooden floor and gave her a bow. 'Charmed to meet you, dear lady,' he fawned. 'Delighted to know that someone has been brave enough to take on my good friend Jack.'

'Jack?'

'William Jackson Ramsey,' William said. 'Isaac has always called me Jack. Have you saved us your best room, Isaac, as I asked?'

Rosamund looked about her. This wasn't at all what she had expected. They were in the bar area; casks and barrels lined the walls, and long wooden tables were already taken by groups of men who seemed to be taking a great interest in her. 'Is there another dining room?' she asked. 'You said you'd booked supper.'

'And so I have.' William took her arm. 'Lead on, landlord, and take us to our accommodation.'

They were led up a set of very narrow stairs to a small landing and then up another even narrower set to the top floor, where Isaac opened a door to a long room. To her relief, it contained a large bed and a wash stand with clean towels, a wardrobe and an easy chair.

'Thank you,' she said in some relief. 'This will do very well.'

'Our best, m'lady,' he said. 'Nothing but the best for our Jack and his lady wife.'

'Draw me a tankard of your best ale, Isaac,' William said, 'and I'll be down to quaff it in two minutes. I've a thirst on me from the drive.' He grinned as he spoke. 'And I'll need several more before the night is over.'

'And for you, ma'am?'

'A pot of tea up here, if you will,' Rosamund said, 'and a slice of bread and butter.'

William took hold of both her hands when the

landlord had gone down, and opened her arms wide as if to look at her. 'Well,' he said, 'here we are.'

'Yes, indeed,' she said nervously. 'It was a tiring journey. I shall be pleased to have a rest before supper.'

'And so you shall.' He indicated the bed. 'A very comfy mattress. And there's no need to change for dinner – we don't dress up here.'

'But you said you'd invited guests!'

'So I have, but you don't need to worry about them. There's no one to hold a candle to you.'

He blew her a kiss and left her, and she took off her boots and jacket, unfastened her waistband and climbed on to the bed, where she lay back and took a deep breath. Why was it, she wondered, that she felt as though she had made the biggest mistake of her life?

CHAPTER THIRTY-FIVE

William tapped on the door just as Rosamund was drifting off to sleep, and told her that their guests had arrived. 'We're eating at seven, so don't be long,' he said. 'I'll wait downstairs. Isaac will show you where we are.'

She rinsed her face and hands and straightened her clothes and hair. Searching in her valise, she found a lace cap and placed it on her head. 'That will have to do,' she breathed, glancing at her reflection in the mirror. 'How I hate to be rushed.'

The staircase was dark and she fumbled her way down the two flights to the bar room. It was full of rowdy men and a few women who turned to look at her. Isaac was busy serving ale and she tried to catch his eye, not daring to venture past the crowd of men. Then a young serving girl pushed past and she asked her where she would find Mr Ramsey's private room.

The girl looked at her blankly. 'Don't know any Mr Ramsey,' she said. 'You'll have to ask Isaac.'

She started to move away, but Rosamund put out her hand. 'Would you ask him, please? I can't get his attention.'

The girl hesitated, but there must have been something in Rosamund's voice that commanded her respect because she nodded and pushed her way to the landlord. After a moment Isaac came hurrying towards her.

'Begging your pardon, ma'am. This way if you please.' He raised his voice. 'Out the way, lads – let the lady through. Mind your backs and your manners. No foul language please, we have quality here.'

His voice had its effect and everyone stood back to make way, some of the men pulling off their caps and hats and some giving a little bow. She couldn't tell if they were mocking her or not, for she was afraid to meet their eyes. Isaac gave a perfunctory knock on a door and opened it to a room full of people. A table was set for supper, with a huge pie in the centre surrounded by several dishes of steaming vegetables and a large jug of ale.

'Here she is at last,' William called out, coming towards her. His face was flushed and she wondered if he had had more than the one tankard of ale he had ordered. 'Quiet, everybody. Kindly be upstanding for the beautiful Rosamund, who did me the great honour of becoming my wife only this morning.' Rosamund blushed as everyone stood and cheered and she was led to a seat at the head of the table.

'Wine, landlord, the best that you have, to drink a toast to my lovely bride.' William pointed a wavering finger at her before bending over her and whispering beerily that he would introduce her to everyone all in good time. Sitting near her was a portly, bleary-eyed man who murmured a name she didn't catch and opposite him was a pretty but rather blowsy young woman with rouged cheeks, wearing a low-cut gown and purple feathers in her hair.

'How d'ya do, Mrs Ramsey?' she purred. 'Marie-Louise Jarvis, but everybody calls me Lou. I'm an old friend of Jack's. You're a friend of his sister, I understand?'

'Yes, I am,' Rosamund murmured, leaning away as a young maid served her a very large portion of meat pie whilst Isaac hovered behind her with a carafe of wine. She was suddenly overwhelmed. This wasn't the way it was meant to be. She had thought that she and William would have a quiet supper together, during which they could have talked and got to know each other better. She looked about her at his choice of friends and knew that they could never be hers. The sooner I can persuade him to come and live in Hull the better, she decided.

As the evening wore on the voices grew louder and more clamorous as the ale and the wine flowed everywhere but into Rosamund's glass, for she refused any more after the first two. A headache was beginning and she wondered how soon she could make her escape. William was sprawled with his elbows on the table talking nineteen to the dozen, yet she hadn't had any conversation with him since she entered the room.

Eventually she got up; of her nearest neighbours, the man was asleep with his head on the table and gravy on his chin, and the woman Marie-Louise had gone to speak to another group and was sitting on someone's knee. She made her way towards William, who looked up as if he were surprised to see her. 'I'm going up to the room, William,' she murmured into his ear. 'I'm very tired.'

He closed his eyes momentarily and gave a nod, his head almost dropping to his chest. Then he blinked at her and blew out his cheeks. 'Right,' he slurred. 'I'll be up as soon as this lot have gone, which will be when the barrel runs dry.' He slapped her rump, making her jump. 'Keep the bed warm for me.'

She opened the door and closed it behind her, steeling herself to face the crowded bar room. She dodged between the drinkers and no one stopped her or made a comment, but when she reached the stairs she had to negotiate her way past a couple sitting in a close embrace halfway up and a hand reached inside her skirt to clasp her ankle. She kicked out and rushed upstairs to the safety of their room, where she closed the door and put a chair against it as there was no lock.

She breathed in. This was a nightmare. Surely in the morning, please God, she would wake and know that it was.

Downstairs in the supper room, Marie-Louise saw Rosamund leave the room and went across to William and put her arms round his neck. He pulled her on to his knee and nuzzled into her shoulder.

'Now then, Jack,' she murmured into his ear, 'and you a newly married man, to a real lady no less.' She nibbled his ear lobe. 'And you with a taste for something more hearty.'

He put his finger over her lips and she opened her mouth to enclose it. 'We need to go up in the world,' he whispered. 'We'll be all right, Lou, trust me.'

She sucked on his finger and said softly, 'Promises! Well, you won't forget us on the way up, will you, Jack?'

The next morning Rosamund awoke to find she was alone in the bed and only on her side had the blankets been disturbed. She heaved a sigh of relief. William had obviously been too drunk to get up the stairs. Someone tapped on the door and a female voice called out that she had brought breakfast.

'One moment, please.' Rosamund got out of bed and put a wrap round her shoulders before moving the chair and opening the door.

'Mr Ramsey said he'd be up in a few minutes, ma'am. He's been seeing to the hosses.' The maid put a tray down on the bed. There was a pot of tea, a milk jug, two cups and several slices of toast.

'Thank you.'

As the girl left, William came bounding up the stairs. 'Good morning!' he said, as fresh faced as if he had never taken a drink in his life, and kissed her cheek. 'You were fast asleep when I came up last night, so I didn't disturb you. I slept in the chair.'

'Really?' She didn't believe him. He couldn't have got into the room without waking her, but she was grateful that he knew he had transgressed.

'Come on then,' he said jovially. 'Tea and toast and then a hearty breakfast before we go off to the races. I want to show off my beautiful wife. I think you'll bring me luck, so we'll have a flutter or two, eh? What do you think?'

'I don't know,' she said. 'I've never been. Is it exciting?'

'Nothing quite like it. And we'll make everyone sit up and take notice when we arrive in the curricle.'

And in spite of herself she couldn't help but smile at his enthusiasm and hope that today would be better.

Downstairs, the inn was as busy as it had been on their arrival the day before. Adding to the babble of conversation was the crowing and cackle of cocks and hens, fastened in crates, and the yapping and warning growls of dogs tied beneath their masters' feet.

'This is a favourite meeting place for the local farmers,' William shouted above the clamour. 'It's where they seal their market deals.'

'I see.' Rosamund followed him into the room where they had eaten supper. The table was laid for breakfast, and as she sat down the maid came in with fresh coffee. Isaac followed her with two plates of bacon, eggs, sausage and chops.

'Thank you,' she murmured. 'But I'm afraid I can't eat all that.'

'Eat what you can and I'll finish it.' William was already reaching for the loaf of bread in the centre of the table and tearing off a chunk. 'Best breakfast in York,' he grinned. 'Isn't that right, Isaac?'

'So I'm told, but not for me to say.' The landlord leaned towards him. 'Put me a guinea on Brass Monkey, will you, Jack, and take the wager out of the winnings?'

'Is it a good bet?' William asked, and when told that it was he agreed that he'd have a flutter too.

They set off after breakfast, William telling her how she was going to love it, and when they reached the Knavesmire Rosamund was quite thrilled with the atmosphere. Besides the racehorses and their trainers, there were more people than she had ever seen in her life, thronging the side shows that had been set up to entertain them with tumblers and clowns, and inspecting stalls selling trinkets and greasy-smelling food.

William found her a place near the rails and said he was going to put on some bets. 'I'll be back in a minute. We always meet friends round here.'

Rosamund looked towards the grandstand. 'Can we not sit down under cover?'

'Not unless you've a few guineas to spare,' he said. 'That's for the gentry, not the likes of us, unless you're very rich, Rosamund.' He smiled. 'But we want to be in the midst of what's going on, don't we?'

He walked away towards a crowd of people clustered about a man in a very tall top hat who stood beside a large board with numbers and names written on it. Rosamund turned to lean on the fence and gazed down the long stretch of track. She hoped she was going to enjoy the day, but she couldn't help thinking that she'd rather be at home. She rather feared that her life was changing, and she wasn't at all sure it was for the better.

Someone was calling 'Rosie, Rosie' and then 'Rosamund'. She turned, and with a sinking heart saw Marie-Louise and her escort from the night before bearing down on her. That was when she knew for certain that life as she had known it was definitely changing for the worse.

Margriet had stood on the steps until the Percivals had turned the corner into Whitefriargate, before going inside and closing the door. She listened. There was not a sound in the house except for the chink of crockery coming from the kitchen. They'll be making a cup of tea now that everyone has gone.

She suddenly felt very alone and wondered what she might do. She'd brought several books home from the library, but she didn't want to read, not yet; she'd look at them tonight. She decided to go out and have a look around town, just as she used to with Papa. Maybe she would see the boy Billy and his friends.

She raced upstairs to change, ignoring what Mrs Percival had said. I'll run if I want to, she thought rebelliously. What did she know about anything? Taking off her muslin dress, she threw it on her bed and looked in her wardrobe. After a moment she brought out a plain skirt she had worn for school, a white blouse and her 'everyday coat', as her mother called it, which was rather short for her now, coming down to mid-calf. She didn't care. She wouldn't see anyone she knew, except perhaps the Sandersons, and they wouldn't notice what she was wearing. In fact, she rather hoped that she might see Julia or Florrie and be invited to tea.

She crept downstairs, deciding that she wouldn't tell Mrs Simmonds that she was going out. She might try to stop her, or tell Jane to go with her, and she didn't want that. Quietly she opened the door and closed it behind her, glad that the kitchen window didn't look over the front of the street. She ran swiftly down the steps, and without in the least planning her route sped off in the direction of Land of Green Ginger.

CHAPTER THIRTY-SIX

Rosamund arrived home just after seven on the evening of the third day, hammering on the door because she didn't have a key. She had never needed one.

'Prepare a hot bath immediately,' she told an astonished Jane, who had opened the door to her, 'and tell my daughter I'm home.'

Jane dipped her knee. 'Begging your pardon, ma'am, but Miss Margriet is out.'

'Out! Out where? It's after seven o'clock!'

'We think she's gone to 'fair, ma'am.'

'What? Alone? Send Mrs Simmonds to me immediately.' Rosamund dropped the blanket she was carrying on the floor, took off her coat and hat and threw those on top of it. 'What on earth is happening? The world has gone mad.' She put her hands to her head; she was shaking with fear and anger and with the battering she had had in the coach from York.

She hadn't expected to spend two whole days at the races. On the evening of the second day William had been very downcast and she guessed that he had lost heavily on the horses. As he drove them back to the inn she had told him she would like to go home. He'd muttered that it was too late now and she replied sharply that she knew that but would like to return to Hull the following day.

'No,' he'd said. 'You don't understand. We can't! These are the last races of the season. I have to make up my losses.'

'And I have a young daughter at home,' she had replied coldly. 'I wish to return.'

He hadn't looked at her but stared straight over the horses' heads as he told her that in that case she would have to catch the coach, as he was going to stay.

She had been shocked. At first she couldn't believe what he was saying, but glancing at him she saw that he was quite serious and not speaking in jest. 'Very well,' she had said, hoping that he would change his mind. 'That is what I will do.'

But he didn't change his mind. He told her he would escort her to the afternoon diligence and make sure she was safely on board before he left her. Except that he didn't, and had asked the landlord to escort her as he'd left early for the races; nor had he told her that the coach journey would take six hours. This information was given to her by Isaac, who was most attentive to her well-being; having discovered that she had not travelled alone before, he had packed a parcel of bread and ham to save her the effort of competing for attention when the coach stopped for refreshments.

She had done some serious thinking as she travelled, huddled beneath the blanket that Margriet had so thoughtfully suggested she bring, and concluded that the only thing in her new husband's favour was that he had not yet ventured into her bed. She would tell him that he could live in York if he pleased but that she would stay in Hull and he could visit her whenever he felt so inclined. She would not give him the opportunity of saying that she refused to live with him.

But now, trembling with fatigue as she sipped the cup of sweet tea that Mrs Simmonds had brought her and waited for Jane and Lily to fill her bath, she wondered what to do about Margriet. Should she inform the constable that her daughter was missing, or wait as Mrs Simmonds had suggested, for Margriet had gone out at the same time last evening and returned two hours later.

'We think she's gone to 'fair, ma'am,' the house-keeper had said, unconsciously echoing Jane. 'I'm really sorry, but short of locking her in her room, I don't know what else I could have done. When she came back last night she told me that she had been with friends, so mebbe she's gone with them again.'

But who were they, Rosamund wondered. The Sandersons? She would have her bath, and if Margriet hadn't returned by then she'd send Jane round to ask if she was there. Her eyes filled with tears and her lips trembled as she realized she had no one to ask for advice. She thought she had never been so unhappy in her life, while the loss of Frederik seemed to loom larger than it had ever done, even when she was first told of his tragic death.

The door was locked when Margriet arrived home at eight o'clock and she had to ring the bell.

Mrs Simmonds answered the door instead of Jane. 'Your mother is home, Miss Margriet,' she said, 'and not well pleased. With any of us,' she added irritably.

Margriet went into the sitting room. Her mother was flushed and seemed exhausted. 'Are you unwell, Mama?'

'Just extremely tired and very anxious. Where ever have you been? Mrs Simmonds didn't know where you were. It was most irresponsible of you not to tell her.'

'I'm sorry, Mama,' Margriet said penitently. 'I've made some new friends and they asked me to go to the Hull Fair with them – and oh, it was wonderful.'

'But alone, Margriet! You should not have gone alone!'

'I wasn't alone, Mama. I told you, I was with friends!'

Rosamund was too tired to argue. She was worn out with the journey, from being jolted and racketed about on the potholed road, and was longing for her bed.

When Margriet had sneaked out after the newly-weds had departed she'd walked swiftly towards Land of Green Ginger, turned the corner and then stood as usual as if waiting for someone, looking up at the window of the Lindegroens' house. The curtains looked rather grey and she hoped they hadn't gone away, as there were many questions she wanted to ask.

She waited a few more minutes but Anneliese did not appear, so she decided to walk towards Market Place. She had gone only a few steps when she heard someone hailing her and turned to see the two girls who had been with Billy on the day she had walked to the pier.

'Hello,' they chorused. 'We've seen you before. We met you with Billy.'

'Yes,' she said. 'I'm Margriet. Do you live round here?'

'No,' one of the girls said, and grinned. 'We're just passing by.'

'Do you?' the other one asked. 'Did you say you lived in Whitefriargate?'

'Yes, I did,' she said. 'I do. Where are you going?'

'To Market Place to see if any of 'gypsies have come.'

'Gypsies? Why?'

'Cos 'fair's coming tomorrow and 'gypsies generally come first and bring their hosses and sometimes they let us have a ride.'

'Oh, of course! It's October,' Margriet said. 'I'd forgotten about the fair. My father used to take me when I was very little.' A sob caught in her throat. It seemed such a long time ago.

'Come with us if you like,' one of the girls said, and Margriet said she'd love to and asked their names. Betty and Mabel, they said, and they were both fourteen.

'I'm nearly fourteen,' Margriet said. 'At least, I will be next January.'

'Come on then,' Mabel said. 'You'll be all right with us.'

She had been all right with them, and they had met up with Billy and some of his friends. They also met the gypsies, who allowed the two girls to have a ride on the ponies, and they shrieked with excitement as the men ran alongside them egging them on to go faster. They had offered Margriet a ride too, but she was too shy and shrank back and they'd smiled and called her a little rawnie. Betty told her later that it meant little lady. They asked her to come with them the next day to see the fair folk arrive and she said she would if her mother would allow it, but her mother didn't come home. Once more she had slipped out in the afternoon and met the others on the corner of Parliament Street and watched as the tumbling clowns, the drummers, the trumpeting elephants, and the roaring lions and tigers in their cages processed down Whitefriargate towards Market Place. She had a moment of fright when she saw Jane and Lily watching too, but they didn't see her in the crowd. It had been a wonderful day, and because she had had the forethought to take a sixpence from her purse before leaving home she had offered to buy tickets to see a side show. Billy, Betty and Mabel had gazed at her in astonishment and shaken their heads and looked at each other. Then Mabel had become the spokesperson and said that if Margriet really wanted to spend the sixpence, would she buy a hot potato that they could share?

'Is sixpence not enough to buy three?' she had asked, and when they said it was she had handed the coin over to Mabel. It was then that Margriet had learned that her new friends not only had no money, but did not have anywhere to live either. They slept wherever they could find shelter, in a basement or a shop doorway; for food they begged for coppers or ran errands, and in the winter went to the soup kitchens that were run by Mrs Sanderson and other ladies.

'She's great is Sandy,' Billy said, scraping the potato flesh from the skin with his teeth. 'We all love her, and Immi as well. They never forget us.'

They didn't buy tickets for any of the events because none of them had any money, but they had shown her how to lift a flap of a tent and creep in to watch without paying until they were spotted and thrown out. She had been scared of doing that as she knew that it was wrong, but nevertheless it was very exciting.

They are vagrants, she thought as she lay sleepless in her bed. She had come across the word in one of the books she had borrowed from the lending library, and later she discovered many other things about the town she lived in that amazed and delighted her.

Papa was right about the king's garden and knocking old houses down to make Parliament Street, when he told me to imagine how it might have been before. What was it he had said? See it in your mind's eye. What a strange thing to say and yet I could – I can. Thinking of her two days spent at the fair, she turned down the lamp and snuggled further into bed. The only question mark was over the name of Land of Green Ginger, because in the book no one seemed to know for sure why it was so called. She gave a secret smile. *But I know.*

But she hadn't told her mother all of this for she knew she wouldn't understand, and besides, Mama seems to be unhappy, and where is Mr Ramsey now?

*

Two days later William turned up, all smiles as if nothing untoward had happened. He greeted Margriet cordially, stayed three days and then went off again, saying he had business to attend to. He continued coming and going over the next few weeks, each time sleeping in the guest room, and Rosamund thought she could cope with that. He was with them on Christmas Day but didn't return until the New Year, on the very day that she received a letter from her accountant.

'I will see him, dearest,' William told her when she said that Mr Clayton wanted to call to discuss several matters. 'No need for you to worry about it.'

'I would be grateful if you would,' she said. 'I really don't have a head for figures.'

William kissed her cheek. 'Why don't you visit my sister whilst I talk to him,' he suggested. 'She was only saying the last time I saw her that you haven't visited in weeks.'

'It's true, I haven't.' The fact was, Rosamund had thought that Lydia had been rather cool towards her when she had called after the wedding. Or perhaps it was her fault; she had been cross with William and perhaps was blaming Lydia. 'I'll send Jane with a card to say I will call, and I'll take Margriet with me.'

'Yes, do,' he agreed. 'It's time Margriet grew up and took her place in the adult world. She's becoming rather wild, I fear.'

Rosamund looked at him and wondered why he had said that, and what Frederik would have made of it, for he had thought his daughter could do no wrong.

It was a bitterly cold day when Rosamund and a reluctant Margriet set out to walk the short distance to High Street where the Percivals lived. Margriet didn't want to call on them, but neither did she want to stay at home with Mr Ramsey, who, to add to her mistrust of him, had completely forgotten her fourteenth birthday.

A man was coming towards them as they walked down Silver Street, and he lifted his hat as they approached. 'Mrs Van— erm, Ramsey,' he corrected himself. 'I was on my way to see you. Did you not receive my letter?'

'I did,' she said. 'Mr Ramsey is at home and he will attend to any matters arising; you know how confused I get with figures.'

'Ah!' he said, putting his head on one side. 'Well, if you're sure? There are, erm, important matters to be attended to.'

She gave him a perfunctory smile. 'Perfectly sure, Mr Clayton. Good day to you.'

CHAPTER THIRTY-SEVEN

'No, nothing untoward,' William told Rosamund on her return from her visit to Lydia. 'Clayton suggested that we might like to sell some of the shares in the company as business is good and the price has risen.'

'In Frederik's company, you mean? But why would we do that?'

'Oh, purely to claim the profit.' He smiled. 'We could buy something, some new clothes, perhaps, if you would like? A piece of jewellery, some gewgaw for Margriet. I forgot her birthday, didn't I?' He pulled a downward mouth.

'Mmm, you did. But there's enough money in my allowance if I wanted to buy new clothes, and I don't. I have enough.'

'Oh, but that is your personal allowance. Clayton suggested that if some of the shares were sold, there would be a nice little nest egg to spend.'

'I see. What do you think, William?'

'Well,' he said seriously, 'shares and business stock go up and down, and at the moment I think we'd be as well selling some.' He lifted a finger. 'Not all of them, of course, just whilst they are so high. We'd be sorry if we didn't and they dropped in price.'

'If that happened we'd lose money on them, wouldn't we?'

'Exactly!' He rubbed his short bristly beard. 'What do you think, shall I instruct him?'

'Oh, dear. I don't know. Yes, if you think it wise to do so. You know more than I about this kind of thing. Yes. Tell him we'll sell. He must think it's a good idea if he made the suggestion.'

William took out his pocket watch and checked the time. 'I'll call round now and tell him, and he can instruct the broker before the end of day.'

'Is that new?' Rosamund asked. 'I thought you had a silver one.'

'What?' He stood up to leave. 'Oh, my Albert chain!' He fingered the heavy gold links. 'No, I've had it a long time. A family heirloom.'

Rosamund was perplexed; she had meant the gold watch, not the chain. It was a moment before she realized that William must have made a mistake – Prince Albert had set the fashion for wearing a chain so William's couldn't have been a family heirloom, because the queen and Albert had only been married for ten years. She gave a little shrug. Perhaps the watch was a family heirloom. A misunderstanding, nothing more.

When he returned, William was furious. 'I wanted to get off to York first thing tomorrow,' he said brusquely, 'but that stupid fellow says that the broker will need your signature to sell the shares. I pointed out that you were married to me now and therefore I could deal with it, but he says not!'

'Oh, there's no need for you to stay if you need

to be in York. When he comes with the papers he'll show me where I should sign.'

'No, I'll wait. Another day won't matter, I suppose.' He chewed on his lip. 'He could lose me a business deal, that's all.'

'Could I not sign something to say that you may deal with any of my concerns?'

'I can in any case,' he barked. 'I don't need your say-so! It's the law of the land. What's yours is mine. It's just that your former husband seems to have made it awkward regarding the sale of shares. I'll have to speak to the lawyer and find out what's going on.'

'I'm sorry,' she gasped. 'I'm sure Frederik only did it for the best. He was a very considerate man.'

He came up close and breathed into her face. 'I dare say he was, but he can't change the law.'

Rosamund was shocked by his attitude, and rather afraid. Although he didn't touch her, she could see how angry he was, but why? She knew that women had few rights, every woman knew that; Frederik was unusual in that he had never used a penny of the dowry she had brought to their marriage, always saying that by rights that should be hers and not his, and he would support her and any children they might have, and he had. Her dowry, as far as she knew, was still intact.

Mr Clayton brought the share papers for her signature the following day. 'I do beg your pardon, Mr Ramsey, and yours too, Mrs Ramsey, for the inconvenience this might have caused, but the matter of buying and selling shares isn't my field at all. It's the broker who does that and he's instructed by Mr

Webster, who has the overall jurisdiction. However, I understand that there is a ready buyer for these and so the monies will be in your bank almost immediately.'

Rosamund signed where he indicated and wondered why Mr Clayton should have suggested they sell the shares if it wasn't his field; it seemed most odd. It was also strange, she thought, that he seemed nervous of William and barely looked at him as he said goodbye.

'I'm getting rid of him,' William said when the door had closed behind him. 'He's useless. I'll look after the accounts from now on. Why should we pay him for adding up figures when I can do it just as well?'

Rosamund nodded. 'Of course. If that is what you think.'

'It is,' he said bluntly. 'And now I'm off. I've wasted enough time already.' His coat was hanging over the banister rail and he picked it up and turned to give Rosamund a peck on the cheek. 'Lots to do. I'll be back in about a week,' and he was gone.

It was three weeks before he returned and he explained that he had been extremely busy. She asked him what he had been doing and he replied vaguely that he had fingers in many pies. For amusement only, he told her, for he didn't really need an occupation as such, but he liked to be engaged in new projects. He didn't ask her to return to York with him and she didn't mind that in the least.

On the anniversary of their wedding in October he insisted on taking her to a country hotel near

Bridlington to celebrate and gave her a gold neck-lace that delighted her. A week later he observed that the catch seemed loose and insisted on return-ing it to the jewellers. She told him that there were excellent jewellers in Silver Street who would be able to adjust it; she hadn't noticed that there was a fault, but he said that it was an expensive piece of jewellery and he wanted a replacement.

It was the month the Hull Fair came, but this time Margriet asked her mother if it was all right for her to visit it with her friends. Rosamund con-sidered that Margriet's behaviour had changed for the better, for she spent a good deal of time reading in her room and sometimes sewed with her mother in the afternoon, so she agreed that she could, providing she went early in the evening and returned no later than eight o'clock.

Rosamund had not met Margriet's friends; she had suggested that they might be invited to tea one afternoon but Margriet had refused on their behalf. 'They are working people, Mama,' she had said in excuse. 'They don't have time for tea.'

That hadn't been the right response, as her mother had then asked what kind of work they did and Margriet was flummoxed. She could hardly say that the girls ran errands or that Billy and the other boys asked for odd jobs in the wood yards or the stables because her mother would then declare that they were not suitable companions for her.

In the week running up to Christmas, Rosamund asked Margriet to walk with her to the bank as she wanted to draw out some money. Frederik had always given the servants a cash bonus at Christmas, but she, unused to handling money, had forgotten about it, and although she had increased their annual wage they hadn't received a bonus since Frederik's death. Now she decided that she should show her appreciation for their faithful service.

Frederik had used Samuel Smith's bank in White-friargate for many years. It was very busy, and they sat down to wait for the queue of businessmen and tradesmen to conclude their transactions. When a teller became free Rosamund asked to make a with-drawal. He took out a ledger and ran his finger down a list, cleared his throat, said, 'If you would excuse me for just a moment, Mrs Ramsey?' and disappeared through a door behind his desk.

She waited, tapping her foot, and gave a little shrug at Margriet at her side. The teller came back all smiles, and asked if she would kindly wait a few more minutes as Mr Blackstone would like a word.

'Mr Blackstone?'

'The manager, madam.' The clerk lowered his voice. 'He won't keep you long.'

They sat down again. 'Why does he want a word, do you think?' Rosamund murmured, more to her-self than Margriet. 'Is that usual? Perhaps he is new and wishes to introduce himself.'

Margriet shook her head. She had no idea.

A few minutes later another door behind the teller's desk opened and a man in a black frock coat and pinstriped trousers came towards them. He gave a courtly bow and said, 'Mrs Ramsey? Good morning. I don't believe I have had the pleasure of meeting you. I knew your late husband Mr Vander-groene very well. Such a loss, such a loss.'

Rosamund nodded. 'This is our daughter, Margriet Vandergroene. You wished to see me?'

'Indeed, indeed. If you would kindly step into my office? Nothing untoward, ma'am, just a little misunderstanding I'm sure.'

Rosamund looked sharply at him, but didn't say anything. Margriet followed her into the office.

'Will you be content to have your daughter with you?' Mr Blackstone asked when he'd closed the door behind them. 'There are one or two – erm – financial matters to discuss. Ideally Mr Ramsey should be here, but as you are a long-standing customer we can make an exception.'

'He's away. On business,' she said coldly. 'What is this about? I simply came in to make a withdrawal to pay my servants a Christmas bonus.'

'Most commendable,' he said suavely. 'But please, won't you be seated? Was it a large amount, Mrs Ramsey, for if not, I'm sure we can accommodate—'

'Not large,' she said, sitting down on one of the two chairs opposite him. 'Why do you ask?'

He seated himself behind his desk and clasped his fingers together, looking from her to Margriet and back. 'The hard fact, Mrs Ramsey, is that there is nothing in the account to withdraw. It is quite empty.'

She gave a little laugh. 'But that's ridiculous! How can it be empty? It is not so long since we sold some shares – surely the money from those went into the account?'

He looked down at the ledger in front of him; there were two separate columns of figures, one column much longer than the other. He shook his head. 'There are no recent deposits, Mrs Ramsey, only withdrawals, promissory notes and bills of exchange, some of them on demand. The account is overdrawn.'

Rosamund leaned forward and whispered, 'What are they for, these promissory notes and bills of exchange?'

'Some payments go back over a year,' he said. 'The first, which took rather a large slice of the capital, was for a—' He peered down at the ledger. 'A curricle, would it be? And pair. Accommodation and wedding feast; racing expenses at York, Doncaster and Beverley; a gold watch and chain; many other items.' He looked up sympathetically. 'A gold necklace!'

Rosamund touched her throat; the necklace had not yet been returned. William had said the jeweller still had it. Blackstone saw the gesture and murmured, 'Perhaps it could be sold to offset some of the expenses?'

She shook her head. 'I haven't got it any longer,' she said throatily, and felt Margriet's hand creep into hers. 'Has everything gone? Is there nothing left?'

'Nothing with this bank,' he said softly. 'Whether there are accounts with other banks I couldn't say. Mr Vandergroene banked with us for many years; to my knowledge he didn't bank elsewhere.' He took a deep breath. 'Mrs Ramsey, I might be out of order in saying this and of course I know nothing of your present husband's circumstances, but if this lapse is not just a matter of careless accounting might I suggest . . .'

Rosamund felt faint. Accounting? Mr Clayton had asked to see her but William had insisted on dealing with him himself. And William had told him that his services were no longer required.

'Mrs Ramsey?' Mr Blackstone was saying as if from a great distance. 'Are you all right? Would you like a glass of water?'

Rosamund shook her head but one was brought anyway. Margriet held the glass to her lips whilst she sipped and she heard him saying, 'And so, if you have any concerns at all, I would suggest that you speak to your lawyer, who will be able to advise you. If, as seems likely, your assets have been eroded, your husband is obliged to maintain you, although not your daughter as she is not his. It is usual for a married woman to have control of any household contents, but other than that, well . . .' He lifted his hands in a gesture of negation.

'Speak to your lawyer, Mrs Ramsey, if indeed he will allow you to consult him without the presence of your husband. Speak to your lawyer immediately.'

CHAPTER THIRTY-EIGHT

'Ask Jane to bring a tray of tea to my room, will you, Margriet?' Rosamund asked as they mounted the steps to the front door. 'I need to sit quietly and think.'

Margriet did as she asked and then went up to her own room and stood gazing out of the window. Her mother was shaking as they left the bank and had had to take Margriet's arm. The account was empty, the manager had said. What did it mean? Could they not afford the next meal? How would they pay the servants? Expenditure had never been discussed, so she had no idea how matters stood. Had her father left money for them and Mr Ramsey had spent it?

Mr Blackstone had read out a list of items and they had all been purchased by Mr Ramsey. Her bracelet hadn't been mentioned. She never wore it; it was still in its box in a drawer. She turned away from the window and went to the chest of drawers, but the box wasn't there. It had been in the same place since it was first given to her, and now it had gone.

She moved the guard from the fire and sat

down. Were they destitute, like Billy and the other children who roamed the streets? But they had the house, they had somewhere to live, and surely they must receive something from Papa's business? But then she was struck by what her mother had said: they had recently sold some shares. Did that mean that they could no longer rely on an income from the company?

The clatter of wheels and a whinnying down in the street alerted her and she rushed back to the window. Ramsey's curricle, the one he said he'd bought for her mother, was outside and he was jumping down and hailing a boy to come and hold the reins. It was Billy. She stood back so as not to be seen, but saw Ramsey shaking a finger at Billy, who touched his cap. Ramsey took the steps at a run, opened the door with his key, and slamming it behind him roared, 'Rosamund! Rosamund! Where are you? I want to speak to you.'

Margriet opened her door a crack and peered over the banister. Her mother's door on the landing below opened and Margriet saw only her back as she came out and stood at the top of the stairs.

'And I want to speak to you too, William,' she said in a low voice. 'Most urgently.'

Margriet opened her door wider and, slipping out, knelt on the landing to see but not be seen.

'I need some ready money,' Ramsey said abruptly. 'I need it now. How much have you got in the house?'

Margriet watched her mother descend the stairs. 'Ready money?' she heard her say. 'What does that mean? You told me that what was mine was yours; well, it seems that what I had you have spent.'

Margriet could see Ramsey's face quite clearly and saw a flush burn his cheeks. 'What?' He frowned. 'What are you talking about?'

'I've been to the bank.' Her mother continued slowly down the stairs until she was just two steps above him. 'I went to get some *ready money* to give to the servants as a Christmas bonus, but it seems that there is nothing left. The account is overdrawn.'

'Hah,' he scoffed. 'What have you been spending it on, Rosie? You naughty girl.'

'Please don't speak to me in that manner.' Her voice was icy. 'I am not a servant girl. My name is Rosamund and I have not spent my money!'

'Oh, hoity toity,' he sneered. 'May I remind you, madam, that it isn't your money, but mine to do with whatever I like. I have had a few expenses, it is true.'

'But the shares that you sold?' she interrupted. 'Where is the money from those? It is not in the bank account.'

'No. Not in that bank account. I've decided not to use Smith's bank. They are not very accommodating.' He looked at his fingernails. 'So, you haven't any cash lying around?'

'Certainly not,' she said sharply.

He put his foot on the first step. 'You would tell me if you had, wouldn't you, Rosamund? You wouldn't hide it from me? No?' He gave a shake of his head. 'Of course you wouldn't. Mmm, well, pity. Oh, by the way, we'll have to sell the house. I was hoping to avoid it, but it can't be helped. We'll get a good price for it, though, and get you something smaller. Or you could rent somewhere; that would be a better idea, less capital expenditure. In the meantime we can get a loan on the strength of it.'

Margriet put her hand to her mouth. Sell the house! She saw her mother sink down on the step and whisper something that she couldn't hear. Ramsey was looking down at her. Then he said, 'Sorry, Rosamund. I'm not cut out to be a husband. But you were quite a catch.' He pursed his mouth. 'I was attracted to you, don't think I wasn't, but it helped that you were well provided for. Don't worry, I'll make sure you're all right, but we'll have to sell, you do realize that, don't you? You wouldn't want the disgrace of a bankrupt husband. I'll see my lawyer tomorrow and instruct him.' He paused. 'I won't stay now; you probably don't want me to in any case. But when this is all sorted out I'll take you off somewhere for a few days, perhaps in the spring, back to that hotel near Bridlington. You liked that, didn't you?'

Margriet slipped back into her room and a minute later the front door banged. She looked out of the window and saw Ramsey run down the steps. He fingered his waistcoat pocket, brought out a coin and tossed it to the waiting Billy, who caught it, looked at it and then at the man who had given it, muttered something, and tossed it in turn to a young lad who was waiting on the opposite side of the street.

She watched Ramsey climb into the driving seat, and as he raised his whip he looked up at the house and must have seen her face at the window. He grinned, cracked the whip and drove away.

Rosamund said she didn't want anything to eat that evening, and stayed in her room. Margriet told Jane that her mother was unwell and asked her to take a bowl of soup and a slice of bread and butter up to her. She herself would also eat in her room, so there was no need to make a fire in the dining room.

Later, she went to Rosamund's room to say goodnight and found her mother already in bed, her hair loose about her shoulders. She looked sad and vulnerable.

'I don't know what we shall do, Margriet,' she said tearfully. 'Where will we get an income if all the shares are gone? If the house is sold, I fear we won't see a penny of the money. I don't know which way to turn.'

'Would Grandmother Vandergroene help us?' Margriet suggested. She knew that her mother hadn't seen her own parents since Frederik's death; when she had written to tell them of it, Rosamund's mother had replied to say that they hoped Frederik had provided for her and her child as they were unable to assist them.

'I wouldn't think so,' her mother said wearily. 'My fault, for I haven't kept in touch with her.'

'But I have, Mama. I write every month. She wouldn't want us to be destitute.' The word keeps cropping up, Margriet thought. I think that destitution is in front of us.

'Do you?' Her mother seemed surprised. 'I didn't know.' Since her marriage she had failed to notice that Margriet and her Dutch grandmother had been corresponding regularly. Oma was the one

326

person who seemed to understand how much she missed her father, Margriet thought, and she always closed her letters with the wish or promise that they would meet again soon. If they did have to sell the house, she would write and tell her and ask her advice.

She decided that she too would go to bed and read. She was absorbed in the history books of old Hull and had found a section on Whitefriargate and why it was so called. She snuggled down beneath her blankets, intent on thinking of something other than the predicament in which she and her mother found themselves. Reading would take her mind off it. If she had to find employment, perhaps she could be a governess like Miss Ripley, she thought, and she could only do that if she absorbed knowledge.

She turned a page; there was an illustration of monks with tonsured heads and dressed in flowing white robes. They were Carmelite friars but often called White Friars because of the colour of their robes. 'We practically live on Whitefriargate,' she murmured to herself, 'and I never thought to question why.'

Sleep was beginning to overtake her but she kept on reading, blinking her eyes to keep awake. Her thoughts began to wander. She pictured the old monks and wondered where their monastery had been; she thought of Miss Ripley and whether she could ask her advice about obtaining a position. But not yet, her common sense told her; you are not old enough. So where would they live if Mr Ramsey sold the house? Who would take them in? She closed her eyes. Who did they know?

A voice whispered in her ear and at first she couldn't understand the words; then it became clearer. 'Come and live with us, Margriet, and bring your *moeder* too.'

She sat up. 'Anneliese?' she whispered. 'Is it you?' The room was dim but firelight shadows danced on the walls and she could see the girl quite clearly sitting in the chair by the fire. She was older now and had lost her round childish features. Beneath a white winged cap, two long fair plaits hung over her embroidered bodice and she wore a white apron over her black skirt. Plain wooden clogs were on her feet.

'Anneliese,' Margriet whispered. 'I haven't seen you for such a long time. Where have you been?'

Anneliese turned to her. 'I've been here all the time,' she said softly. 'Growing up just like you. I'm sorry you lost your papa, but you must be strong. I have spoken to *mijn moeder en vader* and they say you can come and help me in the garden and your *moeder* can help in the kitchen. Will you come?'

Margriet saw again in her mind the king's garden they had walked in when she was so much younger; the small circular lawns and the neat box hedges that surrounded them, the trees heavy with blossom and the bright patches of flowers. She heard the birdsong and the voices of the ladies and gentlemen of the court as they strolled in the sun.

'Where is the king?' she asked. 'Should we ask permission to visit his garden again?'

'No.' The room seemed to be getting darker and Anneliese was diminishing and becoming difficult to see. 'We are too old now to play in his garden, Margriet. You can help me in our garden.'

'But what shall I do? Anneliese,' she pleaded, 'don't go! What shall I do in your garden?'

Anneliese smiled as she gradually faded from sight. 'Why, grow things! That's what you do in a garden; we'll plant flowers and shrubs, and tulip bulbs and ginger!'

CHAPTER THIRTY-NINE

Christmas passed quietly. William Ramsey didn't come and Margriet and her mother dined alone; they ate sparingly as Rosamund was nervous about owing money to the butcher, but neither did she want to alert the servants to their predicament. It was January when Ramsey came again. For some reason he couldn't get his key into the lock and he had to ring the bell. Mrs Simmonds answered the door and he strode past her into the hallway, bellowing, 'What's going on? Rosamund! Rosamund! I need to speak to you.' Plainly he had been drinking; his face was flushed and there was the smell of strong ale on him.

Mrs Simmonds calmly folded her hands in front of her. 'Good day, Mr Ramsey. Please follow me, sir; 'mistress is in 'sitting room. She has a visitor, but asked that you be shown through if you called.'

'Called? What's that supposed to mean? Get out of my way.'

Rosamund was sitting by the fire and Margriet opposite her. On the sofa sat the visitor: the lawyer Hugh Webster. He didn't rise when Ramsey barged in, but gave a smug smile. 'I rather thought you'd be here before the day was out, Ramsey, but I'm afraid you're wasting your time. I explained everything thoroughly this morning.'

Margriet watched from her chair. Events had moved swiftly since Ramsey's last visit. She had gone with her mother to see the lawyer as Mr Blackstone had advised, and Hugh Webster was more than willing to discuss their situation. It had transpired that since then Ramsey had consulted his own York lawyer, who had asked him to obtain a copy of his wife's deceased husband's will before he put the wheels in motion for the sale of the house. Ramsey came to Hull but not to see his wife; he had made an appointment to consult Webster. When Webster was advised by his clerk of the pending appointment and the reason for it, he came immediately to visit Rosamund and brought a locksmith with him to change the lock on the door.

'Forgive me, dear lady, but I can't stay now,' he'd told her. 'I am in a great rush as I have much reading matter to peruse, but trust me when I say that all is not lost. The money in the bank has gone, it is true, and you won't get that back, but do allow me to have your lock changed to protect the contents of your house. Mr Ramsey will most certainly come to see you after he has heard what I have to say.'

Rosamund was very confused; Webster seemed to be very buoyed up by the whole situation, but she allowed the lock to be changed as he suggested, and told him that she wasn't so much worried about the house contents as about the house itself. 'Mr Ramsey wants to sell it!' she exclaimed.

The lawyer had nodded sagely. 'So my clerk

331

informed me when Ramsey made the appointment. We have heard many rumours about Mr Ramsey, sad to say. My clerk, who is the soul of discretion, always has his ear to the ground – not that you would know it, for he has the look of a very mild and unassuming kind of man. I will call on you as soon as I've spoken to Ramsey. If he arrives before I do, then stay calm and act as if you know nothing. It would be a good idea to have your daughter with you.'

As Rosamund didn't know anything, the second part of his instruction would not be difficult to follow, but keeping calm was a different matter altogether. Fortunately, Mr Webster reached the house a few minutes before William's tempestuous entry, and although her colour fluctuated she was able to maintain her composure.

'I'm going to fight this in the courts.' Ramsey pointed a stabbing finger at Webster and then at Rosamund. 'Don't think you can get away with it. In common law everything a woman brings to a marriage belongs to her husband.'

Rosamund clutched her hands together. 'Yes,' she murmured nervously. 'So I believe.'

Webster stretched out his legs. 'Have you come to bully your wife?' he asked mildly.

'No!' Ramsey retaliated. 'I only want what's legally mine. I won't leave her without a roof over her head.'

'Indeed you won't.' Webster sat up. 'You are obliged to ensure that she doesn't have to rely on the workhouse for accommodation.' Rosamund shuddered, but he went on, 'But as I have already explained to you, you can't have this one. This property belongs to her daughter, Miss Margriet Vandergroene, willed to her by her father, Frederik Vandergroene. The only money that Mrs Vandergroene has left from your spending spree is the dowry her father gave on the occasion of her first marriage, and is untouchable by anyone but her.'

Ramsey glowered at him. 'There'll be a way round it. I'll speak to my lawyer.'

'Jameson, isn't it?' Webster said. 'I have received a letter from him asking to see the original will, but he has no just cause to examine it. It is no concern of his, or yours either for that matter, but speak to him by all means. I remember him,' he murmured idly, as if recalling an incident. 'Did you not use him once before over a certain racing scandal? Did you escape prison that time?' He left the question hanging. 'I forget the details. He might take you on if he thinks you can afford his fees on a case he can't win.'

William Ramsey spun round, uttering an oath that made Rosamund blush and Margriet open her mouth in astonishment, and left, slamming the doors behind him.

Webster stood up. 'May I ring the bell for coffee, Mrs Vandergroene? I feel we may need some refreshment whilst I explain the ins and outs.'

'Oh! Forgive me.' Rosamund was flustered. 'Margriet, can you—'

Margriet was already on her feet and reaching for the bell on the wall. She went out to meet Jane in the hall. 'Ask Mrs Simmonds to serve coffee and Dutch biscuits, if Cook has made any, and to bring the brandy decanter and two glasses, please.' Then she stood for a moment outside the sitting room door to get her breath, and reach some understanding of what she had heard. '*Lieveling Papa*,' she whispered. 'Why did you think of that? How did you guess something like this might happen?' She felt choked by the knowledge that her father had had the foresight to make sure they were safe after he was gone.

Mr Webster looked up when she went back into the room. He was standing with his back to the fire and had lifted his coat tails, which made her smile.

'Now, my dear Miss Vandergroene. Do you recall when we first met?'

Margriet shook her head. 'No, sir, I don't think so.'

'Well, perhaps that's not surprising, for you were only' – he waved his hand vaguely on a level with his waist – 'so big! You were with your papa, and you told me about a king's palace in Hull. Do you remember now?'

'Yes,' she said, animated. 'Now I do. Papa had taken me to the Vittoria Hotel near the pier and bought me a dish of ice cream.'

He nodded. 'That was when I told your papa about a certain widow left penniless by her second husband, and the perils that can ensue if families are not well advised.' He turned to Rosamund. 'Frederik came to see me and we redrew his will in favour of Margriet; not doubting for a moment that she would take care of you if such a situation should arise, as indeed it has.' He sighed. 'Of course, we did not expect his death so early in life, but fortunately everything was in place before the tragedy occurred.'

Mrs Simmonds knocked and came in with the tray. Mr Webster looked on approvingly as Margriet poured coffee for her mother and herself and brandy for him. When she handed him the glass he swirled the liquid round and sniffed it appreciatively before taking a sip. 'Excellent,' he purred. 'Excellent.'

'Frederik had a good supplier,' Rosamund said. 'I drink very little myself, but I know that this is of top quality.' She made a mental note to send a couple of bottles to the lawyer's office.

'Now,' he said, sitting down again and turning to Rosamund. 'Some more good news. The shares that you held in Frederik's company and which Ramsey sold; he was told that there was a ready buyer who was prepared to buy immediately if the price was right, and since Ramsey needed the cash he sold them at below the market value. That buyer was myself, on Margriet's behalf, as instructed in Frederik's will. I have all the paperwork,' he added.

'So, if Margriet agrees, bearing in mind that as a minor she must be advised by me, you could buy back those shares with money from your dowry which has lain untouched since you first received it on the occasion of your first marriage. You do not have to decide now,' he said. 'There is no hurry.'

'But if I did that, could William claim them as he did before?' Rosamund asked diffidently.

Webster nodded. 'He could.'

'In that case, *no*,' she said. 'And yet I must have money, and there will be none from Mr Ramsey.' Rosamund drank her coffee and then picked up her glass. For almost the first time in her life she was thinking for herself. 'I can't divorce him, can I?'

He shook his head. 'Sadly, no. But he can divorce you if you give him cause, and if he chooses to and if he can afford to, which I doubt.'

That wasn't fair, Margriet thought. Why should women be so – so . . . She sought for the word to describe the position in which women could find themselves. Inferior, she thought, but said out loud, 'Subordinate! Is that the right word for women, Mr Webster, in relation to men?'

He gazed at her. 'I'm afraid it does describe the position in which they can find themselves, certainly.'

'In that case I might never marry,' she exclaimed. 'There would always be the worry that my husband could take everything.'

'No,' Rosamund objected. 'Not all men are like William Ramsey. Think of your papa, how he considered us constantly, more than I ever knew.' Tears began to run down her cheeks and she started to sob, with relief that her ordeal might be over and with regret that she had never understood how kind, considerate and understanding Frederik had been. 'There will be someone worthy of you, Margriet. Someone, somewhere.'

Margriet put down her cup and sat by her mother with her arm round her shoulder, and was surprised a few moments later when Rosamund, wiping away her tears, said, 'Margriet, would you mind stepping into the hall for a moment whilst I speak to Mr Webster privately? I want to say something not for your ears.'

Webster seemed surprised too but didn't comment, and Margriet left the room. As the door closed firmly behind her, Rosamund took a sobbing breath. 'Mr Webster, I hope you will forgive me, for I am unused to speaking of my private life, but it seems to me that I have very few options.' She moistened her lips with the tip of her tongue and looked down into her lap. 'I do not wish to spend the rest of my life tied to a man I neither admire nor trust. It might well be that Mr Ramsey will come to the conclusion that he doesn't want to be with me either, and so I would like to end this marriage.'

'But the scandal,' Webster said. 'Does that not bother you?'

She gave a little laugh. 'At one time the scandal would have been abhorrent to me, but not any more. It would be a nine-day wonder. However, there are no grounds for him to divorce me, so how can we get round that?'

He frowned. 'A divorce would be out of the question. Only the wealthy can contemplate it and it is a very difficult and contentious situation even for them. A separation, perhaps, on the grounds of infidelity, but I can't see you contemplating anything as sordid as setting up that kind of scene.' He shook his head. 'No, dear lady, I do not see how it can be done.'

'Well then, there is only one thing that I can think of, and that is to blackmail him with innuendo and insinuation.'

'I don't understand. About what?'

Rosamund hesitated. 'His manhood,' she said softly. 'I rather think that he might be vulnerable on that score.' She recalled the woman, Marie-Louise, at their wedding breakfast who she suspected he might have known intimately. Her voice dropped even lower. 'William Ramsey has not once shared my bed, not even on our wedding night.'

'Ah!' He let out a breath. 'An annulment, then, for non-consummation of marriage, and a mutually agreed parting. Yes, my brave lady, I think we can run with that. He wouldn't want it talked about; that would be a scandal indeed. He might turn it on its head, of course, and say that you were the one who denied him.'

'That is a possibility I am prepared to endure,' she said firmly. 'I will scupper Mr Ramsey's boat and see him flounder once and for all.'

CHAPTER FORTY

Margriet lay flat on her stomach on the floor of her room, her nose to one map and surrounded by several others. 'Oh, Papa,' she breathed. 'You were right all along. Here they are, just as you said.' It was as if he were in the room with her, smiling and cajoling and saying, *Well, of course I was right. Would I tell my little Daisy an untruth?*

She had persuaded the librarian to let her borrow the maps for one day only; he had become quite friendly since he realized that Margriet was serious about her desire to learn what had gone before, as history was his favourite subject.

'I'm interested in finding out where Henry VIII had his palace,' Margriet told him. 'I believe it belonged to a wealthy family before him.'

The librarian looked over his round-rimmed spectacles at her. 'Yes, the De la Poles. It was built for them when they lost their home to the sea at Ravenspurn.' He handed her the maps. 'You may take these on condition that you bring them back tomorrow without fail. I'll lend you more then.'

What she had found now on Robert Thew's map of 1784 delighted her, for here was her own

Parliament Street designated as Mug-House Entry as her father had told her, but even better was the area behind Land of Green Ginger, filled with sketches of bushy trees and hedges.

'The king's gardens,' she murmured. 'And was it here that you grew the ginger, Anneliese? Will I ever know?' For in her heart she was beginning to suspect that Anneliese was a figment of her imagination, a spectre of her dreams.

'Haven't I told you already?' The familiar whisper came in her ear, and she turned her head to see Anneliese sitting in her chair. She smiled at her. 'Don't stop believing in me, Margriet,' she said softly.

'I won't,' Margriet breathed. 'Not ever.'

She turned back to the maps. 'Let's see what you have to show me, Mr Speed,' she murmured, looking at the name of the mapmaker and the date, 1610, even earlier than the previous one. 'It's almost too small to read, and there are no recognizable streets.' The old walls and gates of Hull, the Citadel, and the towers of two churches were shown, with ships in the Humber and windmills outside the walls; just like Netherlands, she thought. 'And what's this?' She peered closer. 'Another church? No.' She ran her finger down the index and took a breath. 'King's Place! I've found it! But now it's gone, other buildings have been built over it. There's nothing now but the place names.'

Something else was niggling away. It was something to do with what Anneliese had said about her garden and growing shrubs and bulbs and ginger. What? What was it? She turned to ask her what she had meant, but she had gone, and Margriet's mother was calling for her.

'Margriet? Had you forgotten we have an appointment with Mr Webster?' Rosamund was ready to go out.

Margriet had lost track of the time, but it didn't take long to scramble into her coat and bonnet. Mr Webster's office was only a few minutes' walk away at the top of Parliament Street, and when the lawyer had sent his clerk to arrange a meeting Margriet had suggested that an outing would do them both good, rather than summoning the lawyer to come to them. Somewhat to her surprise, her mother had agreed, and the appointment had been made.

Webster had recommended that they should ask Ramsey to send her a monthly allowance as she had no other income. 'He won't like it, of course, but if his lawyer has any sense he will advise him to do so,' he had said. It was now the end of March and a letter had been received from Ramsey's lawyer, Jameson, and they were meeting with Webster to hear the outcome.

As they walked up the street towards the lawyer's office, Margriet said, 'Mama, I'm sure we don't have to worry too much about managing, even if Mr Ramsey defaults on any payment to you, as I can sell some of *my* shares that Papa left me, and we can live on the money that they bring.'

Her mother wasn't happy about that suggestion and said that her father had probably intended them for her dowry.

'Then I'll have to consider very carefully before I

marry,' Margriet observed, 'and not choose a spend-thrift like Mr Ramsey.'

Rosamund flinched. Margriet was right, of course; she should have been more careful and spoken to the lawyer before entering into another marriage contract. How disastrous it could have been but for Webster's forethought and Frederik's wisdom in taking his advice. The last thing she wanted was to spend Margriet's inheritance, for she would never be able to pay it back. She had done some serious thinking since her catastrophic marriage and realized how easily she might have found herself in an even more difficult situation. When Mr Webster had said that Ramsey had an obligation to keep her from the workhouse, she had had the grace to feel ashamed that she had once regarded its inmates as simply undesirable and unworthy. Now she wondered what circumstances had brought them so low.

'We are a little further forward,' Webster told them when they were seated in his private rooms. 'I have received a letter from Ramsey's lawyer, and Jameson says that in principle Ramsey will agree to an annulment of the marriage.' He glanced at Margriet. 'Do you wish me to continue this discussion in front of your daughter, Mrs Ramsey?'

Rosamund hesitated, and caught Margriet's questioning glance. She considered for a moment and then said, 'In view of Margriet's sensible suggestions regarding our situation and livelihood, I think she's grown up enough to hear what Mr Ramsey has to say.' She turned to Margriet. 'But if you are embarrassed by the subject, which in truth is not something I would wish you to hear under normal

342

circumstances, please feel free to leave the room and wait outside.'

Margriet nodded, and wondered what it might be. She was sorry for her mother; she had always been so genteel and sensitive, but the trauma of this marriage had changed her.

'Very well.' Webster shifted papers about his desk. 'The premise is that Ramsey will consider an annulment of your marriage on the condition that you say it is you who have refused to consummate the marriage and not him.'

Rosamund gave a wry smile. 'I thought as much. He will not want damaging aspersions cast on his . . .' She hesitated, thinking of Margriet.

'Quite so.' Webster cleared his throat. 'I agree. I'm considering . . .' He paused and folded his hands in front of him. 'I think we should give Ramsey a little more time to consider his position should you refuse before we send an answer, but I suggest I tell Jameson to advise him to arrange the details of your allowance immediately, as you are suffering under unfavourable monetary circumstances. In the meantime I will make a few enquiries of my own into the state of his affairs.'

Margriet accompanied her mother home, but then hesitated in the hallway. 'Mama, I'm going to take a walk. I don't need Jane with me,' she added hastily, 'I'm only stretching my legs as far as Market Place. I won't be long.' She opened the door before her mother could object. 'I think you should ring for tea and take a rest. That meeting was very stressful.'

Her mother didn't make any objection and Margriet escaped. She quite often slipped out

343

alone now. We live two minutes from the town, she thought, where is the harm in it?

She also supposed that her mother might like a little time alone to consider Ramsey's suggestion. What a dreadful man he was, using their marriage for his own selfish needs.

It was Tuesday, market day, and the area in front of Holy Trinity Church was thronging with people buying produce from the stalls. The vendors were shouting out the wonderful quality of their goods and the cheap price, and the customers were bargaining for a better one. Margriet wandered between the stalls, enjoying the liveliness and bustle of it all.

'Buy a bunch o' flowers, miss? Brighten up your life.'

Margriet turned. It was Betty, holding out a spray of yellow daffodils. She didn't have a stall but by her feet was a metal bucket holding a few bunches of rather battered-looking narcissi. 'Betty!' Margriet smiled, but Betty avoided her eye.

'Hello, miss,' she muttered. 'Will you buy a bunch o' daffies?'

'I'd love to,' Margriet said, and was struck by the relief on the girl's face. She hadn't intended to buy anything, but she had a few coins in her purse. 'How much are they?'

'Onny a copper,' Betty mumbled. 'Whatever you can afford.'

'Here we are.' Margriet held out a sixpence. 'I'll give them to my mother.'

Betty hesitated. 'They ain't as much as that,' she said.

344

'Then I'll take two bunches, please. She loves flowers.'

Betty chose the best of the daffodils and handed them to her.

'Where do you buy your flowers?' Margriet asked curiously. She hoped they hadn't cost much, because they were not good specimens.

'I didn't buy them,' the girl admitted. 'Old Tom on 'flower stall give 'em to me. They're from Sat'day's market.'

'Oh, I see.' That would account for their bedraggled appearance. 'It's nice to see you again, Betty. You do remember me, don't you? I came to the fair with you.'

Betty nodded. 'Yeh. But Billy said it were best not to talk to you.'

'Oh!' Margriet was incredibly hurt. 'Why? Did he say?'

Betty nodded again. 'He said you weren't like us.'

Margriet sighed. 'I suppose I'm not,' she said, 'but that doesn't mean you can't talk to me. I mean, it's not my fault, is it?'

Betty appeared to consider. 'No, suppose not. I'll tell him.'

Margriet left her and went in search of the flower stall Betty had mentioned. An elderly man was standing behind it, and looked across at her. 'Lovely daffies here, miss. Better than them you've just bought.'

'I haven't much money with me,' she admitted. 'But I was wondering where you bought your flowers.'

He took off his hat and scratched his head. 'Why, from them as brings 'em in from abroad, miss. These weren't grown here; it's a bit early for English flowers.' He picked up a bunch of deep red tulips. 'Now see these beauties, not fully opened yet. They're picked while they're still closed up, then start to open on 'ship that brings 'em over from Holland, and by 'time I collect 'em from Farrell's warehouse they're almost ready. Beautiful, they are.' He gazed at the flowers admiringly. 'Dutch tulips; can't beat 'em.'

'I know,' she said breathlessly. 'And where is the warehouse?'

He frowned. 'Public can't buy from there, onny us that sells 'em on. Tradesfolk, you know.'

'Yes. Yes, of course. I understand. Thank you. I'll come again on Saturday and buy some.' She laughed. 'I'll remember to bring some money with me next time.'

'Aye, it's no use coming to 'market without a copper or two, miss.'

It was as she was walking away that something struck her. Farrell, he'd said. She knew that name, but how? And then she remembered. He was the man who had said that the house in Land of Green Ginger was haunted. Old memories swirled in her head. He had wanted to discuss something with Frederik, but she couldn't remember what.

She walked on down Market Place towards Queen Street and the pier. This was a commercial district, with warehouses, hotels, jewellers, cutlers, coffee houses and tea merchants jostling cheek by jowl and the butchers' shambles tucked through an archway. Surely it was somewhere in this vicinity that her father's office had been situated? He had brought

346

her with him once or twice when she was a child.

The memory clicked into place. Mr Farrell. He had wanted to speak to her father about importing tulip bulbs from Netherlands.

That was it, she thought. That was what Anneliese had said. She said that we could grow flowers and shrubs and plant tulip bulbs and ginger. But we can't grow tulips or anything else, because . . . Her head spun. Anneliese doesn't realize that we haven't got a garden. There are no gardens here any more.

CHAPTER FORTY-ONE

Amsterdam

Hans Jansen straightened his jacket, smoothed his hair and rang the bell on Mevrouw Vandergroene's door.

She had been sitting in her window looking out and had seen him walking down the road by the canal. How handsome he had become, she thought as she greeted him at the door, urging him to come in and saying how good it was to see him. He followed her upstairs to her cosy, cluttered sitting room and returned the compliment.

He sat down as invited and waited for her to return with coffee and cake. His *oma* was just like her: as soon as anyone knocked on the door the kettle which always seemed to be on the boil was deployed for making coffee and a freshly baked cake was lifted from the cake tin.

'It's very good to see you,' she said again as she poured thick black coffee. 'How is Cornelia? Does she keep busy?'

'Yes, she does; she has started to paint again. She said she used to enjoy it when she was young, but she stopped when she got married and had my sister and me and concentrated on her garden, which she loved. Now that she doesn't have a garden any more she has started to paint landscapes, mainly tulip fields, dykes and windmills.' He laughed. 'And she's good. Very good indeed.'

'Ah, I'm so pleased.' Gerda eased herself into a chair. 'And your *oma*?'

He took another sip of coffee, which was so strong it set his heart racing. 'She's well. She sits in her window and knits kettle holders and sometimes warm jumpers for anyone who wants them; she's started sewing again too. Did you know she used to be a seamstress?' He put his hands on his jacket. 'She made this for me, and dresses and skirts for Klara and my *moeder*. She also spins, and when spring comes she puts on her traditional costume and sits outside spinning or knitting and people stop to talk to her. Visitors to Amsterdam always ask her what is she making.'

'Well, my word,' Gerda exclaimed. 'She puts me to shame. And you, what are you doing? You have finished your education, I expect.'

'That's why I have called today, *mevrouw*. I came to tell you that on Monday I begin my first week at the Vandergroene Company of importers and exporters.'

'Splendid!' She clapped her hands. 'I'm so pleased that it has at last come to pass. Frederik told me that he thought you would do very well.'

'I am so grateful that he mentioned my name to Gerben Aarden all those years ago. Aarden actually made a note to remind me if I didn't get in touch

349

myself. I knew I wanted to work rather than go to university, but I did do a year of business studies that I thought would help me in commerce. So here I am, and I can't wait to start. Best of all, I know that my father would have been delighted that I will be working in his old friend's company. It's sad that neither of them is here any longer to know of it.'

He paused, wondering if he should have referred to her son's death in front of her, but she nodded. 'Frederik would have been delighted too, I know.'

'Do you hear much of Margriet?' he asked. 'Like Klara, she must be growing up fast.'

She smiled to herself at Hans speaking as if he were already an adult, but, she thought fondly, he is still a boy. 'She was fifteen in January,' she said, 'and I hear from her quite often; every four or five weeks, perhaps. Her mother had some ill luck in her second marriage.' Her mouth curled downwards. 'She was never very aware; not a woman of the world. Brought up in a very sheltered household, and I suppose Frederik spoilt her too. I don't know the details – Margriet doesn't tell me too much in her letters, but it seems that her new husband took advantage of her. Rosamund's lawyer is handling her affairs so I hope *he* knows what he is doing, even if she doesn't. But Margriet will be all right – I will make sure that she is.'

'I hope so,' he said. 'If ever I get the chance to travel across to England to visit the Hull office, perhaps it might be possible to visit?'

Gerda looked at him. That would be very nice, she thought. She must visit his *oma* and find out more about him. He seemed a fine upstanding young man, handsome, honest-looking, ambitious too, she thought. A good prospect for some young lady.

She nodded and gave a small sigh. 'I'm sure it would be possible. You must let me know if you do go. I live in hope that Margriet might visit me one day, but her mother doesn't travel and her previous companion has found employment elsewhere, which is a pity for I liked her very much.'

He left then, telling her that he would let himself out. Outside, he turned and gave her a cheery wave before walking away.

Yes, she mused. She must visit his *oma*, and his *moeder* too, and have a little chat about those young people.

Margriet was sitting on a bench at the pier looking out at the muddy brown waters of the Humber. Many ideas were swirling in her head, some of them prompted by Betty and her bedraggled flowers, but after finding King's Place on the map, it was Anneliese who was at the forefront of her mind.

Anneliese couldn't be a ghost, she decided, because surely if she were she wouldn't be visible in the Parliament Street house but only at hers. Besides, she looked different now that she was older, and Margriet thought that if she were a ghost she would stay the same age as she had been the first time. She wore more grown-up traditional Dutch clothes, too. And that thought gave Margriet yet another idea.

'Hello, miss!'

Margriet looked up to see Billy and the young

boy she had seen with him on the day Ramsey had thrown him a coin. 'Hello, Billy,' she said, smiling at them both.

'This is my brother Jim,' Billy said. He lowered his eyes. 'I've just seen Betty,' he muttered. 'She says you were upset that I'd said we shouldn't talk to you.' He kicked at a stone. 'I didn't mean owt. It's just that I didn't want 'lasses to get any fancy ideas about you.'

Margriet frowned. 'What kind of fancy ideas?'

He shrugged. 'Well, they can't really be friends wi' you, can they? I mean, you live in one o' them grand houses in Parli'ment Street, don't you?'

'Yes, I do. But we can still talk, can't we? I don't have many friends, and I get lonely sometimes.'

'Do you?' He seemed astonished. 'I'd never have thought it.'

'I know the Sandersons – Sandy and Immi,' she told him. 'Immi's sister Julia is my friend. We went to school together, but I don't see so much of her since we left.'

He nodded. 'She helps her ma wi 'soup kitchen in 'winter,' he volunteered. 'Why don't you call and see her? She lives in Albion Street.'

'Yes, I know,' she said, and thought Billy very well informed. 'Billy, how do you earn money?'

He shrugged. 'I'm willing to do owt. Run errands for traders, hold hosses' heads like I did for that gent outside your house, though it was hardly worth my time for 'pittance he give me.'

'He hasn't any money left,' she said. 'He spent it all on that fancy carriage and pair.' She thought for a minute. 'If something came up, something that might make a difference to your life, and your friends', would you take a chance?'

He laughed. 'Yeh, like a shot. Course we would, wouldn't we, Jim?'

The younger boy was wearing a cut-down coat and a flat hat that came well over his eyes and ears, but he stretched his neck and head back to see her from under it and said '*Yeh*', just as Billy had done.

She asked Billy if he knew where the import and export company Vandergroene had their offices and of course he did; it seemed to Margriet that he knew about most things and most people.

'I'll tek you and show you, if you like,' he offered eagerly. 'It's near 'Pilot Office in Queen Street,' and on impulse she agreed.

'I know someone who used to work there,' she said vaguely, 'and I wondered where it was.'

He led her back to Queen Street and pointed it out, a narrow yet imposing three-storey red-brick building with a shiny brass name plate on the wall beside the heavy oak door. She remembered seeing it when her father had taken her.

'Thank you, Billy,' she said. 'You're a useful person to know.'

'I know all 'streets in Hull,' he said proudly. 'Every alleyway and shop.'

Margriet smiled. 'I'll remember that,' she said, and meant it.

Heading towards home, she reached Parliament Street but walked past her own door and continued to the building where Mr Webster had his rooms. She asked the clerk if she might make an appointment to see the lawyer the following day, but before he could check the diary Mr Webster himself came up from the basement and greeted her in some surprise.

'I don't want to take up much of your time, Mr Webster, but I'd like to ask you something.'

Up in his office he waited courteously as she chewed her lip for a moment, wondering how to start.

'It isn't as if I wish to hide anything from my mother,' she began eventually. 'But until my idea is fully formed, I don't want to discuss it with her. I'd like to embark on a venture of my own, Mr Webster. I realize that I might be too young, which is why I'd like to ask you if it would be feasible, and also if I might have access to a sum of money that Mr Ramsey can't get hold of.'

'There will be no difficulty about that, Miss Margriet,' he said, 'none at all. But you must not give any to your mother. As I have already explained, Ramsey could claim it if you did.'

'I won't,' she said fervently, and went on to explain what she wanted to do.

His shaggy eyebrows rose in astonishment as she outlined her plan, and several times he contended that she might not need any money under the circumstances.

'Oh, but I do,' she said earnestly. 'I want to be as independent as possible.'

'Very well,' he said eventually. 'Leave it with me. Come and see me again, say in a week's time, and we will see how we've progressed. In the meantime, as you have suggested, go along to see the Sandersons. You will find them most supportive.'

'Thank you,' she said. 'And there is just one thing more.'

The following morning, after telling her mother she was going out for a walk, Margriet arrived back in Queen Street and climbed the stairs to the first-floor office of the Vandergroene Company. She knocked on the door and walked into a large room full of desks with a clerk behind each one, all of whom looked up as she entered and as one rose from their seats.

'Good morning, miss.' One of the clerks came towards her. He was dressed, as they all were, in a dark frock coat, striped trousers and a grey waistcoat with a stiffly starched white shirt and high collar. 'May I assist you?'

'I would like to speak to Mr Reynoldson, if I may. Is he at liberty this morning?'

He gave a small bow. 'I will find out for you. Won't you take a seat?'

She sat down, and as she did so the clerks also sat back at their desks.

'Might I enquire your name and business, miss?'

'My name is Margriet Vandergroene and my business is with Mr Reynoldson.'

On hearing her name all the clerks immediately stood up again, and Margriet held her gloved hand to her lips to hide a smile. 'Please be seated, gentlemen,' she said in her best imitation of her mother, and they did so, only to rise again as Mr Reynoldson, unaware of her presence, came out of another room.

She was ushered into his office and offered coffee

or other refreshment. When she refused he said how nice it was to see her again. 'How time has passed! I remember your father bringing you here when you were only a child.'

'I remember too, Mr Reynoldson,' she said. 'And it's good to see that the business is operating so successfully, even after – after . . .' She faltered and fell silent, suddenly overcome by the realization that beyond the walls of the Parliament Street house life was continuing almost as normal without her father.

Reynoldson must have understood something of what she was feeling, for he said softly, 'We still miss him and talk about him, those of us who were here then. It was a great tragedy, but we hope that he would have been proud of how we are maintaining the family name.'

Margriet wiped her eyes and nodded. 'Yes,' she croaked. 'He would have been.'

'So what can I do for you, Miss Vandergroene? How can I be of assistance?'

She explained to him as she had explained to Mr Webster, and he too said that she didn't need any money as she was a major shareholder in the company.

'My mother's lawyer, Mr Webster, whom you know, says that he will take care of the monetary issues if you will agree to the proposal.'

'It will be our pleasure, Miss Vandergroene,' he said, a wide smile on his face. 'And any advice you might need, please feel free to ask.'

He ushered her out of his office, the clerks once more rising and bowing, and escorted her down the stairs. As she turned to say goodbye he too bowed.

'A great pleasure to see you again. I'm happy to think that the next generation of the Vandergroene family will be joining the company, albeit in a small way to begin with.'

She felt cock-a-hoop with success and had begun to march away when she heard her name being called. It was one of the clerks, clutching a large bouquet of tulips.

'Miss Vandergroene! A batch of fresh flowers from Amsterdam was delivered to the office this morning. Mr Reynoldson asked if you would accept these with our compliments.'

She thanked him profusely. What a good omen. So much achieved in one morning, she thought, heading back towards town. She took a huge breath. Now for a visit to the Sandersons and Florrie.

CHAPTER FORTY-TWO

Margriet stood on the top step of the Sandersons' house in Albion Street and waited for the door to be opened. The maid dipped her knee. 'G'morning, miss.'

'Good morning. Would it be convenient to speak to Mrs Sanderson?'

'Come in, miss. I'll just ask her.' The girl tripped her way down the short hallway to a room at the end and put her head round the door, then turned back to Margriet and beckoned to her. 'Come through, miss. Mrs Sanderson is in here.'

Margriet went in and found Mrs Sanderson sitting at a table that was strewn with papers and ledgers, with rather incongruously a knitted giraffe sitting in the middle of it all.

'Margriet!' she exclaimed. 'What a lovely surprise. And what beautiful flowers. Was it me you wanted to see, or Julia? I'm afraid she's out.' She raised her voice to the maid, now back in the hall. 'Fetch a pot of coffee, Hetty, and biscuits, please.'

Margriet smiled. Mrs Sanderson was such fun and still so informal. 'I had hoped that I might say hello to Julia, but it was you I wanted to see really. I need some advice and I thought you could give it.'

Alice Sanderson leaned back in her chair. 'Of course. But tell me, how is your mama?'

'She – she's having some difficulties, I'm afraid.' Margriet's voice dropped.

'With her husband? We have heard rumours about Ramsey.' Mrs Sanderson's voice lowered too. 'We have friends in York.' She nodded significantly. 'I hope the situation is resolved. She has her lawyer on him, I trust?'

'Yes, she has.' Margriet didn't want to discuss it further. Mrs Sanderson seemed to understand, and asked what she could do for her.

'You might think it very strange, Mrs Sanderson, but I wanted to ask if I might borrow Florrie. If she's willing, that is.'

'Borrow Florrie! What a strange request.' She stopped speaking as Hetty brought in a tray of coffee and biscuits, and waited for the maid to leave the room before reverting to the subject.

'What do you want to do with her?' she asked as she handed Margriet a cup and a plate of biscuits.

'I'd like her to accompany me to Amsterdam,' Margriet replied. 'I'd like to visit my grandmother for a particular reason – as well as wanting to see her, I mean. My mother won't cross the sea and I can't travel alone and there's no one else suitable.'

'Well, no, of course you can't go alone, not until you're older, but then you can.' She waved a finger. 'Don't let anybody tell you that you can't, just because you're a woman. Not once you've reached twenty-one, at any rate.'

'But that's years away, Mrs Sanderson, and I really

need to go now. Perhaps if I could explain?'

And so she told of her visits to the lawyer and to the Vandergroene office, and the reasons for them, and about Billy, Betty and Mabel.

'Well, my goodness,' Mrs Sanderson exclaimed. 'That's quite a tall order, but most commendable. We can ask Florrie if she'd like to go with you. I don't see any reason why she shouldn't. Young Richard is rather a handful, just as Hughie was, and now there's Conrad, and I'm inclined to think that Florrie might be just a little bit bored with looking after small boys. Not that she complains,' she hastened to add. 'But she might be glad of a change of routine and Hetty can manage them for a few days, I'm sure. I don't suppose it would be for too long, would it?'

Without waiting for an answer she shifted papers aside and picked up a brass bell that had been hidden beneath them. Hetty came rushing back in in answer to its ring. 'Is Florrie about?' Mrs Sanderson asked. 'If she is, will you ask her to pop down? There's someone here to see her.'

'Sorry, ma'am,' Florrie said when she came down, looking very flustered. Her cheeks were pink and her hair was straying from its usual neat knot. 'Oh, how nice to see you, Miss Margriet.' She turned back to her employer. 'I've put Master Conrad in his cot, but I doubt he'll stay there for long. I've asked Hetty to stay up there until I get back.'

'Draw up a chair, Florrie,' Mrs Sanderson said, 'and help yourself to coffee. Margriet has a proposition for you.'

Margriet was astounded by Mrs Sanderson's attitude towards her staff. She treated them like – well, like the normal people they were. It was no wonder that Florrie liked working for her. Margriet wondered whether even a visit to Netherlands would tempt her away, but she was delighted to be proved wrong. As soon as she had explained, Florrie turned to Mrs Sanderson. 'But – would you mind, ma'am? It would mean leaving Hetty to look after 'boys.'

'I realize that, but I think you might be ready for a change of scenery, and I'm able to do more to help now that Hughie is at school.' She waved her hand across the cluttered table. 'And I shall soon have all this sorted out, after which there are no more projects to fill my time until the winter, when we start the soup kitchens again.'

'Then yes please, I would love to come with you, Miss Margriet. I enjoyed staying with your grandmother. Will it be soon? It would be lovely to see 'tulip fields in full colour.'

Margriet nodded. 'As soon as I can arrange it, if that's all right with you, Mrs Sanderson?'

'Why not? And you're right, Florrie, the tulip fields are wonderful.' She sighed. 'I haven't seen them for such a long time in spite of my husband's being half Dutch.' She shook her head in mock despair. 'I don't quite know what happened to those years.'

Florrie smiled. 'You had your babies, ma'am.'

'Of course I did,' she agreed. 'And they are far more precious than any holiday abroad.'

Margriet couldn't wait to put her ideas into motion. She told Florrie that she would let her know the details as soon as she'd booked a passage. As she left the house, clutching her flowers, she reflected anxiously that the only major task left for her to do was to explain the situation to her mother.

At the Junction Dock swing bridge a ship was passing through the waterway from the Old Dock towards the Humber and the sea. A flock of herring gulls flew in the ship's wake, and as she waited for the bridge to close and let her across she rehearsed what she would say. However, as she headed down Whitefriargate, she glanced up at a clock above a jeweller's shop and realized that she must go on another errand first.

She walked on, hearing an echo of jumbled voices and a clatter of clogs on the cobbles; she passed the end of Parliament Street and it was as if her feet were acting of their own volition as she was propelled into Land of Green Ginger. She stood at her usual corner and was transfixed. Looking down Manor Street, all of a sudden she saw the gardens at the end of it. Ragged boys were pushing heavy wheelbarrows filled with soil and shouting 'Mind your backs, sirs' to gentlemen sporting trim pointed beards, wide-brimmed hats and rich brocade coats lined with shiny bright silk; ladies in long-sleeved, high-necked embroidered gowns strolled or chatted in little groups of two or three, their maids in attendance.

What's happening? Am I dreaming? She looked down at her feet and saw that she was wearing clogs, like the ones her father had brought from Netherlands, and then she looked up at the Lindegroen house and there was Anneliese beckoning her. She crossed the narrow street and approached the door; it was open a finger's width and she pushed it wide to enter. It was as she recalled it from when she had visited as a child. Had she visited? Had she met Anneliese and her mother here when she had slipped out without anyone's knowledge? She was confused, not knowing what was real and what imaginary.

She climbed the winding staircase to the first floor and entered the room overlooking the street, a room filled with dark furniture and tapestry wall hangings. Anneliese turned from the window. 'I thought you were never coming,' she said. 'You've missed the king. You've brought tulips; were they for him?'

Margriet looked down at the tulips. Where had they come from? 'I can't stay,' she said. 'I'm travelling to Amsterdam soon.'

'Oh!' Anneliese whispered, and although the sun was shining through the glass her image faded, becoming illusory and obscure as if she were standing in shadow. 'I wish that I could go with you. It's the place where I was born.'

'You can come if you like,' Margriet said. 'I'm going because of you.' But Anneliese had left, melting and disappearing as if she had never been. Margriet wandered into other rooms, all empty of furniture, although it seemed that someone had recently been there as there were footprints on the dusty floor and fingerprints on the window sills. Slowly she made her way down the stairs and hesitated at the bottom, closing her eyes and listening intently. There was something, faint voices and footsteps. Anneliese was still there, she thought. She hadn't gone away.

Outside, Margriet stood for a moment watching the passers-by. There was nothing strange about them now. People were going about their business as usual, dressed in their everyday clothes; she felt headachy and rather faint.

'Nice flowers, miss.' It was Billy again; she thought it strange how he always seemed to be popping up wherever she went.

She looked down at them. She really should get them home and put them in water. 'They're Dutch tulips,' she told him. 'Just in from Amsterdam.'

'Aye,' he said. 'I know what they are. Are you all right, miss?'

She nodded. 'I think so. You can call me Margriet. It's Dutch.'

'Oh! Are you Dutch then?'

'Half,' she said. 'My father was Dutch.'

'Like 'folks that used to live here.' He nodded towards the Lindegroen house behind her. 'Well, that's what folk say. That's how 'street got its name.' He glanced at her. 'Shall I walk you home? You look a bit dowly.'

Margriet didn't know what dowly meant, but she said yes as she still felt rather faint, and together they walked to Parliament Street and her door. 'Thank you very much, Billy,' she said, and drew one of the red tulips from the bouquet. 'Have you got a buttonhole in your coat?'

He grinned. 'No, but I can slot it through 'hole in my hat.'

Margriet watched him as he snapped off half of the tulip stalk and poked the flower through the hole in the rim of his flat cap, so that it showed bright and cheerful above his forehead. She smiled. 'I'm going away to Amsterdam – to see my grandmother,' she added. 'I'll bring you another cap, like the Dutchmen wear.'

'I can't pay you.'

'I know.' She smiled again. 'It will be a gift.'

CHAPTER FORTY-THREE

'I am so thrilled to see you again.' Margriet's *oma* put out her arms to greet her as she and Florrie stepped off the ship on to the quayside. 'It is good to see you too, Floris,' she said, and Florrie smiled as she thought how nice it sounded. '*Welkom. Welkom.*'

'I'm going to keep that name, Miss Margriet,' she said later as she unpacked Margriet's trunk. 'I really like it; it's much more elegant than Florrie and not as stiff and starchy as Florence.'

Margriet laughed. Just as at Mrs Sanderson's, Florrie was very relaxed in her *oma*'s house. And, Margriet thought, she no longer seems like a servant; she's grown in status and yet is still polite and well mannered. After luncheon, Florrie offered to go out shopping for Mevrouw Vandergroene if there was anything she needed, and was asked if she would collect a parcel of cotton and embroidery thread from the haberdasher.

'I really wanted you to myself,' Oma admitted to Margriet when she had gone. 'There is so much I need to know after so long.' She gave a wistful sigh. 'I haven't seen you since your papa's memorial service. I have asked your uncle Bartel to go and fetch you many times, but he said it would cause a rift between you and your mother. Would it have done, do you think?'

'Perhaps,' Margriet agreed. 'Mama is, or was then, rather sensitive, but she has changed since her second marriage. In any case, I always intended to come when I was old enough.' She gave a sudden smile that lit her face and her *oma* was conscious more than ever of the passing years. Her granddaughter was almost a young woman.

'And then the opportunity presented itself,' Margriet went on. 'In a way, that odious man Mr Ramsey opened my eyes, and my mother's too.'

Gerda gave a startled gasp at Margriet's description of her stepfather, and Margriet apologized. 'I'm sorry if I've shocked you, Oma, but it's true. I never liked him from the moment he began to call on Mama. He was all smiles and affectation. He bought me a fur muff and hat to wheedle me into liking him, and a bracelet which he stole back, and when they married he bought Mama a curricle and pair but she never drove it once and he always took it back home with him to York.'

'Back home to York? Did he not live with you and your mama in Hull?'

'No. He sometimes stayed for a day or two and then went back to York. He always seemed like a guest. And then we discovered . . .' She faltered, wondering if she was saying too much, but she wanted Oma to understand everything. 'We discovered that not only had he sold some of Mama's shares in Papa's company and spent all the money, but he had emptied the bank account as well. It was so embarrassing for Mama.'

Gerda put her hand to her chest. 'I can't believe it,' she gasped. 'Frederik worked so hard to achieve his success.'

'He did,' Margriet agreed. 'But Oma, this is the best part. Mr Ramsey wanted to sell the house too, and he would have, if Papa had not been so very clever.' She gave a triumphant grin. 'He left the house to me, which means Mr Ramsey can't touch it. And our lawyer arranged for me to buy all the shares Mama had left in the Vandergroene business from her because Ramsey can't touch anything of mine. And so he's gone back to York, and although I can't tell you what might happen next, we're hoping to be rid of him altogether.'

'So,' Oma said cautiously, 'how is your mama managing if she doesn't have any money?'

'Our lawyer says that Mr Ramsey will have to pay her a monthly allowance because she is suffering financial hardship, and in the meantime she has her dowry to pay the servants and tradesmen, because no one else could touch that. And of course we are being very prudent and economical.'

'I see.' Gerda's opinion of her daughter-in-law was changing the more she heard, from thinking of her as a frivolous woman unable to recognize a charming fraudster when she saw one, to regarding her more amiably in consideration of her attitude to her servants and tradespeople. 'So how has this man's behaviour opened your eyes? I don't see the connection.'

'I realized that I must try to earn some money

until I reach twenty-one and can claim my inheritance.' She frowned a little. 'But it's not just that. I know some young people of my age who live on the streets. They try to work, but there are few opportunities for them, and they don't have houses to live in or feather beds to sleep on or even a proper meal every day. I thought how lucky I was to have so much, and so . . .' She handed her grandmother a folded sheet of paper. 'I've written it all down for you so I don't miss anything out.' Would her plan seem impossible? Might Oma laugh at the proposal? 'It might not work,' she murmured. 'And I need your help.'

Florrie came back just then, so she fell silent. She was pleased to see that her *oma* continued to glance through her plan as Florrie was talking.

'I love Amsterdam,' she was saying. 'It reminds me of Hull, except there are more waterways, but some of 'buildings seem similar. What I really like to see is 'women in their old costumes.'

Gerda nodded vaguely, her eyes still on the document. 'Not so many here in Amsterdam, but in some villages the women wear the traditional costume most of the time.'

'Yes,' Margriet said, 'and in Gouda the men do too, I remember when Papa took me.' She paused, thinking. 'We brought back some cheese, and we called on . . .'

'Mevrouw Jansen,' her grandmother reminded her.

'Tante Lia! Yes. And Klara and Hans. Klara and I played together but Hans was studying in his room. I liked him; he was very friendly, and polite to my

369

father.' She smiled. 'They called him Uncle Freddy, which I thought very funny.'

Gerda nodded. The child hadn't suspected then or seemingly since that Lia had been her father's mistress. 'They live in Amsterdam now,' she told her. 'Along the Amstel, not far from here, and I see them quite often. As a matter of fact, Hans called to see me only recently to say he was about to start work with the Vandergroene Company.'

'Really? What a coincidence! I would love to meet them again. Would it be possible, do you think?'

Her *oma*, who had picked up on the gist of Margriet's ideas, thought how strange it was that life had so many connections. Not coincidences, she didn't really believe in those, but rather she felt that somehow there was a master plan being developed and worked on so that eventually everything would fall into its proper place.

'I think it is more than possible. Perhaps we could go tomorrow? Floris, would you like another walk? And perhaps you would too, Margriet, to stretch your legs. Why don't you call at the Jansens' to ask if it would be convenient? Mevrouw De Vries, Mevrouw Jansen's mother, will be at home even if no one else is.' Gerda got up from her chair and looked in a drawer for pen and paper. 'She doesn't speak English, so I'll write a note,' she said. 'I've been meaning to call for a few days. How opportune.'

Florrie didn't go with them the following day, and as it was a sunny morning she said that unless Mevrouw Vandergroene had anything she would like her to do, she would take another walk along the Amsterdam canals. 'I don't think I'll get lost,' she said, 'but I'll write down your address just in case.'

Margriet was puzzled to see her *oma* pick up the document she had given her, but Gerda explained that it just so happened that Hans had told her that his grandmother was an excellent seamstress.

'So everything is falling into place,' she said, patting the piece of paper. 'You will go home with everything you require.'

Mevrouw De Vries was sitting in her doorway knitting something bright and colourful. She got up immediately when she saw them and began chatting volubly to Gerda, though Margriet could understand nothing of their conversation. Lia came downstairs to welcome them.

'I am so pleased to see you again, dear Margriet,' she said, and Margriet thought she sounded rather emotional. She gently touched Margriet's cheek. 'You have become a beautiful young woman since I last saw you.'

Margriet dipped her knee and thanked her. She remembered how kind Tante Lia had been, and how easy to talk to. 'It's lovely to see you again. How is Klara? And my *oma* said that Hans is now working at the Vandergroene Company.'

'Klara is out visiting a friend, but she will be home soon. And would you believe that Hans is in England! He rushed home the night before last and said that his manager wanted him to go with him to the Hull office and they were leaving that evening; after Hull they will be travelling on to other towns. He will be so sorry that he has missed you.'

Gerda, whose conversation with Mevrouw De

Vries did not prevent her from listening to Lia and Margriet's, frowned slightly, muttering 'Tsk'.

'I will be coming again,' Margriet said as she followed Lia upstairs to her apartment. 'Oh, this is so nice,' she exclaimed. 'What a lovely view of the canal and the boats and the bridges.' She went to the window and looked one way and then the other. 'I remember the pretty garden you had in your other house,' she said. 'You must miss it, but the view of the Amstel must make up for it, doesn't it? We live upstairs at home too, but we don't have such a view or a garden either, just rooftops and alleyways.'

'But you can have pots and baskets of plants, which is all I have now,' Lia said. 'My tulips are in flower already.'

'Yes,' Margriet said eagerly. 'That's one of the reasons why I'm here – as well as to visit Oma, of course,' she added hastily. 'And I think, Tante Lia, I might ask for your advice on tulips!'

She was invited to sit down in the window and Lia pulled forward a small table so that she might put out a coffee cup and plate for her. Margriet thought wistfully of the time she had visited the Jansens in Gouda with her father, and eaten waffles sitting on a canal wall. Unbidden, tears came to her eyes; she missed him still.

Lia seemed to understand. 'We are both thinking of your father, I think,' she said softly, and Margriet nodded, too choked to speak. 'He was a good friend to us,' Lia went on. 'To my husband, and to me and my children too after Nicolaas died.' Her voice faltered as she continued speaking. 'I – we never thought that losing someone so special could happen again. Life is very hard sometimes.'

Margriet wiped her eyes. 'I feel his presence here very strongly,' she said. 'Perhaps it's because we are in his own country.'

'He loved being with you in England,' Lia murmured, and Margriet nodded, remembering that he had once told her that. 'I think what you are feeling now is the great love that he left behind?'

'Yes,' she said wistfully. 'Perhaps so.'

Her grandmother told her that everything was arranged and that Mevrouw De Vries was willing to help them. 'Mevrouw and I will go out this afternoon, and buy everything that is required.'

Then the plan was explained to Lia, who smiled and said she would help too, as she was also a good seamstress.

'And I can sew a neat hem, and so can Florrie,' Margriet said excitedly. 'She used to let down the hems of my dresses when I had outgrown them. I'll tell her about it and she'll want to help too.'

'So we'll have a sewing circle,' Lia said. 'How long do we have before you return to England, Margriet?'

'Less than a week. Then I must go home to Mama. She'll be lonely without me.'

Klara came home in time for lunch, and then the two grandmothers trotted off to the draper's and the haberdasher. Lia, Margriet and Klara, who tucked her arm into Margriet's, set off for a local flower market, where Lia showed Margriet the stone pots and hanging wicker baskets and how the tulips, hyacinths, primroses and other spring flowers were displayed. 'If you haven't much space you can stand pots one on top of another to make a tower, and plant trailing ivy so that it grows over the edges, or put them on a wall or ledge.'

They saw Florrie on the other side of a canal and called to her, then watched as the young man she was with gave a short bow and left her, lifting his hand in farewell. Florrie crossed a bridge and came towards them, and blushed when Lia teasingly lifted her eyebrows as Margriet introduced her.

'I – erm, the young man asked if I was lost,' she explained, 'and he gave me directions. I got mixed up with the canals.'

In the flower market there was a stall selling refreshments and they perched on high stools to drink piping hot coffee. Florrie gave a sigh of pleasure; there were no such treats for her at home, where she was constantly looking after other people's children. Margriet told her about her idea, which seemed to be coming to fruition.

'I can help,' Florrie said. 'I make my own clothes, and things for my sister's children too. And I'm quick. I can hem a skirt faster than anyone I know.'

'Well, there's a challenge.' Lia laughed. 'Wait until we tell your *oma*, Klara; she thinks no one can hem faster than her.'

When they trooped back to Lia's house they found that the two grandmothers had arrived first, and the table in the ground-floor apartment was strewn with a mound of black woollen cloth, a heap of white and striped cotton, a box of different-coloured silk thread and bobbins of white and black cotton.

Mevrouw De Vries took a tape measure from a

drawer, and gave Margriet's grandmother a pencil and notebook to write down the figures. She stood Margriet on a stool to measure her from waist to feet, and then asked her to stand down so that she might measure her shoulder width, front and arms, and lastly her head.

She nodded in satisfaction, went back to the drawer and flourished a pair of scissors, saying something that Margriet couldn't understand. She looked questioningly at Lia.

'And so we begin,' Lia translated.

CHAPTER FORTY-FOUR

They cut and stitched and cut and hemmed, and Lia threaded coloured silk and embroidered patterns of padded stem stitch, blanket honeycomb and French knot in various shades of green and blue and gold on to black cloth and they all looked and admired.

Then Klara took Florrie to the kitchen and they made starch in a deep bowl and plunged in squares of white cotton which they squeezed and partially dried and then pressed with a hot iron that drew off steam but didn't scorch, and took them back to Mevrouw De Vries, who tucked and turned and stitched then ironed again so that the item stood up on the table crisp and taut without falling over.

In between times, Lia or Klara made coffee or brought lemonade, biscuits and cake, and now and again one or other of the group would get up and walk round the table to help their circulation, and then Mevrouw Vandergroene called out 'One finished'. An hour later, Mevrouw De Vries called '*Twee afgewerkte*', and Florrie smiled and translated 'Two finished', and the Dutch ladies laughed and clapped their hands. Then, as the day darkened and a lamp was lit, a third was finished and they sat back and sighed.

'Now only the boys,' Klara said, and her mother declared that the rest could be completed the next day.

'Thank you,' Margriet said. 'I can't thank you enough.'

'Come then, Margriet,' Lia said. 'Let us see the fruit of our labours. Klara, will you begin to make supper? We have soup, ham, cheese and herring.'

'I'll make pancakes too, Moe,' Klara said. 'Everyone likes those,' and Florrie said she would help.

Lia gathered up an armful of finished garments and asked Margriet to come to her bedroom. 'There's a cheval mirror in there and we can see how you look.'

Margriet followed her into her bedroom. It was a pretty room, with landscape paintings of high mountains and green meadows adorning the walls. A white lace covering was spread over the bed and on this Lia draped the garments. Margriet raised her arms to undo the buttons at the back of her bodice and out of the corner of her eye she thought she saw her father. He was smiling.

She must have made a small breathy sound because Lia turned quickly. 'Something wrong?' she asked. 'Margriet, *lieveling*, are you all right?'

'Y-yes. Thank you. I turned a little dizzy, that's all.'

'You are so pale.' Lia was concerned. 'You have been sitting for too long.' She opened the window and a soft breeze rushed in, bringing with it the scent of hyacinths and narcissi. 'You must take a short walk before we have supper. Perhaps you would like to do that now?'

'No, no, it's nothing, really. Could you – would you mind unbuttoning my gown?' It had been the sudden movement that made her feel dizzy, she thought as Lia unfastened the buttons at her neck. But why would I think of Papa now, especially here where he has never been?

She stepped out of her skirt and took off her bodice and Lia helped her into the black cotton blouse and wool skirt. Then she slipped on the embroidered waistcoat that Lia had so patiently stitched, and fastened the striped apron round her waist. Next she stepped into a pair of Klara's clogs and then Lia turned her to face her and carefully pinned on the white starched winged cap.

'Every area has its own style of cap or bonnet, did you know?' she asked, smiling at her, and Margriet felt a mystical sense of déjà vu.

'Turn round,' Lia murmured, 'and see what I see.'

Margriet slowly turned to look in the long mirror and saw the reflection of a Dutch girl in her traditional costume, but the face looking back at her was not her own. It was Anneliese.

After supper, Margriet, Oma and Florrie walked back to Gerda's house. Margriet still felt rather strange, her head empty of meaning and understanding. She couldn't understand why she had visualized her father; his image was so strong that he had seemed to be in the room with her. She had wanted to ask Lia if she had seen him too, but thought it would be a senseless question, for why

378

would she? There would be no reason at all, for Lia and her family had only moved to Amsterdam after his death. And then to see Anneliese too, but surely that was simply a trick of the mind. Whenever she thought of Anneliese, she always pictured her dressed in Dutch clothing.

The other finished garments were parcelled up with hers ready to be taken back to Hull, and the final two would be completed the following day. She was beginning to have doubts. Maybe it was a silly idea and the intended recipients wouldn't agree to her plan, but Mr Webster and Mr Reynoldson, and Oma and Lia, seemed to think it would work. And she had to do *something*.

Gerda was speaking. 'Such a pity that Hans was away,' she said. 'He told me he would let me know if he might be travelling to England.' She sighed. 'But Lia said it was very short notice, and I suppose he didn't have time.'

Margriet nodded. It was the second time Oma had mentioned Hans. 'Never mind,' she said. 'I'll come again.' She turned to Florrie. 'If you can come with me?'

'If Mrs Sanderson will allow it,' Florrie said. 'She is my employer, Miss Margriet; I can't take advantage of her good nature.'

'You look after her children, yes?' Gerda asked. 'You like this work?'

'I like working for Mrs Sanderson,' Florrie said. 'She includes me in her family arrangements; she's not like an employer.' She glanced at Margriet and added hastily, 'I don't mean that I didn't like working for your mother, but I didn't want to stay

379

after Mr Frederik – that is, when Mrs Vandergroene married Mr Ramsey.'

'I know, Florrie,' Margriet said gloomily. 'I didn't want to stay either.' She stopped. She had said too much; she certainly could not tell Florrie that she hoped the situation might have changed by the time she arrived back home.

'Well,' Gerda said, 'if you ever get tired of looking after other people's children, Floris, perhaps you would consider coming to live with me? As a companion? Until such time as you might perhaps want *kinderen* of your own?'

'Oh!' Florrie stood stock still. 'Oh, goodness. I would – I do!'

Margriet looked at her with fresh eyes. Why had she never considered that Florrie might want a life of her own? Her own home with a family who belonged to her, instead of always serving others. She wasn't so very old, maybe only in her twenties; and Margriet thought of the young man Florrie had been talking to on the other side of the canal. Perhaps she might make a good match here in Amsterdam.

'And then, *mevrouw*,' Florrie continued, 'we could travel to Hull together; you to visit Miss Margriet and I to visit my sister and her family.'

Margriet could hear the contained excitement in Florrie's voice and felt pleased that there might be an opportunity opening up for her; one day, she thought, there might even be such a possibility for herself. She wasn't unhappy, but she couldn't help wondering if there might be something more to life than she had now.

The week passed swiftly, and on the last day the new clothing was packed into parcels to take home. Margriet told her grandmother that she would come again as soon as she could, but explained that she wouldn't want to leave her mother alone for too long. 'I think she is very vulnerable without me. And I'm afraid that Mr Ramsey might come back.'

'It seems to me,' Gerda said practically, 'that he won't come back if there is no money to be had, and if he can't get his hands on the house.'

'How do we learn to trust, Oma?' Margriet asked. 'What will I do, for instance, if someone should ask for my hand in marriage? How will I know whether he wants me or only my property, like Mr Ramsey with Mama?'

Gerda hid a smile as she gazed at her beautiful, innocent granddaughter. 'Well, *lieveling*, if he loves you he will not be able to hide it. And if you love him too you will know it without any doubt, and it won't matter whether he is rich or poor. Though try to love someone rich,' she added hastily, only half teasing. 'But whichever he is, you will know if he is the right one.'

'Did Papa know, do you think, when he met Mama? I used to think sometimes that their fondness for each other had died.'

Gerda gave a small sigh. She didn't know Frederik's wife sufficiently well to comment, but she had got the impression that she was a cold woman, whereas – of course she would think well of her son – Frederik had always been a loving child.

'Your papa was full of love,' she said softly. 'I can't speak for your mama. Love has to be shared or it can disappear into thin air.' She leaned across and kissed Margriet's cheek. 'Don't be afraid, *lieveling*. You will find a love to last.'

It was early morning when the ship docked in Hull; both Margriet and Florrie had woken in time to watch as the ship rode out of the German Ocean and into the calmer waters of the Humber estuary. The sunrise lit the low-lying meadows of Holderness, the reclaimed Sunk Island and the rooftops of still-sleeping villages, until it reached the windmills and church steeples and touched the tall buildings and warehouses of Hull with a warm glow as the ship slipped silently through the locks and finally into Junction Dock, two minutes from home. Margriet asked Florrie to find a porter for their luggage. 'I know it isn't far,' she said, 'but the parcels are quite heavy.'

Florrie looked round for someone to carry their luggage from the dockside to Parliament Street, and then Margriet spotted a boy with a handcart. 'There's Billy!'

'Billy, is it?' Florrie said. 'Do you know him, Miss Margriet?'

'Yes. He's one of the boys I was telling you about.'

'Well, in that case . . .' Florrie raised her voice. 'Billy! Come and give us a hand here.'

Billy came up at a trot and grinned at Florrie as he skidded to a halt. 'Yes, miss, what can I do for you?' Then he saw Margriet and touched his hat and she noticed that he still had the tulip threaded through it, though it was rather limp and withered now. 'Miss,' he acknowledged.

'Can you tek this lot to Parliament Street?' Florrie lapsed into her native Hull dialect.

'Certainly can, miss.' He began to load the luggage and parcels into the cart.

'Is this your handcart, Billy?' Margriet asked. 'Or is it a borrowed one?'

'It's mine, miss,' he said. 'I found it some weeks back. I didn't pinch it,' he added quickly. 'It had a leg missing, but I found a piece of wood that fitted, more or less, and nailed it on. It's a bit lopsided and 'wheels are skew-whiff, but it does 'job all right.'

Billy was right: it leaned to one side and the wheels seemed to go any way but straight, but he seemed quite adept at pushing it and within minutes he was pulling up outside Margriet's house ahead of them.

'How does he know where you live?' Florrie asked. 'You must be careful he doesn't tek advantage, Miss Margriet.'

Margriet laughed. 'You sound just like my mother, Florrie. I'm surprised at you.'

'Well, if you're in my charge, Miss Margriet,' Florrie said firmly, 'I must tell you what's right and what's not.'

'Of course you must.' Margriet kept a straight face and wondered what Florrie would think if she knew that she had spent time on her own with Billy and the two girls, without a chaperon. 'I do understand that you are responsible for me.'

Billy and Florrie carried their luggage to the top step and Margriet took money from her purse to pay him. She thanked him, and just as the door was being opened she managed to murmur, 'I need to speak to you about something, Billy. Will you and Betty and Mabel meet me tomorrow at about noon in Trinity Square?'

He seemed surprised but he nodded, touched his cap, collected his cart and, whistling, wheeled it wobbling and rattling down Parliament Street.

'Mama!' It was a shock to see her mother. Answering the door wasn't something she normally did. Florrie too expressed surprise.

'Where's Jane, ma'am? She hasn't left you?'

'No,' Rosamund said. 'But we're spring cleaning and I told her that I would do it. I was hoping it would be you.' She smiled at Margriet. 'It's lovely to have you home again. Do come in, Florence. We'll ask Mrs Simmonds to bring coffee and you can tell me what you've both been up to.'

Margriet and Florrie exchanged glances. Margriet couldn't think of a time when her mother had been so bright and cheerful, whilst Florrie was astounded to be invited to take coffee with them. 'I'll go down and make it, ma'am, if that's all right?' she said. 'I don't think Mrs Simmonds will mind if she's busy.'

'Of course she won't,' Rosamund said cheerfully. 'And ask Cook if there are any biscuits, although,' she turned to Margriet and said pensively, 'I don't suppose they'll be as nice as the ones you've been having in Amsterdam.'

Margriet kissed her mother's cheek. 'Cook makes lovely biscuits,' she said. 'And it's really nice to be home again.'

'I have something to tell you, Margriet.' Her

mother lowered her voice as they went upstairs to the sitting room, even though Florrie had gone off to the kitchen. 'William Ramsey has been here again.'

CHAPTER FORTY-FIVE

Surely he wasn't coming back? Mama couldn't have forgiven him? She wouldn't, would she? Questions flew around Margriet's head, but she couldn't voice any of them whilst Florrie was there, talking about Amsterdam: the fine old buildings, the canals, the pots and troughs and baskets of spring flowers that adorned the waterways.

'It sounds lovely,' Rosamund said regretfully. 'If only I could rid myself of my great fear of crossing the water. My husband – my late husband, I mean – really wanted me to visit his country of birth.'

'You'd love it, Mrs Vandergroene,' Florrie said, completely forgetting that Margriet's mother had changed her name on marriage.

Margriet and her mother exchanged glances. 'I'm Mrs Ramsey now, Florence,' Rosamund said. Florrie began to apologize, but Rosamund told her there was no need. 'Sometimes I forget too, or try to,' she said wryly.

As soon as Florrie had gone, Margriet demanded to be told more about Mr Ramsey. Rosamund took a deep breath, and nodded.

'I had a visit from Mr Webster shortly after you

left,' she began. 'He has been very helpful with advice and reassurance, and he warned me to expect another visit from Mr Ramsey.' Margriet noticed that she no longer referred to him as William. 'He told me very firmly that if he came I must send for him at all speed.' Her mother seemed filled with nervous energy. 'So I told Jane to fetch Mr Webster at once, without referring to me, if Mr Ramsey should call.'

Margriet was astounded. She was quite sure that at one time, confronted by such a situation, her mother would have retired to her bed whilst someone else attended to the matter. But now, of course, there wasn't anyone.

'And so he came,' she prompted. 'What did he want? Did he ask if he could stay – or I suppose,' she said slowly, 'I suppose he didn't have to ask, thinking that he had every right to be here as he's your husband?'

Rosamund shuddered. 'He did think that, and so did I, and he sat here, very nonchalantly, in that very chair where you are now, and told me what we were going to do. He said he would leave his lodgings and we would rent a house in York because surely I could scrape some money together from somewhere, and I was still saying it was impossible when Mr Webster arrived.' She took a moment to compose herself. 'I can only trust that he was telling the truth when he said, before he even got through the sitting room door, that he had firm instructions from Miss Vandergroene that Mr Ramsey was not to be admitted to her property under any circumstances whatsoever.'

Margriet smiled. 'I told him I didn't want Ramsey

in my house, but it sounds much better in legal language. And so did he leave?'

'He looked as though he was about to make a fuss, but then Mr Webster told him that he was following up certain information he had received regarding a Marie-Louise Ramsey, formerly Jarvis, who he had been told would testify that she was legally married to William Ramsey six years ago, resulting in four children and that she was expecting another.'

Margriet drew in a breath. 'No! So he married you illegally. Can he go to prison for that?'

'I don't know,' her mother admitted. 'He made a very swift departure, and Mr Webster hurried off too. He said he had much to do, and his last words to me were "Don't worry, dear lady".' Her voice dropped. 'I have met this person,' she said, 'this Marie-Louise Jarvis, and I believe she might have been a party to this deception.'

'I'm so sorry, Mama.' Margriet came and knelt by her chair. 'It means more difficulty for you.' Scandal too, she thought. She wasn't sure her mother could withstand the shame of it.

But Rosamund stroked Margriet's head. 'I shan't mind too much,' she said quietly, 'if it means I can undo the mistakes I have made in my foolishness.'

They both sat mulling over the circumstances, until Rosamund remembered something and gave herself a little shake. 'But that is not all my news,' she said. 'I had another visitor, the day after you left; your ships must have crossed mid-sea.' She smiled. 'It was Mr Hans Jansen, the son of a friend of your father's. Do you remember him? He said you had met some years ago, when Frederik took you to Netherlands.'

'We did,' Margriet said. 'And did he tell you that he is working for the Vandergroene Company in Amsterdam? His mother and sister live there now and I met them again on this visit.'

'He was a charming young man,' Rosamund said. 'He reminded me of your father, not in looks but in manner, although your papa would have been older than him when he and I first met.'

'He'll be about nineteen or twenty, I think,' Margriet said. 'His sister is maybe seventeen, a little older than me.'

'And are they a good family?' Rosamund asked cautiously.

Margriet laughed. 'I believe so,' she said. 'He's the only son. Don't start matchmaking, Mama, please! Oma Vandergroene has begun already.'

'Has she?' Her mother looked askance.

'Hans Jansen, it seems, is just perfect. But you might as well know now that I don't intend to marry. Not if I have to give everything I own to my husband.'

Margriet invited her mother to look over the clothes she had brought back from Amsterdam; it was time to explain the plans she had for the street children. 'Except they are not children now,' she said. 'They are my age if not a little older, except for Jim, who's maybe about twelve.'

'And they live on the streets?' her mother asked dubiously. 'Where? They must surely have a roof over their heads?'

'I think perhaps a doorway if they can find one, but sometimes they're moved on. People think they make the town look untidy.'

Rosamund said nothing. That was what she had always thought when she hurried past homeless people. She had told herself that someone should do something about them, but it had never crossed her mind that it should be her. And now her daughter was considering helping them, might even be putting herself in danger by mixing with them.

'Are you intending to wear these clothes to attract attention to their plight? I don't see what good it would do.'

'No, Mama,' Margriet said patiently. 'I'm going to try to show them a way that they can help themselves to make a living without waiting for charity.'

That night, before she climbed into bed, she hung the skirts, tops and trousers on hangers on her wardrobe door so that they wouldn't crease. She was hoping that if her friends agreed to dress up in this way people would notice them and buy from them, so that they would feel they were earning money rather than begging for it, and gain some self-respect. She was nervous, but Mrs Sanderson believed in the idea and Florrie was going to ask if she would allow them to meet at her house.

So many ideas were buzzing in her head as she planned what she would say to Billy and the girls the next day that she tossed from side to side in bed, unable to sleep. She looked at her clock and it was twelve o'clock and then it was two, and when she was finally drifting off she thought she heard someone knocking on her door. She got up and looked out on the landing but there was no one there; she listened at her mother's door but all was silence. Then she heard the knocking again and went back to her room for her dressing robe, put it on and padded barefoot down the stairs.

'Who is it?' she whispered at the front door and a voice answered but she couldn't make out what it said. She held her ear to the wood. 'Who?'

'Anneliese. Open the door.'

She drew back the bolt and turned the key, opening the door a crack. Anneliese was dressed as usual in her traditional garments. 'You're back,' she said. 'I've been looking for you. Come along.' She held out her hand. 'I've something to show you.'

Margriet closed the door quietly behind her and followed Anneliese down the steps. The street was quiet and there were no people about, and although it wasn't dark there was a grey mist hovering, making the street and houses shadowy, and clouds were covering the moon.

'Where are we going?' Margriet asked as she was led towards the top of the street, where there didn't appear to be a way out because of the dilapidated buildings in front of them, but Anneliese put her finger to her lips. 'Shh,' she said. 'Not anywhere you will remember.'

The moon suddenly appeared from behind a cloud and lit up the street. 'It's the Lenten moon,' Anneliese murmured. 'The last of the winter.'

Margriet was confused. This was her own street where she had lived all her life, but now she barely recognized it. It was smaller and narrower than it should be, and had passages and alleyways off it that she had never noticed before. 'Where are we?' she asked. Anneliese didn't answer, but took her hand and led her down one of the alleyways, which led into another, both of which had buildings on each side with small yards in front and in each yard were children playing who didn't look at them as they passed. They went up another narrow alley and came out on the road where Margriet thought the Old Dock would be. Except that it wasn't.

'I don't know this place,' she told Anneliese. 'I'm lost.'

'Don't you see? Look.' Anneliese pointed across the open space in front of them. 'Here is where the dock will be,' and then Margriet saw men working with picks and shovels, and wheelbarrows full of soil and debris that had come out of the earth; there were markers and ropes and fences to show where the dock would be and in the distance were allotments and trees and shrubs.

'These gardens will be gone soon,' Anneliese told Margriet, 'but I'll show you some others. That's what you like, isn't it? You like to see the gardens?'

'There aren't any,' Margriet said. 'There used to be.'

'No, they're still here if you know where to look, and allotments too where people can grow vegetables as well as flowers.'

Anneliese set off in an easterly direction and Margriet tried to make sense of where they were going. Their clogs clattered on the cobbles and Margriet looked down at her black skirt. She couldn't remember putting it or the clogs on. She touched her head and found she was wearing one of the starched caps. Anneliese, she noticed, was wearing a white bonnet with a frill that covered the back of her neck.

'This is the back of Land of Green Ginger.' Anneliese pointed. 'Look, there is Hanover Square and Manor Alley where you can get to my house, and here are the gardens where my father grows his tulips and ginger.'

And there they were. Small gardens, it was true, but they were filled with colourful red and yellow tulips and white narcissi, blue hyacinths and some bluebells too, and in between the flowers were the thin green shoots of ginger. Margriet clasped her hands together in delight. 'How lovely,' she exclaimed, and wondered if these were the same gardens she had glimpsed on the day she had been to the Vandergroene offices and then wandered into Anneliese's house.

'Have I seen these gardens before, Anneliese?' she asked.

Anneliese shook her head and smiled. 'No, you're not old enough.'

'Did you come to Amsterdam with me?'

'Yes, of course I did,' she said. 'Don't I come everywhere with you?'

CHAPTER FORTY-SIX

The next morning Margriet's mother came into her bedroom. She was fully dressed and had already had her breakfast.

'Margriet, are you awake?'

Margriet turned her head and opened her eyes to see her mother standing by the bed, looking anxious.

'Jane said you were fast asleep when she came to open the curtains so she didn't disturb you. Are you unwell?'

Margriet pulled herself out from under the bed-clothes and stared around the room, seeing the Dutch costumes hooked on the wardrobe and one black skirt half off its hanger as if put there in a hurry. She frowned. Had she worn it?

She gazed glassily at her mother. 'Tired, I think. Am I going somewhere today?'

'You said you were meeting those children. Margriet, I'm having second thoughts about this. Perhaps you should cancel the arrangements; you don't seem yourself.'

Margriet threw back the sheets and swung her legs out of bed. 'I'm not unwell, Mama. I – I had a restless night, that's all. I'll be all right as soon as I've had breakfast. May I have coffee and Oma's *poffertjes*?'

'What? What are they?'

Margriet huffed out a breath. 'Sorry! I'm still half asleep. Oma gave me little pancakes for breakfast and that's what she called them. I'll have porridge as usual, please. I'll be down in ten minutes, Mama. I'm perfectly all right, really.'

She hadn't meant to sleep so late and still felt tired and headachy, her mind hazy with something only half remembered. Did she really go out walking with Anneliese in the dead of night? She drew back the curtains and looked up and down Parliament Street. It looked the same as usual and yet she remembered – what? A different street from this one; much older, with dilapidated buildings and no way through to the dock. But there was no dock, there were no ships.

She sat on the edge of the bed. What's happening to me? Why does Anneliese take me on these journeys? Her comprehension, now that she was no longer a child, told her that she was imagining these things, and yet she was loath to lose her friend, real or not. She could see her so clearly; she had grown up with her.

Cook had said that the porridge was now cold and not worth eating, so she'd prepared some rashers of bacon and lambs' kidneys which were hot and waiting under a dish on the dresser.

'I asked Cook about the pancakes,' her mother told her, 'and she says she'll make some for tomorrow's breakfast.'

'Really?' Margriet was once more surprised that

her mother had taken the trouble over what was probably a sudden and obscure whim on her own part. 'Thank you, Mama.'

Just before noon, Margriet packed the Dutch garments and white caps into two parcels and set off for Market Place. I hope they all come, she thought. What if they didn't? What if Billy thought she was just playing a game and didn't bother to tell the others? Maybe he thought she was just a rich girl with nothing better to do.

But he was there, with Jim, Betty and Mabel, all waiting by the church gate or sitting on the low wall. Margriet approached them diffidently. 'I've had an idea,' she said. 'I hope you think it's a good one. It's to help you earn a living. Or at least, it's a start, and it might lead to better things.'

'I've got a job,' Billy said. 'I'm me own master. Don't have to kowtow to anybody except 'customers.'

'You mean like carrying people's luggage or looking after somebody's horse and carriage and hoping you'll be given a copper or two?'

'Yeh,' he said defiantly. 'Just like that.'

Margriet nodded. 'Then I think you could be put in charge of this plan and make it work, because I can't, not without you.' She turned to the girls. Betty was concentrating on biting her nails and Mabel was sitting on the church wall idly swinging her legs. 'Not without any of you. Oh, and the other thing is that we can talk about it at the Sandersons' house.'

Instantly they were alert and ready to go. 'Is Sandy in on this then?' Billy asked eagerly. 'Cos if she is then it'll be all right.'

'She doesn't know all the details yet, but yes, she approves.'

They were ready to move off immediately, and Margriet wondered if they were motivated by the prospect of food at the Sandersons'. Billy offered to carry her parcels, and she handed them over to him. 'Don't drop them in a puddle, Billy, whatever you do.' Then she asked him if his handcart would be available.

'Aye, it will be if 'wheel doesn't drop off,' he said. 'Why? Will there be summat to carry?'

'Yes,' she said. 'There will be, but I think the cart will need a lick of paint first.'

'Oh, I can do that,' he said, 'except that I've no money for paint.'

'All right. We'll have to make a list of what we need, but we'll go over everything once you've heard about the plan. If you don't like it, well,' she gave a little shrug, 'it will only be a pipe dream.'

Billy looked sideways at her as they walked along Whitefriargate. 'This means a lot to you, doesn't it?' His forehead wrinkled as he considered. 'Are you doing this just for us?'

'I think I'm doing it for myself as well, Billy. For all of us.'

As they had hoped, Mrs Sanderson had provided food. Huge plates containing beef and chicken and thick slices of bread were ready and waiting on a flowered tablecloth on her dining room table, along with pots of jam and marmalade and two types of cake.

'Eat up,' she said heartily, 'and then we'll hear

what Miss Margriet has to say about her project. I'm going to talk to her while you have breakfast.'

'Don't you know about it, Sandy?' Billy asked. 'We thought you did.'

'Only some of it,' she said. 'But it sounds like a wonderful idea if you can make it work.'

Margriet smiled, pleased Mrs Sanderson had said that. It would make the others think it was their concern and not just hers.

When she thought they had almost eaten their fill, Margriet picked up her bundles and slipped out of the room and upstairs to Julia's bedroom, as agreed with Mrs Sanderson. Julia was waiting for her.

'I can't wait to hear all about it,' she said. 'Can I help you change?'

Margriet slipped out of her own clothes and into the costume and Julia quickly plaited her hair and pinned the cap on her head. 'Oh,' she said excitedly, 'how lovely.' She took another breath. 'Oh, Margriet, can I have one too? I'm a quarter Dutch after all.'

'There's not much time.' Margriet looked in the mirror and was pleased with what she saw. 'Can you sew?'

'Of course. You know my mother. Immi and I had to learn to knit and sew and make do and mend all kinds of things. Nothing is ever wasted. I could make a skirt very quickly, and I've got a white blouse that would go very well and Papa has a black waistcoat I can borrow.'

Margriet laughed. Everything was falling into place. 'Well, why not?' she said happily.

When they went back into the dining room, everyone stopped talking and fell silent. Betty and Mabel stared at Margriet with their mouths open, whilst Billy frowned. 'Is that you, Miss Margriet? You look different.'

'I do, don't I? And,' she hesitated, 'I hope I've done right, but I've had costumes made like this for Betty and Mabel, and for you and Jim some black trousers and waistcoats. I had to guess the sizes.' She began to open the parcels, and Betty and Mabel took out the skirts and held them against themselves, looking at each other with wide eyes.

'Are these for us, miss?' Mabel said breathlessly.

Margriet said they were, and handed Billy and Jim their garments and then opened a smaller bag and brought out two peaked caps like the ones she'd seen the cheese porters wear at Gouda. 'I said I'd bring you a cap, didn't I, Billy?'

'You did, miss,' he said, and she sighed a little. They were never going to call her anything but miss. 'But what 'they for?'

Margriet hesitated. If they did not like her suggestion, her whole plan would collapse. 'If you agree, you're going to be flower sellers. I'll provide the flowers: tulips, narcissi, hyacinths, whatever's in season. I have a contact with some suppliers and they've agreed that we needn't pay them until the flowers are sold, and then whatever money is left over will be yours.'

Billy flipped his bottom lip with a finger as he thought about it. 'Is there a catch?'

'I don't think so,' Margriet said. 'The Dutch costumes are because so many flowers come across from Netherlands, and people will be interested when they see you and stop to talk, and then they'll buy your flowers.'

'What will 'market traders say?' Betty said. 'They'll think we're pinching their trade. And besides, don't you have to register to be a trader?'

Mrs Sanderson raised her eyebrows. 'I think we can sort that out, Betty,' she said, for she saw by Margriet's expression that this was something she hadn't thought of. 'We'll say it's a try-out to help you street children earn money, and you'll apply for a licence if it works well. We know a few people we can talk to.'

Margriet smiled. They were warming to the idea; she could tell by the way they were turning to each other and murmuring. Then Betty said, 'Can we try them on?'

'Julia will help the girls,' Mrs Sanderson told them, 'and Billy, there's a small lobby near the kitchen. You and Jim can change in there.'

They all rushed off after Julia and Mrs Sanderson smiled at Margriet. 'It's going to work,' she said softly. 'What a splendid thing to do. It will lift their spirits.'

'I hope so,' Margriet said fervently. 'It's already lifting mine. Now we have to get hold of baskets and buckets and tubs and paint Billy's handcart, because I'm going to suggest that he'll transport the flowers and keep the girls supplied when they sell. By the way, Julia would like to wear a costume too.'

Mrs Sanderson laughed. 'I rather thought she might. If you don't object I think she'd be an asset.'

'That would be lovely. I would be so glad of her

help,' Margriet said with some relief, as she had thought that she might have to keep everyone's confidence up on her own if sales were low. Julia was such a positive person, just like her mother. 'Thank you so much, Mrs Sanderson. You've been so kind and helpful.'

'It's my pleasure,' Mrs Sanderson said warmly. 'You've given these young people a chance of something good in their lives. You have given them hope.'

CHAPTER FORTY-SEVEN

Hans Jansen followed Stephen Reynoldson as they stepped down from the train at the newly opened and imposing Paragon Station, which was closer to town than the older Kingston Street railway terminal. They had caught the earliest train from Leeds and it was now just after midday. He had been surprised when Reynoldson had written to ask if he could come again so soon after his last visit, but the manager had told him he had made a valuable contribution to the business and some of their clients had asked to see him again. This second trip had gone even better than the first. He had been introduced to contacts in Wakefield and Leeds and persuaded them to export more raw wool and woollen cloth through Vandergroene's. Import companies had placed new orders for Dutch cheese and Genever, or gin as they preferred to call it, and market garden suppliers who were already buying tulips had increased them. Reynoldson was delighted, and fully concurred with Gerben Aarden's view that Hans Jansen was a young man to watch for the future.

On the way back from Leeds, he had suggested

that Hans might like to come and work temporarily at the Hull office, so that he could see how it linked with the one in Amsterdam. 'It's important that we all know what the others are doing,' he had explained. 'I spent some weeks in Amsterdam myself after Vandergroene died, to acquaint myself with the business there, and it was very beneficial.' Hans was pleased and flattered, and promised to consider the proposal.

As they stepped out of the concourse, Reynoldson turned to him and said, 'I'd like to take a stroll to Market Place if you're not in a hurry to get back to your lodging. It's market day and there's something I'd like you to see.'

Hans said he was in no hurry at all. 'What's happening?' he asked.

'Well, you might not know this, but Frederik Vandergroene had a daughter. She's still only young, but she's recently begun to take an interest in the company.'

'Ah, Margriet! Yes, of course. Is it today? The Dutch day?'

Seeing Reynoldson's surprise that he knew about the Dutch day, he explained that he had known Frederik very well as he had been a friend of his father's, and Margriet had been to their house as a child. 'I called on Frederik's widow when I came last time, but Margriet had left for Amsterdam to visit her grandmother. Mevrouw Vandergroene is a friend of my mother's, and on my return home I was told of the Dutch plan. I'd love to meet Margriet again.'

The covered stalls stretched down the long road

of Lowgate and Market Place and spilled into the square under the shadow of the ancient parish church of Holy Trinity which, Reynoldson told him, was presently undergoing urgent restoration. The market was packed with traders of fruit, flowers and vegetables, meat, fish and livestock, as well as those selling cloth and fancy goods; shoppers picked and bargained and inspected the fruit for bruises or maggots, whilst the stallholders called their wares and wrapped them in brown paper or popped them into waiting baskets and held out a hand for payment.

The two men wandered into the square and Hans thought he might not spot Margriet in the crush of people, but then he saw young girls on the brink of womanhood dressed in Dutch costume and white caps, as they might have been in Gouda or Volendam, or even Amsterdam, walking about the square with baskets of tulips in their arms. His mother had told him of their sewing session.

'Why Dutch?' he had asked.

His mother had put her head on one side and said, rather wistfully, 'She wants them to be noticed, but I feel that the way she has chosen to do it might be in remembrance of her father.'

He spotted a young errand lad dressed in baggy breeches like those he used to wear himself when he was a child. The boy wore a striped shirt under a black waistcoat and a red kerchief round his neck; he had clogs on his feet and a peaked cap was slipping over his ears. Another boy, a few years older, was pushing a bright green handcart decorated with paintings of tulips and windmills and filled with real tulips, narcissi and other spring flowers, replenishing the girls' baskets.

'Have we supplied the flowers?' he asked.

'Yes, but they'll be paid for,' the manager answered. 'Miss Vandergroene insisted. She said that the young people had to learn that it was a business. I did give her a small discount, though. After all, she's one of our chief shareholders.'

Hans nodded. He also had a small number of shares. He hadn't known until recently that Frederik had left him and his mother and sister a stake in the business. Not enough to make them rich, he supposed, but a token of Frederik's esteem, and of his love for Lia.

And then he saw Margriet. He knew her instantly, even though he hadn't seen her for several years. She had lost the childhood plumpness in her cheeks, revealing her high cheekbones, and her eyes seemed larger as she looked about. Her shining hair, dressed in a single plait, hung over her shoulder almost to her waist, and her mouth . . . He stopped and gazed. Her mouth was soft and smiling . . . *She's lovely.* She had been a pretty child, but now she was beautiful.

He forgot about Reynoldson, who had gone to buy something from one of the stalls, and began to walk towards her, shouldering his way past the shoppers, many of whom were carrying bunches of tulips and sweet-smelling hyacinths. The press was so great that it seemed as if something or someone was trying to push him back, but determinedly he continued, ploughing a path towards her, watching her progress through the throng.

'Margriet!' he called, and she turned in his direction. '*Goededag! Herinner je mij?*' Hello. Do you remember me?

She paused. 'Is it Hans? Is it you? It is!' She held out both hands and he clasped them fervently. 'I hoped you would come again, but didn't expect it to be so soon,' she said ardently. 'My *oma* said you had come to England whilst I was in Amsterdam.' Then she laughed, and he felt a soaring joy. 'My *oma* and yours spoke of you constantly. Klara was cross and said that you were your *oma*'s darling boy!'

'I'm afraid I am.' He laughed as well. 'But she loves Klara too. How good it is to see you, after such a long time, Daisy.'

'*Daisy!*' she murmured. 'I haven't been called that since Papa—'

'Oh, I'm so sorry.' He gently squeezed her hands, which he was still holding. 'He – your father often referred to you as Daisy when he was speaking of you.'

'It's all right.' She smiled and reluctantly he released her hands. 'I like it, but no one else has ever called me that.'

'Not your mother?'

She shook her head, her eyes lighting up with amusement. 'Certainly not my mother. She's very proper.'

'She was very welcoming when I called.'

Margriet laughed again. 'Don't tell Klara, but you made a good impression on Mama. I think you know how to charm the ladies.'

He looked at her and hoped he could charm her too. But perhaps she was still too young – as he also was, he supposed. He must not frighten her away.

'You've done very well, Margriet,' he said. 'Your friends must be pleased. How many are there? I've counted three girls in costume plus you and the two boys.'

'Yes,' she said, looking about her. 'My friend Julia wanted to help; the other girls are Betty and Mabel, who have nowhere they can call home. The older boy is Billy and the other one is his brother Jim.' But she kept miscounting. She'd seen another girl dressed in Dutch costume, looking cross, pushing into Hans as he walked towards her. She thought it was Anneliese.

Hans was saying something, but she didn't hear him, her eyes searching the crowd for her friend. But then Betty was in front of her saying something too and she felt confused.

'Sorry, what?'

'I said I've run out of everything and I can't find Billy. And I've got this heap o' money.' Betty jingled the cloth bag in front of her. 'What shall I do with it?'

Margriet mentally shook herself. 'I'll take it until Billy gets back – he's volunteered to look after all the money until you can have a tally-up at the Sandersons'. He won't be long – he's just gone to fetch more flowers.'

'Yes, but what shall I do now, miss? I'm all fired up and nowt to sell.'

Margriet had an idea. 'You know Tom, don't you? His stall seems to be busy. Why don't you go over and ask if he'd like you to assist him until Billy gets back?'

407

Betty seemed doubtful. 'Tom wasn't too pleased about us selling flowers and tekkin' his trade.'

'I'm sure he'd be glad of the help; he doesn't appear to be managing very well on his own.'

'Work for nowt, do you mean?' Betty frowned.

'Yes, if necessary,' Margriet said. 'He might not be able to pay you this time, but on the other hand I'm sure he'd be very grateful.'

'All right,' Betty said. 'I've nowt else to do,' and she wandered off towards the flower stall.

They watched as she spoke to the old man, and although he frowned at first and shook his head, he listened for a minute or two and then beckoned her to his side of the stall. The difference in Betty was immediately apparent. She seemed to grow in maturity as she called out for shoppers to come and buy Tom's blooms.

'Come to owd Tom's,' she shouted. 'Best in 'market. Come on. What 'you waiting for?'

She's in her element, Margriet thought. She's amongst people she knows, people like her, who talk as she does, and today she's proved that she can work.

Hans was watching too. 'You've given her a chance to show what she can do,' he said. 'Behind that costume she has found herself.'

Margriet nodded, still watching Betty at work.

'I'm coming to work in the Hull office,' he murmured. Until that moment he hadn't made up his mind about Reynoldson's offer, but now he knew that it was what he wanted. 'I'll start in a month's time.'

She turned to him with a question in her eyes,

and then she smiled. 'Good. Would you like to come to supper later?'

As the market began to close, Margriet's little group gathered together and made their way to the Sandersons' house to sit around the kitchen table, count the money and work out if they had made a profit after expenses. They had, a small one which they shared out between them. They were all excited by the success of their first business venture and to have some money in their hands. Betty was the last to arrive and when she did she had a huge beam on her face. 'Owd Tom's offered me a job every Sat'day,' she announced. 'With wages,' she added as if amazed to be thought worthy of payment. 'But can I keep 'costume, Miss Margriet? I've nowt else decent to wear.'

'Yes, of course,' Margriet said. 'They were made for all of you, no one else. Though you don't have to wear the cap if you don't want to.'

'I like wearing it,' Mabel said. 'It keeps my hair tidy. Miss Margriet, you know that you gave us some money to have a bath at them new baths in Trippett Street before we wore 'costumes? Well, it was lovely – all that hot water. First time I've ever had a bath. So I want to earn money to do that every week if I can, or maybe once a month anyway,' she added as an afterthought, as if appreciating the enormity of spending money so recklessly.

'I've been offered work as well,' Billy said. 'In a joiner's shop. It's somebody who meks cupboards and toys and all sorts of things, and wants somebody to paint 'em. He saw 'handcart and liked 'idea.

I'm good at painting,' he said. 'Or,' he mused, 'I'll see how it goes and mebbe do it for myself one day.' He turned to his young brother. 'I'll show you how to as well, our Jim.'

Julia offered them all tea and cake, but Margriet excused herself since she and her mother had a guest coming for supper.

'It isn't that dashing young man I saw you talking to, is it?' Julia asked curiously. Margriet pretended she didn't know who she meant, but her blush gave her away. Betty had seen him too, and nodded knowingly.

'He's an old friend,' Margriet explained. 'From when we were children. He's Dutch.'

'Gets even better,' Mrs Sanderson broke in. 'And I should know! Off you go then. Say thank you to Margriet, everybody.'

They all stood up, Billy, Jim, Betty and Mabel. 'Thank you, Miss Margriet. Thank you very much.'

CHAPTER FORTY-EIGHT

When Margriet arrived home her mother was in the sitting room, her chair drawn up by the fire, her sewing lying idle on her lap. She looked round when Margriet entered the room and greeted her cheerfully, but Margriet was not deceived; she thought her mother had been crying.

'What's wrong, Mama? It's not Mr Ramsey again, is it?' She couldn't rid herself of the thought that he might try to find a way to worm his way back into their lives.

'No, no.' Her mother gave a weak smile. 'Mr Webster assures me that we won't see him again, except perhaps in court.' She hesitated. 'But it seems to me that Ramsey has in effect shown me what a foolish woman I have been.' She wiped her nose delicately on a lace handkerchief as Margriet sat down in the chair opposite her. 'I didn't realize how lucky I was to have had your father, so patient and kind as he was with me, and to have you too, my lovely daughter.'

'What has brought this on now, Mama?' Margriet asked softly. 'Something has upset you.'

Rosamund nodded. 'I was sitting here alone and

I suddenly thought that if I didn't act now that was how I would be for the rest of my life: alone.'

'You'll always have me,' Margriet assured her, but her mother shook her head.

'You have a right to your own life, not one that is for ever tied to mine.' She saw that Margriet was about to say something and hurried on. 'Whatever path you choose, you won't waste your life as I have done. So,' she took a breath, 'I put on my coat and hat and ventured out.'

'On your own?'

'Yes.' Rosamund lifted her head. 'Quite alone. I thought that if you could do it, and Mrs Sanderson often goes out by herself – I've seen her from the window – then why shouldn't I?'

'Bravo, Mama,' Margriet said softly.

'And it was a revelation, such freedom! I actually wouldn't have cared if Lydia Percival should have seen me without a maid accompanying me. But I didn't see anyone I knew, which was rather disappointing.' She sighed. 'However, I came to Market Place and saw your – your . . .' she hesitated, '*friends* from the streets and thought how energetic and busy they were, and – and *clean*. Then I saw Mrs Sanderson and her daughter, and Florence too, who was very surprised to see me, and I wondered . . .' Again she hesitated. 'I wondered, if Mrs Sanderson hasn't done so already, perhaps we, that is if you and she agree, could form a committee to help other young people?'

Margriet was astonished. Mrs Sanderson had in fact broached the subject with her already, but she was already committed to other projects and would need more help if she were to take on another. 'What a wonderful thought, Mama.' Impulsively she got up and kissed her mother's cheek. 'But why did that make you cry?'

'Because I saw you speaking to the young Dutchman, Mr Jansen,' her mother said wistfully. 'And I saw how he looked at you, and knew that sooner or later your life would be changing, if not with him, then with someone like him.'

Margriet sat up straight in her chair. She couldn't believe that after all the trouble her mother had had with Mr Ramsey she could say such a thing. It was true she found Hans very personable, but she hoped that it would be possible for a grown woman to have a gentleman friend without marriage coming into it.

'Do not even think of it, Mama,' she said. 'I am not considering marriage. Papa left me this house so that you and I could be safe and comfortable, and although we won't have much money until I come of age, we'll manage. So why would I consider marrying *anyone* knowing that a husband can claim everything I own?'

'But Margriet, your papa—'

'Wanted us to be secure and if he hadn't planned for that then Mr Ramsey would have taken *everything* we owned.' Margriet hadn't realized that she had raised her voice, nor that she was so angry that English law condoned such an unjust state of affairs. 'And,' she went on, 'although Hans Jansen is very pleasant and I would very much like him for a friend, and, by the way, I have invited him for supper tonight, I will *not* be considering marriage with him or with anyone else, *ever*!'

413

*

They had a very agreeable evening, for Cook had excelled herself on being told that a young Dutch gentleman was coming for supper. 'I'll give him English lamb,' she told Mrs Simmonds. 'I won't try anything Dutch tonight, but maybe if he comes again, then I might.'

'You could try those little pancakes for a dessert,' the housekeeper said. 'Those might impress him.'

Cook pressed a floury hand to her forehead. 'Are we trying to impress him? Surely Miss Margriet is too young to consider a suitor?'

Mrs Simmonds pursed her mouth. 'Well, this is 'second time he's been. He called when Miss Margriet was away visiting her gran in Amsterdam. Besides, you know what folk such as 'mistress are like – they make plans well in advance.'

Upstairs, Rosamund was very conscious of the need not to appear to be making plans but to treat Hans as she might any visitor. She asked him about his work with the Vandergroene Company and expressed surprise and pleasure when he said that he was coming to work in the Hull office.

'I won't be here permanently,' he explained, glancing at Margriet, 'but it is very good experience for me and will also improve my English.' He too knew that he had to tread cautiously, and when Rosamund went on to ask about his mother and sister he answered as briefly as he could, careful not to reveal that he knew far more than he could possibly tell her.

And then, to Margriet's astonishment, her mother asked if he had ever met Margriet's grandmother,

414

who also lived in Amsterdam. He said that he had, having introduced himself when he joined the company. 'I was told that she took an active interest in her son's business, and as we live within a short distance of her I thought it polite to do so.'

'Good,' Rosamund said. 'It's nice to know that Margriet has contact with her Dutch relatives, and friends too. So very important, is it not?'

Margriet was astounded. Her mother had been averse to any contact between Margriet and her *oma* for years. It was almost as if she had been jealous of her. Now she was positively encouraging the bond, so when Margriet said goodnight to Hans and asked him to come again, she meant it. She wanted him to be her friend, and she thought from the way he pressed her hand that that was what he wanted too.

She didn't go to sleep straight away that night, but lay wide awake, thinking of the day and how successful it had been. The shoppers in the market, on seeing the young people in the Dutch costumes, had stopped to talk to them and then bought flowers. Betty, Mabel and Julia had flitted about between the stalls – and so had Anneliese. Anneliese had obstructed Hans as he walked towards her.

'I tried to push him away,' a voice whispered in her ear.

Margriet shook her head and covered her ears. 'I must stop this,' she muttered. 'I'm too old for childish games.'

'I am not a game,' Anneliese said. 'We don't need him. I'm your friend, not him. Tell him to go away.'

'No.' Margriet spoke aloud. 'I won't.'

'Please! Let's go to my house. You like it there. You can come and see my garden again.'

Margriet shuffled down under the sheets and blankets and covered her ears. 'No. Go away. You're not real.'

But Anneliese's soft voice persisted. 'But of course I am. Margriet, please come with me,' and as Margriet drifted to sleep she knew that she would; she would once again be drawn into Anneliese's world.

CHAPTER FORTY-NINE

Despite her hopes, Margriet saw Hans only once or twice more that year, as he was still working in the Amsterdam office. Aarden had vetoed the move to Hull, saying that he wasn't ready to give Hans to England yet and he should travel to France and Germany first. Although Hans appreciated all the experience he was getting in those countries, he longed to see Margriet again. On the rare occasions when he could find an excuse to do so, he would visit the Hull office and call to see her and her mother.

Margriet, Rosamund, Mrs Sanderson and Imogen set up a committee for the welfare of the street children, and were joined by two other well-meaning ladies and three retired gentlemen. From the evening that Hans came for supper it became increasingly apparent to Margriet that her mother had completely changed her outlook on life and was no longer the formal, shallow person she had been. She was still fearful of giving offence and maintained her standards of good manners and refinement, but she was warmer and kinder than she had ever been, and was touched and pleased by how people now responded to her.

Margriet suggested inviting Billy on to the committee too, as he knew more than anyone what the street children needed if they didn't want to live in the workhouse: a roof over their heads, a chance of paid work, and food. 'It doesn't seem like much to ask, does it?' Rosamund said at the first meeting. 'Not when the rest of society expects and receives those things as a right.'

Margriet had smiled at the comment and thought how her mother's eyes had been opened to what was just and what was not. She had become stronger because of Ramsey's behaviour. Mr Webster was still pursuing his enquiries, but he occasionally called to inform her mother of his progress, telling her that he hoped to have news very shortly.

It was almost Christmas, and Margriet and her mother were looking forward to a better one than they had had in recent years. Margriet had received a letter from her grandmother, and another from Hans. She had asked her mother if it was all right to receive his letters, and Rosamund had told her that Hans had already written to her, to ask her permission to correspond with her daughter.

'He's a friend, Mama,' Margriet had insisted. 'Nothing more. Please don't think I have changed my mind about marriage, because I haven't.'

'You are still far too young to consider marriage in any case,' her mother said prosaically, 'so I am not thinking about it. Perhaps you would care to read your friend's letters aloud?'

Margriet was taken aback. It was not that there was anything in them that her mother might take exception to – he merely described where he had been and told her how cold it was in Amsterdam now that winter was here – but they were private letters, written for her.

But someone else in Margriet's life took exception to her receiving them. Anneliese had begun to visit her more frequently at night and became cross when Margriet didn't want to talk to her. Strangely, she always seemed to know when Margriet had received a letter from Hans, or replied to one, for she bombarded Margriet with commands insisting that she must tell him to go away.

'But I can't,' Margriet said miserably, her pillow wet with tears. 'I don't want him to go away. He's my friend.'

'*I'm* your friend,' Anneliese said vehemently. 'You don't need another.' Margriet knew that Anneliese would soon become even angrier, for in his last letter Hans had told her that he would be coming to work in the Hull office early in the following year.

It was Christmas Eve afternoon, and they had just lit the lamps when the doorbell rang. Rosamund stiffened; she had not yet got over her fear of Ramsey's returning and causing trouble. Margriet looked out of the window into the street and remarked that it wasn't Ramsey, unless he had walked, as there was no carriage there.

Jane knocked and opened the door. 'It's Mr Webster, ma'am. He asks if it's too late to call.'

'Oh, no, not at all. Please show him up; and make tea, will you please, Jane?'

Mr Webster was shown in; there was a covering of snowflakes on his shoulders and top hat. He apologized profusely for the lateness of the hour. 'I would not have come so late on a Christmas Eve, dear lady,' he said, 'except that I have in this last half-hour received a messenger directly from York. He brought me news from Ramsey's lawyer, who, I might add, is Ramsey's lawyer no longer. The man has flown.'

'Flown?' Rosamund said breathlessly. 'Ramsey?'

'The same,' the lawyer said, chuckling. 'Last seen boarding a ferry to France with his wife and children scurrying after him.'

'So what does it mean for my mother?' Margriet asked urgently.

'It means that Ramsey is a bigamist and that your mama is free of him, though not of the scandal. But as he was a York resident and not from Hull, it is the York newspapers that will run it – indeed are already running it, for bigamy is a rare felony. By the time Christmas is over his escapades will be old news and of no interest to the readers of the Hull *Packet* or *Advertiser*. It also means,' he continued, warming to his subject as he was invited to take a seat, 'that he is unlikely to return to these shores. If he does, the law will have him, not on one count but on two, for he is being chased by another lady – and I use the appellation lightly – whom he also *married*. The only thing in his favour, begging your pardon, madam, is that it appears he did not consummate that marriage either.'

Margriet saw by her mother's drained and ashen face that she was on the point of collapse, such was her relief at hearing the long-awaited news. 'And if by chance he dared to come back?' she asked quietly.

420

'Then he has no claim on your mother, none whatsoever. I propose, if I may, dear lady,' he went on, turning to Rosamund, 'that you insert a small advertisement in the newspapers to say that henceforth you are to be known only as Mrs Vandergroene, and no other name will be recognized.'

In late February, Hans wrote to say he was now working in the Hull office and had obtained comfortable lodgings in the town. 'I am at present travelling with one of my colleagues, but I hope to call and see you one day soon.'

Margriet was delighted to hear from him, but tried not to think of him too often in order to keep Anneliese quiet. She sometimes thought she must be hovering on the verge of delirium, for surely this was not normal. For the first time she began to wonder why she could still see an imaginary childhood friend, whom she herself had named Anneliese. As she slipped between the bedsheets that night, she thought she knew that Anneliese was not real, but imaginary, and yet she appeared when she least expected her. As a child she had conjured up a companion because she was lonely, but she was no longer lonely.

'But *I'm* lonely,' Anneliese whispered. 'You don't think about that, do you? Just because you have new friends doesn't mean you can abandon me. Come with me, Margriet. Come out and play.'

Margriet sat up and saw Anneliese sitting at the foot of her bed. 'I don't want to. Anneliese, please stop. I'm grown up now and you must grow up too.' She stopped speaking as Anneliese began to weep at her words and her form became shadowy and indistinct. 'I'm sorry,' Margriet said, reaching out a hand towards her. 'I don't want to hurt you, but you must try to understand.'

Where Anneliese had been sitting was a shadow, dissolving like grey mist over water, but Margriet knew she was still there. She hadn't gone away; she was still there, waiting for her.

When Hans arrived back at the Hull office at the beginning of March he was greeted by the news that there had been an outbreak of influenza in the town and that they should avoid crowds. 'It has been in Amsterdam also,' Hans said, 'as has cholera, but it was contained.'

After finishing work for the day he went back to his lodgings in a house in Grimsby Lane, that ran between Market Place and High Street, run by a widow and her daughter. He dropped his bag there, wrote a note to Margriet, changed his formal business coat for a casual one and went out again, his intention being to put the note through the Vandergroenes' letter box, asking if he might call the next day, a Saturday.

He looked up at the topmost windows of the tall house in Parliament Street and thought he saw a shadow against one of them. He waved a hand in case it was Margriet, ran up the steps, and slipped the envelope through the letter box before turning and striding down the street again. He would have supper at a hostelry in the town, and then go back to his lodgings for an early night. The last few weeks had been very busy, with much travelling and many meetings with potential clients.

The next morning he rose, had breakfast and wandered into the town. He bought a posy of flowers from a girl at a stall who smiled and thanked him as he paid her, and then made his way to Parliament Street. He was shown into the sitting room, where Mrs Vandergroene greeted him warmly, and he remarked how well she looked as he handed her the posy.

'I am very well indeed,' she said. 'Thank you. How very nice of you to call. Won't you be seated? Margriet will be down very shortly. She was up late this morning, but seemingly she didn't sleep well. In fact I heard her call out once and went to her, but she didn't wake – dreaming, I suppose.'

'I'm sorry to hear that. I wondered if you would allow her to come for a short walk with me this morning, Mrs Vandergroene, just into town or by the river. Perhaps you would like to come too?'

'Oh, no, thank you, it's still far too cold for me. But perhaps you should avoid the river,' she said cautiously. 'I understand there is influenza in the town, and the Old Harbour is always packed with ships and boats. You can't be too careful: foreign sailors and travellers might well be carrying the infection. You could of course walk by the estuary, if you don't consider it too far. It is very open there, if very breezy. Margriet used to like going there with her papa when she was a child.'

Hans hid a wry smile as she spoke; she obviously didn't think of him as a foreigner or a traveller, even though he was foreign and indeed had been travelling. The door opened and Margriet came in and greeted him, then apologized for her lateness. He was struck immediately by her pallor and dull eyes. He gave a short formal bow. 'How nice to see you, Margriet,' he said. 'I asked your mother if you might like a short walk, but I understand that you have not slept well, so perhaps . . .' His question hung in the air, weighted with his disappointment that she might not come.

She sank down on the sofa. 'It's true that I didn't sleep well, I often don't, but a walk in the fresh air might waken me up. I might be very dull company, though.'

He assured her that she wouldn't be, and then was startled when she asked if he had arrived back from his travels this morning. 'Yesterday,' he said. 'Did you not receive my note asking if I might call?'

Margriet looked at her mother, who shook her head. 'I'm sorry,' Margriet said. 'I did not. When did you send it?'

'Last evening at about six thirty. I brought it myself. Did I not see you in an upstairs window?'

She smiled. 'No. Mama and I were having supper at that time.'

'I waved. One of the maids perhaps, looking out?'

She drew in a breath, then shook her head and murmured, 'I don't think so. Perhaps a movement of the curtain?'

He agreed it could be that, and didn't mention that the window had been closed. She went to get a warm cloak and a shawl and he told Rosamund that he wouldn't keep her out long, as she did look very tired. He thought they might have rain, and he wouldn't like her to get a chill. Rosamund was gratified by his concern and said she would place her daughter in his safe hands.

When they reached the street he asked Margriet if she would like to take his arm, and wondered why she looked back at the house before she said, 'Yes, thank you, I will in just a moment.' She fiddled with her gloves and shawl until they turned the corner into Whitefriargate, then put her arm through his.

'Where would you like to go?' he asked. 'Your mother suggested the estuary.'

'That would be lovely,' she said. 'Could we go to the hotel and have hot chocolate? Papa used to take me there.'

'You must still miss him,' he said. 'I miss my father very much. Sometimes I want to ask his advice on something and forget, momentarily, that he's no longer here.'

She turned and looked up at him. 'Oh, so do I miss mine. I used to think that I was the only one to feel such things, but of course I'm not. It's so hard, isn't it, especially if you have had a good relationship, as I did.'

'But you have your mother; she seems very protective of you.'

'She was so protective when I was a child that I was not allowed to have friends,' Margriet told him. 'She didn't want me to go to school, but I think my father must have insisted.' She hesitated, as if she might have said more, then asked him about his work in the office.

She was glad when they reached the pier, for she felt quite chilled. The wind was strong and the estuary water rough, and seeing her shiver Hans suggested they go into the hotel to have a hot drink and get warm.

'This is the place where Papa brought me,' she said. She remembered too that it was here that she had met Mr Webster; something stirred in her memory and she wondered if it was then that he had warned her father about making his will watertight. What a clever, dear man he was to be on the side of women and fight the injustice inflicted upon them. She was glad he was now their friend as well as their lawyer.

There were few people in the hotel and they had the room overlooking the estuary to themselves. Hans thought that Margriet seemed unwell; she had drawn her shawl tight about her shoulders, and as she drank her chocolate she glanced around the room from time to time.

'Are you uneasy about something, Margriet?' he asked quietly. 'Is something bothering you?'

She passed her tongue over her lips. 'Not exactly,' she murmured. 'But I think I am perhaps unwell.'

'Then we must get you home immediately.' He started to rise to his feet, but she forestalled him.

'No!' She didn't mean to be brusque, but thought that was how it sounded. 'I'm sorry. It's nothing, really.'

'*Ow!*' Hans rubbed his thigh and shifted in his chair. 'Something sharp in the upholstery,' he said, running his hand over the fabric. 'A pin left in maybe. *Ow!*' he said again as he felt the pain, and was astonished when Margriet hissed, '*Stop it!*'

'No, no, not you, Hans,' she said. Her eyes filled with tears and her mouth trembled.

'Margriet! What is it? What's wrong?'

She shook her head and tears spilled down her cheeks. 'I can't tell you. I can't tell anyone.'

He leaned forward and took her hand. 'You can tell me anything—' As he began to speak he felt a slap on the back of his head, sharp enough to make his ears ring. 'Ow! What's happening? I think we had better leave.'

'I will explain,' she wept. 'But you must promise not to tell anyone, and I will understand if you don't believe what I say.'

'I believe that something nipped and slapped me,' he said softly, 'but I don't know what it was, for there's no one else in the room. Is this place haunted?'

'I don't think so. It's me,' she croaked. 'I'm the one who's haunted, and I don't know what to do.'

'You're going to have to explain, Margriet.' Once more he reached for her hand and again he felt a sharp pinch on his thigh. 'Trust me,' he whispered. 'Tell me.'

And so she began.

CHAPTER FIFTY

Hans listened carefully to the long tale of the mettlesome spirit who had penetrated Margriet's thoughts and imaginings since she was a child. He had no reason to disbelieve it for he had felt the pinches, but he was inclined to believe there was some other explanation. Margriet, he considered uneasily, was certainly unwell and troubled no matter what the reason. He called for the bill, and led her to the door. It had started to rain, so he put her cape hood over her head and fastened his own scarf round her neck to keep it in place.

'Where is the nearest cab stand?' he asked the post boy, and when the lad pointed across the road he hurried Margriet towards it with his arm about her, almost carrying her towards a waiting carriage.

'Parliament Street, quick as you can,' he ordered the driver, who cracked the whip and set off down busy Queen Street, through the throng of shoppers heading for the market.

'Don't tell Mama,' she urged fearfully. 'Please don't tell Mama. Only say that I have a chill. It's true,' she muttered. 'I'm so very cold.'

He put his arm about her again and drew her

close. This wasn't the way he had imagined holding her in his arms, but she was trembling and shaking, unable to keep her body still, and he was struck by the sudden fear that she might have influenza.

The cab cut down Silver Street into Whitefriargate and Margriet lowered her head to her knees as if she didn't want to be seen as they passed the end of Land of Green Ginger.

'Don't tell Mama,' she implored again as they reached her door. 'She won't understand. She doesn't know about her.' She turned a stricken face up to him. 'But I think maybe Papa did.'

He kept his thumb on the bell, which made Jane come running. 'Miss Margriet is ill. Please fetch her mother immediately, and then she needs hot bricks in her bed and a fire lit in her room.'

'Yes, sir.' Jane bobbed her knee. 'And a hot posset?'

He didn't understand what she meant and she told him it was hot milk with added spice and wine. 'You must ask her mother about that,' he said. 'She will know.'

But Rosamund didn't know any remedies for colds and it was left to Cook to decide. She heated milk with a dash of ale and a sprinkling of nutmeg whilst Mrs Simmonds took Margriet upstairs to her room, undressed her, wrapped her in a blanket and put her into her bed, which Jane had warmed with a warming pan filled with hot coals from the kitchen range and hot bricks wrapped in an old blanket.

'I think you must send for a physician, Mrs Vandergroene,' Hans told her quietly. 'We cannot rule out the possibility of influenza. Better to be safe than sorry. If you will tell me where he lives I will go myself.'

'You must ask Mrs Simmonds,' Rosamund said, confused by this development. 'We rarely see a physician. Ask her for Dr Johnston's address. I seem to recall Margriet liked him when she was a child. We haven't seen him since . . .' She put her hand to her head. 'You don't really think—'

But he was gone, running to the kitchen and then out of the door. She went slowly upstairs to sit by her daughter's bedside.

The doctor came within the hour and felt Margriet's burning forehead. Rosamund watched anxiously. 'Do you think it is influenza, Dr Johnston?' she asked him. 'I don't know how she could have caught it.'

'I don't know,' he said. 'She's certainly feverish, but you have done the right thing by putting her to bed. How are you feeling, Miss Vandergroene? Are you able to describe your symptoms to me? Do you have a cough or a sore throat?'

She shook her head. 'No,' she said weakly, and he watched her nervous eyes search restlessly around the room and saw how she trembled. 'I'm cold, and I'm hot.' Her body ached too with the shaking but she didn't tell him that; it was as if she was being pulled in several directions.

'I'll come again tomorrow,' he told Rosamund. 'Keep her quiet and warm but not overheated and give her plenty of cool drinks, lemonade or boiled water. I'll see myself out.'

He went down the stairs to the young man wait-ing in the hall. 'I don't think Miss Vandergroene has influenza,' he said, assuming he was a relative. 'But she has a fever, I'm not sure what kind. It's strange,' he added, rubbing his hand over his chin. 'Is she prone to hallucination? She seemed to be looking at someone in the room.'

'No,' Hans lied. 'She is rarely ill.'

'Mmm, that's what her mother said,' the doctor murmured. 'But I've seen something similar before. Ah well, we'll see. I'll call again tomorrow.'

Hans sat in Mrs Vandergroene's sitting room after the doctor had left, not knowing what else to do. Jane brought him a tray of tea and a plate of bread and ham. He wasn't hungry, but he drank the tea and wished it were coffee. He paced about the room and longed to go up and sit by Margriet's bedside, but he knew that would be unacceptable. Another hour went by and Mrs Simmonds came in.

'The mistress asked if you were still here, and when I said you were she asked if you'd mind going up.'

Instantly he was on his feet. 'If you would follow me, sir,' Mrs Simmonds said primly, 'I'll show you 'way.'

He followed her up to the top of the house, where he waited on the landing whilst the housekeeper went into the room, closing the door behind her. He remembered when he had looked up at the window and seen the shadow. You're being absurd, he told himself firmly, but a doubt crept in.

Mrs Vandergroene came out, looking ashen. 'She is no better, Mr Jansen,' she said. 'I am so worried. She keeps talking about someone I have never heard of.'

'Is there anyone I can fetch to sit with you? A friend or a relative?'

She nodded and swallowed hard. 'That is why I asked for you,' she said in a low voice. 'Would you be kind enough to take a message to someone? I feel sure she will come if she is able. She works for someone else now but she knows Margriet very well. She looked after her all through her childhood. Florence is her name. If I give you the address?'

He put his coat on again and asked Jane for directions, but was unable to remember the litany of shortcuts that followed. When he left the house he raced down Whitefriargate to the Junction Dock, where he picked up a cab to take him to Albion Street. He asked the driver to wait, and it was Florrie herself who opened the door. She listened to what he had to say, asked him in and ran down the hall to a room at the end, returning with a woman he guessed was the mistress of the house in spite of her dishevelled appearance.

'Is there anything you need?' Mrs Sanderson asked. 'Anything I can send for the poor child?'

'Your prayers,' he said, 'and strong thoughts to make her well.'

She nodded. 'It is done.'

'I have met your mother and sister,' Florrie told him as they rattled back. 'I'm going to work for Miss Margriet's grandmother. As her companion,' she added. 'I sail in a month.'

He nodded, barely listening, and murmured something, but he had no idea what.

Rosamund wept when she saw Florrie. Hans saw the sensible and caring young woman put her hand on her former mistress's shoulder and pat it gently before she ran upstairs.

'I'm so afraid,' Rosamund wept. 'What will I do if she doesn't recover?'

He was struck with fear, but murmured comforting words as he led her into her sitting room. 'Rest for a while,' he said. 'You are overwrought.' He hesitated, and then asked, 'May I go up? If Florence is there?'

She sighed and wiped her eyes. 'Yes, of course. What does it matter if it is the done thing or not? I don't care about anything as long as Margriet gets well again, and I know how highly she regards you.'

He sped upstairs and this time he knocked on the door. When he entered Florrie was kneeling by the bed and murmuring something to her charge, who was thrashing about, her face running with sweat and her hair wet and bedraggled.

'There's summat up, sir,' Florrie whispered. 'She keeps calling out a name, but it isn't anybody I know. It sounds Dutch, but I don't ever remember her meeting anybody with that name.'

'What is it?'

Florrie shook her head. 'Sounded like Anneliese. It's Dutch, isn't it?'

'Yes, it is.' He watched as the girl leaned over the bed.

'Miss Margriet,' she said softly. 'It's Florrie. You know, your Florrie who looked after you when you were just a little bairn. Did I tell you that I'm going to see your *oma* soon? Now then, I don't want to have to tell her that you're ill. She won't be happy to hear that, will she? She'll want to hear that you're fit

433

and well, so what we going to do about it? Will you tek a sip of water?'

She fumbled for the glass at the side of the bed. Hans reached and handed it to her so that she could put it to Margriet's lips. Margriet took a drink, running her tongue about her lips as if her mouth was dry.

She said something, and Hans and Florrie listened intently. 'There, she said it again,' Florrie murmured. 'Who is it?'

'It's someone she used to know,' Hans hedged. 'Her name was Anneliese.'

'No.' Florrie shook her head in denial. 'Nobody I knew of.'

'Someone in Gouda whom she met at my mother's house,' he said desperately, and was relieved when Florrie seemed to accept it.

They were both startled when Margriet suddenly sat up with wild eyes and shouted, 'No! I won't come. I'm staying here.'

Hans rushed to the other side of the bed and took her hand. 'Hold her other hand, Florence,' he urged.

'It's Florrie, sir,' she told him. 'Only Mrs Vandergroene calls me Florence.' But she took Margriet's hand as he asked and held it tight.

'Don't let go,' he said. 'She's fighting. Hold her fast.' He spoke firmly. 'Margriet. Tell Anneliese to leave. Tell her it is time she went home.'

Margriet shook her head, her neck stretched back. 'She doesn't want to,' she said wildly. 'Not without me.'

Open-mouthed, Florrie gazed with startled eyes

434

from one to another as Hans said, 'Tell her you are staying here with me and your mother and everyone who loves you.'

Margriet let out a cry. 'She won't *listen* to me. *You* tell her,' she shrieked. 'It's because of *you* that she wants me to go with her!' She dropped back on her pillow as if exhausted. 'You tell her,' she said again, her voice faint but her eyes still searching the room. 'She'll listen to you.'

Hans swallowed and licked his lips, and held Margriet's hand in both of his. 'Very well,' he said quietly. 'I'm going to tell her to leave now and you must hold fast to my hand and to Florrie's and let Anneliese go without you. Do you hear me, Margriet?'

She didn't answer. He looked at Florrie appealingly and saw she was afraid, her breathing swift and short as if she had been running.

'Anneliese,' he called out in his own language. 'You must leave now. Your time here is over. You have been a good friend to Margriet but now you must go back where you belong.' He spoke firmly, and although his voice wasn't loud it was strong and determined and unwavering and filled the room with resonance. 'Say goodbye. Go now and leave her in peace.'

They watched as Margriet shook and shuddered and lifted her arms in entreaty, but still they held her fast. Moments later the tremors passed and they felt her go limp; she closed her eyes and lay still.

'Oh, sir,' Florrie breathed, and her voice caught. 'She's not – not . . .'

Hans gently touched Margriet's cheek. It was

435

warm, but the fever had passed. He smiled, and his throat tightened as his eyes filled with tears. 'No,' he said, his voice choked. 'She is well. She has come back to us.'

CHAPTER FIFTY-ONE

1854

On a sunny Saturday two summers later Hans and Margriet strolled through Market Place and Trinity Square.

Margriet waved to Betty, who was working full time with Tom on his stall and had moved in with him and his wife, becoming the surrogate daughter they had long been denied. Mabel, with the help of the committee, had found work with a florist. She and Billy, who was setting up his own signwriting business, were planning on getting married and living above the rented workshop with Jim, who was apprenticed to a joiner. Julia Sanderson was also to be married later that year, while her sister Imogen said she wasn't going to marry but instead intended to set up a charity to house orphaned children.

Margriet had taken several weeks to recover fully from the unaccountable fever, as the doctor had called it, but was now fit and well and could remember little of what had happened. She recalled that she had felt drained and empty when she was at last able to sit up in bed, and had built up her strength with Cook's chicken broth, coddled eggs and syllabub.

Hans had been her constant visitor until she was once more downstairs with her mother. He was fully committed to his work with the Vandergroene Company, and was expected to take a leading position in the years to come. On one of his trips home to Amsterdam he had brought Gerda Vandergroene back to England with him and she had stayed with Margriet and her mother, building bridges with her daughter-in-law at last. When she returned home, Florrie had gone with her. Floris, as she was now known, had never fathomed what had happened to Margriet, but wisely did not try to understand something completely beyond her comprehension.

'I miss not seeing Floris,' Margriet remarked as they strolled past the church. 'And . . .' She hesitated, wondering what Hans would say to this confession. She was eighteen years old now, after all. 'Sometimes I miss Anneliese too. She was my constant companion for so long.'

He looked down at her. 'Am I not your constant companion now? Have I not taken her place?'

She didn't answer his question but said, 'She was jealous of you, you know; that's why she changed. We played very happily when we were children – or at least I think we did. She's becoming a distant memory.'

Hans breathed a small sigh. How reassuring and comforting it was to hear her say so. Not once had he implied that Margriet had conjured up this being from her imagination because she was lonely, nor ever suggested that Anneliese wasn't real, but

Margriet wasn't quite over her. She still hurried past Land of Green Ginger and never looked down it.

'So,' he said again. 'Have I not become your constant companion?'

She smiled and bent her head. It was time, she thought, to explain a few things to him. 'You have, it's true. Shall we walk to the pier? We can sit there and watch the ships sailing past.'

He stopped first and bought Margriet a bunch of sweet-smelling roses. She pressed her nose to them. 'They're lovely,' she said. 'Thank you.'

Gallantly he pressed his hand to his heart. 'It is my utmost pleasure,' he declared. 'I would be happy to bring you flowers every day.' At twenty-three, Hans was already a kind, thoughtful young man.

She smiled but didn't respond and they walked on in comfortable silence until they reached the pier, where they sat on a bench and watched the ships and barges sailing down the estuary, the smaller market boats tied to the timbers below the pier lapping and bobbing on the water.

Margriet looked down at the roses. 'You know, don't you, Hans, that I have made a pledge never to marry. I have mentioned it often.'

He nodded solemnly. 'Indeed you have, Margriet. I have heard your comments regarding the plight of married women many times.'

'Mr Webster says that one day in the not-too-distant future, the legal status of married women will change and Parliament will be forced to bring in new and fairer rules.'

'So I understand. But,' he said, holding in a smile, 'what I don't understand is why you think that I should be interested in this English law. Or is it that you intend to inform every man you know of what is or might be happening?'

'Oh, well.' She flushed, and seemed a little flummoxed. 'It's just that I feel I should make it plain that I could never marry. Not even you, Hans, though you have my utmost respect and' – she took a deep breath – 'affection.'

'I see.' He covered his mouth. She is the sweetest, most darling creature I have ever met. 'But, Margriet' – he turned to look at her but she had lowered her head and he couldn't see her face for the rim of her bonnet – 'I wasn't aware that I had made you an offer of marriage.' He paused before continuing. 'And in view of your lack of trust of any man who might wish to exchange wedding vows with you, regardless of the deepest love he might have for you, then I am grateful for your warning and am mindful of the rebuff that would be given should I foolishly think to ask you.'

Although to begin with he had been teasing, his last few words held a certain tonal quality as he realized that he would be deeply upset if she thought that he would marry her, or any woman, for her property.

She turned to him and her face was a picture of dismay. 'I've hurt you. I didn't mean to – I'm sorry, so sorry. I wouldn't ever want to hurt you; what we have is very special, our friendship and understanding, and . . .' Her lips parted. 'I do love you, Hans,' she whispered. 'Very much.'

He closed his eyes and put his head back, exhaling a great breath of deliverance. Then he gazed at her and smiled. 'You love me but don't trust me? Not with your life when I would honour it above all else? Or is it only with your property that the difficulty arises?'

She nodded and then shook her head and began to weep, and gently he wiped away the tears with his fingertips. 'It is because of my mother and Mr Ramsey. I know in my heart that you are not like him.'

'Margriet,' he whispered. 'I love you and want to marry you. Give your house to your mother, give her your shares and your money and all that you own and come to me with nothing but your love, because that is all I want. One day in the future I will give you a house where our children will play.'

'And a garden?' She continued to cry.

'And a garden filled with flowers if that is what you desire.' He kissed her palm. 'Not quite yet, as I have not earned enough, but I will, and until then, if you will marry me, we will rent a house that neither of us can own where you'll feel safe and we'll be happy together.'

She wiped away her tears and then blew her nose, leaving it pink and blotchy. 'I will marry you, Hans, if you choose to ask me. If you do, we wouldn't need to rent another house – I can give mine to my mother and we could live with her there. She could live on the top floor in my old nursery schoolroom and have my bedroom, and we could have the rest of the house until such time as— What? Why are you laughing? I'm perfectly serious.'

He put his arms around her, regardless of any passers-by, and kissed her cheek. 'Life with you is going to be fun, unpredictable and full of love, Margriet, and I just can't wait. Let's go now and ask your mama for her permission. Will she be pleased, do you think?'

'She will be delighted,' Margriet said joyously.

Rosamund had indeed been delighted. She felt safe at last from the clutches of William Ramsey, thanks in great part to the advice of Hugh Webster, who had become her very good friend as well as her lawyer. She occasionally accompanied him to official functions and dinners, and both were happy in the knowledge that there was no commitment on either side: Webster was a confirmed bachelor and Rosamund intended to remain a widow for ever more.

Lydia Percival had written to Rosamund from an address in Wiltshire; the letter was carefully couched so as not to admit any blame on her own part, either for the introduction to or the indiscretions of her brother. She went on to say that in her opinion Rosamund's virtuous reputation would not suffer in the least from the scandal, as she had had such a good name prior to her involvement with William Ramsey. In Lydia's opinion William's weakness should be laid entirely at the feet of his first wife, Marie-Louise Ramsey, as he had previously led a blameless life. She explained that she and Vincent would be staying quietly in Wiltshire for an indefinite period but that she would be pleased to hear from Rosamund should she care to write.

Rosamund read the letter carefully. Had Lydia known or guessed there was something wrong?

Perhaps she had, although not at first, and then dared not say out of fear for her own reputation. Rosamund screwed the letter into a ball and committed it to the fire, where with some satisfaction she watched it burn.

The wedding of Margriet and Hans was to take place the following summer and there was much coming and going between Hull and Amsterdam as arrangements were made. There were also regular passings up and down Parliament Street as Margriet visited Hugh Webster, climbing the stairs to his rooms overlooking the rooftops, entries and alleyways to discuss her inheritance. She had decided that if she really wanted to show her love and trust for her husband-to-be they should share everything they owned. She also asked Hugh Webster if he would give her away, to which he replied that he would be honoured.

On a glorious day in August the bells of Holy Trinity rang out and English and Dutch friends and relatives gathered outside to await the bride's arrival. Margriet's and Hans's grandmothers wore traditional Dutch costume at their grandchildren's request. Lia wore pale green silk and Rosamund silver grey and the two walked into church side by side, united, had Rosamund but known it, by Frederik's constant love. Julia and Klara, as Margriet's attendants, both wore soft blue.

Floris had helped Margriet into her crinoline gown of rose silk and dressed her hair with rosebuds and a wispy veil. She was very happy, she confided to Margriet, as she was being pursued very seriously by a kind young Dutch man.

After the service, as they stood outside the church door, Margriet lifted her face to receive a kiss from her handsome husband and both laughed as they were covered in flower heads thrown by Betty and Mabel. She looked around her. Everyone she cared about was here: her mother, the Sandersons, the street children, the clerks and managers of the Vandergroene Company, but most of all her father's family – her *oma*, Anna and Bartel and her cousins – and the Jansens whom she loved so dearly. On the edge of the crowd, two others hovered, whom she could only see mistily as if through diaphanous gauze.

'Papa.' Her lips formed the word. 'Anneliese.' Her father smiled, and then he put his hand on Anneliese's shoulder and she raised hers as they moved away.

Hans touched her cheek and turned her towards him. 'Margriet?' he said softly.

'Yes.' She smiled up at him. 'I'm here.'

The house in Parliament Street was renovated over the next few years. Rosamund loved being on the top floor, where she felt safe in the knowledge that her daughter and husband and growing family were living below. She wasn't alone as she had feared she might be. Sometimes as she lay awake in her bed at night she heard the chatter and laughter of her grandchildren and it was almost as if they were in her sitting room next door, which had once been Margriet's schoolroom. That was nonsense, of course, for they were tucked up in their own little beds on the floor below, and so their voices must have been echoing through the walls and ceilings. She sighed contentedly as she turned on her pillow; it was a very comforting sound.

AFTERWORD

The spirit that had been Anneliese slipped back through the layers of time to the very beginning. She drifted by the damp river bank, pausing momentarily by the rough shelters where she watched children playing by the camp fires and women stirring the contents of pots or pounding grain. Wild boar penned in enclosures snuffled and grunted and men sawed timber to make stronger cabins for their families. They would be staying here, had found their shelter, and would build a town.

She passed through many centuries and the cabins became more solid, built with brick and stone. Royal personages came by ship and saw this place as a safe haven, barricaded it with walls and ditches against enemies from across the northern sea and named it King's Town upon Hull. Decades passed in the blink of an eye; rich merchants and traders made their homes here and royalty returned; the common people bowed or knelt as courtiers and gentlefolk rode by on their fine steeds towards their manor houses and imposing palaces. She did not bow to them, but simply melted away.

She bowed to the white-robed Carmelite monks

who walked the long street of White Friar Gate where their house was situated and to those dressed in the black habit who lived close by the estuary. As she bowed her head they looked cautiously in her direction, as if they were unsure or even slightly afraid.

The lonely child who had called to her had not been afraid but had welcomed her presence. What pleasure we had together; the girl reminded me of myself when I was once a child. I showed her so many sights and she loved the royal gardens, the neat hedges and lawns and scented flowers, and more than anything she loved the scent of the ginger plants, the tulips and narcissi that my father once grew in his garden.

We had a brief but happy time together, but I knew I was losing her. I knew she would no longer need me on that day when the tall, broad-shouldered young Dutchman, my own countryman, came striding towards her. I tried to detain him, to push him away, but he was intent in his purpose. It was as if he saw me and said, No, she is mine. I became bedevilled in my attempts to be rid of him, which wasn't ever in my former nature, and even tried to take her with me, but he was stronger than I. When Margriet at last turned and I showed myself to her, she bade me a sad goodbye and I knew I must leave. She will miss me.

Like a breath of a breeze the spirit drifted through warrens of dark and murky alleyways towards Market Place, whence came the clamour of reverberating voices; the strident shouts of traders, children mewling and crying, women gossiping, the clatter of clogs on cobbles and the snapping snarl and growl of dogs as she passed them by.

Onward she wandered towards the short street named for her family and the house she had once called home. People took short cuts through the passageways and some, more aware than others of a presence amongst them, turned their heads or inhaled a sudden breath as they felt a ghostly visitant lingering near.

I have been here for far too long, and yet I wanted to stay; but now my time here is finished and I am ready to rest. She paused by the house. The door was open to admit her as it had always been, and she went in search of what she had left behind. The upstairs rooms were empty, cool and welcoming to her. She listened; she could hear the echo of her mother's voice calling to her and was glad. They had had so little time together before Anneliese had to leave, before the fever had taken her away.

The shade of Anneliese ran her fingers across the wall and put her cheek against the coolness and whispered, *Moeder, I am here. I have come home.*

AUTHOR'S NOTE

Land of Green Ginger is the strangest of addresses
hidden away in the heart of the old town of Hull.
According to Sheehan's history of Hull, early
inhabitants of the town once described it as a place
where green ginger was sold.

In very early maps it was designated as Old
Beverley Street and lay within the district where the
illustrious family of De la Pole – having lost their
home to the sea at Ravenspurn at the mouth of the
Humber – built their new home, Suffolk Palace. This
was a magnificent mansion with a tower entrance,
splendid rooms, courtyards, pleasant flower and
kitchen gardens and ornamental fish ponds. It
is said that during the reign of Henry VIII, who
acquired the palace and kept court here in 1540,
the house and gardens were extended and renamed
the King's Manor. It is also conjectured that green
ginger was grown in the royal gardens as a luxury
for the monarch's table.

There have been, and still are, many commercial
connections between the Netherlands and the town
of Hull. Therefore it is more plausible, though
less romantic, that a Dutch family by the name of

Lindergren or Lindegroen resided here in this street, and so Lindergren Ganger (Lindergren Walk) became corrupted to Land of Green Ginger.

From these historical facts and my imagination I have attempted to create a fictional tale. After all, who are we to say that it might or might not have been true?

Val Wood

SOURCES

Books and websites for general reading and information:

History of the Town and Port of Hull, James Joseph
    Sheehan, 1866
Property Rights of Women in Nineteenth-Century
    England, www.123helpme.com

Hello and thank you for joining me. I hope you are enjoying or about to enjoy *Little Girl Lost*. Has anyone noticed that this novel is set at a slightly earlier period from my other books, and that it also includes a dreamlike sequence of a former time?

There is of course a reason for this; there is always a reason why an author writes of specific things; rarely do we write on a *whim*, there has to be a purpose. My purpose for doing this was because of the vast amount of rich history in the city of Hull and although my favoured era for creating fictional history is mid-nineteenth century, I felt that I would like to explore even further back, to give a flavour, a sense, of an earlier time and this I did through my central character Margriet.

When we first meet Margriet, she is an intelligent, curious, yet lonely child without siblings and with few friends. Her mother is strict, determined to bring Margriet up to be a lady, whereas Margriet's father, Frederik, is an easy going Dutchman, insistent that his daughter should be allowed freedom, whilst at the same time giving her an education as he would have done with a son, if he had had one.

Frederik begins the task by teaching her of the ancient history of Hull and as he does so, shows her the seemingly ordinary street with a notable name, Land of Green Ginger. A street Margriet has passed many times without noticing it. When she does become aware of it, she also becomes conscious of a little Dutch girl living there, a child that no one else can see. Is Anneliese therefore a spirit child or an imaginary friend conjured up by Margriet's loneliness?

Land of Green Ginger is well known by the residents of the city of Hull and there are numerous theories given as to why the street was so named; I give two in my story, one that a Dutch family once lived there and their name Lindegroen, was corrupted to become Land of Green Ginger and the other with an association with King Henry VIII who acquired a splendid palace close by, with gardens where ginger was grown as a delicacy for his table. We shall never know which, or if any of these stories are true, but what matters is that all of these old tales bring a rich tapestry of life as it once was.

As with all of my novels I am writing of life and characters of another era, and in many instances apart from the huge advances in science and knowledge, people themselves are much the same today, with joy in their lives or sadness and tragedy to bear and in *Little Girl Lost* I have tried to convey these emotions through my characters.

Frederik is saddened and frustrated by the coldness of his wife and only strengthened by the love of his daughter; when he finds love with someone else, he is filled with guilt and anxiety over an impossible situation.

On his tragic death, not only is Margriet distraught over his loss, his widow Rosamund is too and unable to cope alone. Being unaware of the pitfalls of inheritance and legalities of property rights that widows could fall into during that time, she was a sitting target for an unscrupulous 'wife hunter'. It is left to Margriet, now a young woman, to assist her mother in untangling the web of deceit and law in which they are trapped and in doing so, must consider her own future, a future which is beckoning from her father's kinsfolk. But Anneliese, her constant life companion, has other ideas and her hold over Margriet is increasing to a perilous degree.

Is Anneliese therefore real in the spiritual sense or a figment of a highly charged imagination? Dear Reader, I leave it to you to decide.

Sincerely,

Val

I was born in the mining town of Castleford, spending my formative years there before coming to live in East Yorkshire as a young girl, and just like a stick of Scarborough rock I'm Yorkshire through and through.

I was such a dreaming child, living in my imagination and through books. My education was dire, and I had the distinction of failing my Eleven Plus – twice. My saving grace was my writing and reading ability; given an essay to write I was in my element, and as for books, I couldn't get enough of them.

In my adult life I took myself off for Further Education to achieve for myself what my teachers couldn't teach me. But, rather than go on to take a university degree which had been my original intention and because I had re-discovered my love of writing, I joined a writers' workshop to polish and hone my writing skills and importantly be with like-minded people.

Prior to this I had in the meantime worked in fashion, trod the catwalk, danced ballroom competitions, married Peter and had two daughters and a grandson. I had lived a full life before taking my writing seriously, but once I did it became my passion. This was the time too when I became a hands-on volunteer and a supporter of various charities, some of which I still support today.

I began my first novel, *The Hungry Tide*, in about 1988 and in the several years of writing it I became completely absorbed in the nineteenth century and the way of life. That novel became the catalyst of what was to come; in 1993 I entered and won the Catherine Cookson Prize for Fiction and was propelled into becoming an author of regional historical novels.

Having lived in the country district of Holderness for most of my married life, I now live in the lovely old market town of Beverley. It featured in my book *The Kitchen Maid*; I've always had a soft spot for Beverley and I have the advantage of both town and country on my doorstep. I have a small gravel garden where I can sit and ponder or retreat to my summerhouse, and I always have a book with me. Old habits die hard.

What was your favourite book growing up?

Louisa May Alcott was my most favoured author when I was growing up and *Little Women* my favourite book. I didn't realize then that I was reading Literature, nor that I would be inspired to write books with similar themes, including that of a family and a mother coping at home without a husband. Another strong woman.

How do you research your novels?

Research is very important to me and we're lucky enough in this area to have good libraries and two excellent venues to gather information, the Hull History Centre and the Carnegie library. Both have archives of local and national interest. For researching places abroad, like America or Europe, the internet is a great source of information, especially for detail of the nineteenth century.

What themes are important to you when you write?

Poverty and injustice are my pet hates and these were prevalent in the nineteenth century. I also like to write about strong women. They had to be strong in order to survive.

Do you have any favourite characters you'd love to write about again?

Sometimes a character stays with me long after I have finished a book, and not always the chief protagonist. This happened in *The Hungry Tide* and the character

Annie, who I felt that, despite appearing to be weak and a hopeless case, had more to offer given the chance – and in her own book in her own name, Annie became strong, warm and with a great humour that hadn't been apparent in the first book. In *His Brother's Wife* there is a child, Daniel, whose forebears were unknown. I had to write about him in order to find out just who he was and what had gone before. This became *Every Mother's Son*.

What advice would you give an aspiring writer?

To anyone aspiring to write, I'd say take a pen and paper or a blank page on your computer screen and start to put ideas down. Write about what is important to you, what stretches your imagination, choose a period in which you feel comfortable and is of interest to you, be it the present, the past or the future, and fill it with characters. Give them a name and they'll come alive. Recently, I have promoted two short story competitions in my local area in order to encourage creative writing, and I provided a sentence to be included in the story, for would-be or first-time writers don't always know how to start. The winner and runner-up had never written before and were thrilled to receive their prizes.

Fall in love with
The Kitchen Maid
by Val Wood

Jenny is determined to make her own way in the world, and she secures a job as the kitchen maid in a grand house in Yorkshire. Gradually, she gains the attention of the young master of the house, and they fall in love. But slowly their dreams turn to nightmares, culminating in a scandal that will force Jenny to leave behind everything she knows.

Cast aside by her own family, Jenny faces many difficulties until an unusual promise changes the course of her life: Jenny the kitchen maid becomes mistress of her own grand house. Although she tries to fit in with this new world, however, she never forgets the words a gypsy once told her: that one day she will return to where she was happy – and discover her true love . . .

But will the tragedy of her past stand in the way of her happiness?

The Kitchen Maid will be available with a beautiful new cover in June 2016

Far From Home
by Val Wood

Can she make a new life away
from everything she knows?

When Georgiana Gregory and her maid, Kitty,
make the long sea journey from their native Hull
for New York, they hope to escape the confines of
English life and savour a land of opportunity.

But in New York, Georgiana finds she isn't far from
home when she encounters a man passing himself
off as a local mill-owner's son, Edward, who has
fled to America. Georgiana recognizes the man
standing before her as Edward's valet Robert –
Edward himself appears to have vanished.

As Georgiana and Kitty pursue the adventures
of the frontier, and Edward tries to flee his
enemies, are the dangers of this new
country too much to cope with?

Far From Home will be available with a
lovely new cover in October 2016

Every Mother's Son
by Val Wood

**Can new beginnings bring
fresh hope to his family?**

Harriet and Fletcher Tuke have worked hard to
raise their children well. Daniel, the eldest son,
has always known that his birth father died
soon after he was born, and that Fletcher
raised Daniel as his own.

But as Daniel comes of age and begins to fall in
love with childhood friend Beatrice, he can't help
but wonder about his heritage – his olive skin and
dark eyes reminding him daily of the difference
between him and his siblings, and between
his and Beatrice's families.

Daniel's wish to learn about his past takes him
to Europe, where decisions about his future
take shape. But will it be one he can share with
Beatrice? And as Harriet hopefully awaits his
return home, she could never imagine that
answers to questions about her own family
are also just on the horizon.